SHAMEEZ PATEL PAPATHANASIOU

THE LAST FEATHER

Book One in the *Selene* Trilogy

This is a **FLAME TREE PRESS** book

Text copyright © 2022 Shameez Patel Papathanasiou

FLAME TREE PRESS
6 Melbray Mews, London, SW6 3NS, UK
flametreepress.com

US sales, distribution and warehouse:
Simon & Schuster
simonandschuster.biz

UK distribution and warehouse:
Marston Book Services Ltd
marston.co.uk

Publisher's Note: This is a work of fiction. Names, characters, places, and
incidents are a product of the author's imagination. Locales and public names
are sometimes used for atmospheric purposes. Any resemblance to actual
people, living or dead, or to businesses, companies, events, institutions, or
locales is completely coincidental.

Thanks to the Flame Tree Press team.

The cover is created by Flame Tree Studio with
thanks to Nik Keevil and Shutterstock.com.
The font families used are Avenir and Bembo.
Map design by Jaylynn Ruiters.

Flame Tree Press is an imprint of Flame Tree Publishing Ltd
flametreepublishing.com

A copy of the CIP data for this book is available from the British Library
and the Library of Congress.

HB ISBN: 978-1-78758-710-6
PB ISBN: 978-1-78758-708-3
ebook ISBN: 978-1-78758-711-3

Printed and bound in Great Britain by Clays Ltd, Elcograf S.p.A

SHAMEEZ PATEL PAPATHANASIOU

THE LAST FEATHER

Book One in the *Selene* Trilogy

FLAME TREE PRESS
London & New York

For Nashreen, who lit up a room with her laughter.
I'll miss you forever.

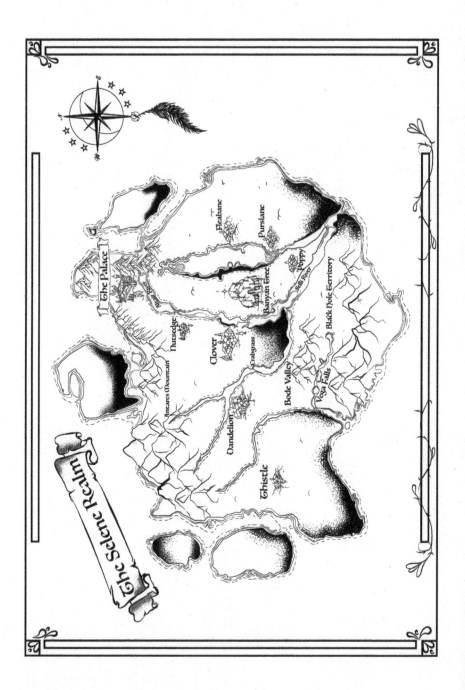

The Selene Realm

CHAPTER ONE

Another dream.

Cassia opened her mouth to greet him, to say something, but it didn't matter. These dreams had become so commonplace that she knew there was no point in talking to him because she couldn't hear him anyway.

Instead, she relaxed her mind, stopped trying and enjoyed what was essentially a silent one-man movie starring her best friend, Lucas Williams.

Lucas leaned forward toward her, drawing his dark eyebrows close before dipping his head. A bright white light behind him peeked through over the top of his messy black hair and then he lifted his head and all she could see was him.

He opened his mouth and she could hear him sighing. Well, she couldn't actually hear him, but she knew what it would have sounded like. Everyone knew what Lucas's loud and dramatic sighing sounded like. Taking in every detail, she noticed the way his dimples came out when he pursed his lips and shook his head at her as he usually did. She memorized everything in the few seconds she had with him before waking up.

★   ★   ★

Cassia awoke with a fright, thrashing about on the couch, causing the blanket to twist between her legs. A blanket she didn't remember putting there. She didn't remember falling asleep either. The cold air on her exposed skin sent a shiver through her warm sleepy body and she stretched her legs outward, purposely allowing the chill to work its way into her spine and eventually reach her brain, giving her the motivation she needed to move.

The television across from her was on with the sound muted, thankfully, giving her a moment to collect her thoughts as she pushed herself up and slouched over, with her elbows resting on her knees. Slowly straightening her back, she enjoyed the feeling of it cracking softly. She rolled her neck, listening to the light pitter-patter walking toward her.

"Hey," she said, without turning around.

"Are you awake?" the small voice asked.

Cassia rolled her eyes at her younger sister, Calla, as she walked around the couch. "Well, I'm not sleep talking," Cassia said, rubbing her hands across her face, wiping off the sleep.

"You were literally just talking in your sleep, and fighting by the looks of it," Calla countered, sitting down next to her, bundled in their late father's oversized nightgown. She put her tiny hand on Cassia's knee and asked, "Was it Lucas again?"

Cassia nodded. The dreams started a few days ago and since then, every time she closed her eyes, she saw his. Those dark eyes she was all too familiar with. The eyes that she had looked to for help, regardless of the situation, boy trouble, cheating on tests, a sparring partner, whatever she had needed, he had been there. Until one morning, he wasn't.

The loud ping of the microwave interrupted her thoughts and Calla jumped up and skipped to the kitchen. She returned with a plate of fried eggs and mushrooms. "Mom made us breakfast before she left for the hospital. She took your lunch with her."

"Where's your breakfast?" Cassia asked, digging into the eggs. The chili flakes stung the insides of her mouth pleasantly. She only had a few minutes before she had to be back at the hospital.

Calla shrugged and Cassia knew that it meant one thing. She was nauseous. She was always nauseous.

"You need to eat, Calla."

"I remember him, you know," Calla said, looking up carefully.

Her hazel eyes seemed glazed over and Cassia couldn't tell if they usually looked that way. She made a mental note to bring it up with one of the other doctors, or she would research it herself.

"I know I was only seven, but he was always really nice to me. He was like my brother."

Cassia smiled. Her heart squeezed the way it usually did when she discussed her best friend. "You were his little sister. He was there the day you were born. He stuck a piece of gum between your neck folds and when Mom found it, she was so mad, she banned him from visiting us for an entire week. It felt like a lifetime."

Calla laughed. It was Cassia's favorite sound in the whole world. Her high-pitched giggle bubbled up in her throat and then exploded out of her mouth and bounced off every surface, spreading light.

"Do you think they'll ever find him?" Calla asked softly, leaning back on the couch and stretching her legs toward the coffee table. Her feet couldn't reach the edge. She slouched down and eventually managed to get the tips of her toes onto one of the corners of the table.

Cassia shrugged. She didn't like thinking about it. But when she did, she only had one question: *How does someone just disappear?*

She was there with him. Well, she was with someone else, but she didn't want to think about that. The point was, he was there, and a few hours later, he was gone.

"It's been almost four years," she said, standing up. "I think if they were actually looking, they'd have found him by now." Stepping over her little sister's thin brown legs, she added, "Come on, you're coming with me to the hospital today. Mom and I are both working late."

★   ★   ★

When they reached the hospital, Calla ran inside confidently, as if visiting a family friend. In a way, it was like that. She was instantly swept up by a group of nurses who loved her entertaining, and mostly fictional, stories.

Cassia followed closely behind, shaking her head at the way Calla had all the nurses wrapped around her tiny fingers. She made her way into the locker room and slipped out of her leggings and into her blue scrubs. She haphazardly shoved everything into her locker and her bag spilled its contents all over the floor. The mixture of medication, chocolate cookies, hand sanitizer, pens, notes, receipts and books made her wonder, for a moment, if that's what it would look like if her mind were cracked open and spilling out.

Probably fewer receipts and more chocolate cookies.

Her mother, Maya, appeared at her side, giving her a quick kiss on the cheek. "Here's your lunch. I can take off at eleven if you want," she said, and touched the plait that lay on Cassia's shoulder. "I like this. Anyway, come find me." Before Cassia could greet her, or agree to seeing her later, her mother whipped out of sight in a blur of tan skin and mostly black hair, all wrapped in a small pair of pink scrubs.

Her mother was the best nurse anyone could ever ask for, but people rarely asked for her. They only ever requested their doctors by name.

That was part of the reason Cassia wanted to study medicine – to do what her mother never had the opportunity to do. She wanted to save the world and be there on time for the people who needed saving. She knew now that if the paramedics had arrived sooner, her father would still be alive. He should still be alive.

Regardless of her motivations, her mother was ecstatic at the thought of having a doctor in the family. She was there every step of the way, from the minute Cassia started filling out university applications to her first failed exam when she had almost given up. Her mother's unwavering support saw her through it all and was the reason she could neatly stitch up a wound before she even had the chance to kiss a boy.

"Yo, Khan."

She turned around to face one of the other interns rushing toward her, a stack of papers in one of his hands and an energy drink in the other. "Your sister's blood work came back. All negative," he said.

Cassia scanned through the results. Something must be wrong.

They must have misread the results or used the wrong sample. *How could everything always come back negative?* She made a mental note to run the tests again and this time, she would do it herself.

Every doctor they took her to agreed on one thing.

Calla was dying.

She was dying and they didn't know how to stop it. They gave it all sorts of names. For the first few months they thought it was her imagination. They thought she was lying about her nausea and her pain, but when she had visible weight loss and increased inflammation, they finally decided to look into it.

They ran her through an MRI, and did every blood test they could think of.

There was no cancer, no heart defects, nothing. It was a medical mystery and whenever someone thought of something new to test, she was there, being tested and treated symptomatically.

"I'm sorry," he said, brushing his fingers through his shoulder-length hair. "We'll figure it out. I saw her in the hallway, she's looking better…. Stronger."

"She has good days." Cassia smiled politely and rushed off to rounds, rambling off answers without having to think about it. Her memory was excellent. It had always been, but over the last few years it had become photographic, or *videographic*, if that were a thing. She could clearly recall a sequence of events as if watching a video, like the ones her dad had recorded of her and Lucas's shared childhood birthdays.

After a ten-hour shift, Cassia found Calla sitting in the break room, her eyebrows furrowed over a geometry problem. Her sleeves curled over her hands and all that peeked out were her little fingers angrily gripping a blunt pencil.

"Need some help?"

"Stop showing off that you're good at math," Calla joked, and groaned loudly. "I hate this. I'm never going to use it."

"Math is extremely useful," Cassia said as she picked up the thin notebooks and shoved them into the superhero-themed backpack.

"Not if you're dead."

Cassia flinched, but said nothing. Calla had taken to making comments about her death and Cassia had no idea what the appropriate reaction should be. Realizing her mouth was open, she slammed it shut, grinding her teeth as Calla walked ahead of her.

After dragging her family out of the hospital, Cassia drove them home in silence. They were all too tired to talk. Her mother's eyelids slowly dropped and a quick peek in the rearview mirror told her what she already knew – Calla was out cold, her wavy black hair bunched around her small face. Cassia wanted to brush it back, pin it up and expose her pretty face, which she so seldom showed. She and Cassia had the same wavy black hair, inherited from their father, but their tan skin, that was all their mother.

Taking the long way home, she gave them all a few extra minutes to release the stresses of the day even though all she could think about was resting her head and falling asleep, hoping she would get those few minutes with Lucas.

CHAPTER TWO

Lucas visited her again. At least, that was what she liked to call them. *Visits.* She wasn't ready to face the fact that he would never visit her again, not in real life. Where she would be able to hug him, or punch him, depending on her mood and how annoying he was being.

During one of the many sessions where she sat on that worn-out leather couch, her therapist had suggested it was a harmless coping mechanism. Her brain was simply trying to make sense of his sudden disappearance and searching for closure.

This *visit* went as they usually did; he spoke, and it looked like he was saying her name, or *Cass* as he called her. He was the only one she allowed to call her that, he and his mom, Aunty Rosheen, since she came up with it.

She didn't bother trying to respond. She just smiled at him, watching him huff and puff, before he dragged his large hands across his face in frustration. Sometimes she reached out toward him, and he would reach back, but their hands never made contact, like trying to touch light.

His dark hair was longer than when she last saw him. It brushed over his ears and flicked in all directions when he ran his hand through it. A thin layer of stubble had crept over his jawline. By the time he'd turned eighteen, he still hadn't grown much facial hair. This wasn't the eighteen-year-old boy who had gone missing who visited her. He looked the way she imagined he would look now, if he were here.

★   ★   ★

Cassia awoke to a sudden shriek. She launched herself out of bed, stumbled over her scrunched-up sheets, and crawled to the door. She flung it open as she climbed to her feet and ran in the direction of the all-too-familiar scream: Calla's room.

Calla was curled up tightly, looking even smaller than usual, in the middle of her bed. The room felt damp and cold, even though the heater was on. Cassia ran to the bed and wrapped her arms around her sister.

"Calla, talk to me, talk to me," she said, trying to keep her voice calm and steady.

Calla's screaming sent bolts of pain into Cassia's chest and the bedroom shook as if being shattered by the sound.

Using all her force, she flipped her sister onto her back, and peeled her thin arms and legs away from her chest. Cassia placed her lips on her sister's forehead – she was burning up. Cassia checked for any obvious injuries but could not find any.

"Calla, please, please, tell me what's hurting?" she shouted through her ringing ears.

The screaming stopped, as did the writhing. Cassia checked her pulse; it seemed fine, slower than her own, she'd bet.

Cassia collapsed on the bed next to her sister, panting as if she'd forgotten how to breathe. Half the time she wasn't sure if she was awake when these things happened.

As usual, after screaming for a few minutes, Calla would fall asleep, or, more accurately, lose consciousness, since Cassia was never able to wake her.

★   ★   ★

A few hours went by and her sister's eyes were clear when they finally opened. "Morning," Calla squeaked. Cassia cursed loudly and rolled onto her side to face her sister. "I'm sorry," Calla said, and turned to her side so that they were facing each other. Scrunching her little face up, she continued, "I did it again, didn't I?"

"Are you okay?" Cassia whispered. It was all she could manage. It was also all she cared about.

Calla nodded. "I think so."

Cassia closed her eyes and willed herself to wake up. This was surely a nightmare. "It's happening more regularly," she said, more to herself than to Calla. She opened her eyes and looked at her sister's pained expression. This was real life, unfortunately.

"I know," Calla replied, and cupped her older sister's face in her hands. "I'll try not to scream next time."

Heartache sliced against Cassia's chest. Blinking away tears before Calla could see them, she said, "Don't be silly. It's not your screaming that upsets me. I want to figure out how to make your pain stop." She shook her head angrily. "It doesn't make any sense."

"Lots of things around here don't make sense anymore. I'm glad Mom wasn't here."

That was a relief. Their mother struggled to accept what was going on. Instead, she did what any sane person would do to maintain that sanity – she ignored it. After spending months speaking to every doctor who owed her a favor, of which there were many, she eventually gave up and spent all her time at work. Solving medical problems she knew could be solved. No one could blame her; Cassia often wanted to do the same thing.

They pulled themselves off the single bed and started getting ready for the day when Calla suddenly announced, "I don't want to go to school today."

"Come on, please don't fight me today. You're terrible at math, so let's not pretend you're smart enough to skip class." Cassia playfully leaned on her sister's shoulders as they entered the kitchen.

"You know, I will grow and you won't be able to do that anymore."

"If you're anything like Mom, you're almost at your full height," Cassia said with a laugh. Teasing her sister felt natural, and for those brief moments she almost forgot about everything unnatural about their situation.

"You're one to talk. You're not that much taller."

Cassia dragged Calla to school, much against her will, and watched as everyone stared as she climbed out of the car. They'd had to inform the school about Calla's unknown medical condition, and since then, everyone, including the other students, treated her strangely. Cassia's heart twisted in guilt. If her classmates had looked at her that way, she wouldn't want to go to school either. Granted, she never had many school friends, but she had Lucas. He was all she needed.

Calla shot back a look of anger.

So small, so fierce. They got that from their mother. At least that's what her dad used to say.

Cassia held up her hand in a wave that was meant to be encouraging, but Calla was already gone, with her dark hair bouncing angrily behind her.

★   ★   ★

With five hours free before her shift started, she should have gone home to sleep, but after their stomach-twisting morning, she was too buzzed. Her hands steered the wheel against her mind's better judgment and instead of going home, she found herself driving along the narrow mountainous road that took her to the place where her life had been flipped upside down.

Twin Peaks Camping Grounds.

The sign looked just the same as it did that night, four years ago. White fading letters on a dark green background, mounted on two rusting steel poles. And unlike that night, the parking lot was empty.

Cassia turned off the car and climbed out without hesitation, fueled by something she didn't understand. Perhaps it was because of the dreams, but for some reason, she needed to see it again. She needed to understand what happened to him.

The uneven stone stairs stretched down a steep path and below it, in the distance, the water shimmered. Luring her in as it had that night. If she closed her eyes, she could picture Lucas lifting her up in the water and dunking her under. She remembered swimming back up to the surface and shoving him. He lost his footing and stumbled underwater, pulling her back down with him.

There was a full moon that night and the light scattered off the water like shooting stars. The air was thick with excitement, celebration and teenage sexual tension. She remembered Jay wrapping his arms around her and whispering in her ear before leading her back to her tent. One side of Lucas's mouth had curved upward into that familiar lopsided smile, his dimple practically daring her to do it. He knew exactly what Jay wanted and he thought she wouldn't go.

So, she did. Partially to prove him wrong and partially because she was rather surprised that Jay, one of the hottest guys at school, was interested in her.

A typical cliche. Losing her virginity on the night of her eighteenth birthday. *Their* eighteenth birthday. Her stomach twisted awfully at the memory, wrapping around itself, crippling her.

Lucas had literally been there from the second she was born. Their mothers gave birth on the same night, in Rosheen's living room. While the details were always fuzzy, she knew Lucas was a few hours older than she was, because he liked reminding her of that.

He was always there.

How could he suddenly not be?

Cassia walked over the flat grass where their tents had been erected. Her tent was next to Lucas's and in the middle of the night, after what was one of the most awkward and uncomfortable experiences of her life, she crept out of her tent and into his.

He wasn't there.

No one knew where he was. She'd left him right there. In the water. Surrounded by his friends.

What happened?

It was the question that had haunted her for years.

Shaking the memories from her head, she inhaled the fresh smell and walked to the edge of the water. She stared at the last spot where she'd seen him and, without thinking, pulled off her shirt and threw it to the ground. Suddenly, it was a need, not a want or a simple curiosity. She needed to feel the water. The same water that took him. Urgently, she kicked off her shoes and tossed her phone and keys onto the pile of clothing. The second they landed, she already had one foot in the water, without bothering to check the temperature first.

The coolness of the fresh mountain water threatened to freeze her extremities but she soldiered on as the numbness set in. She swam to where she had last seen him and looked down at the crystal-clear water. So clear that she could see beyond her toes as she gently treaded, keeping herself afloat. She could even see the rocks far below covered in green moss. Closing her eyes, she dropped down, and water gushed into her ears as her toes landed on the rocks below, slipping on the slimy moss.

Had he slipped?

No, he couldn't have.

Lucas was an excellent swimmer and a big guy. Someone would have seen him go down.

Someone would have, at the very least, found his body.

Surfacing, she inhaled deeply, rubbing her icy fingers across her wet face, and swam back to where her clothing lay.

Staring across the swimming area while she pulled her dry clothes over her wet body, she marveled at the size. The lake wasn't that big or that deep, but she had swum through it for days after, searching alongside the official search-and-rescue team. She had continued searching long after they gave up. When no one had found him, a strange mixture of loss and relief filled her. If they hadn't found him, surely it meant he could still be alive, somewhere.

But she knew the truth.

He would never leave without telling her. He would never willingly leave her.

★   ★   ★

After her unplanned detour and another twelve-hour shift, her feet ached as she unlocked her front door and walked into the living room.

Calla was on the couch with a laptop balanced on her legs, and their mother was cooking in the kitchen, keeping an eye on Calla in the living room over the marbled island. The smell of ginger and garlic smothered her senses, making Cassia's stomach growl loudly. Sleep could wait. She needed food first.

Her mother's friendly voice jumped across the kitchen island. "How was your day? You look terrible."

"Thanks, Mom," Cassia murmured. Her mother was both her biggest supporter and critic. Balance. Her mother laughed, looking up at her, eyebrows raised as she waited for the rest of her answer. "Oh," Cassia continued, "my day was…." She hesitated, and then blurted out, "I went to the camping site today…to Twin Peaks."

The sound of the wooden spoon vigorously stirring against the sides of the pot suddenly stopped. All that remained was the sound of the onions sizzling. Even Calla sat up straight and turned around to stare at her.

"Why?" her mother asked, the friendly tone she'd used just a minute prior vanished.

"I had to," Cassia replied, shaking off her backpack and dropping it to the floor. "I wanted to."

"It's dangerous. I told you. I begged you, Cassia. I begged you to never go there again." Her mother's voice climbed in pitch, until the last few words of her sentence were almost too high-pitched to hear.

Cassia pulled up a barstool at the kitchen counter and climbed up. "I know how to take care of myself, Mom. Dad made sure of that."

"He taught Lucas too, didn't he? It didn't make a difference," her mother snapped, her hazel eyes wide with fury. She turned back to the pot and stirred viciously. Cassia was glad that the meat she'd tossed into the pot was already dead before taking that beating.

"Mom." Cassia prepared her apology. She stretched an arm across the counter and said, "I'm sorry. I just want to know what happened to him."

Her mother reached out her hand and briefly squeezed Cassia's fingers. "Promise me you won't do it again. Promise me. Nothing good can come from it."

"I promise," Cassia said, unsure whether she meant it.

"I promised her I would keep her boy safe," her mother said, tears bunching at the corners of her eyes. "It was her dying wish." She swallowed hard and exhaled a shaky breath.

"You lost your best friend and a year later, I lost mine...." Cassia mumbled.

Her mother locked eyes with her and said, "Death comes, as it does, without warning. My work prepared me for that."

"He isn't dead! He's missing."

Her mother looked back to her pot and stirred, slowly, as her eyes glazed over. "I was supposed to keep him safe...." she repeated. "She kept you safe that night."

"The night I was born?" Cassia asked. They'd spoken about this a number of times and each time the story differed slightly, leaving her with more questions than answers.

Her mother nodded. "You could have died. You were seven weeks early."

"I know," Cassia replied, "but I still don't understand how she saved me or how she helped you, considering she'd just given birth."

A few seconds passed as her mother stared at the stove, without stirring. She looked at Cassia. "I don't remember the details, it was years ago. What I do remember is how Lucas screamed. Big lungs on that little baby. I don't know who was screaming louder, me or him, but the second you were born, the second Rosheen lifted you up, he stopped crying and looked at you. It was like he already knew you were going to be his best friend."

Cassia laid her head in her arms, flat on the counter, and allowed the tears to overwhelm her. Her chest ached, tugging at every part of her, forcing her to acknowledge the loss.

Her mother walked around the kitchen island and rubbed her back gently. "I'm sorry, baby, I didn't mean to make you cry…. Supper's ready, let's eat. You'll feel a bit better."

Cassia fell asleep that night, purposefully picturing the shimmering water. Not the water she had seen that afternoon, but from that night with the moonlight shining across it. She welcomed Lucas into her dreams, wishing and hoping that perhaps this time she would be able to speak to him, hear him and finally ask him about what had happened.

CHAPTER THREE

Lucas

Lucas slammed his fist on the dark wooden table, sending a shudder through the large dining room.

Cass still couldn't hear him. She seemed to have stopped trying. When she occasionally tried speaking, he couldn't hear her either. He sighed with annoyance, watching her stare at him, mildly amused.

If he wasn't so desperate to get hold of her, he'd have found it amusing too.

Blinking a few times, she disappeared. Presumably, she'd woken up. He often found himself wondering whether it was for work, or university. He hoped she'd gone on to study medicine just as she said she would, even though he'd used every opportunity to try to convince her to take a gap year with him and backpack through Europe.

"That's it," Lochlan said, exhaling loudly. "I'm going to fetch her myself."

Lochlan hovered behind him like a shadow. Overwhelming him not necessarily with darkness, but a lack of light.

Lucas pushed his chair back suddenly and stood up. He turned to face Lochlan, meeting his hard gaze.

Lochlan's unnatural blue eyes flashed brightly. "Your plan isn't working. I'll fetch her." His tone was hard and unkind.

Discomfort grew in Lucas's stomach. If he had his way, he wouldn't let Lochlan near her. Even though Lochlan said he needed Cass here as much as they did, he was still a First.

"Back off," Lucas replied. "We're doing this my way." He took a step toward Lochlan and while Lochlan, being a First, was already taller than the average person, Lucas towered over him.

Lochlan raised his hands in surrender as a playful smirk covered his smug face. "All right, your Highness."

"Don't call me that," Lucas countered. A muscle in his jaw hardened and he willed it to relax. He wouldn't let Lochlan's taunting get to him, not today.

Lochlan rolled his eyes and said, "I thought it would be wise to teach you some manners, since you always conveniently forget to address me properly." He grabbed the end of his maroon-and-gold cloak, lifting the Firsts' insignia, a full moon surrounded by six stars, to his chest, and vanished.

Lucas marched upstairs to the library, seething. This was usual after any interaction with Lochlan. The library door swung open at his command and the lights turned on. Shelves extended as far as he could see. He had been here for about four years and there were parts of the library he still hadn't had the chance to explore.

Books and scrolls lined the walls from floor to ceiling. The dark shelves absorbed light and ushered in a quietness that was unshakeable. He slid his hand across the book covers; dust flickered off and disappeared into the darkness. He found the *Book of Visionaries* exactly where he had last seen it and made his way over to the desk in the corner. He sat down and opened the heavy book from the beginning, for the third time. There had to be a way he could speak to her in her dreams. He must be missing something.

Maybe he wasn't powerful enough, maybe she wasn't, or maybe their bond wasn't as strong as he thought. Whatever the problem was, he had to solve it. Too many lives depended on it.

"Lucas?"

He spun around, recognizing the deep voice. Xo stood behind him, casually leaning against one of the shelves, a shelf filled with smut.

"These are my favorites," Xo said, sticking his thumb out, pointing at the shelf behind him.

A laugh escaped Lucas, against his better judgment. "You must be the one who's been putting them in here."

"All literature should be respected," Xo replied with a wide toothy smile, his white teeth contrasting with his dark skin. His broad body pushed off the shelf as he made his way toward Lucas. "No luck?"

"Nothing. Same as always. I don't think she can hear me." Lucas slammed the book closed and stood up. "According to this book," he said, throwing it toward the shelf, where it levitated and settled in between two other books perfectly, "it's unlikely that I'd be able to reach her, since I'm not a Visionary. It was a long shot anyway. We need a new plan."

"How about a bit of lunch before we get started, yeah?" Xo replied, his brows furrowed, as he walked over and casually slapped Lucas on his back.

Lucas sighed and nodded. Xo always knew when to step in. If it weren't for him, Lucas would not have survived on this side. Lucas arrived here, in the Selene Realm, in the midst of a hurricane. Little did he know, he was the cause of it. If Xo hadn't managed to calm him down, he would have destroyed himself and everything around him. Xo took full advantage of this fact.

They made their way down the long passage in silence. The house, or more accurately, the manor, was different from the home he grew up in. It was old and worn, but he didn't mind. There was a sense of familiarity.

Every crack in the wall, or scuffed linoleum flooring, had a story to tell and every story was far more interesting than the life he used to live.

Xo sniffed loudly and cheered. "Brie's baked something," he said, increasing the speed of his walk until he broke into a full-fledged run. Lucas shook his head in amusement as his stomach growled at the scent of the freshly baked bread. Since he arrived here, he was almost always hungry.

They entered the kitchen as Brie was removing the steaming loaves of bread. Her hands were covered in red oven mitts she had knitted herself and a soft smile covered her pretty face as she set the bread down on the table.

Lucas and Xo waited eagerly, their mouths watering as they watched her slice through the bread. "Watching me isn't going to make it go any quicker, boys," she said.

Lucas jumped up to slice some cheese and Xo quickly intercepted the knife and said, "Let me do it."

"I know how to slice cheese," Lucas replied, slouching back into his seat.

"Yeah, but I'm better at it," Xo said, tossing the knife into the air and catching it, without breaking eye contact with Lucas.

"Nice," Lucas said. "Excellent use of your skills."

Brie sat down next to Lucas and asked, "Hey, still no luck?"

"If everyone could stop asking me that, it would be great," he snapped, and immediately regretted it. He looked up into Brie's big blue eyes – naturally blue, he noted, unlike the bright blue eyes of the Firsts. "I'm sorry, I just don't know what to do."

She covered his hand with her own and gave him a sympathetic smile. "You're not doing this alone. We're all here for you, remember."

"Yeah, you don't actually need any of them, you have me," Xo said, that smile fixed on his face as he prepared their sandwiches. "Brie, we're gonna need another bread."

"I baked five of them, but you can get it yourself," she snapped, narrowing her eyes at Xo. He blew her a kiss in response and she rolled her eyes. Lucas stifled a laugh. This was usual for every mealtime.

"Maybe we can do this without her?" Brie asked, turning her attention back to Lucas. Her blond hair fell into her face and Xo reached out to push it back. He nearly lost a hand in the process. Brie was as good with a knife as he was. "We don't even know if she can help us. It's all a big risk," she said.

"She needs to be here. She'll be able to help. Plus, I…" Lucas hesitated, swallowing down his sandwich before continuing, "I want to help her sister."

Brie sat back, understanding clouding over her eyes. She crossed her arms and before she could say anything, Xo spoke.

"Is she hot?" he asked, wiping a few crumbs off his chin.

"She's eleven."

"Never mind, then. What about Cassia. Is she hot?"

"We're not allowed to interfere with what happens on their side, Lucas," Brie said. She bit the inside of her cheek. Her sandwich was still untouched. "If the king finds out…."

"I know, but I have to. Her sister shouldn't be in that much pain, especially when we know what it is. We know how to fix it! Why should she suffer? Why should Cass suffer with her?" Lucas noticed the fear entering Brie's eyes. He felt Xo's heavy hands drop down on his shoulders. He hadn't seen Xo move to stand behind him.

"Sorry," Lucas mumbled. He knew he'd done it again. He'd tapped into the power that equally impressed and frightened them.

"It's okay…it's fine…. I suppose asking for her help goes against the rules anyway, so we may as well break all the rules while we're at it," Brie replied, standing up. At full height, she still wasn't much taller than Lucas when he was sitting down.

"The blue eyes suit you," Xo teased, glancing over at Lucas. "So sexy. If I were you, I'd tap into those powers just to get the eyes."

"Lochlan agrees, you know, that she could help us," Lucas said, purposely ignoring Xo's comment.

"That's what I'm worried about," Brie said.

"He wants to end this massacre as much as we do. He's the one who warned us about it," Lucas said, standing up. He towered above both Brie and Xo.

"Why?" Brie replied, her chin raised. His height didn't intimidate her at all. "He's a First! And not just any First, but Prince Lochlan Firdra. You couldn't pick a *worse* First and I don't trust him."

"Neither do I," Lucas snapped, "but we need all the help we can get. We can't let what happened to Sevin, Alyssa, Jean…." Brie paled when he mentioned the last name. "We can't let it happen to anyone else, to everyone else."

Lucas tried his best to shake off what Brie said, but he knew. He knew that trusting Lochlan was risky. It was no secret that the Firsts hated the Reborns, but this curse, these monsters – it affected the Firsts too, according to Lochlan. They had as much to lose as the Reborns. They had more to lose, since they had everything and owned everyone.

"I'm worried he has an ulterior motive. Find out what it is before we get ourselves into deeper trouble," Brie said.

Xo slapped him on the back, nearly knocking the air out of him. "Come on, let's take your mind off things for a moment, yeah? How about you join me for a hunt? Nisa's busy, Jun's still recovering from the last time we went out and Brie doesn't want to hunt with me." Xo eyed Brie and she narrowed her eyes at him.

"Why would I want to hunt with you after what you did last time?" she asked.

"It was just a small-to-medium-sized roach. They can't hurt you." Xo laughed and Brie stomped out of the kitchen. For someone so small, she sure made lots of noise moving around.

"Where are we hunting?" Lucas asked.

"We won't cross the Selli River. I don't want to go too far carrying such precious goods," Xo said, raising an eyebrow at Lucas playfully. He grabbed a hunting sheath and shoved it into Lucas's hands as they made their way out the front door. Lucas sucked his teeth. If he could flash his eyes, he would have, just to scare him, but Xo's smile only grew wider.

Upon reaching the front garden, Lucas put his fingers in his mouth and whistled loud enough for the sound to carry around to the stables at the back. Three Baskian wolves came running from behind the manor in a blur of black, gray and white. Ruq, the largest of the three wolves, reached them first, bowing down and trying to slip his head between Lucas's legs, like he used to do when he was a lot smaller.

"Calm down, boy. You're way too big for that now." Lucas rubbed his hand in the gray wolf's fur and Ruq licked him in response.

Zuq and Willis nuzzled Xo; they both loved joining on hunting trips. "Let's take all of them," Xo said. "They need a walk anyway."

"We need to leave at least one of them here, in case of an emergency," Lucas replied, mounting Ruq. The wolf's tail wagged happily when he realized he was chosen for the trip.

"Fine," Xo replied. He marched back into the white manor and came out carrying an entire roasted chicken. "Willis, you're staying behind this time, okay?" He tossed the chicken and the wolf opened his mouth, nearly swallowing the entire thing in one bite.

★   ★   ★

It was a sunny day, as most days were. There was barely a cloud in the sky. They rode to one of their usual hunting spots and jumped off the wolves. Lucas rubbed his hands together; the wolves understood they should melt into the shadows and wait on his call.

He followed Xo as he tiptoed through the woods. The surrounding trees were short and full of bloodberries. Xo swiped off a handful of the red berries and tossed them to Lucas, who pulled out the bag they had brought along and filled it. He popped one into his mouth, savoring the taste. It reminded him of a sweet strawberry, albeit with an ominous name.

Xo gestured to his left, where a kudu was nibbling on bloodberries behind one of the bushes. His long fingers gracefully and silently drew back an arrow. Upon exhalation, he released it, without bothering to reach for another. He didn't need it. The arrow shot through the air and landed in the animal.

'One-shot Xo', that's what they called him.

Kneeling beside the fallen animal, they closed their eyes and thanked the kudu for the food it would be providing, for the energy it would give them and how that energy would give them the ability to use their magic to protect themselves.

"What are you gonna do if you can't reach her?" Xo asked as he started skinning the kudu. His nose scrunched up in distaste as he wiped his knife clean on the animal's fur.

Lucas shook his head. He unsheathed his knife to assist and speed up the process. "I don't know."

"Look, I don't trust the guy, but sending Lochlan would make all of this a lot easier."

Lucas pressed his lips together. He already knew that. "Are you sure she won't get stuck on this side?"

"She'll have the necklace," Xo said, looking up from the kudu.

"Even if Lochlan is the one who brings her here?"

Xo nodded and said, "Besides, I mean, we kind of need her stuck on this side, don't we?"

"Her sister needs her more." Lucas grabbed his waterskin to wash his hands. The sight of blood on his hands made him lose his appetite. "I want it to be her choice to come over. Plus, there's no way she'd go with him willingly. You have no idea how stubborn she is and if he hurts her, I'll kill him. I don't even want him near her."

"We're running out of options," Xo replied, holding his hands out and waiting on Lucas to pour water over them too. "Don't think I haven't noticed that you wreck your entire bedroom every time you have a nightmare."

"I have it under control, okay?"

"Lucas."

"I don't want him near her."

CHAPTER FOUR

The guilt Cassia felt for allowing Calla to skip school disappeared as soon as she saw the smile spreading across her little sister's face. Calla had been screaming, again, and it didn't seem fair to either of them to fight with her about going to school.

"Can I use your laptop to watch movies on in the cafeteria?" Calla asked as they reached the hospital. Her eyes were still puffy from crying, as were Cassia's. Cassia pulled out her laptop and handed it to Calla, who held it to her chest tightly.

Cassia greeted a few people on her way into the hospital. Some of them she'd met when she started studying or interning and others she'd known for as long as she could remember. Every single nurse and doctor knew her by name and many of them, much to her embarrassment, remembered her as the child who was caught sneaking into the morgue to see a dead body.

Lucas had obviously been right behind her. Or in front of her, leading the way. She often lost track of who instigated the trouble they so regularly landed themselves in.

The cold white walls and floors always put her at ease. She could fall asleep listening to heart monitors beeping and the hum of the constant air-conditioning. She often did.

She wrapped her arm around Calla, shocked at the heat radiating from her sister's neck. She leaned downward to place her lips on Calla's forehead, but Calla shook her off. "I'm fine."

"You're burning up."

"Then use a thermometer. There are like a hundred of them in this building," Calla said, turning around to stomp off, but quickly looked over her shoulder and repeated, "I'm fine, stop worrying and go study. Save lives. Fill out forms. Do whatever it is you do here all day."

Cassia walked off to the locker room and felt her phone buzz. It was likely her mother, the university or a promotional text. No one else ever contacted her. While walking, she took out her phone. Promotional text. She deleted it and made a mental note to take a day to unsubscribe from everything. She looked up just before walking into something hard.

Not a wall.

Simon.

She'd have preferred a wall.

Simon was a few years ahead of her. Top of his class and stereotypically handsome. Every minute spent outside of the hospital was undoubtedly spent at the gym.

"Cass," he said, his lips curling into a smile, "if you wanted to feel my body, you could have just asked."

"Don't call me that."

"We should go out for coffee, you know," he said, looking down at her. She stepped back, before shaking her head and sidestepping him. He grabbed her wrist. Closing her eyes, she knew she could break away from his grip, even though he was bigger than her. Playing it through her mind, she pictured the look of shock that would cover his smug face if she ever did any of the things to him that her dad taught her to do.

"Cass, come on. We're both here all the time and it's a shame for two people as pretty as we are to not be having sex." His grip on her wrist loosened as he trailed his fingers along her arm.

"Bold of you to assume I'm not having any sex."

Truthfully, Cassia hadn't even been on a date in years and she hadn't had sex since that night, four years ago, and that night was not something she thought about fondly.

"Regardless," he continued as she pulled her arm away, "I could show you a good time…you're so tightly wound. I would love to be the one to unwind you." He licked his lips and she looked down at her hand, curling her fingers into a fist.

A punch in the center of his perfect face would be the highlight of her day, but instead, she did what women everywhere were forced to do to get rid of a man. She uncurled her fist, smiled and nodded. "Yeah, I'll think about it," she said, hating the lie as she said it.

She definitely would not think about it, but pretending that she would was a lot easier than ever convincing him that she wouldn't and even easier than the alternative, breaking his nose. The worst part was that she would probably be the one who would have to fix him up.

The corridors were bustling with nurses, doctors and cleaning staff rushing around, pushing beds where they were needed and wiping off every single surface all the time. The lingering smell of disinfectant was something she expected both at home and at the hospital.

Snaking her way through the building and dodging nurses, she finally reached the corner of the hospital that was quieter and emptier. Even the lights felt dimmer.

It was her own secret break room. The only place she knew she would be alone. It was why she often studied at the hospital. It was where she studied throughout school too. The room, for some unknown reason, smelled of brown sugar. It was comforting, a trigger to help her focus.

She pulled out her notes and dropped them on the small table she had moved into the room ages ago. There were fewer distractions at the hospital than at home. Home had a TV, a shelf full of books she promised herself she would get to and a bed. Her bed. However, if she were being honest with herself, home had far too many memories of Lucas. She was afraid to pack away the framed photos, the notes, the ticket stubs, because after four years, she was afraid she would forget about him. If it weren't for the dreams, she might have. Everyone else seemed to.

The break room light flickered every few minutes, casting the shadow of her head onto her notes. It wasn't surprising; even the handyman rarely came into this room. She highlighted another paragraph. At the rate she was going, the entire textbook would be highlighted in shades of yellow and green and it would be easier to identify the sentences that weren't highlighted.

She tapped her pen on the table, softly repeating the sentences back to herself, while scribbling key words onto her notes. Her handwriting was quickly becoming the scribble she'd once complained about doctors having.

The faint sound of shoes on tiles pulled her from her notes. At the doorway stood a man. Though she was someone who was rarely at a loss for words, she found herself speechless. Struck by his beauty. His strong jawline. His defined cheekbones and his curly brown hair, which brushed the top of the doorframe. He was handsome in the most obvious of ways. Except it was his eyes that knocked the air out of her. They were blue, but not blue in a way she'd seen before.

"Can I help you?" she choked out, offering him her best polite smile as she tried to make sense of what looked to be a royal warrior's cosplay with a long maroon-and-gold cape pinned at his broad shoulders. Perhaps he was here to entertain the pediatrics department.

"Dark hair, hazel eyes, and a pretty smile," he said, his voice smooth, wrapping around her. "You must be Cass."

The nickname pinched at her heart and then flared up irritation.

"Excuse me?" she said, frowning in confusion as she looked up at the sculpted stranger.

"Ah, yes. The nickname is reserved only for Lucas, then?" he replied. The corner of his mouth tilted up into half a smile and a shallow dimple graced his cheek. He edged closer toward her as the cape swayed to the side, revealing black leather pants and a black shirt, clasped together in the middle with three golden clips.

If hearing Lucas's name didn't send her into shock, the color of the man's eyes did. As he stepped closer, they shimmered, reminding her of a blue flame. Something about him told her he was as dangerous as one too.

"Who are you?" she asked, feeling her heart rate pick up.

"It's a long story, and you won't believe me anyway. But I need you to come with me." He edged closer and Cassia stood from her seat. He took another careful step closer, his heavy leather boots now barely making a sound as he moved smoothly, like a cat.

She mimicked his movement, taking one step back for each step he took toward her, maintaining the same distance between them.

"Who are you? How do you know Luke?" she asked.

"I am a...friend of his, I suppose, using the word 'friend' loosely. Very, very loosely." He lifted his hands casually as he spoke and his cloak swayed open, revealing a knife that looked too sharp to be a prop.

"I know every single one of his friends." Cassia's grip around her pen tightened. "I'll call security if you don't tell me who you are."

He sighed dramatically and said, "While I don't enjoy cliches, it's rather fitting at this point." He took another step closer. "We can do this the easy way, or the hard way."

Cassia stepped back. The back of her sneaker hit the wall. Cornered. Cursing at herself, she focused on her breathing, just like her father had taught her to.

Stay calm. Evaluate the situation. Find the exits.

The exit was right behind him, and the room was not wide enough to get around him.

"Easy way," she said, and walked toward him casually, flashing her best smile as her heart pounded against her rib cage. "How can I help you?"

He smiled, a smug smile that made her stomach jump. She was in trouble. She knew that much. Faster than she expected, he grabbed her elbow and pulled her close. Using all the energy she could muster, she lifted her knee and it met his groin. He grunted, doubling over as his hands flew down to shield himself in case of a second attack. She made a run for the door, but he spun around, grabbed her at the waist and pulled her into his chest. Her fingers tightened around the pen she was still holding and she drove it into his thigh, feeling it pierce the hard muscle. A low growl escaped him. The depth of the sound vibrated through her body but he would not let go.

"Oh, Cass," he said, his voice still smooth and calm, despite the pen still firmly embedded in his leg.

"Stop calling me that," she snapped and spun around even though he held her tightly. She threw her head forward against his chin. The dull pain spread across her forehead and blinded her for a second, but it must have blinded him too as his grip loosened.

She ran.

Before she could take even two steps, he appeared in front of her.

Appeared.

Without walking.

Appeared.

And then, he laughed.

"Oh, you are a fiery little lady," he said, running his hand through his messy brown curls and then wiping the blood off his bottom lip. He inspected the blood and smiled. "I'm impressed."

Cassia staggered back until her thighs knocked against the edge of the table. "W-what," she stammered, "what are you?"

"Cassia, your laptop died. Could I get the charger?"

Calla stood at the entrance and panic overwhelmed Cassia. The tall man who stood in front of Cassia vanished and reappeared a finger's width from Calla's face.

He bent over and whispered, "Boo."

Calla screamed.

Her scream triggered Cassia into action. She ran up to him. She wouldn't let him hurt Calla. Whoever he was. *Whatever* he was.

He stood and faced her as she reached him. "That's about enough of that," he said. His hand gripped the back of her neck as he pulled her into his hard chest and whispered, "Time to go, little lady. This is going to feel a bit weird."

Writhing to get free, she cried out, "No! Stop! Please!" Her body recoiled in his grip a second before her soul was pulled from her body and her body was pulled apart. And then she passed out.

CHAPTER FIVE

Pins and needles startled her awake as the tingling in her chest spread outward, traveling along every nerve in her body until it reached the tips of her fingers and toes. She became aware that she was not breathing. She could not inhale or exhale. Her body was not her own. She tried moving, but her limbs still felt detached, her eyelids sealed shut.

She remembered the fight. The man. The man with the blue-flame eyes who claimed to know Lucas. Calla was there…screaming.

Was it all a dream?

Fingertips brushed across her forehead, trailed down the side of her face, across her jawline and then stopped. The faint salty smell of the ocean tickled her senses, reminding her of all the time she'd spent at the beach.

"She's in one piece, as required."

That voice. It was him. Her attacker. Once again, she tried to move, to run, but her body and brain were not co-operating.

"I told you not to touch her. I warned you," another voice replied aggressively. Another voice she recognized.

Four years. It had been four years since she'd heard that voice, aside from the numerous videos she'd watched over and over.

Luke.

Cassia willed her eyes to open once more, focusing on every last ounce of strength to reactivate her body.

"It was supposed to be her choice," Lucas said in a tone she'd rarely heard him use before. "How did you even find her?"

"I can be very convincing when I need to be," the other man replied in that smooth and calm voice, seemingly unaffected by the bite in Lucas's voice.

And then she felt it. The air whirring back into her body with a force. Had she not been lying down, she would have been slammed onto her back.

Her body shot upright as she gasped for air, gripping the grass on either side of her legs. Her lungs expanded as if it were the first breath she'd ever taken. She looked around, her eyes immediately falling on a broad back with wide shoulders. The same shoulders she had sat on at festivals. Dark tousled hair brushed along the nape of his neck, the same hair she had on a few occasions shaved off, both with and without his permission.

Lucas turned around to face her, his almost-black eyes widening as a smile took over his face. He walked toward her and dropped to his knees. "Cass."

She was dreaming. She must be dreaming. Her dreams had simply evolved and started including made-up characters from all the novels she read. A quick glance over at the man she had fought with proved that. He was still there, in costume, raising an eyebrow at her. The corner of his mouth kicked up into a smirk.

"Cass?" Lucas said again and reached out to touch her. She took in his long-sleeved brown t-shirt and darker brown pants. Her eyes fell on every part of him, every strand of hair and defined muscle. It was Lucas. Not the one she remembered, but the one from their *visits*.

She sat quietly, knowing she wouldn't feel his touch. She never did.

His hands cupped her face and she felt it. The warmth of his fingertips spread through her cheeks. "Cass, are you okay?" Lucas asked her gently and looked over his shoulder at the man standing behind him. "What did you do to her?" he growled.

Tears streamed down her cheeks and onto Lucas's hands. He broke away from his glare and looked back at her, his features instantly softening.

"Luke?" she whispered, so softly she might as well have not said anything at all.

He smiled at her again, both of his dimples making an appearance, and a fresh wave of tears pricked at the corners of her eyes.

Lucas pulled her into his strong embrace and it took her a few seconds to clock that it was him. That she was safe. She wrapped her arms around his neck and inhaled, expecting the apple-scented shampoo he had always used. Instead, he smelled fresh, like the ocean.

"Cass," he said again, into her ear this time. His voice was deep and familiar, taking her back to a time when her life was simple. When her biggest problem was which university she would go to.

"I see. So, it's okay when *he* calls you that?"

She opened her eyes and found those chaotic blue eyes staring at her. A wicked smile spread across his face.

Cassia unwrapped her arms and pushed down on the ground. Her eyes darted between Lucas and the man in the maroon-and-gold cape.

Lucas stood up to face her attacker. "Leave. Now."

Cassia had never heard him use that tone. It was deep and aggressive. It was a warning.

"Seems I've struck a nerve. Can't imagine why, since no harm was done," the man replied. The smirk was still plastered to his face. "Well, except for my leg." He gestured to the hole in his leather pants. "That's going to take a couple hours to heal. Can't say I've ever been stabbed with a pen before." He dragged his teeth over his bottom lip and added, "It was almost delightful."

Cassia opened her mouth to respond but her eyes fell on the big old manor behind him. Vines crawled up the walls and every uncovered section was scarred with cracks and chipped paint. The undersides of her legs were tickled by the freshly cut grass, which stretched all the way to the front of the house. She glanced upward at the blue sky; there wasn't a single cloud in sight.

She had absolutely no idea where she was.

"Lochlan," Lucas said, taking a step closer to the man.

"Fine, I have to go anyway. My father will be looking for me," Lochlan announced. "Thanks for the scuffle, little lady. I do hope we'll get another chance at that."

Before either of them could reply, Lochlan vanished.

Just like before. Like he had done in the hospital. She was sure she saw it correctly this time.

Cassia stood slowly. Her legs felt as though they might give in underneath her and then they did. Her knees buckled and the ground approached quickly, but before she hit it, Lucas caught her, grabbing a handful of the front of her hoodie and pulling her back to her feet. He wrapped an arm around her and dragged her close.

"Lean on me. Your legs will take a few more minutes to realize they belong to you."

Cassia leaned her head on his chest and listened. His heartbeat was steady. His chest was warm, just like his fingers had been. This dream was different. It was better.

"Cass?" Lucas asked, glancing down at her.

She looked up at him and smiled, enjoying being able to feel him, smell him and hear him. She could get used to this.

Narrowing his eyes at her, he said, "This isn't a dream, dammit. Don't give me that stupid smile. I've spent days trying to get you to do something other than smile at me. It drove me fucking nuts."

A classic Lucas rant. The laugh started in her belly and while she tried to suppress it as she watched his face redden with frustration, she couldn't stifle it. She burst out laughing. Obviously, she'd lost her mind. There was no other explanation.

Lucas stopped mid-rant and his hearty laugh joined hers. He brushed her black hair away from her face.

"What in the world is going on?" Cassia said to herself and looked downward. Her eye caught on something unusual. She was wearing the same clothes she had worn that morning, a black hoodie with black leggings and white sneakers. But there was something else. A long thin chain hung around her neck. A bunch of red and orange feathers about the length of her little finger drooped together at the lowest point. "What is this?" she asked, lifting the feathers to her face. They were soft, much like she expected them to be.

"Oh, yeah, we have a lot to talk about," he replied, touching the feathers gently.

She looked up at him, amazed that she could hear him and he could hear her.

"It's not a dream, Cass," he repeated, his brows knitting into a frown.

"This doesn't make any sense," she said, her own fingers reaching for the red feathers, and overlapping with Lucas's fingers. He grabbed her hands in his own and squeezed them. "Where are we?" she asked.

"I really missed you," he said quietly, "and I'll explain everything, but I just need a minute to look at you, and touch you." He squeezed her hand again. "And just convince myself that it's really you, that you're really here."

At least he was as shocked as she was. His calloused fingertips grazed across her knuckles. This couldn't be a dream. It felt too real. He felt too real. "Go on then, bask in my presence and then please tell me what the hell is going on," she said.

Lucas led her toward the manor. Her legs wobbled with each step. "Welcome to the Selene Realm," he said casually, as if it weren't the most shocking thing she had ever heard.

"You gonna elaborate or do I need to beat it out of you?"

He chuckled and said, "We're in another realm. It runs on the same timeline as your world, so we're still the same age, kind of. Physically, I'd start aging slower at some point."

"*Our* world," she corrected him as they climbed the three face-brick stairs leading to the front door.

"It's not *my* world anymore." He paused at the entrance to the manor and pulled her aside to sit on a patio bench. Birds chirped happily and a sense of peace washed over her. The grass she had been lying on stretched ahead of the manor for miles. A small white picket fence bordered the property and beyond that, all she could see were trees in the horizon.

There were no skyscrapers; there were barely any structures. A gravel path swept through the grass to her right and left, but there were no formal roads.

"Did you die?" she asked, her voice catching in her throat. "Did I?"

"Kind of…." he replied. "It's not that simple. That night, on our eighteenth birthday, I don't know, maybe an hour after midnight, something told me to swim underwater."

"What do you mean 'something'?"

"A voice. So I went under and when I came up for air, I was in this realm, coming out of the Selli River, and then there was this hurricane…." He paused and gestured ahead of them. "Never mind the hurricane. I'll show you the river a bit later."

Cassia nodded even though none of what he was saying made sense. "And I was wearing the same feather necklace," he explained, poking at the feathers.

"What does it mean?"

"The state that you're currently in, you're called a Guest. You can leave whenever you want, by ripping off each and every feather. Unless you want to get stuck here, you have to leave before the last feather drops. It looks like you have eight of them."

Cassia felt her jaw tighten. "So you had the same necklace?"

Lucas nodded.

"Did you choose to stay?" she asked. Understanding crept over his face and glanced downward. "Did you choose to leave me? To be here?" He nodded again without lifting his head to look up at her. "Why? I needed you!" Cassia shouted, unable to control her emotions. "I walked out of that tent, after what was one of the weirdest and most awkward experiences of my life, and you weren't there. I really needed you." She swallowed back the instant tears and shook the thought from her head. A fresh wave of anger and pain flowed through her veins, pushing her onto her feet. "When my dad died a few months later, I needed you again and you weren't there. I mourned my best friend, my dad, and then on top of everything, Calla." Her voice cracked on the mention of Calla's name. She needed to get home. *What's going on?*

She wanted to stomp off but had no clue where she'd go. Despite his explanation, she still had no idea where she was.

Lucas stayed seated and eventually looked up at her before wrapping his arms around her and pulling her down onto the bench. "I know, I'm sorry. I'm so sorry, I wish I could have told you. I wanted to. It killed me that I couldn't. I know, I know—"

"No," she interrupted, trying to break out of his embrace, but he held on too tightly. She considered stepping on his toes, but she didn't actually want to hurt him just because she was hurt. "You don't know. Calla's dying and I need to get home. Take me home and stay here in your weird world, you complete asshole." She pushed him back, feeling suffocated in his arms. "And let me go!"

Cassia stood again and mentally prepared herself to say goodbye. Her stomach turned at the thought. As she wrapped her fingers around the bunch of feathers, he finally spoke.

"We can save Calla."

CHAPTER SIX

"What?" Cassia said, frozen in place, her previous anger forgotten, and stared into his eyes. It was like looking at the night sky in the middle of the day.

"Well, we can help you save Calla…. It's why I wanted you here. Well, one of the reasons at least." Lucas stood up and straightened his back. He was taller than anyone she knew.

"Tell me how," she breathed, desperate for information. It was the first time she'd had any hope of saving her sister. "How am I supposed to help her?"

Lucas took a step toward the front door and she followed, her head spinning with thoughts, throwing her off balance. He dropped his hand to the small of her back and gently nudged her along with him, keeping her from toppling over. "I know this sounds ridiculous... and I know you're not going to believe me, but you can heal her."

Cassia shot her friend an incredulous look. "That is ridiculous and I don't believe you. What are you talking about?"

He opened the large front door. Its dark wood was engraved with the same leaves that covered most of the face of the building. It creaked loudly enough to let anyone there know that they had guests.

A bulky staircase wrapped around the back end of the foyer; each dark wood baluster was intricately carved. The walls beside the staircase held multiple paintings of animals and people she'd never seen before. The only things she recognized were a fluffy white cat and rows of blue roses. Before she could look at them all, Lucas interrupted her thoughts.

"Come on, Cass. Didn't you ever wonder why you have an affinity toward healing people? Treating them? Why you're – and I'm guessing here – studying medicine and damn good at it?"

"What are you trying to say? I'm the top of my class because I study, something you never even attempted to do," she snapped, but she knew, she always knew that certain things came too easily to her. She imagined it was because of her photographic memory or due to her mother's influence, that it was a natural talent or that growing up in a hospital meant all the other doctors' skills just leaked into her bones via osmosis.

"You're a Healer."

"This is definitely a dream," Cassia blurted out.

"Oh, and a Visionary." Lucas looked down at her and rested his hands on her shoulders, forcing her to look up at him.

"What?" she asked, as if she hadn't heard what he said.

"It's why I could contact you in your dreams," he said, letting go of her and leading her up the long staircase. Her white sneakers settled in on the worn red velvet carpet that clung loosely to the stairs.

"You didn't contact me, you just visited. I couldn't hear anything," she complained, her hand trailing the intricate patterns on the handrail.

"Well, I tried contacting you. Your powers weren't strong enough and you don't know how to control them.... It failed, miserably."

They reached the top of the staircase. A long passage stretched out ahead of them, doors lining either side, all of them closed. The dark green walls contrasted the dark wood and red carpet and yet, something about it felt familiar. It felt *homey*.

"You wanted to tell me how to save Calla?" she asked, her own question pulling her from the surrounding distractions.

"Yeah, amongst other things," he said, furrowing his brows. "Anyway, now that you're here, we can teach you how to control your powers to heal Calla, and we'll brew the suppressant tonic."

Cassia stared up at Lucas. She was growing tired of asking questions.

He caught her look and grinned. "I'm sorry, I've been here so long I forget how unbelievable it all sounds. A suppressant tonic will keep Calla's powers under control, until she's old enough to properly learn how to use them."

"Powers?" Her heart rate quickened.

"Empath."

"What?"

"Is that the only word you're going to use?" he asked as he opened the door to a library. At least that's what she assumed it was. Shelves lined the walls and books lined the shelves farther than she could see. The room was dark and musty. The smell reminded her of the inside of their old piano, which no one ever used. The dim lighting and uncanny silence gave her the sense that she was sneaking into a forbidden library in the middle of the night.

"Hold on, prepare for your mind to be blown," he said, bouncing both his eyebrows before lifting his right hand and curling his fingers toward him. A book flew down from the shelf and landed directly in his open hand.

Cassia jumped back, her eyes wide with surprise and fear.

"Pretty cool, huh?" he said, offering her two of his dimples in exchange for one smile from her. "Telekinesis, which is the coolest power, if we're being honest."

"No way. This isn't real. None of this is real...or I'm dreaming or I'm dreaming and my mind is combining all the conversations we've ever had into this weird dream," she said. She thought back to how he had always said he would pick telekinesis as his superpower, while she argued teleportation was a far better choice, imagining all the time she could save if she could skip the traffic.

"It's not a dream, Cass," Lucas said quietly as he dusted off the front cover and showed it to her.

Strange symbols on the black leather cover blurred and transformed into the words, *Book of Empaths*.

"It's like a thousand pages long and the text is tiny enough for you to need your specs, so I'm hoping you're wearing your contact lenses," he said with half a smile.

She was.

They walked toward one of the many desks. There was only one chair and before they reached it, he gestured quickly and a chair from another desk slid across the floor and stopped in front of her. Cassia gasped, jumping out of the way.

"It wasn't going to hit you," he said, gesturing at the chair. "Sit."

"Now you're just showing off," she said. She sat and opened the book.

A small lamp was fixed on the end of the desk. The light was dim and yellow, providing just enough for her to make out the tiny letters. The book wasn't written in English; it was not even written in a script she could recognize.

As with the title, the scripts blurred and reappeared in her own language. She glanced up at Lucas questioningly.

"It'll only appear legible to those who have been given permission to read it by one of us...." he said and then added casually, "Protection charm."

"And what exactly are you? A wizard?"

Lucas frowned as if he hadn't thought of that. "Something like that, without the wands and the broomsticks, although we do brew potions in cauldrons, so the stereotype hit that one on the head," he said with a laugh and flipped through the book. Multiple bookmarks lay between the pages. "Ah," he breathed, and then read aloud, "*An Empath may exhibit physical side effects should they be unable to control their ability. The younger the Empath, the more severe the side effects. Continuous exposure to a negative emotional and mental state could lead to death. It is recommended that the Empath's abilities be suppressed to avoid further damage.*" He paused and glanced sideways at Cassia. "Does she go to the hospital with your mom the way we used to? I'll bet there's loads of negative emotions there."

'Negative emotions' was putting it lightly. Calla was surrounded by death, by grief, by everyone's constant exhaustion and inability to deal with their medical bills. Cassia had basically dragged her sister to her coffin almost every single day.

"How do we suppress it?" she choked out, guilt eating at her.

He turned to another bookmark. The ingredients and instructions were listed for the suppressant tonic. "We have about seventy percent of these ingredients on hand. We have sage, rosemary, whiskers of a lire, petals of a nerine…. I've been hunting down the other ingredients, but it hasn't been easy….And there are some other distractions…."

Cassia touched his arm gently, still shocked at the sensation of physical contact. He glanced at her and she nodded. "Cool, cool, cool. Sounds cool. Everything sounds extremely cool."

"Are you freaking out?" he asked, closing the book and sending it back to the shelf with a flick of his wrist.

She shook her head, watching the book float away and land exactly where he had summoned it from. "No, why would I freak out? I'm a Healer and a Visionary and my sister is an Empath and it's killing her but we have a tonic, or seventy percent of a tonic and uhm, my best friend has telekinesis and…am I missing anything?" She paused, "Oh, yes, there's this." She reached down to the feather necklace. "So, no, not freaking out, nope. Nothing to freak out about, nothing at all."

"Cass."

"What if the last feather falls before we finish the tonic? Before I learn how to heal her? How sure are you that I can heal her? How sure are you that she is an Empath? Why is she an Empath? Why did it suddenly start affecting her? Actually, why am I magical? Why are you? Is everyone secretly magical?"

"Cass."

"What happens if I die in this realm? Do I go back to my realm? If I go back to my realm, can I get back to the Selene Realm? Are there other realms? Could I end up there accidentally?"

Lucas pulled her in for a hug so tight it squeezed the air and anxieties out of her. He did it every time she started panicking. "I've really missed you."

"Sorry to interrupt."

Cassia turned around to face a handsome, dark-skinned man with a friendly face. He instantly smiled at her and she couldn't resist smiling back.

"Xo Tembo, meet Cassia Khan." Lucas released her and gestured to the man, who took a few eager steps toward them and stuck out his hand. Cassia reached out her hand too. Xo shook it firmly. It was another person, other than Lucas, that she could hear and touch.

She was starting to realize that all of this might be real.

"Finally. It's good to meet you, Cassia. I heard so much about you and I can't wait to hear some more, but…" Xo said with what felt like genuine interest before he turned to Lucas. "Lochlan is in the dining hall waiting on you. He says it's important."

Lucas sighed loudly and looked to the ceiling.

"He has that threatening look in his eyes, boss. I wouldn't take too long," Xo said, raising his eyebrows.

"Fine. Stay up here," Lucas said to Cassia.

"He specifically said he wants to see her," Xo said. "He's a second away from teleporting through the house, so…."

"I'm not scared of him," Cassia said as her heart thumped wildly, and, much to Lucas's obvious displeasure, she inhaled deeply and walked out of the library, curious to see what Lochlan and his blue-flame eyes wanted from her.

Lucas ran up to her and led them back downstairs. The dining room must have taken up about half of the manor. A twenty-seat table stood in the center of the room, made out of the same dark wood that covered the rest of the place. Red velvet seats surrounded the table, matching the rug, and in one of those seats sat Lochlan.

He stood as they approached and crossed his arms, tutting loudly.

"What do you want?" Lucas asked, protectively stepping in front of Cassia.

"You haven't covered her scent, you absolute ape. If I can smell her, so can the rest of the Firsts and we're not the only ones you need to be worried about," Lochlan said, his eyes fixed on Cassia.

"I covered her scent the second you arrived with her," Lucas spat.

"It didn't work," Lochlan said, resting his hands on his hips.

"I can smell her too," Xo stated softly, his head dipping slightly. Lucas turned around to look at him and then looked at Cassia.

THE LAST FEATHER • 43

"Why wouldn't it work?" Lucas asked.

Lochlan rolled his eyes. "You probably did it wrong." He took a step forward and said, "Step aside, your Highness."

"Don't you dare touch her."

"The royal guard will be here in a minute. If any of them can teleport, they'll be here in a second. You know that."

Lucas stepped aside and said, "If you—"

"Blah blah, don't hurt her, et cetera," Lochlan mocked as he opened both of his hands in front of her, his long fingers spread apart. He pulled them back, just an inch, before pushing forward. A burst of cold air wrapped across her skin as the smell of burning wood filled the air.

Xo sniffed loudly and said, "Firewood?"

Lochlan smiled at Cassia and said, "To suit that fiery personality."

Cassia narrowed her eyes at him. If Lucas didn't trust him, neither did she and she wanted him to know that.

"You can go now," Lucas said firmly.

Lochlan tutted again and said, "Not so fast. Has she seen anything yet?"

"She's not ready yet."

"Time is running out," Lochlan said, resting his hand on the table for a second before drumming his fingers. The sound echoed through the dining hall in a way that heightened her anxiety with each tap.

"She's still got eight feathers. Back off," Lucas replied, lifting his chin. The large room suddenly seemed much smaller. Much too small for these two men to be arguing.

"Very well, I shouldn't be here when my half-witted half brother arrives. It will simply add to the list of reasons he would like to kill me." Lochlan sighed and looked at Cassia. "The cover-up isn't enough. She needs to change her clothes, if that's what you would call *that*," he said, looking her up and down. "Have her shower and she needs to eat some of our food to keep her original scent hidden."

Without farewell, he vanished, just as he had before, leaving the subtle smell of vanilla and violence in his wake.

"Who is he?" Cassia asked, leaning against the maroon-carpeted wall, still staring at where he'd stood.

Lucas's shoulders were tense as he turned to face her. "Long story, but he's right. You need to get into the shower. Now. I'll bring you something to eat and wear." He grabbed her wrist and led her through the house at such a speed that her feet were barely touching the ground. They arrived at the doorway of a spacious bedroom, a four-poster bed at one end, but before she could look around, he shoved her into the connected bathroom. "Shower works just like a normal shower. Mostly. Use the soap. Wash your hair." He grabbed her shoulders and made eye contact. "Be quick. Be quiet."

CHAPTER SEVEN

Lucas

Lucas ran to the kitchen and grabbed two of Brie's freshly baked chocolate chip cookies.

"I think this should fit her. We'll find something better later," Brie said, holding up clothing that he didn't bother looking at. He took it and launched himself upstairs.

Lucas knocked gently. There was no answer. Entering the room, he kept his head down, just in case. The coast was clear. He heard the shower turn on, immediately followed by the sound of Cass muttering something to herself.

"Cass?" he called into the bathroom.

"Still busy!" she replied quickly. "Is it okay if I get the feathers wet? I couldn't remove the necklace."

"It's fine," he said, walking into the bathroom, still looking at his feet.

"Don't come in!" she said.

"I won't look, but take this." Lucas looked away. He rolled up his sleeve and blindly stuck his hand through the shower curtain. He'd seen Cass naked once when he'd barged into her room unannounced. They never spoke of it.

"Why are you passing me a cookie in the shower?"

"Just put it in your mouth," he replied, annoyed at the water dripping down his hand, trailing down his arm and into the sleeve of his shirt.

"That's what *he* said," she replied, laughing at her own joke.

He resisted a laugh; there wasn't time for jokes. "Cass, please, just—"

"Okay, okay," she said, the sound of her words muffled by the sounds of chewing. "I will have you know, this is the first time I'm eating in the shower."

"Clothes are on the bed, and another cookie. Remember, be quick, be quiet." Lucas rushed out of the room and closed the door behind him. He listened for a few moments while he caught his breath. Cass was here, in his world. As he let out a long sigh, the sound of the shower water running stopped.

Voices traveled upstairs, unfamiliar voices. More than one. He walked downstairs as casually as he could, even though he was aware that he was moving faster than usual.

If they sensed he was anxious, they would know something was up. He shook it off and schooled his expression.

Nisa, a Reborn whom they'd only recently recruited and who was a few years younger than him, stood at the open front door. Two of the royal guards stood in front of her, blocking all light from behind them.

"Hey, boys," Lucas said plainly as he reached the front door and then he rested a hand on Nisa's shoulder. "Nisa, Brie's looking for you in the back garden."

She looked up at Lucas appreciatively, curtsied and left.

"We smell a Guest, a female Guest."

Lucas recognized the speaker as being Lochlan's younger brother, Kain, although he looked at least a few years older. Age meant nothing to Firsts.

"You just missed her." Lucas leaned against the doorframe, his heart still thumping wildly.

"There was one?" Kain asked, his blue eyes wide. The blue eyes and fair skin were about the only things that resembled Lochlan. He licked his bottom lip, exchanging a glance with the other First before looking back at Lucas. "Where did you find her and where did she go?"

"I just stumbled upon her while out hunting and uh, she ripped off the necklace." Lucas shrugged casually and then added, "Poof, gone."

"Why?" he growled. The guard standing beside him rested his hand on the golden hilt of his sword.

"She didn't want to be here," Lucas replied, picking at imaginary fluff on his wet sleeve.

"You have to report all Guests to the king," they shouted in unison.

"I don't *have* to do anything," Lucas spat, feeling his power building. He looked downward, shutting his eyes just in case.

A familiar heavy hand slapped him on his back. "What's going on here? We paid our taxes, yeah? And we have no kids."

Lucas exhaled in relief hearing Xo's deep voice.

"Let me deal with these clowns," Xo whispered and looked at the two Firsts, who scrunched up their noses in disgust.

"Mind if we take a look around?" Kain asked, a hungry smile spreading across his lips. While it was phrased as a question, they both knew that denying them was not an option.

Xo snuck a look at Lucas and then nodded confidently and shrugged as if it were no big deal.

Lucas's mind raced to his bedroom, to Cass. He would trade his telekinesis for teleportation right now. He would trade his life for hers.

They led the royal guards through their home. Kain strolled through every room, sniffing loudly, using his telekinesis to move furniture around, open curtains and cupboards. The other guard used his sword to push items around. They reached the bedroom and Lucas squared his shoulders. He would fight them, if he had to. He would kill them, even though killing a royal guard, let alone a prince, was a crime of the highest degree. He wouldn't let them take her.

His stomach twisted as Xo opened the door and they walked inside, but the room was empty. The clothes were missing from the bed. The windows were wide open, letting in a crisp breeze. They surveyed the room, peeking into the still-steamy bathroom, and moved on.

Kain spun around and unsheathed his sword, his maroon-and-gold cape lifting and falling at the sudden movement. The point of his sword pressed against Lucas's neck, the cold metal sending a shiver down his spine. "Next time, call us, or you will be invited to the palace for disobeying the king's orders, and I am sure you don't want to find out how that goes," Kain spat.

The thrashing of Lucas's power inside him grew wilder. He shut his eyes and Xo stepped in between them, gently lowering Kain's blade, his other large hand raised in surrender. He said, "Yeah, yeah, we hear you. She wanted to leave, ripped off the necklace before any of us could stop her."

Lucas exhaled the breath he had been holding and nodded. "Of course, your Highness." He bowed, appealing to the prince's inflated ego.

Kain shot him a final look of distaste before marching out of the manor.

Lucas slammed the door behind him hard enough for the hinges to complain.

As soon as he was sure Kain was far away enough, he ran through the house. He couldn't smell her anywhere.

Xo ran ahead of him, surveying all the rooms they had just checked with the royal guard and Prince Kain.

"Are they gone?" Nisa asked, intercepting them in the library, her light brown eyes wide with fear. She almost always looked scared, but Lucas had come to learn that was rarely the truth.

"Where is she?" Lucas asked desperately.

Nisa smiled reassuringly and said, "She's okay, we hid her..." she paused and grimaced before continuing, "...in the dungeon. It's the only place we could think of that they don't know about."

Relief washed over him. He rubbed his hands across his face, and then it hit him. "The dungeon?" he asked. He didn't want her in the dungeon. He didn't want her anywhere near the dungeon.

"Brie's in there with her. She said it would be fine," Nisa explained, brushing a loose dark brown curl behind her ear. "I'm sorry, I knew you wouldn't want her in there."

Lucas offered Nisa a polite smile and ran downstairs to the dungeon, taking three or four steps at a time. The staircase went down three floors. Each floor it became narrower and narrower until it was only wide enough for one person.

Moving so fast, he could barely stop himself before colliding with the metal door. He grabbed the cold handle and felt his skin prick in the center of his palm as it drew blood. It didn't make him flinch anymore. The metal bars shifted before he heard the familiar click signaling that it was unlocked. Flinging the door open, he walked inside and found Cass collapsed in the middle of the dungeon on the floor, barefoot with her loose, wet hair strewn across her face. Brie sat beside her, cross-legged, a stern expression across her dainty features.

"She's okay, I think today's been a lot for her." Brie stood and walked toward the dark shadowed corner of the dungeon. "She seems fine. She told me she thinks she had a vision, but then she collapsed before she could say anything else."

Lucas nodded, but Brie's focus was already elsewhere. He brushed Cass's black hair from her face and trailed his finger along her freckles as he did when he first saw her in this realm.

When she was asleep, she looked exactly as she had when they were kids.

After a few moments, her eyes fluttered. The flecks of green in her hazel eyes seemed brighter than usual. He pinched her chin and a confused smile spread across her face.

"I had a vision."

He smiled at her. "I heard. Do tell."

"Of you, talking to two men who were looking for me or for a *Guest*. I could see it clearly, I could hear you clearly," she said, confusion covering all her features, but still, the smile remained. "It happened when I put this shirt on." She pulled at the oversized beige t-shirt she was wearing and sat up. Her eyes were wide and filled with questions, questions he was afraid he might not be able to answer.

"That's my shirt," Lucas replied, touching her arm. He still couldn't believe she was here. There was no time to process it. "It must have triggered a vision about me."

"I know. It smells like the ocean." She straightened her legs and wiggled her toes. "Why do you smell like the ocean and why do I smell like firewood? Why couldn't I smell like vanilla, like Brie?"

Brie came out of the shadows and giggled.

Lucas chuckled nervously, glancing toward the dark shadows of the dungeon. It was quiet, at least.

"I smell like vanilla because I was baking. My chosen scent is pine trees," Brie said, grabbing his shoulder affectionately before turning to head upstairs. "I'll get some food ready."

"You chose the ocean? Why?" Cass asked, standing, practically drowning in his t-shirt.

"Reminded me of you, of us, of summer at the beach, surfing, ice lollies...reminds me of home," he said and stood up. She walked into his arms and he wrapped them around her.

"What's the point of the chosen scents?"

"To blend in, but it doesn't always work," Lucas said, fiddling with the ends of her wet hair. "I don't actually know. Xo just asked me to pick a scent before he covered mine. Anyway...." Lucas released her and gestured for her to follow him to the dungeon door, but she hesitated.

"Luke," she said, biting on her bottom lip the way she always did when she was nervous, "I had another vision, when I walked in here."

Lucas waited in the doorway. "No wonder you collapsed. You need to be careful about overusing your abilities."

"Not like I asked for it." She looked up at him and said, "I saw a man in a cage, screaming, and while I don't hear anything right now, based on what I could see in the vision, I think it's this dungeon and Brie wouldn't let me go in that direction...." She pointed at the dark shadowed corner.

Lucas felt his stomach somersault. "It's nothing."

"You can't lie to me."

He bit down. He had no idea how to explain this to her. "Can we go upstairs and eat something and I swear I'll explain everything after...." He sighed, turning back to the door. "I need some food in my stomach before we have this conversation."

"Well, that's not ominous at all," Cass joked and he smiled, opening the dungeon door and waiting for her to walk through. He closed the door behind them. He heard the sound of the metal parts locking in immediately.

Brie was in the kitchen slicing onions. She looked up as they entered and smiled, teary-eyed. "Food won't be done for another half an hour at least, maybe a bit more."

"Do you need some help?" Lucas offered and Brie shook her head, her eyes landing on Cass, who was walking around the kitchen, looking at everything. "I think your hands are full enough as is."

Cass turned around and looked at Brie. "Thanks for the clothing and for taking me to the dungeon," she said, offering up one of her best smiles. The one that always got her out of trouble. Kind and soft.

Brie replied with a smile as kind and soft, and pointed at a loaf of bread on the counter. "Lucas, could you make her a sandwich? I'll bet she's starving and too embarrassed to admit it."

Cass looked as though she would protest and deny her hunger, but instead she simply nodded.

Lucas walked up to the counter and patted a barstool. Cass climbed onto it. He sliced the bread and she was practically salivating. Reaching out to the fridge, he grabbed a block of cheese.

"I don't see any power lines," Cass said, eyeing him. "How is your fridge powered?"

"Solar panels out back," Lucas replied. He stretched out his hand and summoned a jar of butter. He unscrewed the lid and buttered both slices of bread, the way he knew she liked it.

"Huh," Cass said, "that's interesting…everything seems kind of… rural."

Lucas laughed and sliced the cheese. "It is, but the Firsts have access to pretty much everything in your realm. We get the solar panels from the Firsts when we register our villages. It's part of the agreement."

"So, are these people here, are they your village people?" she asked.

"We're called Thistle," Lucas said with a sigh. "And before you ask, no, we didn't get to choose the name. The king assigns them… flowers for the First villages, weeds for the Reborns." Cass's mouth dropped open and Lucas shook his head, uninterested in discussing the king. "Never mind that."

"Every time you answer one of my questions, you know you give me ten more, right?"

"I realize. Can you please eat? Your stomach growls keep giving me a fright." He placed the sandwich on a plate and cut it down the middle. He slid the plate across the counter toward her. Cass was about to argue when her stomach grumbled loudly. She pulled a face at him, picked up the sandwich and hungrily bit into it.

"Luke, what's my mom going to think when she can't find me?" she said with her mouth full as if the thought had just struck her.

Lucas leaned on the counter and sighed again. He knew Aunt Maya would freak out.

"I'll be gone for days, I assume. Is there a way I can contact them? Or go back there and then come back here?" she asked, shoving the last bit of the sandwich into her mouth. She dusted the crumbs off her face and chest onto the table and then brushed it into her hands.

Lucas held out his hand and she gave him the crumbs. "I don't think there's a way to contact them and no, as far as I know, you can only be a Guest once…. There isn't a standard rulebook. I don't know." He emptied his hands into the bin in the corner of the kitchen. He grabbed a kitchen towel and wiped the counter.

"So, they'll think I'm missing, like you went missing?" Cass pursed her lips up on one side, nervously. The pain across her face pulled him into sticky guilt.

"I'm sorry, Cass…I really am…. But unlike me, I'll make sure you go back. And you'll be able to help Calla. It'll be worth it. Promise." Lucas walked up to her and extended his hand. Cass took it and he led her back down to the dungeon. "Speaking of promises, I promised you I'd tell you what's going on in the dungeon. But before we go inside, know that what I'm about to show you is scarier than anything you've ever experienced."

She nodded warily.

They walked through the dungeon and to the dark shadowed corner she had asked about. "Luke," she said. He could hear the fear in her voice. "Could you tell me what it is? What's so scary?"

Lucas sighed softly. He looked up for a moment. He didn't know how best to explain it. "It's our friend, Jean. He's going to die or he's going to bite one of us and become one of them."

"A First?" Cass asked, walking closer toward the dark shadowed area.

Lucas shook his head, the frown line between his brows deepening as the pain curled around his heart. "Like Rahlog. A monster."

CHAPTER EIGHT

"Explain," she said firmly. Her mind buzzed with all the information it couldn't process and she had a feeling Lucas's explanation was only going to make it worse.

"Rumor has it, King Idis cursed Rahlog, a Reborn man, with the intention of culling us," Lucas said, his voice low. Cassia gasped lightly and he continued, "But King Idis couldn't control him and so he accidentally released the deadliest monster our kind has ever seen."

Lucas walked with her into the darkness until they reached a solid door. He gestured forward and the door flung open. Screams suddenly echoed through the chamber, shaking her with fear. "If they bite you, you either die from the illness they spread, weakening your immune system and dragging you through a hell of pain, or you bite someone else and complete your transition into what we now call a Rahlog, who by the way, feasts on us to survive and so the cycle continues."

"Like a zombie?" she shouted above the screams, shutting her ears.

"No, not really, you aren't dead. Like Jean, you're still completely sane, completely in control, except with the desire for human flesh."

Lucas led her into the room, where she saw the source of the screams coming from inside a cage.

"If he's sane and in control, then why do you have him locked up?" she asked as they reached the small cage Jean was being held in. Her hands were still pressed against her ears as the screams traveled through her soul. Jean's pale hands gripped the metal bars until his knuckles were completely white. He threw his head back and screamed again, opening his eyes only to stare directly at them for a second before throwing his head back and screaming some more.

Lucas lowered his head and dug into his pocket. He pulled out a vial and apologized to Jean before rolling it inside. Jean threw himself down and cried. He scrambled for the vial and downed its contents.

Within a minute, he collapsed, leaving Cassia and Lucas standing there in eerie silence. Her legs were still shaking as she pictured his mouth wide open in her mind, his lips pulled tight across his teeth and his eyes popping. It would haunt her forever.

"He asked me to. He said he'd bite us if the pain got too bad, and it did. We administer as many pain suppressants and sleeping tonics as we can, but it's not enough," Lucas said. His shoulders slumped as he looked down at Jean.

"This is torture," she whispered, her skin crawling as Jean writhed in his medicated sleep. His dark brown hair stood in every direction as if he had been pulling at it. The clumps of hair on the dusty floor confirmed it.

"We were hoping to figure something out. We were hoping you could help us. With your visions, maybe you could see something useful…especially if you could be around him, it could trigger something…" Lucas said as he hung his head. "When you have more control over it, at least."

She swallowed hard, pulling her focus from Jean to Lucas. "How can I help? Do I need to touch him?"

Lucas pursed his lips before saying, "You could try."

She knelt down beside the cage and reached forward to gingerly touch Jean's fingers, which lay loosely against the bars. She closed her eyes and tried to focus, having no idea what she was trying to do.

There was nothing. Just the image of his face contorted in pain. She shook her head. Lucas placed a hand on her shoulder and kissed her temple. "We'll get there," he said and started making his way out of the dungeon and back upstairs. Defeated. Her friend was defeated. The Lucas she grew up with was rarely defeated. On her darkest days, he'd always been there motivating her. This time, she needed to be there for him. But right now, all she could do was follow him upstairs in complete silence while she figured out how to control these visions.

*   *   *

Later that day, Lucas led her to her bedroom. The room was similar to the last one she had been in, which she found out, was his room. Part of her had hoped they would be sharing, even if it was only because after being away from him for four years, she was afraid to let him out of her sight.

Her room was smaller, but equally clean, with another four-poster bed at one end. After pulling back the thin blankets, she climbed in, rubbing her cold feet against the sheets to create warmth and get her blood flowing. She let her eyelids relax as she willed herself to sleep, but her stomach growled uncomfortably, as if she hadn't eaten in days. She'd skipped dinner, having had no appetite, as all she could picture was Jean and his face frozen in constant pain. His screams echoed through her mind every time she closed her eyes. That was the problem with having a memory as good as hers.

She sat up in bed and stared into the dark room. There was no way she would fall asleep. She still couldn't understand where she was and the house was full of people she didn't know or trust.

There was a thud at the door. Her heart raced and she tumbled out of the bed and crouched down low behind it. *Stay calm. Evaluate the situation. Find the exits.* She searched her memory of the room and recalled a letter opener on the dresser. It was about three steps away; she could get to it if she needed to.

The door handle squeaked as it turned and she leapt toward the dresser.

"Cass?"

"Dammit, Luke. You nearly gave me a heart attack," she said, slouching back onto the bed as her heart plummeted back to its normal rate.

"Thought you might be hungry," he said as he walked in with a plate of steaming food. The door closed behind him without him touching it. "Roast chicken and potatoes. You'll need your energy...." She curled up on the bed. It was all too much. "I know it's been a lot," he said, sitting down next to her, "but please, eat. I cooked it by myself."

"What? No way," she replied, looking up at him. Even in the dark, she knew he'd be smiling.

"I'm just kidding, I knew you would easily accept magic and monsters but draw the line when it comes to me cooking."

"Remember that time we tried surprising our mothers with dinner?" she asked.

He laughed loudly. "They were surprised all right," he said. "And I'm still surprised they ate it."

He held the plate out to her and she took it. It instantly warmed up her fingers and she put it down on her lap. It heated her thighs pleasantly.

"Think you're ready to start summoning up some visions?" he asked, lying back onto the bed. Without warning, the bedside lamp turned on. Cassia looked at him and he raised his eyebrows. "It's pretty cool. I know."

"So cool," she said, biting into a potato, crispy on the outside and soft and fluffy on the inside. "I'd like to focus on my healing power first, if that's okay?" I know you need my help, but I'm worried I won't learn enough before I get back to Calla. I have to save her."

She picked up a piece of chicken and bit into it. It was tender and delicious; she couldn't chew quickly enough. She'd never been this hungry in her life.

"Of course," he replied. "We have time. You still have eight feathers, right?"

Her hand shot up to her chest and she slipped her fingers through each feather as she tried to avoid getting them covered in gravy.

Seven.

Meeting Lucas's gaze, she said, "It seems I've lost one."

CHAPTER NINE

Lucas stood and surveyed the room, the muscle in his jaw fluttering as he clenched and unclenched. She turned around, following his gaze, which moved from the floor to the bed.

"Ah," he said, reaching across the blankets and lifting the bright orange and red feather. "Here it is."

Cassia looked down at her chest as Lucas tossed the feather onto the bedside table and climbed back onto the bed. "Seven," she said. "Does that mean another seven days.... Or?" She polished off the tender chicken and resisted the urge to lick the plate. He was lying flat on his back; he would not even know. She brought the plate up to her lips and heard him chuckle quietly.

"It's unpredictable. Some fall off quicker than others. All of mine fell off within a day.... Brie's took almost a month," he said, shifting up the bed and stretching out. "I can sleep here tonight, if you want?"

"I was hoping you'd offer," she said and lifted the plate. "I'm going to take this to the kitchen and rinse my hands...and face."

Since she had no idea where the light switches were and decided it wasn't worth the walk upstairs again, Cassia navigated into the kitchen in the dark. The moon cast a cold blue light across the kitchen sink. Assuming the tap worked the same way regular taps worked, she turned to open it slightly and rinsed her plate. Grabbing the sponge, she washed the plate and added it to the drying rack before washing her hands and marveling at the menial task amid the magic and chaos. Her mother would be proud.

As soon as she closed the tap, the silence returned. Complete silence. She rushed back upstairs and found Lucas exactly where she'd left him, with his chest rising and falling steadily. Sliding her hand along the bedside lamp, she searched for a switch. Lucas flicked his wrist and they were wrapped in darkness. She crawled onto the bed and turned to face him.

"Tell me everything. From the second you got here," she said, tucking her hand underneath her head.

"I will." Lucas leaned forward and placed a quick, soft kiss on the top of her head, "But not tonight. You need sleep if you're going to be of any use to us tomorrow."

Smiling at him, she knew he was smiling at her too. She grabbed one of the many pillows and shoved it in between them and he laughed. Inhaling the ocean, she closed her eyes, picturing summers on the beach and the sand between her toes. Finally, sleep took her.

★　★　★

The next morning Cassia woke up when Lucas threw one of his heavy arms over hers and the sheer force of it startled her. "You're crushing me," she complained, wriggling away from him.

His mouth opened in a wide yawn as he ran his hands over his face and grumbled. She stifled a giggle. He was never a morning person; even a magical world could not change that.

"I don't know about you, but I slept well," she said.

"That's the best sleep I've had in years," he said, pushing his messy black hair away from his face.

She smiled at her best friend, missing him even though he was right there with her.

"What's going on in your mind, weirdo?" he asked quietly.

"You never said what made you choose this world. Why didn't you come home? You promised me you'd always be there for me, so what was so important? You know our side doesn't have flesh-eating monsters, right?" Lying on her back, she stared up at the patterned ceiling and the small chandelier hanging in the center of it. She looked back at him, noticing that his smile faded slightly, and she instantly regretted her question, "Never mind."

"My mom and…kind of my dad too," he replied softly.

Joseph.

She never knew Lucas's dad, neither did he. He died before Lucas was born; there wasn't a photo or an item of clothing left behind to remember him by. All they knew about him was that that was where Lucas got his dark hair and eyes from.

Lucas propped himself up on one of his elbows and the smile returned. "Come on, before you ask me ten thousand questions, let me show you." He rolled out of bed and stretched, nearly touching the ceiling.

"Your mom's here? Your dad? Why didn't you say so?" She crawled out of bed and slipped on the shoes they had found for her, a pair of worn-down brown leather boots. They were a bit too big, so she tightened the laces as tight as they could go. Since she slept in the clothing they gave her, she was ready to go.

"I think she's here, on this side, but she's not *here*," he said, gesturing around him.

"And your dad?"

"My mom wasn't lying when she said he died, but she neglected to mention that he was murdered…by King Idis."

"Shit, Luke…."

"Go downstairs. I'll meet you in the kitchen for breakfast with some more answers for you," he said and made his way out of the room.

Before she left, she grabbed the letter opener and tucked it into her pocket. Her limbs ached as if she had been fighting and then she realized that she *had* been fighting…with Lochlan. A chill traveled down her spine as she pictured those blue eyes.

The paintings above the staircase caught her eye again and this time, she took a moment to look at them. The white fluffy cat looked smug, as if it knew it was being painted. As if it knew it was beautiful.

The artist was apparently a lover of felines. Another painting depicted a big cat that reminded her of a lion, but not entirely. The creature's black fur looked soft, making her think of their neighbor's fluffy black Maine coon, but around its face wrapped a golden mane, just beyond which two sharp black ears stood tall.

Unlike her neighbor's cat, Billy, this beast didn't look like anything she'd want to pet. Its snout was longer than those on the lions she was accustomed to seeing, similar to a wolf's, and its eyes were big and dark. The beast was crouched down low, its long fangs exposed, as if ready to attack the artist.

"Hi, you should come and join us for breakfast."

Cassia's head snapped down to the man on the ground floor looking up at her. Her eyes immediately fell on his white shirt, which was completely stain- and wrinkle-free. The only thing out of place was his shaggy black hair.

Anxiety kicked in and her hand slid down to the letter opener.

Suddenly, she felt her heart rate slow down to its usual pace.

He smiled gently. "Is that better?"

"What?" she asked, confused at the calmness washing over her..

"I'm Min-Jun Lee, but most people call me Jun. You're Cassia, right? Calla's sister."

"What do you know about Calla?" Cassia asked defensively, studying him. He looked older than she was, perhaps in his mid-thirties.

"I know she's an Empath, like me." Min-Jun walked up to her and held out a brochure. "I was looking for you. I made this for you, for her."

Cassia reached out and took the brochure.

So, you're feeling too many feelings and you're feeling them too intensely? You might be an Empath.

"Lucas said she's quite young, eleven, I think he said…. I was trying to summarize it and make it fun. Not sure I succeeded." He ran his hand through his messy hair as if that would help tame it. "Anyway, seeing as you're unlikely to finish the *Book of Empaths* before you have to go, I picked out all the important bits for her."

"Thank you," she mumbled, still feeling unusually relaxed.

"Stop it, Jun," Lucas said as he walked up behind her and placed a hand on her shoulder, leading her down to the ground floor.

"My apologies, I didn't want her to freak out before I got to introduce myself," he explained, and raised his hands in surrender.

A rush of panic returned, doubling her heart rate immediately. With wide eyes, she looked up at Lucas, who chuckled lightly and said, "You'll have to set some boundaries with him. Empaths have a dirty habit of spreading calm and joy wherever they go."

Min-Jun laughed and she felt light bounce off the walls. There was only one other person who laughed like that: Calla.

They reached the large dining room where they had met with Lochlan the day before. Cassia sat in the chair Lucas summoned and he sat beside her at the grand dining table. Min-Jun sat on the other side of her.

Brie, Xo and Nisa walked in carrying dishes of food. Eggs, toast, sliced tomato and avocado. Cassia's stomach rumbled again and she held her hands over it, wishing it would mute the sound.

"Eat," Lucas said, dishing up a portion of scrambled eggs and swiping her a slice of toast before the rest of it disappeared.

Greedily, she inhaled the food in a few minutes and even after that, she was still hungry. It was as though she'd eaten nothing. Everyone at the table giggled.

"Goodness, Lucas. Give her some more food. You remember what it was like," Brie said and he filled Cassia's plate with another serving of eggs and some cheese. Cassia looked up at Lucas curiously. She was becoming tired of asking questions.

He seemed to realize this and launched into an explanation. "Using magic exhausts you. You'll find you're a lot more tired and hungry than usual," he said, spreading butter onto his slice of toast. The butter soaked into the bread and she salivated. He handed the slice to her. "Oh, go on. I can't have you lusting after my toast like that."

She wanted it so badly, she didn't bother arguing.

"So, Cassia, how are you feeling?" Nisa asked. Her light brown eyes were kind. "It's a lot to take in."

Cassia smiled automatically and nodded. "Fine, thank you." She had more to say, but she was too hungry to pause her eating.

"Lucas, are you joining us for a hunt today? We could use an extra set of hands," Xo asked, pushing back his chair. He wiped a napkin across his mouth and smiled widely.

"You promised me answers, boy," Cassia warned Lucas in between swallows, and Xo laughed heartily.

"You could join us on the hunt," Xo said and Lucas frowned, shaking his head. "What? It will be good for her to look around and we haven't had any trouble in a while...."

"Yeah, sure. That sounds great," Cassia answered and looked up at Lucas. "We can talk on the way."

"It's dangerous," Lucas replied. He blew out a slow stream of air after finishing his breakfast.

"I can handle myself," she said, standing up. If she didn't leave the table, she was afraid she might never stop eating. Even the table would be eaten at this rate.

"Great. You'll need some weapons and maybe some armor." Xo paused, scrutinizing her. "Can you use a bow and arrow?"

She shook her head. "No, they don't teach that at human school."

"I take it you can't ride a wolf either."

Her mouth dropped open. "Excuse me?" Surely, she didn't hear that properly.

Xo flashed Cassia another smile and said, "Oh, you are in for a treat."

"She can ride with me," Lucas said, standing up and walking over to a tall closet. He gripped the handle and waited a second before he opened the doors, revealing rows of daggers, a couple of bows and quivers. He pulled out a few daggers and called her over, offering one of them to her. "At the very least," he said to Xo, "she can handle a knife."

"My kinda girl." Xo beamed as Cassia rolled the copper knife around in her hands. The curled handle made it easy to grip. Her experience with knives lay in the small pocket knife her father had insisted she carry, but all knives worked in the same way. Use the sharp end.

Bashfully, she slipped out the letter opener and Lucas guffawed. She pulled a face at him as Nisa offered to find her something more suitable to wear, stifling a giggle as well.

She followed Nisa into her bedroom, which was painted a peaceful lilac color, and Cassia immediately realized that was what Nisa smelled of. The sweet, heady scent of a lilac. "Cassia," Nisa said, "you can wear this, for a bit of extra protection." She offered Cassia a bundle of black leather garments.

"We'll meet you down at the stables, out back," Xo called out from downstairs. "I'll get the wolves ready."

Wolves.

He'd definitely said wolves.

That couldn't be true.

Nisa left the room and Cassia slipped into the leather pants, which were lined with cotton on the inside and more flexible than she'd have imagined them to be. She threw the leather jacket over the oversized t-shirt she was wearing.

Cassia walked back downstairs and twirled around in a circle, wondering which direction would take her to the stables. Min-Jun came downstairs and smiled kindly. "You can reach the stables through the kitchen door. Follow me."

She followed him into the kitchen and exited through the door. The stables stood at the back of the manor. A red face-brick building, the size of a small house.

Xo and Lucas walked out of the stables, followed by three enormous wolves. Each wolf was easily longer and taller than a cow.

Frozen in place, she watched them closely as they saddled the wolves. One of them howled as it looked in her direction and a small shriek escaped her.

Lucas sighed and gestured her over. "Are you sure you want to come along?" he called.

"Yes," she answered, attempting to hide the fear that laced her voice. Min-Jun chuckled quietly behind her and her fear disappeared instantly. She looked up at Min-Jun appreciatively.

"Fine," Lucas breathed and gestured for her to come closer again. Now that she could move, she took a few steps forward, hyper-aware of the wolves eyeing her.

"They're going to want to sniff you," Lucas said.

She groaned.

"How are you going to ride the wolf if you're too afraid to have them sniff you?" Lucas asked. Xo finished saddling the other wolves and led them up to her. Cassia closed her eyes as the wolf's snout traveled up and down her body until she felt its hot and sticky breath huffing onto her face. "Open your eyes, Cass. Ruq wants to see you."

Cassia opened her eyes and looked straight into the wolf's golden eyes. "Ruq?" she squeaked.

"This is Ruq," Lucas said from beside her. He scratched the enormous gray wolf's ear. He pointed at the white wolf and the black one. "That's Zuq and the other one is Willis."

"Ruq, Zuq and...Willis?" Cassia looked between the three wolves. Xo chuckled.

"Willis was named by Xo. Don't ask. Poor thing."

Lucas lifted Cassia onto Ruq and climbed up behind her. Xo and Min-Jun mounted their wolves and the wolves slowly trotted along a gravel path toward a lush forest in the distance.

Cassia held onto the reins and Lucas reached around her. "Hold on, they go pretty fast."

The wolves' speed kept increasing and increasing until they were going fast enough for the air to chill Cassia's nose. She shut her eyes; there was no point keeping them open, everything was a blur. Pushed against Lucas's chest, she wondered how wolves of this size, moving at this speed, could be so silent.

"Perfect for hunting," Lucas whispered into her ear, reading her mind.

After what felt like a few minutes, they reached the forest she'd seen in the distance.

Tall trees lined an obvious worn-down path and swept across her vision as the wolf zoomed past, slowing down slightly. She had no idea where they were riding or how much time had gone by when the tall trees were replaced by flat, grassy plains. It felt as though they had been travelling for under an hour. The sun was still rising and had not reached its peak. Granted, she wasn't sure whether the sun moved the way it did in her realm.

Xo stuck out a hand and the wolves stopped suddenly. Lucas's arm around her waist was the only reason she wasn't thrown off. Soundlessly, they climbed off the wolves and Cassia followed their gazes to where a herd of white-tailed deer stood, completely unaware that they were being hunted.

Xo, Min-Jun and Lucas crouched down low, almost crawling. Cassia mimicked their movements, having never been hunting before. Holding her breath, she was afraid that even the sound of breathing would alert the deer.

Min-Jun and Lucas drew their arrows. Xo unsheathed two daggers and Cassia pulled out her dagger, unsure of what she needed to do with it. Turning the dagger around her hands, she trailed her thumb along the engraved *JW*. Xo lifted his hand, gesturing for her to throw her dagger when he threw his. He stuck out his free hand to do a countdown.

Three.

Two.

One.

Arrows were released and Cassia aimed and threw with all her force but the dagger went completely off target and then stopped in midair. She noticed Lucas flicking his fingers as the dagger spun around and flew straight into a deer's neck.

Min-Jun launched himself off the ground before the animals fell. He reached the deer and touched them, closing his eyes for a moment, before burying his dagger in their hearts.

"They don't feel much pain when he's around," Lucas whispered and joined Min-Jun. "You can stay here, if you like. It gets a bit messy."

Cassia stood back. It was the first time she had seen an animal being hunted and she felt bile rising in her throat. She glanced at Xo, who casually sat back down on the grass.

"I don't like the skinning bit. When those two are around, I kick back."

"How long have you been here?" she asked, settling down on the ground alongside him.

"About seven years," he said, lost in thought for a moment. "Yeah, I died when I was about your age, twenty-two, right? Same as Lucas?"

"You died?"

Xo nodded. "Yeah, most of us died in your realm to get here."

"I'm sorry."

"Don't be," he replied, flashing a smile of perfectly straight teeth. "Some people just die and that's the end of it, but look at me now...a second chance, magic.... It's not so bad."

"But Lucas didn't die, did he? He said he didn't."

Xo cut off bits of grass using his dagger. "No, Lucas didn't die. A First invited him here. Firsts can travel between both realms and can move others around too, like Lochlan did with you." Xo frowned at the mention of Lochlan.

"What's the deal with the Firsts and Lochlan?" she asked while looking at Min-Jun and Lucas. Their hands and arms were completely covered in dark red blood. She looked back at the grass beside her instead.

"The Firsts were always here, I think they divided the realms. The magic in this realm is linked to them and they like to remind us of that." Xo tutted, stabbing his dagger into the soil. "For a while, it was only them. They traveled to your realm for supplies and to occasionally interfere if they thought it was necessary. You can thank them for paracetamol."

Xo drew his knife out of the soil as two men approached Min-Jun and Lucas and then quickly tucked it away and relaxed. Lucas extended his one clean elbow as a greeting and Min-Jun nodded happily.

"After thousands of years of their boring existence, they started opening portals to mingle with your realm...and by mingle, I mean...." Xo wriggled his eyebrows.

"I get it, keep going." Cassia shook her head.

"Turns out, mixing people from your realm, which we call Talm, with people from Selene results in a very fertile combination and, uh, accidents happen and the magic can be transferred through generations, even unactivated." Xo chuckled and said, "Kind of like genetics, you know, you might have the same curly hair your great-great-grandmother has, but no one else in your family has it."

Cassia nodded. "So, not everyone from Earth, or Talm, comes here?" she asked. "It's not like heaven, is it? Is this hell?"

Xo laughed lightly and shook his head. "It's a parallel realm on the same timeline as the one you came from and no, not everyone has access, only those with Selene magic that's been activated in their bloodline. When you die, that magic brings you here where it thinks you belong.... And we *do* belong. But, since we're not born here, we get the choice, with the feathers. If you choose to stay, you become what we call Reborn, since we're born as magical beings in this realm. More and more of us started popping up and initially, the Firsts were more than happy to use us to farm and hunt and so forth, but now, the Firsts fear they will soon be outnumbered and overruled. Amongst themselves, the Firsts aren't as fertile as we are.... It's why they keep culling us, but taking Reborn children wasn't enough and now we're stuck with Rahlogs."

"What do you mean by taking Reborn children?" Cassia gasped. The bile that was already making its way up her throat climbed higher.

Xo shook his head angrily and a low growl vibrated through him. "Your firstborn gets taken by the Firsts around the age of ten years old. They get put to work at the palace and in the homes of the Firsts I guess. I have no idea.... We never go any farther than the palace garden and other than Lochlan, we don't speak to any of them either."

"Did Lochlan invite Lucas over? Why?" Cassia asked.

"It wasn't Lochlan."

"Who was it?" Cassia asked.

"His mom."

CHAPTER TEN

Lucas

Neil pointed at Cass and asked, "Who is that?"

"A Guest, a friend of mine. My best friend from Talm, actually," Lucas answered as he cleaned off his hands. "Let me introduce you." He looked up at Neil and smiled as he remembered. "You've always reminded me of her dad."

"What was his name?" Neil asked, still looking over at Cass and lifting his hand to wave. Cass exchanged glances with Xo before returning the wave.

"Deo Khan," Lucas replied, rubbing his hands on his gray tunic to dry them off before making his way back to where Cass and Xo sat.

Before reaching her, Neil called out, "It's been a while since we had a Guest. How do you like our side so far?"

Judging from the flicker that crossed Cass's eyes, Lucas knew that he wasn't the only one who was reminded of Uncle Deo. He walked up to her and offered her the copper dagger he had cleaned. She rolled it around in her grip as she answered Neil distractedly, "Yeah, it's cool."

"Sorry," Neil apologized and stuck out his right hand. "I'm Neil Paleker. I forgot my manners."

Cass shook his hand firmly, the way they'd been taught to do the night before their first awards ceremony in preschool. "Cassia Khan," she said smiling at him, but Lucas could sense her heartache.

Neil pointed at the man behind him. "And that's Zidane."

The wolves howled in the distance. A warning howl. Lucas felt a chill thread across his spine and shut his eyes a second before the screaming started. He spun around to see a horde of Rahlogs running toward them. Taking a step in front of Cass, he stuck two fingers into his mouth and whistled. On his right, Xo whistled too.

On his left, Neil and Zidane unsheathed their swords.

Jun ran up to them and handed them their quivers. Wordlessly they drew their arrows and sent them flying across the plains toward the monsters. His heart was pounding louder every time he realized Cass was behind him. The arrow slipped as he released it and he guided it with his wrist into the head of one of the Rahlogs. He glanced down at Cass to see her knuckles whitened around her dagger, her breathing short and quick, much like his. "It's okay," he said, hoping it came across as convincing. It wasn't okay. None of this was okay.

The wall of Rahlogs got closer and Xo and Jun exchanged their bows for daggers. Lucas dropped his bow and opened his hands in front of him, stretching his fingers apart. He inhaled deeply and swung his hands forward, exhaling as he did it, forcing his magic through his fingertips, embracing the feeling of it and the way it whirled inside him before release. The Rahlogs that had almost reached them were thrown back into the others behind them, but the screams got louder.

The Rahlogs got closer.

Lucas ran forward. He needed to keep these monsters away from his friends. He gestured toward one of the nearest Rahlogs, a man, and flung him into the Rahlog alongside him. Lifting his other hand, he glanced over at the abandoned quiver and lifted the discarded arrows, sending them into the heads of the Rahlogs.

A quick bolt of pain traveled up both his arms and he leaned forward, shutting his eyes as he tried to inhale.

"Don't overdo it, man!" Xo shouted. "We've got this."

A Rahlog grabbed the back of Xo's shoulder, opening his mouth in a scream or preparing to bite. Xo dropped his hand and stabbed the Rahlog in the abdomen, sending him tumbling. Another Rahlog pounced on him and Xo kicked him off, digging his dagger deep into the Rahlog's head.

Lucas looked up before a Rahlog reached him and saw another one approaching Cass. Summoning his fallen dagger, he drove it into the Rahlog, desperate to get to her. The Rahlog grabbed her and she dropped her dagger, likely out of fear. Lucas felt his magic building up in an unpleasant way as he watched her tug her arm toward herself, trying to break the grip, but the woman she was up against hung on tightly. He broke free and sprinted toward her, but he was blocked by another two Rahlogs.

Cass assumed a fighting position, picked up her dagger and held it out in front of her.

Another Rahlog grabbed her from behind. His teeth neared her neck as Lucas leapt toward her and drove his knife into her attacker's head.

Finally, the wolves arrived, circling him, and Lucas gripped Cass around her waist and threw her onto Ruq. He pulled the wolf close and whispered, "Home." Ruq would know what to do.

"Hold on, Cass," he said to her and whistled again before she could respond or fight him on this. Ruq sped off, gaining speed quickly, and Lucas turned around, raising his hands and preparing to fight. He slumped over for just a second to catch his breath as his head spun.

He knew bringing Cass along on this hunt was a bad idea. Cursing at himself, he inhaled deeply and squared his shoulders despite the pain shredding through his head. Each of the Rahlogs approaching had the same crazed look, which made it impossible to distinguish their leader.

His skin buzzed as it always did when he used too much of his magic. He risked a glance behind him and saw that Ruq, along with Cass, was well out of reach. There was no way any Rahlog would be able to keep up with a fully grown Baskian wolf.

A Rahlog approached him with a pained smile stretched across what used to be a pretty face. Now she was covered in dirt and blood with wounds that hadn't been tended to. Lucas recalled the woman she once was. He couldn't farm and she couldn't hunt. They had traded rabbits for tomatoes, potatoes and peppers. It had become a regular monthly trade until one morning, when he'd arrived carrying two extra rabbits, she wasn't there. Her daughter had informed him that she had been bitten and had run away during the night to prevent herself from biting the rest of their community.

Now she stood in front of him, staring at him. The light eyes that had once joked with him had vanished.

"Lucas," she growled, her mouth covered in deep red blood that was likely not her own.

"Rita."

"I can't help myself, you know that, right?" she said, her voice rubbing against his skin like sandpaper. Her once-sweet voice was hoarse, as all of their voices were, because of the screaming.

"I have to defend myself, you know that, right?" Lucas unsheathed his dagger. The copper hilt fit in his palm as if it were made for him. He wasn't sure he had the capacity to use any more magic. Not without pushing himself further than he was used to. Further than Xo recommended.

A flash of sadness crossed her dull eyes. She nodded sympathetically and said, "I am so hungry."

Before he could respond, she leapt on top of him, pushing him to the ground. His head slammed on the grass, and his mind was encircled with pain. The chatter of her teeth sent a shudder through him as she neared his skin. He raised his dagger and forced it into her abdomen. She cried out and he winced at the sound, shutting his eyes as he choked on his heartache. She stumbled off him, grasping at her gaping wound and Lucas apologized before swiftly pulling her close and stabbing his dagger into her heart.

The color drained from her skin and he leaned down next to her, bowing his head. He hated this; the killing was all too much. Especially when he recognized the person they were before. He took her thin hand in his own and held on to it, wishing she'd had a different end. He started reciting the Selenic Farewell to the Dead as a sharp sting scraped the back of his neck. He spun around, his hand extended in front of him, as his power shot through his palms and flung the Rahlog back. Lucas collapsed on his knees, shaking the ground underneath him. Too much power was used. The pain coursed through his entire body. Every joint ached. Every limb seemed to want to detach from him.

His magic wanted to break out of his body.

But there were more Rahlogs approaching. Xo was overwhelmed, fighting off two Rahlogs at the same time. Jun and Zidane were each fighting one, and Lucas couldn't see Neil anywhere. The wolves howled in the distance and Lucas scanned the area for them, finding them surrounded by Rahlogs. With struggle, his magic built up in his chest and escaped, not only from his palms, but from his entire body, pushing outward and flinging the remaining Rahlogs into the air. They dropped down, falling to their death as the sounds of skulls cracking etched itself into his mind. All of them were dead, except one.

The Rahlog stood up slowly, twisting his neck and stretching his spine before he looked down at his fallen brethren. "You will pay for this by being the first new member of my pack, since you killed the rest of them," he said, smiling although the smile never reached his green eyes. He was a Reborn, but not one that Lucas had ever met.

The Rahlog ran toward him, his lips curling upward in anticipation, and Lucas clumsily reached for his dagger, but it was too far away. The Rahlog reached him, throwing his arms forward and scratching Lucas across his face, drawing blood. The monster's nostrils flared as he smelled the blood and launched forward, his mouth wide open. Stumbling back, Lucas hit the ground as the Rahlog landed on top of him. He summoned the last of his magic and called for his dagger, which flew straight into his grip. But his limbs were aching, frozen with pain, with weakness.

The whine of a sword whipped through the air, slicing through his fear. The crazed eyes lost their green shimmer as the Rahlog's head rolled off his neck, his blood splattering onto Lucas's face and shirt. What was left of his body collapsed onto the ground and behind him stood Zidane with his sword drenched in blood.

"Neil," Zidane choked out, looking at the lifeless body of the Rahlog. "They got Neil, they bit him, Lucas, they bit—" Zidane paused and looked up at Lucas. He dropped his sword.

"Where is he? Where's Neil?" Lucas asked, standing up and spitting out the blood that had made its way into his mouth. He dragged his sleeve across his face while looking around. There must have been about twenty lifeless bodies scattered around them, most of them Rahlogs, except one. Neil.

"Your—your eyes," Zidane stammered.

Lucas slammed his eyes shut and willed himself to calm down. He covered his face with his hands, his fingers aching with pain as if every bone in his body was broken.

"Your eyes," Zidane said again, his voice shaking violently.

"They mean nothing," Lucas said, looking up as he felt his power draining. The numbness set into his bones and he knew within a few moments, he would be unconscious.

"You're one of them."

Xo walked over. The wolves followed, each of them dragging a deer in their mouths.

"I'm not one of them," Lucas spat as Zuq padded to his side. He rested his head on the wolf.

"But your eyes." Zidane leaned over to lift his sword from the sandy ground. He wiped it across the chest of the decapitated Rahlog before strapping it to his waist.

"I'm not one of them," Lucas repeated, his voice muffled by the fur as he climbed on top of the wolf. Xo tied the strap around him.

"It's not what you think," Xo said while tightening the straps, "and if you tell anyone, you'll be the reason we all get killed."

CHAPTER ELEVEN

Her stomach lifted as the wolf rode off. Spinning around, Cassia couldn't see Lucas and his friends at all.

She'd given up on shouting for the wolf to stop. She raised her hand the way she had seen Xo do it, but the wolf continued running. Leaping off wasn't an option either; she wouldn't survive the landing at this speed.

Leaning down, she wrapped her arms around the wolf's neck, burying her face in its gray fur and hoping she would see her friend soon.

The large wolf slowed to a surprisingly gentle stop in front of the manor, but Cassia was too scared to look up, she was too scared to let go. The gray wolf lowered itself to the ground to make it easier for her to get off, but she wouldn't budge. Instead, she rubbed her face deeper in the soft fur as frustration and fear stung her eyes. Ruq trotted up to the front door and bowed again while howling.

She had to go back to Lucas. What if he needed her help? She needed to save him.

"Take me back to Lucas," she said to the wolf, but it ignored her. "Ruq, please!"

The front door opened and Nisa stood there, looking at Cassia quizzically.

"Cassia, what happened? Where is everyone?" Nisa asked and walked up to her. Cassia hesitated, wondering what she could tell Nisa. Perhaps she could help. She knew Lucas lived with these people, but she was not sure how well he knew any of them.

Lucas wasn't always the best judge of character. He trusted too easily. But she was out of options and Nisa was the only one here.

Cassia lifted her head, aware of her puffy eyes. "Nisa, I— There—

Rahlogs, so many Rahlogs, and then Luke, uhm and I wanted to stay, but—" She stumbled on her words, gesturing between herself and the wolf but all she could picture were those monsters and how close she'd come to being bitten.

Nisa touched her arm gently. Her clean, trimmed and painted nails looked out of place against Cassia's bloodied and muddied arm. "It's okay, take a deep breath," Nisa instructed her with a voice as shaky as her own.

"I didn't abandon them, I swear," Cassia choked out, her voice cracking. She slid off Ruq awkwardly and he curled up at the foot of the bench, rubbing his head gently at their legs.

"I know," Nisa said and let go of Cassia's arm. She brushed her dark hair behind her ears and her light brown eyes glazed over for a moment.

"We need to help them. I don't know how we got there exactly, but we rode through a forest and it was at these plains, we were hunting—" Cassia rambled, straightening her back and wiping away the last of her tears. Nisa touched her arm again and gave her a small smile.

"I know, I know."

"How?" Cassia asked, guessing the answer, but needing to hear it anyway.

"I'm a Telepath," Nisa responded shyly and turned toward the open door. "Come on, let's get you into a shower, or wait, a bath. I think you need a long bath. Your muscles will thank me tomorrow morning." Nisa walked inside and Cassia followed, her mind racing with confusion.

"What about them? We can't just leave them. They were heavily outnumbered. They could be dead," Cassia shrieked.

"They're alive," Nisa replied while walking upstairs. "I spoke to Jun. He said they're okay and they'll be coming home soon. So, let's get you clean in the meantime."

"Can you communicate with people telepathically?" Cassia asked, following Nisa up the dark wooden stairs, tramping muddy footprints into the carpet. "Sorry," she mumbled.

Nisa smiled kindly and waved her off. "I can't communicate telepathically to just anyone, but in addition to being an Empath, Jun is also a Telepath, so he and I can talk. Telepath and Empath abilities often go together. He said he thinks my Empath powers will activate at some point…" Nisa turned to face Cassia. Her eyes were soft and Cassia felt herself relaxing. Perhaps Nisa was already an Empath.

"Jun," Cassia said and corrected herself, feeling slightly uncomfortable calling him by his nickname, "I mean, uhm, Min-Jun didn't mention that he was a Telepath too." She paused at the top of the stairs to admire the portrait of roses once more. It was such a striking blue. She'd never seen a rose like that in real life.

"Yeah, we don't tend to. Makes people kind of uncomfortable knowing we can peek into their minds with a simple touch." Nisa smiled and led Cassia to the main bathroom. Cassia wondered what Nisa had seen in her mind, and whether Min-Jun had taken a look too.

"Sorry, we haven't redecorated. It's pretty outdated, but the water is always warm and that's all you really need after a near-death experience," Nisa said, and then laughed. It felt entirely out of place, and yet infectious.

The floor of the bathroom was tiled pale pink, which met beige painted walls. The Victorian tub took up the entire back section of the bathroom, its golden footings complementing the tiles. Sconces hung on the walls, casting a warm yellow light over the room even though the sun was shining outside.

"What did he say?" Cassia asked. She wished she could have spoken to Min-Jun herself, or better yet, directly to Lucas.

"He said not to worry, Lucas is okay and they'll be here soon. I'll come and get you as soon as they arrive." Nisa turned around and left.

Cassia closed the door and leaned against the cool wall of the bathroom, steadying her breath. It was unsettling taking a bath after what had been the scariest moment of her life.

Shaking the thoughts from her head, she kicked off her boots and peeled off her leather pants. Flakes of hardened blood chipped off as she pulled her t-shirt over her head. Her hand slid across the area of her neck where the Rahlog's teeth had touched her. The mere thought of it sent a shudder through her entire body. A breath away from being bitten. A breath away from becoming one of those *things*.

Lucas would have had to kill her. Calla would never get the help she needed. Her chest tightened in panic and she shut her eyes. Part of her wanted to open her eyes and be in the safety of her home, of her hospital, but a much bigger and louder part of her wanted to be here, with Lucas, with the chance of saving Calla.

She released her long black hair and stared at herself in the mirror. Her skin was inflamed along her side where she had taken a knock. The reddish color was bright against her tan skin.

Leaning into the tub, she turned on the hot water, the loud gush creating a white noise that, for a moment, calmed her. She reached atop the shelf and grabbed a bar of soap and a bottle of shampoo.

There was a light knock at the door. Cassia stood behind the door and cracked it open slightly.

"Towel, some new clothes, and I figured you may need some conditioner. I don't leave it in the bathroom because the boys use it to wash their entire big, stupid bodies," Nisa said, and Cassia couldn't resist laughing.

Nisa was definitely an Empath, whether or not she knew it yet.

Cassia laid the clothing on the counter and put the towel in reach of the bathtub. She opened the cold water tap as well and swept her fingers through the water until the temperature was perfect. When she climbed in, the water wrapped around her aching muscles like velvet. She rested her head on the hard porcelain edge of the bath and closed her eyes, knowing that if she kept them closed for a minute longer, she would fall asleep.

She slipped her head underwater and came up to wash her hair. She ran her fingers through her wavy hair and it got painfully caught in knots that would take years to untangle by hand. Thank goodness Nisa had brought the conditioner.

Using the soap and a washrag, she scrubbed her body aggressively, as if trying to scrub off the memory of the screaming people. The blood and dirt scraped off into the water, turning it a shade darker as it swirled with her fears. Quickly, she stood and drained the dirty water, along with the unwanted memories of open mouths and gore.

"This is madness," she whispered to herself. "But it's real. I can do this. I can do this."

She turned on the attached shower and rinsed herself off before stepping out into the steamy bathroom. Strangely enough, something as simple as steam was comforting. Normal.

The clothing Nisa brought was a pair of black pants, a black cotton vest and another baggy t-shirt that smelled like the ocean. She sniffed it, inhaling summers spent with Lucas and their families and exhaling whatever her life was right now.

Magic, monsters and a feather necklace.

She pulled the door open and made her way out of the bathroom while towel-drying her hair, and found Nisa waiting outside.

"They're almost here," she said.

Instantly, Cassia's heart rate sped up and she followed Nisa out of the front door, wanting to break into a sprint, but Nisa kept walking leisurely. Cassia stared out into the horizon, but there was nothing, and no sound, other than the whistle of the wind.

Zuq and Willis arrived in a blur, a cloud of dust spinning around them as they stopped, nearly flinging Xo, Lucas, Min-Jun and Zidane from the saddles.

Where is Neil?

Xo jumped off, pulling Lucas down along with him, and Cassia ran to his side. He was bloody, but not bleeding. His pulse was there. Stable. Quicker than it should be, but nothing concerning. She needed to see his eyes.

"He's okay, he just needs a bit of rest and some patching up.... He overdid it, is all," Xo explained as she peeled his eyes open. She exhaled in relief and let go of him. Xo's big arms struggled underneath Lucas's weight and Cassia threw one of Lucas's arms over her shoulder and helped carry him inside.

Min-Jun and Zidane climbed off the black wolf and Cassia heard Nisa gasp loudly. Before she could turn around to face her, Nisa grabbed her arm and asked, "Is there any chance you know how to use your healing abilities?"

"Not really, why?" Cassia replied, looking up at Nisa's face, which was white as snow. Zidane groaned and Cassia glanced in his direction to see him catching Min-Jun just before he could hit the ground.

Min-Jun's eyes were slowly drooping and the clothing in the center of his abdomen was soaked in dark, red blood.

"One of them got hold of a dagger and, well…I don't think he was bitten," Zidane said quickly. "I didn't know it was such a deep gash. He was fine a moment ago."

Cassia dropped Lucas into Xo's arms and ran to Min-Jun's side. She glanced back at Xo, who nodded at her reassuringly. "Lucas will be fine," he said, the concern on his face clearly directed at Min-Jun. "The ride back probably caused more bleeding. Can you help him?" He shifted Lucas from one side to the other.

"I can try," Cassia said and looked up at Zidane. "Lay him down," she ordered as she felt Min-Jun's racing heart. "Do you have a first-aid box, anything I could use to disinfect the wound and stitch him up?"

Nisa ran into the house and Cassia pulled her t-shirt over her head, grateful for the vest she wore underneath, and applied pressure to the wound.

"Everything is going to be okay," she said gently, wishing Min-Jun could use his own abilities on himself. Min-Jun smiled briefly and closed his eyes, sweat droplets forming on his brow. "Stay with me, Min-Jun. Tell me about your family back on my side," she said quickly, remembering her training in the trauma unit.

She knew she could save him, if she worked fast.

Nisa returned, carrying as many medical supplies as she could carry. Xo followed behind her with another armful of supplies. He must have left Lucas somewhere, but now wasn't the time to find out where.

Cassia disinfected her hands and the wound. Min-Jun writhed underneath her touch. At least it meant he had the energy to do that.

"Nisa, get over here," Cassia called as Min-Jun winced again, whimpering with every touch. "Use your powers on him. Remove his pain."

Nisa stammered, "I'm, I, I'm not an Empath, I don't—"

"You are," Cassia replied, disinfecting the needle she would use to stitch the wound. "Focus your mind. You can do this. He needs you to do this."

Nisa picked up Min-Jun's right hand and held it in both of hers, lifting it to her heart.

The needle pierced his skin and he screamed, fighting against Xo and Zidane, who pinned him down by his arms and legs. He had more strength than she'd expected.

Nisa closed her eyes and inhaled loudly, which turned into a gasp when Min-Jun suddenly stopped struggling. Her teary eyes flung open in a panic and Cassia checked his pulse. He was alive.

"Good job," Cassia whispered and Nisa smiled, tears streaming down her cheeks before she closed her eyes and continued channeling her power into Min-Jun. His eyes fluttered open and closed every few seconds as he fought unconsciousness.

Cassia stitched up the rest of his wound and wrapped the bandage around his waist. They exhaled in unison and she felt her panic subside. Falling backward onto the grass, she let relief lap over her.

But before she could catch her breath, Xo leaned across her and raised his bloodied hand for a high five. "Don't leave me hanging," he said playfully.

Weakly, she raised her hand and he high-fived her.

"That's how we do it!" he cheered, and in one quick motion, he lifted Min-Jun and carried him inside.

Nisa followed behind them, saying, "I'll take care of him and get him cleaned up."

"He'd like that," Xo said, earning himself a tut from her.

*　　*　　*

Cassia pulled herself up off the grass and walked inside. Lucas was lying on the couch, unconscious. She slumped down on the armrest next to him, checked his vitals and listened to his breathing. Everything seemed fine. Except for the scratch at the back of his neck and the three smaller scratches across his jaw. The three slashes weren't deep enough to require stitches, although it looked like they were made by an animal.

"Do scratches turn you the way bites do?" she asked Zidane.

He ran a hand over his smooth head. "Only bites. They need to drink from you."

She rolled Lucas onto his stomach and fetched the medical kit. After brushing his hair away from his neck, she cleaned the wound, just in case. His hair was soft and familiar, but longer than usual. She wondered who cut it on this side. Back home, it was usually her mother or his. He never trusted Cassia with a pair of scissors.

Sitting on the floor, she leaned against the couch and dropped her head onto his shoulder.

"Where's Neil?" she asked.

Zidane collapsed onto the armchair and gave her a slight shake of his head. The same head shake she'd give to the family of patients who didn't survive the night.

Cassia looked away. The pain in his eyes was too much for her to bear and while she had barely said anything to Neil, there was something about him that reminded her of her father. Her heart ached with longing. "I'm sorry," she said.

"Thank you," he said. "We sent what was left of him down the river. We couldn't leave him there. It felt like the right thing to do." He dropped his head into his hands and his shoulders shook. "I'm not looking forward to explaining this to his family."

Cassia bit back tears. She remembered being on the receiving end of news like that and finding out that her father was not coming home.

Looking up, she saw Zidane stretch the neck of his shirt across his left shoulder. A dark tattoo circled his upper arm. "It was my first time laying someone to rest on this side," he said.

Cassia opened her mouth to ask about the tattoo as a hot breeze swept through the room, wrapping around her, and before she could say anything, a voice asked, "What did I miss?"

CHAPTER TWELVE

Lochlan stood in the center of the living room as if he owned it. A golden crown was perched on top of his head and underneath it, his brown hair curled outward at the edges as if trying to get away from him.

His mouth turned up into the same smirk he'd greeted her with previously as he bowed slightly, his maroon-and-gold cape opening up to reveal the elaborately gold-and-black-patterned shirt underneath.

Zidane was on his feet in a second with his sword extended in front of him, which only elicited a laugh from Lochlan. He didn't even bother looking at Zidane. While maintaining eye contact with Cassia, he lifted his hand and flicked his fingers as if shooing a fly. Zidane was lifted off the floor and thrown against the wall behind him. The room shook as he landed with a heavy thump, the sound echoing across the wooden floors.

Cassia broke eye contact with those blue eyes and rushed toward Zidane. Even though the living room wasn't large, it felt like it took far too many steps to reach him. She placed her fingers on his pulse; the quick beat put her at ease, but then she noticed the thick dark blood pooling toward her knees.

"Whoops," Lochlan said. "That was a bit harder than I intended. He should be fine though, in the hands of a Healer." He took a step closer to her and she looked at the doorway. "No one's coming, little lady." He twirled his hand and a ring of blue fire surrounded them. The heat of the fire stung her eyes, but the fire was perfectly contained, wrapping them in a sphere of heat as the ring of flames grew around them. "So, unless that big brute of yours wakes up, and I know he won't, it's just you and me." His smirk widened into a full smile, showing off his perfectly straight teeth as he added, "And there are no pens around."

"What do you want?" Cassia bit out, hovering over Zidane as the blood soaked into her pants. "He's bleeding out, I need to—"

"Need to what? Heal him?" Lochlan asked, his blue-fire eyes challenging her. Shimmering, as they did in the hospital.

"I haven't learned how to do that yet," she snapped, gently pushing a scatter cushion underneath Zidane's head and turning him onto his side. "Please, help him."

"Me? Help him? I'm not a Healer."

"Then get one," she said. The sound of screaming echoed outside the sphere and she stood up to face him, squaring her shoulders and clenching her jaw. "Get one."

"There she is, that fire." Lochlan smiled again and both dimples showed up on either side of his mouth. She risked a glance at Lucas, willing him to wake up.

"He won't be waking up and I won't be getting a Healer, not because I don't want to, and please, understand that I definitely don't want to, but I won't be getting a Healer because there are none." Lochlan took a step forward and just like at the hospital, she took a step back. Zidane's sword lay on the opposite side of the room. It was too far for her to reach. "You're the first Healer in decades."

Lochlan sat in the same armchair that Zidane had been in a moment ago. He casually crossed one long leg over the other with an air of such royalty that the vintage green armchair was transformed into a throne.

"I don't know how," she said, glancing around the room for something that could help her, but she couldn't see beyond the fire that surrounded them.

"You haven't even tried."

She spun around and fell to her knees beside Zidane to investigate the wound, Her fingers were coated red. She closed her eyes and breathed slowly, willing herself to calm down. "I don't know what to do," she mumbled, more to herself than to him. Her heart fell into her stomach as she tried focusing her mind and stilling her thoughts.

The air around her shifted as Lochlan appeared behind her and hovered above her for a moment. "Come on, little lady, it's just a small head wound. It should be easy."

She hung her head. Her breath raced through her body and yet it felt like no oxygen was reaching her lungs, or her brain.

Lochlan kneeled down behind her, whispering in her ear, "Close your eyes."

His breath tickled her and she pushed back against him, knocking the air out of his chest. "Get away from me," she ordered through gritted teeth.

He leaned closer and whispered, "Do you want to save him, or not?" His lips brushed against the back of her ear. "Close your eyes and take a deep breath."

She closed her eyes, aware of her back against his chest. If she had a knife, she would turn around and dig it straight into his smug face.

"You're a doctor. Visualize the healing process, the stitches, the removal of stitches and eventually, the scar.... Visualize each step. Convince yourself that it's happening," he whispered softly. His voice was smooth, washing over her senses, and she found herself listening and believing him. "It's about intention."

A rush of warmth spread to the tips of her fingers. They buzzed, guiding her to Zidane's head. She slipped her already slick fingers along the wound and watched as his tan skin pulled together, blending upon meeting, until a shiny scar was all that remained.

The same buzz from her fingers now appeared in her mind as an image entered it. She saw Zidane screaming, throwing himself at a group of men dressed similarly to Lochlan. Their eyes glowed blue. Another man grabbed Zidane and held him back as the men approached him with a thick whip and landed a lash across his chest. He collapsed on the ground, crying out, his arms stretched out as he watched a small boy being dragged away.

Cassia choked out a cry as the vision disappeared. She leaned back against Lochlan's hard chest.

"You know, when you're this close and all you're wearing is this little thing, I can still smell your original scent," he said.

Her momentary lapse of judgment ended when she recalled who she was leaning against. She dropped her elbow forcefully, digging it into his hard stomach. Lochlan stumbled back, coughing and then laughing.

"Always a pleasure," he said with a bow and then looked at Lucas. A muscle in his jaw fluttered. "Please send him my regards. I am sure his Highness over there would hate that he missed me."

Lochlan vanished, leaving behind the soft scent of vanilla as the flames dissipated. Outside of where the flame barrier had been, Xo lay on the ground, barely conscious. Nisa sat beside him, her hand placed firmly on his shoulder as the smell of burning flesh spread through the house.

"He tried running through to get to you," she said, looking up at Cassia. "I don't know what to do."

Cassia ran over to Xo and kneeled down next to him. She closed her eyes, as she had moments ago, inhaled deeply and imagined the skin healing. She had never personally treated a burn victim, but she had been allowed to observe the process. She pictured the end result of new, healthy skin and her fingers buzzed with the magic. Xo had tried saving her. She needed to do this for him.

"Wow!" Nisa said excitedly. "You did it!"

Cassia opened her eyes and found Nisa staring at her. Xo pushed himself up. He inspected his new skin and looked up at her with a smile. "She sure did." He hopped to his feet and pulled Cassia into his arms. She froze; she wasn't used to hugs. Xo looked over her shoulder, let go of her, and ran toward Zidane.

"Zidane's okay. I, uh, I healed him too," Cassia said, as her legs started shaking. Her vision blurred and the room spun.

"Rockstar," Xo said, and a second later, she collapsed.

★   ★   ★

Cassia cracked open her eyes and stared at the ceiling, except this time she couldn't make out the patterns due to her blurry vision. She blinked a few times, trying to clear them, but it didn't help. She realized she hadn't cleaned her contact lenses since she'd arrived and while they were made for extended wear, she didn't want to risk an eye infection in a strange realm. She pushed herself up and attempted to swallow, which caused a coughing fit instead as she struggled with the nonexistent cotton wool in her throat.

She climbed out of bed and her head spun, each movement banging her brain against her skull as if there wasn't enough space in there for it. She was in the same bed she had slept in the previous night and she had no idea how she'd got there.

Blinking a few times, she hoped her eyesight would clear, but it was no use.

What happened?

She climbed out of bed and made her way downstairs, barefoot and still wearing blood-soaked clothing. Her knees threatened to give in every time her feet hit the ground.

She stumbled into the living room. Lucas was still asleep on the couch and Xo sat in the armchair. He flashed a big smile. "You should rest a bit more. You weren't out for very long," he said.

"I'm fine," she said as she looked around for Zidane. Her hand cradled her head. The pain was unrelenting. Xo stood and offered her the two paracetamols and bananas that lay on the coffee table.

Cassia ate the banana with her eyes closed, willing the headache away. She threw the pills into her mouth and drank them down with the icy water, which seemed to freeze her from the inside out. She opened her eyes to see the others watching her in silence. Her vision was still blurry. "Any chance you have saline solution or contact lens solution?" she asked.

"Nope," Nisa said and stood. "But we can try to make some."

Nisa left the living area and Cassia followed her. They walked into the kitchen, where Nisa took out a small pot and filled it with water. She reached under the counter and lifted a large bag of rock salt. Cassia blinked constantly, trying to clear the blurriness.

"Could you give me a small bowl? I'd like to remove them now; they're irritating me," she said, and Nisa handed her a small glass bowl.

Cassia took the small bowl and washed her hands thoroughly before turning to the large window to look at her reflection. She lifted her fingers to her eye and pinched the lens, grateful that it slipped off easily, considering it could have dried out overnight. She blinked a few times, and relief washed over her left eye as she dropped the lens into the bowl. She looked back at the window, confused by the difference in her vision. She shut her left eye and everything blurred. She opened her left eye and shut her right eye.

Crystal clear.

Leaning closer to the window, she looked at her hazel eyes close enough to see the green flecks. Reaching up, she pinched out the lens in her right eye and dropped it into the bowl.

Now both eyes were clear.

Am I imagining this?

She turned around to face Nisa, who had steam rising above the pot of water she boiled. Cassia walked around the kitchen looking at every item. She could see the cracks in the paint, the crumbs on the counter. She looked back to where she'd left the glass bowl and could see the daisies painted on it.

"I can see," she said, and Nisa turned around to face her.

"What do you mean?"

"I can see," Cassia said again, and pointed at the lenses in the bowl. "Without them. It makes no sense. Does everybody in Selene have good eyesight? None of you wear spectacles."

Nisa shook her head. "I know a few Reborns who need spectacles." She pursed her lips up for a second and then widened her eyes. "Cassia! You healed your own eyes!"

"Oh," Cassia said, thinking back to what she'd done, to healing Zidane, to healing Xo. "Are you sure? I didn't mean to."

"I don't know," Nisa said with a small laugh. "But it makes sense though. Why else would you be able to see without your lenses when you've just managed to activate your healing abilities? Sometimes our magic has a mind of its own."

"I suppose I don't need the solution anymore," Cassia said, and Nisa smiled widely, before taking the pot off the heat.

"Guess not. Let's go tell the others!" she said and walked back to the living room. Cassia followed behind her.

By the time they got there, Xo sat in silence. He looked up as she approached and frowned. "What did Prince Lochlan want this time?" he asked. He nearly spat at his use of the word *prince*.

Cassia shook her head and instantly regretted it as it ached at the movement. "I don't know."

Nisa walked over to a large wingback chair and sat. "Probably just came to stir, get us riled up before the Tribute. Don't give in to it, Xo. If you get mad, he wins."

"I am mad," Xo said and then pointed at Lucas, who had not even moved a muscle. "And he's going to be even madder."

"Shit," Nisa said and Xo echoed it, dropping his head into his hands. The burns had healed, but the scars remained.

"What's the Tribute?" Cassia asked. This seemed more important than whether or not she needed her contact lenses.

"There's an event at the palace tomorrow. It's called the Tribute. On the first Sunday of each month, all the towns' leaders need to attend and pay their taxes or tributes to King Idis and the royals and then listen to him preach about how we're the plague and also how we have to allow all the Firsts to look at us as if we're worse than the cockroaches they so eagerly step on." Nisa exhaled. "I haven't been there. This is what Brie has told me."

"Brie was spot on," Xo replied, still investigating his newly scarred skin. "I kinda like the scars, Cassia. It adds to my warrior aesthetic."

Cassia offered Xo a small smile and then closed her eyes. "What happens if you don't go?" she asked. She wanted nothing but to lie down on the couch next to Lucas, but there wasn't any space.

"They show up and take what they want," Zidane spat as he walked back into the living room. His thin lips curled back, exposing his teeth.

He sat on the floor and crossed his legs. Cassia breathed a sigh of relief; he was alive and he was speaking. There was no slurred speech and it seemed as though he was functioning coherently. "They're really powerful. We tried in the past to fight them, but it never ended well. But I'm starting to think that we need to fight again.... Because Lucas is.... You know, Lucas is powerful. We may even stand a chance. Our numbers are growing."

Xo threw a warning look in his direction.

"He was brilliant with the Rahlogs earlier, more powerful than I had ever seen him and I could see he was holding back too," Zidane said.

Xo stared at Zidane, his usual friendly face set in a frown. Zidane looked at his feet. "Thanks for healing me, Cassia. I owe you my life."

"It wasn't a life-threatening wound...." she said. Although it probably was.

Lucas stirred and the room went quiet. All eyes watched him as his eyelids fluttered open. He rubbed a hand across his face a few times and then scratched his head.

"Why are you all staring at me?" he asked, sitting up slowly. Cassia sat next to him, allowing herself a moment of relief that he was back. When Ruq ran off with her, she thought Lucas was done for. He smiled at her, his dimples now reminding her of Lochlan. She shook the thought from her mind.

Again, she instantly regretted the unnecessary movement of her head.

"Good news or bad news?" she asked while smiling back at him. She knew he would pick good news first; he was the only person she knew who did that.

"Good," he said, his voice scruffy.

"I really am a Healer."

He exhaled quickly and wrapped an arm around her, pulling her close. "You did it? You did it! I knew you could do it." He placed a hard kiss on the side of her head. "Come on, no bad news can ruin that."

Xo scoffed.

"Lochlan was here," she said, inhaling the sea scent and wishing they were home together.

His grip around her stiffened. "Why?"

She shrugged. "He didn't say why, but let's just focus on the fact that his unwelcome visit led to me learning how to heal.... Bright side, yeah?"

Cassia heard his teeth grind. "Yeah, sure," he replied.

Reaching around the back of his neck, she touched the scratch and felt the skin close underneath her fingertips.

He looked up at her, his smile returning. "That's incredible. I could feel that."

"Does anyone have wounds for me to heal?" she asked, and everyone laughed.

"Take it easy, big shot. You may not realize it at first, but it will drain you really quickly," Lucas said, his tone getting harder with each word as his gaze fell on Xo's scarred skin.

Cassia nodded. Her entire body was still heavy.

A second wave of drowsiness hit her like a thick layer of fog settling in on all of her senses. The sound of Lucas speaking became muffled. She stood and her knees went weak. Strong hands gripped her and someone was talking to her, but she couldn't hear a thing.

Her blurry vision returned a second before everything went black.

CHAPTER THIRTEEN

Cassia woke up alone in her bed, but the smell of the ocean lingered. She stretched out her arms, rubbing them over the bedsheets, which were still warm. She climbed out of bed and into the shower. Her hands were clean, but Zidane's dried blood was still stuck underneath her fingernails.

Touching the feathers, she counted them, making sure she had not lost another one while she was asleep. There were still seven feathers. A strange mixture of relief and dread flooded her. The longer it took, the more time she had to help Lucas and get the suppressant tonic for Calla...but it also meant more time she would be away from Calla and her mother and she had no idea what they were thinking or how they were dealing with her disappearance.

Especially since Calla had seen Lochlan. She wondered whether Calla told her mother about it and what they would do.

She rummaged in the cupboards for something to wear. The cupboards were lined with clothing, pants, dresses, ranging from practical to evening wear. Surprisingly, there were even high-heeled shoes. Cassia found a long pair of soft beige woolen pants and a brown tunic. She rolled up the bottom of the pants. It wasn't flattering, but it would have to do.

Opening the drawers, she found a golden hairbrush. The gold on the handle and the gold on the top end of the brush differed slightly in color. As with her copper dagger, there were initials engraved in the handle, *RW*. She twirled it around in her hand and the handle twisted. When she twisted it farther and tugged it gently, the handle slipped out, revealing a small sharp blade. She was not the least bit surprised. In fact, the high-heeled shoes surprised her more than a knife concealed in a hairbrush. She reconnected it and brushed through her hair, which only made it frizzy. Patting her hair gently, she tried to calm her unruly mane.

But it didn't matter.

Who cared what her hair looked like when she was fighting off a deranged man trying to take a bite out of her?

And yet, she picked up the brush for one more round.

Back in her world, she didn't care for dating, so much so that her mother kept introducing her to doctors around the hospital and on occasion, even handsome patients. Which was always embarrassing.

She wasn't interested in sex after what happened with Jay. The memory of their bodies awkwardly rubbing against each other, of her discomfort and his unfamiliar hands touching her made her shudder.

After that, she threw herself into her studies and away from the eyes of men. Even though everything inside her desired that escape other people seemed to find in love and lust, she couldn't. She just couldn't.

She opened the drawer again, found a piece of string and tied her hair up before making her way downstairs.

The smell of food pulled her toward the kitchen. Brie sat at the table, forking eggs into her mouth with her right hand while furiously paging through a book the size of the dinner plate with her left.

"Hey," she said, looking up. Her blond hair fell beautifully around her face. "You can dish up for yourself. Everything is in the kitchen, all cooked."

Cassia smiled and mumbled her appreciation. Her stomach agreed audibly.

"Heard you had quite the day yesterday," Brie said, closing the book and sighing. "Congrats on learning how to use your powers, though."

"Thanks…. I can't say I have the hang of it, but it was definitely a start." Cassia grabbed a plate and filled it up with more food than she was proud to admit to. "What are your powers, by the way?"

"Nothing really. I'm still hoping something will show up. I have the basic stuff that comes with being a Reborn. We're faster and stronger than a regular human." Brie dragged another book across the white wooden table and started paging through it. "Everyone says my potion brewing must be a power, but I'm just following the recipes, the same as I do with baking. I think they're all lazy."

Cassia chuckled and Brie smiled. She was beautiful.

"So, even though you're here because you're linked to magic, it doesn't necessarily mean you have a magic power?" Cassia asked.

"Yeah, because with Reborns, the magic is diluted with regular humans and while your magic brings you here, there's no way to say how much of it you have or where you got it from. Whereas the Firsts all have telekinesis and some of them have one or two other powers. They're also faster, stronger and they heal quicker than we do," Brie said without looking up from the book.

Cassia sat across from Brie and started eating. She looked at Brie and hesitated. Brie looked up at her, scrutinizing her expression.

"You can ask me about Calla's suppressant. I would, if I were you."

Cassia sighed in relief. She was thinking about it, but was almost afraid of the answer. She chewed her food, staring down at her plate.

"It's coming along. There are a few ingredients missing. I'll chat to Lucas about who to send to get them," Brie answered without being asked.

Cassia nodded even though she wanted more information. She made a plan to go up to the library and look at instructions in the *Book of Empaths* once more.

"Where is Lucas?" Cassia asked, shoving a piece of bread into her mouth while reaching for another slice. She was surprised he had not come to join her at breakfast.

"On his way to the palace," Brie said, frowning deeply.

Cassia's head snapped upward. "What? I wanted to go with him, in case of...I don't know...."

Brie let out a dry laugh and met her gaze. "Absolutely not. The very last thing any of us would want is for you, a Guest, a *female* Guest, to go to the palace." She shuddered dramatically.

"You mean...." Cassia knew what Brie was insinuating, but she needed it to be confirmed.

Except she couldn't get the words out.

"Sex with a Guest is more satisfying, apparently. King Idis gets dibs on all female Guests that he can get his hands on and when he's done with them, he passes them on to his sons and then the guards until they get lucky enough to rip off their feather necklaces."

Disgust gnawed at every part of Cassia as she stared down at the food on her plate. Her appetite, for once, disappeared. Her mind raced to Brie, to Nisa, and knots appeared in her stomach.

"You don't have to worry. We won't let that happen to you. The Reborns have mostly figured out how to hide Guests." Brie stood up and walked to the kitchen. She filled the kettle with water. "Also, don't worry about Lucas. He isn't alone. Nisa and Xo have both joined him."

"Brie?" Cassia called, standing up and walking toward the kitchen island. Brie turned around with a cup of coffee in her hand and offered it to Cassia. She raised an eyebrow in question. "Why does Lochlan address Lucas as if he were royalty? Is he? Like amongst the Reborns or something?"

Brie tilted her head thoughtfully. "Lucas is well-loved amongst the community for sure and maybe it's because of that…. But, to be quite honest with you, I think Lochlan just does it to irritate him since none of us ever refer to Lochlan by his actual royal title." She sipped on her own coffee and added, "I'm sorry you had to deal with him yesterday, he can be quite terrifying."

"He doesn't scare me," Cassia said distractedly, as she recalled their interaction. She sipped some coffee, stinging her tongue. That would burn for the next few days. In her mind, she visualized what her tongue felt like before sipping the coffee, before the numbness, and then she buzzed, feeling her magic for a second, before the sting in her mouth disappeared.

What an excellent use of my powers.

"By the way, how are you feeling?" Brie asked, sitting down on the barstool across from her and propping her elbows onto the table. "It's supposed to be pretty tiring when you first start using your powers."

"I feel fine, just hungry all the time. It's like there's a hole in my stomach," Cassia said, and popped a piece of cheese into her mouth.

Brie nodded knowingly. "There's more fruit than we can manage. Jun seems to be exceptionally good at growing bananas. We think it's got something to do with him changing the plant's feelings, but he won't admit it and bananas are his favorites."

"How is he?" Cassia asked, the memory of stitching his skin flashing across her mind.

"He's okay, but it would be nice if you could speed up the healing process, if you feel up to it?" Brie asked, and tossed a banana at Cassia.

Cassia caught the banana and nearly ate it with the peel on.

★   ★   ★

Min-Jun was sleeping peacefully when Cassia entered his room. It was set up differently from the other two she had been in, aside from the four-poster bed, which seemed to come standard. The walls had a fresh coat of light turquoise paint, reminding her of the sky on a summer's day. There were no doors on his cupboards. The contents of each shelf were neatly folded or hung up. On his dresser were scattered sheets of paper alongside pieces of worn-down charcoal and sketches of a woman with long straight hair.

She sat on the chair beside his bed and wriggled her fingers before slowly placing her hand on top of the bandaged area.

His eyes opened when she touched him. He looked at her curiously, pressing his lips together before saying, "You figured out how to use your healing abilities. Can't say I approve of the method, but it got you there."

Flinching back, she realized he had looked into her mind.

"Sorry, bad habit with a new mind. I'll try not to read it again," he said and looked away guiltily.

"It's okay, I guess," she said, reaching out steadily and closing her eyes. She inhaled slowly and focused on feeling that buzz in her fingertips, which lay on his abdomen. Instead, the buzz spiraled outward, traveling in every direction, and edged into the base of her head, trickling into her mind as a vision presented itself.

She saw Min-Jun. In her vision, he was wearing a perfectly tailored black suit, standing beside a beautiful woman in a big white dress. It was the woman from the sketch. His face wore an even wider smile than she had become used to.

The buzz of her fingers snapped the image from her mind and she gasped, pulling her hand away. Min-Jun shot upright, his cheeks reddening.

She stammered, wondering whether she should tell him but before she could decide, he said, "I saw what you saw. Sorry, my power pulled me in against my will this time…." A shadow of the smile she had just seen appeared on his face.

"I didn't mean to."

"It's okay. When you're starting out, powers tend to overlap until you can control it." He started fiddling with the bandages, undoing them. "Thanks for fixing me up."

"Wait, don't get up," she said. "I don't know if it worked."

"It worked," he said cheerfully, and she felt his happiness envelop her. He removed the last of the bandage and revealed a shiny new scar. "See?"

"Wow," she said, feeling silly for being amazed by her own powers.

She stood and her head spun. Min-Jun kicked himself off the bed and steadied her, guiding her back down to the chair. "Take it easy. It may seem like something small, but your body has just learned how to convert its energy into something healing and then decided to take a peek at my past at the same time…. It's incredible. I've never seen a Healer or Visionary in action before."

Letting her head drop backward, she tried smiling, but wasn't sure if her face was co-operating. "Yeah, I hear I'm the first one in ages."

"First one since the previous queen," Min-Jun said, twisting his back and sighing at the satisfying crack. "Shit," he said suddenly, "it's the Tribute tomorrow. Has he left already? I need to be there."

"Yeah, before I woke up," she replied. "Nisa and Xo went along, so Lucas isn't alone."

"Has Nisa got control over her Empath powers yet?" he asked, a deep frown line crossing his forehead.

"I don't know, I think she kind of does." Her eyelids were becoming increasingly heavier.

Min-Jun cursed again. Even his curses were gentle. "Lucas is going to need it," he said.

★   ★   ★

Cassia woke up on Min-Jun's bed and walked downstairs with a fresh idea. She made her way down to the dungeon, reached the door and grabbed the handle. Something sharp pricked her palm and she pulled her hand back. Her blood dripped into the handle. After a moment, she tried turning it, but it wouldn't budge.

Perhaps she needed to withstand the prick. Gripping it tightly, she inhaled deeply, ignoring the small zing of pain and tightening her grip.

Still nothing.

She turned around to find Brie watching her from one floor up.

"What's up?" Brie asked. Her smile was fixed and polite, but even from a flight down, the concern in her eyes was clear.

"I wanted to see Jean…. My powers are all over the place. I thought maybe I would be able to see something. It might not be useful, but it's definitely activated at the moment."

The smile faded and Brie sighed and nodded. "Good idea," she said in a small voice. "I was just about to administer his pain suppressant. It usually puts him to sleep. I can wait, if you need him to be awake?"

"I have no idea how any of this works," Cassia admitted.

Brie closed the distance between them and stepped around her, gripping the handle. The door opened as it swallowed her blood and Brie gestured for her to go ahead. Cassia walked inside, followed by Brie, and the door slammed closed behind them, making less noise than she expected.

Hesitantly, Cassia walked toward the dark corner. Noticing her reluctance, Brie led the way quietly. Cassia had prepared herself for screaming the second they opened the door, but there was none.

Jean was on the floor, lying on his back, his arms and legs sprawled out alongside him. His eyes were glazed over, but the alarming part was that his mouth was closed. He wasn't screaming. Cassia ran up to the cage and said, "Let me in."

"Absolutely not. Lucas will kill me," Brie replied, her face twisted in anguish as she looked away from the cage.

"Look at his chest, it's moving," Cassia said desperately. "Barely. I need to check on him."

"I won't open the cage."

Cassia took another step toward the cage, stretching her arm through the gap between the bars to see if she could reach him. He turned suddenly, rolling over and pushing himself up onto all fours before leaping forward. Cassia stumbled back, pulling her arm out of his reach. His fingers grasped for her and then wrapped around the bars. The screams returned.

Covering her ears with her hands, Cassia glanced at Brie and found her unmoved, standing in exactly the same position, her arms crossed tightly around her waist as if cradling a stomachache.

Inhaling deeply, Cassia crawled back toward the cage to reach out and touch Jean's exposed, reddened knuckles, which were still firmly wrapped around the bars. Focusing on her magic and her breathing, she reminded herself of what it felt like healing Min-Jun and summoning that vision. Willing the buzz to appear in her mind.

Nothing happened.

She closed her eyes and tried again.

Brie placed her hand on Cassia's elbow and the gentle buzz crept up her neck as a vision entered her mind. She saw Jean in the manor's kitchen, cooking alongside Brie. Her hair was slightly shorter than it was now. He was slicing onions and she was tapping her foot, with a wide smile across her face. He tossed the onions in the hot pan and while it sizzled, he pulled her into his embrace.

Sharp nails scraped along Cassia's hand, pulling her out of her own mind. Her eyes flung open and she quickly withdrew her hand and took a few steps back. Jean pushed himself up against the bars and stretched his arms out toward her, his screams growing in volume.

"You saw something. What did you see?" Brie asked, her blue eyes wide with concern, her arms tucked tightly once more.

Cassia shook her head. "Nothing." It didn't feel like something she was supposed to see. Much like Min-Jun's wedding.

Brie uncrossed her arms and dug into her tunic's breast pocket, retrieving a small vial with a green liquid. She rolled it nervously between her fingers.

The buzz was still traveling through Cassia's body. She hazarded another touch before it disappeared. Gingerly, she touched the tips of Jean's outstretched fingers and immediately, she was pulled into another vision. This time she saw a large gathering of people. No, not people, Rahlogs. Some of them were screaming and others were talking to each other normally. They looked like regular people, aside from the blood and dirt smeared everywhere. She could barely make out any of their features; it was dark as night.

Jean swiped at her again, but she'd been expecting it and retracted quickly. He threw his head back and howled before collapsing onto the concrete floor. Brie's knees shook slightly as she dropped down beside the cage and whispered, "Jean, please, if you can hear me, take this pain suppressant, okay? It will help." She rolled the vial into the cage and stood up as she said, "I'm so sorry. I'm so sorry."

Grabbing Cassia's wrist, she pulled her out of the dungeon as Cassia's head started spinning.

"Wait," Cassia protested. "I was seeing something."

"Let's get you something to eat," Brie answered, quickly wiping the tears that wet her face. "You look like you're about to pass out."

"I'm fine, Brie, let me go." Cassia pulled out of Brie's grip and went back to Jean.

He picked up the pain suppressant and crushed it in his hands. The glass cut into his palms and red blood splattered onto the gray floor. Brie's entire body seemed to cave in.

"I'll be okay down here, by myself," Cassia said quietly.

Brie's red eyes welled up with a fresh batch of tears. "I'm sorry, I hate seeing him like this…it's been almost a week but it isn't getting any easier. It's actually getting worse." She shoved her hands into the pockets of her pants and bit her lip. "I can't leave you down here by yourself. I don't know whether he'll get hungry enough to break out of that cage. Lucas will kill me if something happens to you."

"I just really wanted to help," Cassia said. "I'm so sorry."

"No need to apologize."

"Actually, earlier when you touched me, I saw you and Jean, cooking together…." Cassia admitted.

Brie's mouth twisted into a smile as her eyes flooded with tears. "What were we cooking?"

"He was chopping onions, there were peppers on the table and you were wearing a blue dress. Your hair was shorter."

"Gosh, that could be anything." She looked upward. After a few moments, she said, "He threw himself in front of a Rahlog for me. Because I let my guard down. We weren't even dating anymore, but he still did it. He still protected me."

Cassia reached out and rubbed Brie's shoulder, willing her magic to stay out of Brie's memories or future. She noticed the scratches bleeding on her own hands and healed them with a touch. Her magic complained as her eyes drooped.

Brie led her out of the dungeon and back into the living area. She turned on one of the lamps. "It's the middle of the day, but this house is so dark," Brie said, gesturing to all the dark wooden furniture.

"Who built this place? How did you end up here?"

Brie laughed as she fell onto the big couch. She kicked off her shoes and curled her feet underneath her. "The manor is enchanted, so I figure it must have been owned by a First at some point…. Xo found it, I think. He collected the rest of us and it felt like home, even though none of us grew up with enchanted manors."

Cassia sat in the lone armchair. She understood what Brie meant; it felt homey, even though it was large, mostly empty and cracked. It felt loved. "Did you die to get here?" she asked, unsure of whether that was impolite.

Brie nodded. "About three years ago."

"I'm sorry."

"You ask a lot of questions, although I can't say Lucas didn't warn me."

Cassia tutted. It would be Lucas to exaggerate her curiosity. "How long before Lucas gets back?" she asked, feeling her drowsiness overwhelm her. "I'm worried about Calla...."

"A day, maybe two, depending on how many people he picks up on the way and whether or not he keeps his cool with the king."

CHAPTER FOURTEEN

Lucas

Lucas left before Cass could wake up to avoid having to answer all the questions he knew she'd ask about why she couldn't go with him. She always managed to trick him into agreeing with her; it was one of her other superpowers. Taking her on a hunting trip was one thing, but taking her directly to the palace would be a disaster waiting to happen.

It already upset him that Xo insisted he and Nisa both join him. Lucas wished none of them would have to expose themselves to that disgusting excuse of a man they called king.

It especially upset him that Nisa was sent to monitor his emotions, something they thought he hadn't realized, but Jun found an excuse to tag along with every month. The irony was that the only person who could help him keep calm was the one person he couldn't bring along with him.

That reminded him, he needed to speak to Cass. There was so much he needed to explain, but being around her, even after not seeing her for such a long time, felt so normal it was hard to remember the abnormal things he needed to talk to her about. All he ended up doing was smiling at her like a fool. Even though he was aware of it, he still couldn't help himself.

Ruq halted on Xo's command outside the Dandelion village. Lucas slipped off the wolf and walked up to the community leader, Petri, who stood outside the boundary of their village. "Lucas!" Petri called as he approached, sticking out his hand. "How're you doing?"

Taking his hand, Lucas nodded. "As best as I can under the circumstances," he said, and let go of Petri's equally large hand. It was odd that his hands were as large as Lucas's but he barely reached Lucas's shoulders.

Petri chuckled politely and shook his bald head. "I despise these meetings. You know, I considered merging our village with yours. That way I wouldn't be the one elected to attend these things anymore." Petri attached his cart to two of his other horses. The cart was filled to the brim with apples, oranges and pieces of folded material.

"Our home is always open to everyone, you know that. We're still only five people in Thistle. How are the rest of the people of Dandelion doing?"

Petri climbed onto his horse. "We're settled in. The kids know the land." He gestured to the newly built walls and said, "After losing so many of our own, we built up to protect ourselves from the Rahlogs.... It would cause too much chaos trying to move everything now." Petri grabbed the reins and added, "You could always join us, though."

"Thank you for the offer," Lucas said. It was something he'd discussed with Thistle, but they weren't interested. They loved the manor. They all did.

He realized Petri was ready to leave, alone. He hung his head as the memory of Neil filled his mind. Neil used to join Petri to the Tribute. "I'm sorry about Neil...." Lucas said, quietly. "He went down fighting bravely...."

Petri blinked back tears and nodded. "Zidane told us all about it.... Thank you for honoring his death." His voice was thick with emotion and the grief they'd all become accustomed to.

After a moment of silence, Lucas mounted Ruq and leaned down to whisper to the wolf, reminding him to go slow since they too had carts attached.

Ever since the Rahlog attacks increased, Lucas promised some of the other leaders along the route that they would travel together. The trek all the way north to the palace had become a risky journey and everyone felt safer traveling in numbers.

"Need to get me one of those wolves," Petri commented, lovingly stroking the black mane on his golden stallion. "The one I had wouldn't listen to me."

Lucas smiled and scratched Ruq beside the ear. "It takes a while to get them to understand you. We've had them since they were puppies."

"We need to get going if we're going to join up with any other leaders before sundown," Xo said as he and Nisa rode up next to them. Their wolves sniffed each other affectionately before Zuq nibbled on Ruq's ear, eliciting a low growl.

They rode slowly, well, slowly compared to what Lucas was used to. Xo and Nisa rode together on Zuq and Petri followed on his horse. Their carts dragged loudly behind them as the wheels wobbled over loose stones and uneven ground. They crossed over to the northern side of the Selli River and stopped at all the small communities along their way to collect their leaders and feed the animals.

The next village, Clover, was quiet. Strangely quiet. Signaling for the others to stay back, Lucas slid off Ruq and motioned for Xo and Nisa to stay mounted, to stay ready. He had a bad feeling about this. It was all far too quiet and even though the sun was setting, there were no lights on. No sounds of children playing or parents calling out to them.

Just absolute silence.

The gravel path took him into the center of the village. He walked up to the nearest house and peeked through the window. It was too dark to see anything inside, and he couldn't hear any movement either. He reached the door, knocked gently and waited a moment, but no one answered. A quick flick of his wrist turned the handle and he found that the door was unlocked. Stepping inside slowly, he looked around, straining his eyes in the darkness. Furniture was scattered around the small lounge. The couch was shredded and dark stains coated the gray carpets that he remembered. Walking quickly, he peeked into the bedrooms and slammed his eyes shut, wishing he hadn't seen that everything was stained red.

He couldn't look at it anymore. He spun on his heel, and kept his head low as he made his way outside, quietly closing the door as he exited.

Xo looked at him from the pathway and Lucas shook his head. Their heads dropped. Lucas walked back up the path and Nisa looked up and held up her palms, signaling that he should wait. He motioned that they should continue on, but Nisa kept her hands raised. She reached out her hand and he touched it, opening his mind to her.

Someone is still around here, she said into his mind. *Check the other houses.* Her thoughts tickled as if she was whispering directly into both of his ears at the same time.

How many? he thought.

I sense two souls, she replied.

Are they Rahlogs? he asked.

It doesn't work that way. I just know that there is life that way.

Lucas let go of her hand and pulled out his dagger. He walked beyond the first house and checked each house the same way. A gentle knock, before entering. Every house greeted him with blood-spattered floors. Occasionally he found a chewed-off hand or an arm that was left behind. In some of the houses, he found dead bodies, ripped into pieces. Nausea swirled in his stomach as he ran out of the house and threw up outside on the gravel path.

Sometimes the Rahlogs couldn't control their hunger and instead of biting and turning someone, they simply feasted until there was barely anything left.

Aside from the putrid smell, the shredded bodies were better than the empty houses, for the empty homes meant that the residents were turned and that new Rahlogs would be born.

After emptying the contents of his stomach, Lucas kept checking the houses, but there was no one left. Nisa's powers must be faulty. Perhaps she was sensing an animal or getting confused with one of the others.

He turned around and started walking back to the rest of them when his eyes fell on the stables at the back of one of the houses. He heard the familiar sound of a horse clip-clopping. Crouching low, he walked into the stables, light on his feet, his copper dagger in his right hand, his left hand raised and ready.

Instead of a Rahlog, instead of just a horse, he found a middle-aged woman and a little boy, fast asleep. The boy was curled up in his mother's arms. The horse neighed as soon as it spotted him and the woman sat upright, gasping as she fumbled for her knife.

"I'm a Reborn," Lucas said quickly.

Her black hair was pulled into a neat bun, but everything else she and the boy wore was torn and dirty. "Please," the woman begged, spreading her arms backward to reach her child, who hid behind her, "Please, please don't hurt us and don't tell anyone about us. Please, they will come for him. They don't know about him. Please."

"I won't," Lucas replied softly, squatting close to the ground, setting down his dagger and stretching out his open palms. "My name is Lucas Williams and I stay at the old manor on the southern side of the Selli as part of the Thistle village."

"With Brie?" the woman asked and Lucas nodded. It amazed him that everyone knew Brie and he had been in this realm longer than she had been.

"What happened here?" he asked.

"The Rahlogs came and they—" Her voice cracked. "And I was too scared to go out. I can't protect myself and my child. I have invisibility, but I can't do it for both of us for very long...."

"I'm sorry," he said quietly as he looked at the scared child peeking out from around her waist. "We're on our way to the palace for the Tribute. You're welcome to travel with us."

"I can't go near the palace with him! They don't know about him. He's a firstborn and my only child." She lifted her knife as if Lucas would call the royal guard and expose them.

"Okay, I understand," Lucas said. He'd heard of some Reborns who had managed to hide their firstborn children. They were rarely successful. "There's another village en route, Nutsedge. You could wait there. I know the leader of the village. He's friendly and his people seem happy. I'm sure they'll be able to accommodate both you and your boy, and if not, you can always come back with me." Lucas tucked his dagger away and stood.

The woman wiped her tears spreading more dirt across her face. She stood and her son wrapped his arms around one of her legs. "It's okay, baby. It's going to be okay. This is Rio," she said, pointing to the boy and then to herself, "and I'm Fila."

Lucas smiled and gestured for them to stay behind him. He led them and their horse to the village entrance and explained the situation to the others. They all offered their smiles and sympathies. Lucas tossed a bag of bananas to Fila and watched as Rio gobbled up three within the space of a minute.

"We have to keep Rio hidden. He's her first and only child," Lucas said.

"How?" Petri asked Fila, his brown eyes glazing over for a second. "How did you do it? How did you stop them from taking him?" He swallowed hard as his voice shook and everyone turned away, unable to bear his pain or to face their own.

"I have invisibility. I hid him every time the royal guards came around for inspections or collections. I know it will cost me my life if they find out I've been hiding him, but I had to try," Fila replied as she lifted Rio onto their horse. "It's not fair that they take our children. They're just children!"

"I'd have done the same thing if I could," Petri choked out, and looked down at his hands as his tears fell.

The rage shook through Lucas's body as his heart thundered in his chest. Inhaling deeply, he tried controlling the power that shot through him. He closed his eyes just in case they were changing color, changing to that very recognizable color. He couldn't have this here.

Not now. He begged his power to subside.

But it wasn't right. The Firsts shouldn't be able to get away with this. They shouldn't be able to do something so cruel. He wouldn't let them. He had to stop them. His magic howled within him, begging to be released.

"The Rahlogs won't strike the same place twice, so this might be the best place to camp for the night," Xo announced and, as it had been a long day of traveling in the heat, everyone agreed. Xo rode up to Lucas and casually slapped him on the back before sliding off Zuq and leading the wolves and the rest of their group into the village and to the stables. Which was, at the very least, free of human remains and the wolves and horses could fit comfortably.

Xo prepared the firewood and one of the other leaders blew over it and fire appeared. "Why didn't I get cool fire power?" Xo huffed.

"I'll take first watch," Lucas offered.

"You need rest. I'll take the first watch."

The scent of the firewood reached Lucas, reminding him of Cass and then instantly of Lochlan. Ignoring the irritation that came along with thoughts of Lochlan, Lucas turned to Xo and said, "I'm fine, stop worrying."

"Saw your eyes flash blue earlier, Lucas. We don't need the leaders of the Reborns to see that."

"I'm fine. Besides, the whole point is to get me tired before we get there. The more power I release now, the fewer chances there are of it showing up there," Lucas said as he prepared a flask of hot coffee for everyone.

Xo leaned closer. "I brought a mild power suppressant. It should last a few hours, just enough to get you through the Tribute."

Lucas hated the idea of being there, entirely powerless, but he couldn't risk having everyone see his eyes either. He couldn't risk having the king trigger his powers, especially since Nisa might not be strong enough to counter it. She'd only just learned how to use her Empathy.

Settling into his sleeping bag, he looked up at the night sky. The stars sparkled against the black sky. The moon was round and almost golden. There were almost certainly more stars in Selene than Talm. Cass would absolutely love this. They'd spent so many nights camping, so many nights staring at the stars discussing their hopes, their dreams and all the things she wanted to achieve.

None of which included an alternate realm.

★　　★　　★

Lucas awoke the next morning to find everything had been packed up and everyone was already mounted and ready to go. Everyone except him.

"You didn't wake me," Lucas complained to Xo as he stood up, brushing off some of the dirt.

"Didn't have to. There were plenty of other people willing to take watch."

They joined the Nutsedge village leader, Roland, and Lucas explained the situation with Fila and Rio.

"Of course, of course. We have space," Roland said to Fila. "You're welcome to stay as long as you like."

Two of their village people dragged out their cart and tied it to the two horses, then waited while Fila and Rio hopped off and thanked Lucas profusely. He wished them well and promised to stop at the town on the way back to check in on them.

They were so close to the palace now, they could see the tall golden walls from Nutsedge village, and Lucas couldn't imagine staying so close to them. A reminder of his time in the mines. A reminder of how many Reborns had lost their lives mining gold.

It was likely why he loved the manor so much. It was about as far away from the palace as he could be without living in the ocean.

When they finally reached the palace boundary, the royal guards stood at the entrance, waiting to search everyone who needed to enter. Their blood-red uniforms contrasted the clean, shining wall. One guard adjusted his crisp white shirtsleeves as they walked up to him. Every Reborn was thoroughly patted down before being allowed to enter the palace grounds. The blond guard ran his hands up and down Lucas roughly without making eye contact. "Go," he said, and Lucas stepped through, watching as the guard searched Nisa. Her eyes widened as the guard slipped his hands behind her and slid them down.

"Touch her again and you'll regret it," Lucas bit.

The guard scoffed at Lucas and said, "I will be sure to tell them you threatened me."

"You'll be dead before the message reaches them," Lucas snapped, and Nisa grabbed his arm, sending a wave of calm over him.

"Let's just go, please. It's not worth your life," she said.

"Listen to your little friend," the guard chirped as Nisa dragged him away still firmly holding his arm and wrapping her calm around him.

They entered the palace garden. It was easily the size of a large stadium, maybe even larger. Lucas was only ever allowed in the garden and had never ventured farther than that, but he'd seen the old palace map they kept in the library and the garden was just the tip of the iceberg.

The grass on either side of the paved pathway was perfectly green and trimmed, as it always was. The edge of the grass was met by blue rose bushes, the only other thing he had seen as blue as the Firsts' eyes. Beyond that, flowers of every kind were scattered around the garden, with red roses definitely being one of King Idis's favorites.

He continued along the path behind their royal guard escorts, who looked over their shoulders every half a second to ensure they were still following close behind.

Ahead of them, at the end of the pathway, the royal family sat upon a golden dais. It shimmered in the sunlight, nearly blinding every Reborn who looked upon it, and yet gazing away was considered disrespectful.

The First king stared at the approaching Reborns, a look of disgust and anger settling on his cruel, scarred face. A map of scars covered the right half of his face, left by the scratches of Rahlog, the man he turned into a monster, before he was released upon the Reborns.

Queen Lila sat on his left, admiring her nails as if she were waiting for dinner. Rumor had it, she had been one of his mistresses, the only one who bore him a son, filling the position of queen as soon as Queen Maeve died.

On either side of them sat the princes. Kain mimicked the look of his father, swiveling a sword around in his lap. Lochlan sat with that familiar smug look on his face. He raised an eyebrow upon seeing Lucas approach and bowed his head slightly.

It was all a game to him.

Lucas couldn't believe he'd let Lochlan know about Cass. Then again, Lochlan was the reason she was here.

Lucas ran his hand through his hair and sighed. He wished he hadn't taken the power suppressant. He wished he could have knocked that look off the king's and his sons' faces.

Kain stood up and shouted, "Attention!" The Reborns quieted down and turned their focus to the dais. The king stood to address the crowd, revealing the golden throne behind him, fitted with red cushions and marked with the First insignia, the full moon surrounded by six stars. Lucas dropped to his knees and bowed his head. The grass was as soft as he knew it would be. The sound of Reborns gasping out in pain echoed through the garden as the royal guards leapt forward to beat anyone who didn't immediately bow down to their king.

King Idis sneered in delight as his guards attacked a handful of Reborns. He waited a moment, allowing for the torture to continue on for his amusement. "Up," he commanded, and the Reborns scrambled to their feet before being whipped by the guards again for not doing it quickly enough.

Lucas wiped the sweat off his brow. While he knew the king had no control over the weather, he was sure that the Tribute was always planned for the hottest or wettest day of the month. The sun slapped the back of his neck and he wondered whether Cass could heal sunburned skin.

"Before we begin," the king said, his blue eyes devoid of any emotion, "I would like to take this opportunity to remind you that if you do not adhere to the rules of the Selene Realm, you will be removed." Lucas scoffed as the sea of blue eyes accompanied wide smiles, excited at the idea of it. "And now for the entertainment. Enjoy the performance." King Idis raised his hands and summoned a mixture of blue and orange flames. He released the fire into the sky, making the already unbearable heat even worse. The flames spun around in the air above them, forming the silhouettes of dancers and gymnasts.

A spectacle to remind them how powerful he was, how using that much magic was as easy to him as breathing.

The fire dancers pranced into the crowd and the Reborns tried their best not to flinch as the dancing flames swirled a mere breath away from their faces. But the fire dancers were the least of their concerns. It was what came next that broke Lucas, that broke all of them, time and time again.

The *Praise the Firsts* dance.

More than one hundred stolen Reborn children shuffled out of the two exits on either side of the back end of the garden. Dressed in black and blue, with the royal insignia displayed on their backs, they made their way to the clearing in the center of the crowd. This forced them to walk by their friends, their families, their parents.

A child no older than ten stepped forward and began to sing. A howl of pain shuddered through the audience, followed by a woman's voice, screaming, "My child! Alice! Alice! My child! My girl!"

Alice continued singing with silent tears streaming down her face as the rest of the children joined her in song. The guards silenced the woman who'd cried out her name and any other Reborn who attempted to reach their stolen child. Lucas bit his tongue so hard he swallowed blood. If he hadn't taken the suppressant, he would surely have killed everyone.

Beside him, Petri's eyes darted among all the faces of the children. Much like many of the Reborns here, Petri had lost his firstborn child to the Firsts. The children were taken from families around the age of ten and were forced to clean, cook and entertain the Firsts' every whim. Some of the chores could easily have been performed with the Firsts' powerful magic, but the king did it to induce fear and mostly to discourage the Reborns from having children. It was as effective as could be.

With one long leg crossed over the other, and his blue eyes flashing with enjoyment, the king leaned back on his throne and played with the ball of fire in his hand, watching it morph from blue to orange and back to blue.

The dreadful performance came to an end and the children shuffled away. To their rooms? To their cells? It was too much to think about. The Reborns received absolutely no updates, except for these monthly performances.

Kain stood up and sheathed his sword, a steel sword of about three feet long, the golden hilt tucked tightly at his waist. He spent the next hour spitting about the Reborns and all the resources they consumed. "The more you consume, the more you need to produce. Therefore, we expect an increase of ten percent next month in tributes."

Lochlan rolled his eyes and yawned. Torturing Reborns was apparently much too boring to entertain that spoiled brat.

"Moreover, applications for extensions to grounds will be limited to grounds used for agriculture. Extension of villages will not be accepted."

Less space. More food.

It was all the same, really.

When the younger prince was finally done, he started calling up the village leaders, who were divided into groups to streamline things.

"Fleabane, Poppy and Purslane," the royal guard called, and two men and one woman stepped forward. Lucas recognized one of them; they had crossed paths once while hunting.

The three Reborns walked up to the golden scale, which was the size of a standard bus. They packed everything onto their side of the scale. The same things Lucas had packed and had waiting: fruits, vegetables, wood, grain, materials, anything they could find that seemed to be valuable.

The king smiled and turned toward Lochlan, who closed his hands into a fist and lifted a boulder, nicknamed the King's Weight, onto the other end of the scale. Everyone watched in anticipation as the weight dragged down the opposite end of the scale, lower, lower, lower...but not lower than the Reborns' packed scale. The three village leaders burst into a cheer and Lucas and the rest of the Reborns cheered alongside them.

The royal guards standing behind the scale stretched out their arms together and lifted the items the Reborns had packed, tossing them into a crate at the far right of the garden. A crate he knew the Reborn children would end up having to sort through.

"Dandelion, Thistle and Nutsedge," the royal guard called, and Lucas, Petri and Roland walked up to the scale and packed everything they had brought along with them. When they were done, Lucas stepped back, wiping the sweat off his brow with his tunic sleeve.

Lochlan lifted the King's Weight and dropped it on the opposite end of the scale and Lucas watched it fall. Between his anticipation and the heat of the sun, he was afraid he might pass out.

The weight tipped the scale, lower and lower, and for the first time in months, the King's Weight dropped lower than the scale they had packed. It took him a few moments to register it. To realize that they were in trouble. A unified gasp echoed through the crowd as King Idis smiled widely. His blue eyes glistened in the light of the sun, flashing wickedly.

Lucas hung his head, cursing loudly. This couldn't be happening. *Why is this happening?*

They had packed enough, as always. They had been eating less, drinking less, working harder to produce new materials and antidotes, everything to meet the requirements.

Petri started apologizing under his breath and Lucas glanced toward him. "I'm sorry, Lucas, with all the people we lost, we haven't been able to produce…. I'd hoped it would be enough…but I suspected it might be too little…." he rambled.

"Who will be accepting the punishment?" the king called, tapping his fingertips together excitedly as his eyes traveled over the Reborns.

"I accept it," Lucas called before Petri could open his mouth. He glanced at Petri's left hand. His wife's name, Sarah, was wrapped around his ring finger. Petri had a family, a wife and a toddler. A family who had just had their firstborn taken from them.

The king couldn't do anything to Lucas that he wouldn't be able to handle. He'd handled it once before.

He walked up to the dais and squared his shoulders.

"Lochlan, go ahead. Make an example of him," the king said.

Lochlan remained seated, staring skyward while saying, "Really, Father? It's not like we need more food from Reborns anyway."

"Are you questioning me?" the king asked, narrowing his eyes. "I command it."

Lochlan stood up quickly and stretched out his hand, palm wide open and fingers spread out. A whip flew out of the palace, across the heads of the Reborns, and the handle landed in his hand. The whip wrapped itself gently around his arm. It was nearly thicker than his wrist. Lucas resisted his body's urge to shudder and instead, he clenched his fists.

He would not let them see him struggle. He would not give them the satisfaction of his screams.

"This is going to hurt," Lochlan said, and leaned closer to whisper, "but luckily for you, I taught your girl how to use her healing abilities."

"Don't even fucking mention her," Lucas snapped.

"Oh, don't worry, she's no use to me dead," Lochlan replied, and then added in a voice Lucas almost couldn't hear, "Maybe you should keep your eyes closed. We wouldn't want everyone to know your little secret power."

Lucas resisted a growl, but shut his eyes, hating his power at that moment. Hating bending to Lochlan's will. The whip sang as Lochlan flung it upward.

Before it landed, the king said, "Wait."

Lucas opened his eyes and stared up at the king. Surely, this wasn't going to be the first time the king showed mercy. Something twisted in his stomach as Lochlan crossed his arms and waited. "My guards tell me you have Baskians. A wolf might tip the scale in your favor." King Idis licked his thin lips.

Lucas's heart thundered against his chest so loudly he barely heard himself beg, "No, please, I'll take the punishment and next time I'll bring extra. I'll bring double, please."

"Oh, begging. Well, now I really want the wolf," the king said, and gestured to his guards, who left and reappeared pulling in Ruq and Zuq. One of them was the same guard whom he had threatened.

Fuck.

The wolves growled loudly, but the guards flung their whips across them, silencing them.

"Please," Lucas begged again as he struggled to find his voice. He could barely breathe, let alone speak. He dropped down to his knees. "I've had them since they were pups. Please, please. If there's any humanity in you, you'll punish me instead."

The royal guard pulled Zuq in front of the king.

"Do you really want a wolf, Father?" Lochlan asked, daring a glance at Lucas. "They stink." Lochlan unwound his whip and pointed at Lucas. "I'll give him a proper punishment. I don't care for the wolf."

The king considered this for a moment and smiled wickedly. He looked at Kain, raising an eyebrow at the sword he dangled in his grip. Without hesitation, Kain ran up to Zuq and in one heavy stroke, he sliced it across the wolf's neck.

A scream loud and foreign escaped Lucas, tearing at his vocal cords, crushing his heart, shredding every part of him. If it weren't for the power suppressant, he was sure he would rip the entire palace apart and everyone in it. He stood up and launched himself at Kain. "I will fucking kill you!" he shouted, his voice hoarse from screaming. "I'll get you for this, you pathetic son of a bitch." He didn't care about the consequences, he didn't care about punishment, he wanted Kain to pay for this, to undo what he did. He watched as Zuq bled out onto the ground and Ruq howled wildly as the guards held the gray wolf in place using the combined force of their telekinesis.

"Lochlan," the king said, turning to face Lucas, "teach him a lesson for his insolence."

The whip struck the air out of him and he welcomed it. The physical pain was nothing in comparison to what he was feeling.

Pure rage.

CHAPTER FIFTEEN

Cassia figured it was the perfect time to explore the grounds, and wandered through the back door of the manor. Instead of walking toward the stables, she followed the red paved path to where the tall banana trees were planted. While it seemed rather silly now, she realized she had never seen a banana tree in real life. She had only ever seen bananas wrapped in plastic, in bunches of six, alongside the packs of apples at the grocery store.

Behind the lush banana trees, of which there were many, the path continued, zigzagging between garden beds that housed lettuce, spinach, peppers and tomatoes. Strolling farther, she spotted the tops of carrots, and a variety of herbs. Straight down the middle stood a row of apple trees leading to the back end of the garden, which was bordered by another row of banana trees. They were right; Min-Jun was exceptionally good at growing bananas.

On her way back to the manor, she came across a cabinet. On top of it sat a pair of gloves, shears, and other small gardening tools. Grabbing the shears, she decided to pick an apple. Another thing she'd never done was eat an apple straight off a tree. She picked one and rubbed the bright green apple against her shirt until she could see her reflection in it. She sniffed it and turned it around in her hands as her stomach growled. Her mouth was already watering at the crisp and zingy taste she imagined it would have.

"It's safe to eat."

She lifted her eyes to find Min-Jun, holding two cups in his hands and smiling at her from the entrance to the garden. He closed his eyes and suddenly his smile faded. "Lucas is almost here," he said, a deep frown forming across his smooth forehead. "Eat the apple. You're going to need your powers."

As she bit into the apple, her eyelids fluttered closed in delight and her mouth filled with the sweet and sour taste. "Why?" she asked, crunching as she took another big bite.

"He's hurt, but it's nothing to worry about, according to Nisa. Although," he said, the frown line deepening, "she said it's more than just physical…. She's run out of energy and is struggling to keep him calm." He shook his head quickly to move his shaggy hair out of his eyes.

"What happened? Is he okay?" she asked, rushing through the last of the apple, eating it down to the core before tossing it into the compost heap.

He pursed his lips. "I don't have any more information, but he is okay, or he will be…."

When she reached the entrance, he passed her one of the cups he'd been holding and she inhaled the familiar scent of coffee.

"It's safe to drink," he said playfully, as he watched her swirling the dark brown liquid in the cup.

After blowing out a slow stream of air, she said, "Every now and then I get freaked out about everything that's going on." Lifting the cup to her lips, she took a small sip. Everything else here tasted better, sweeter, fresher, but the coffee was just the same as it was back home.

She followed him inside and waited on the couch in the living room. "Has she said anything else?" she asked, feeling her anxiety heighten, She wished he hadn't left without her. She wished she could have been there with him to help him immediately.

Min-Jun sat opposite her in the armchair and closed his eyes for a moment. "No, I think she's too drained. Do you want me to take care of your anxiety?"

"Makes me feel in control, if that makes sense," she said, throwing her head back on the couch and staring at the brass chandelier. If she closed her eyes, she would probably fall asleep again. All she had been doing was eating and sleeping and all she wanted to do was tell

Lucas about what she had seen and then go back into the dungeon to see more.

But taking Brie down there again wasn't an option, and Min-Jun had mentioned that he struggled when he was there because of the intensity of the pain Jean was feeling. He wasn't always able to switch his senses off, especially when the emotions reached out to him.

The air was knocked out of her as she thought about Calla screaming in pain, a pain none of them could understand. But Min-Jun understood it. At least, that was how he explained it, but Cassia was fairly certain that at least some of the time, he opened himself up to it willingly out of sheer curiosity. She always felt exposed around him, as if he were constantly reading her, as if every touch gave him a piece of her mind.

The front door flung open and Lucas barreled inside. His shoulders were wide and low, his tunic was ripped in every direction and drenched in dark blood. She could barely look at his wounds because she was too distracted by his unfamiliar eyes. They were bright blue.

Min-Jun inhaled quickly and closed his eyes. Cassia could almost see the calmness he was projecting toward Lucas. Lucas's eyes flickered back to their familiar black color and he looked at Min-Jun aggressively before they flashed blue again.

"Don't do that unless I ask you to," he said, his voice nearing a growl.

Min-Jun raised his hands and retreated. "Just trying to help."

Lucas hung his head and left. A minute later they heard his bedroom door slam. It would be surprising if the door remained on the hinges after that. Cassia glanced at Xo and Nisa and they both looked as though every limb, every muscle, every part of their bodies was struggling under an unseen weight.

Nisa finally spoke. "Go to him, he needs mending."

Cassia ran up the stairs, taking them two at a time, afraid of what she would find. Lucas being angry was one thing; she'd been the cause of it on multiple occasions, but she had never seen him exude such an aggressive energy. Almost animalistic.

Upon reaching his bedroom door, she stopped. Should she knock? Usually she'd call out a warning and barge in, like he'd do with her.

But there was something else he'd do too, when she was in need of cheering up. She cracked the door open slightly and stuck her hand in, pinching her fingers together to imitate a duck. "Luuuuke," she said, using the same deep voice he used when they were children.

"Not now, Cass. They killed..." he said, choking on his muffled words, "Zuq. They killed him."

Dropping her hand, she fell silent. The poor wolf. Her poor friend. She opened the door fully and found him lying on his stomach with his face buried in a pillow. His body shook slightly. She had only seen him cry a few times, when they were kids and his dog died, later when his mom died and once when she accidentally broke his favorite Batman figurine.

She kicked off her shoes and crawled onto the bed next to him. He was still bleeding, the red stains spreading farther across his tunic. Through the tears in the material, she could see his exposed skin was red and inflamed. Long cuts stretched across his back in every direction, creating a grid of blood and pain. In her years of being in the hospital, she'd never seen wounds like this before.

Gently, she placed a hand on his back and he flinched, wincing. "What happened?" she whispered, feeling the magic build up inside her. He stayed silent. She lay down next to him and placed her hand on his back again. Her fingers buzzed with magic and she watched the wounds close until only light, shiny scars remained.

"They just killed him for no reason." His voice was small and reminded her of the child she found whimpering in the cupboard on Father's Day, hoping to celebrate her father since he didn't have one of his own.

"Did they hurt you anywhere else?" she asked, and Lucas turned around. His chest was as violated as his back had been. He clenched his jaw, grinding his teeth.

She tore his shirt off and he gasped.

"Oh come on, the shirt was already ruined. It was easier than getting it over your enormous head," she said. He laughed lightly and she placed her hands on his muscular chest. It wasn't the same chest she had seen in the rock pools all those years ago. This was the chest of a warrior who had been fighting for his survival and the survival of his people for four years.

"You always wanted rock-hard abs," she joked, knocking lightly on his abdomen, surprised by the hardness. He had muscles she didn't know existed.

"I am in pain, Cass. Heal me, dammit." Lucas laughed softly and she slid her right hand across the large slices in his skin. Her eyes swept along every part of his exposed chest and landed on two black bands circling his left bicep, similar to the tattoo Zidane had flashed her. She looked at them closely.

"What are these?" she asked as she trailed her fingers across them. They were each about the width of a finger. "Zidane has one."

"One marking for every loved one you put to rest," he said.

She touched his face gently, wiping the stray tear, and used her other hand to heal the last remaining slash across his chest.

The buzz of magic entered her mind and she realized she was having another vision. She saw herself staring into blue eyes a second before lips collided with hers, the subtle taste of something pleasant and sensual entered her mouth with an urgent kiss.

She gasped loudly. Then the room came into focus once more, pulling her out of her mind.

"Cass, are you having a vision right now?"

She snapped back to the present, her heart pounding so fast she feared it might break through her chest. She looked at Lucas, at his dark eyes, and shook her head. It wasn't Lucas in the vision, surely not. Although he did have blue eyes earlier. But she and Lucas would never kiss. It made no sense. He was like her brother and she was sure the feeling was mutual.

But who else could it be?

Her mind flitted to the other set of eyes that she'd seen shine as blue. Lochlan. But it couldn't have been Lochlan.

Although, Brie mentioned that all the Firsts had those eyes. It could have been any of them.

That seemed worse.

Her mind raced through the options and her heart rate increased as she revisited the vision. An unfamiliar fluttering started in her belly.

"Cass, are you okay?" Lucas asked, propping himself up on one elbow.

Cassia nodded, heat rushing up to her cheeks. "I'm fine," she said, looking away. She couldn't look into those eyes and remember how blue they were when he arrived. She was tired and stressed and he was hurt. Her mind was simply playing tricks on her and making the most of being around him, in the wrong way.

He flopped back down on the bed. A frown formed as he glanced down at her cleavage. Her cheeks flushed and she looked down. "You lost another feather...." He lifted the fallen red feather and counted the feathers remaining. She whacked his hand away and he looked at her with his brows drawn close in confusion.

"Six left," she said quickly and sat up, swinging her legs over the bed's edge.

"Where are you going?" he asked, his eyes still red and puffy.

"I just, I thought maybe you wanted to sleep a bit.... I know I do," she said. It wasn't a lie.

"Stay," he replied. He tapped the bed next to him and a soft smile spread across his lips. Were those the lips in her vision? She couldn't tell. She was too busy staring into those eyes. "It will be nice to have some company...."

Cassia hesitated but the pain across his face, the pain caused by wounds she couldn't heal, was still deeply embedded in his features.

Maybe she could help by being there. She lowered herself back onto the bed, facedown.

"Why are you acting strange?" Lucas asked.

"Just go to sleep," she mumbled into the pillow, feeling a familiar drowsiness take over.

"Fine," he whispered, and placed a soft kiss just above her ear before whispering, "I'm really glad you're here, Cass."

CHAPTER SIXTEEN

Lucas was already at the breakfast table by the time Cassia made her way downstairs. She purposely chose to sit as far away from him as possible. Unfortunately, that still put her directly across from him, and every time he looked up at her, the memory of her vision clearly played through her mind. She cursed her photographic memory.

"Have you told him yet?" Brie asked, taking a seat next to her, gesturing to Lucas.

"No, tell him what? There's nothing to tell him," she rambled awkwardly with a mouth full of avocado. She shoved another piece in so that she was unable to say anything else.

"About your vision with Jean."

Of course, she thought.

Lucas's head shot up and he stared directly at her. "You went down there without me?" His dark eyes made her look down at her plate. "It's dangerous, Cass."

"I managed to have a vision yesterday while touching Jean," she said. "I saw a group of Rahlogs. I don't know if it was a memory of his or a vision of the future. I don't know how to tell the difference...."

"Can't have been a memory, he's never been at a Rahlog camp...." Brie commented, pursing her lips together. She tapped her fingers anxiously on the table.

"What did you see?" Lucas asked. He stood and leaned over the table. "We need to find the camp."

"It was nighttime, so it was really dark. I couldn't see anything behind them...uhm...."

"How many Rahlogs?" Xo asked, bringing a basket of freshly picked fruit to the table.

She closed her eyes and replayed the vision. She counted them slowly before answering, "The vision only lasted a few seconds, but there are at least twenty-three of them."

Min-Jun grimaced and Lucas shook his head. "It's gotta be one of their camps. I know there's more than that." He sat back down again and exhaled slowly. "What else did you see? Anything identifiable? Anything will help."

Again, she closed her eyes and scanned through the vision. "It was dark...it's too dark to see...."

"Did you hear anything? The sound of water, perhaps? Maybe birds or something?" Nisa asked.

"I was a bit distracted by the sound of screaming."

Lucas huffed. "This isn't a joke, Cass."

"I know, I'm sorry." She ran through the vision again, but it wasn't a full view; it never was. "I don't see anything noteworthy." She opened her eyes. "Maybe I should go down there and see if I can get anything else from him."

Lucas nodded, finishing off his slice of bread. "Okay, but I'm coming with you."

They all followed Lucas down to the basement and to the corner where Jean was held. Once again, he lay flat on the ground, his arms and legs outstretched, his mouth agape, just like he had been when she and Brie were there last. There was only one difference; this time his chest was not moving.

Cassia stretched her arm through the bars and touched his ankle, sending her magic through to him. It came back blank. She felt nothing; no energy, no injuries, no life to save. Gasping, she withdrew her hand and Brie immediately read the look on her face and ran upstairs without saying a word. Cassia's heart plummeted when she pictured the smile Brie wore cooking alongside Jean.

Lucas sighed deeply and looked at Cassia. She shook her head, her throat tightening as she struggled to get the words out. She didn't know Jean, but she knew he was innocent. She knew he didn't deserve this death. She knew he was loved.

Lucas grabbed the handle and held it, waiting for the cage to unlock. Lucas knelt down beside Jean, lifted his friend and carried him out wordlessly. Cassia walked behind him, as did everyone else.

Lucas carried Jean slowly up the stairs and out of the house. He paused, looking ahead, and Nisa ran upstairs and called Brie. When she arrived, he continued moving.

They walked across the front garden. The sun was already shining and the heat beat down on them, but Lucas did not slow or quicken his pace. He carried Jean off the manor's property and along the gravel pathways. They walked for a long time, following the beaten track as it twisted and turned in between trees and other bushes. Orange and pink flowers scattered across every single bush. Under different circumstances, Cassia would have thought it was a beautiful day. The birds sang happily, as if the life of an innocent man had not been lost. Had not been taken by an evil king.

Death on this side, it seemed, was the same as on her own side. It came unexpectedly and turned the lives of a select few upside down, while the rest of the world carried on, completely unaffected. When her father died, she wanted to scream at the birds to stop singing, at the cars to stop driving.

Did they not realize that someone amazing had died? Did they not care?

The only difference was that this time, death was a mercy.

They reached the riverbank and Lucas kept going. He soldiered down the bank and walked straight into the water, fully clothed. The current of the river tugged at the edges of his clothing as the water washed by him.

He spoke to Jean, softer than Cassia could hear, and gently used the river water to clean off the dried blood and dirt with one of his hands as he held on to Jean with the other, keeping him from being pulled away by the fast-flowing water. When Jean was clean, he looked over his shoulder at Brie. "Do you want me to send him off?" he asked quietly.

"Can I do it with you?" she asked, and he nodded. She walked forward and into the water. Standing next to Lucas, she was near to Jean's head. She leaned down and whispered something, before placing the softest kiss on his forehead.

Together, they said, "Death came for you as it will come for me. Death is not defeat. Rest your soul, my dear friend, until death decides when next we'll meet."

Brie's right hand shot to her upper left arm and she walked out of the water. Her wet pants clung to her shaking legs as she joined the rest of the group. She stood in between Min-Jun and Nisa, both of them holding on to her. The buzz of their magic was almost tangible.

"Rest your soul, my dear friend, until death decides when next we'll meet," Brie said again as tears streamed down her red cheeks.

Lucas kissed his friend on the forehead and released him into the river. His body was quickly dragged away by the current.

Lucas stood in there for a moment longer. His shoulders were slumped and his head hung low. Cassia and Xo stepped forward at the same time and they walked up to him together. The river water was ice-cold.

"You okay, man?" Xo asked, resting his hand on Lucas's back.

"I wish there was something I could do. I'm so tired of death."

"I'm so sorry," Cassia whispered, touching him gently. Lucas stayed quiet. "I'll try again," she said, "to find their camp. I'm so sorry."

Lucas pulled her in for a tight hug and she felt his warm tears wash over her cold wet face. "I let him down, Cass."

"You?" Brie asked. A sarcastic, broken laugh escaped her as her face contorted in pain. "You let him down? He died because of me."

Lucas let go of Cassia and walked out of the river and over to Brie. She walked into his arms and he held her tightly as her entire body shook violently.

Cassia knew that this time she could not heal Lucas by comforting him. She needed to see something; she needed to help him and his friends. She couldn't leave him in this world, in this mess.

CHAPTER SEVENTEEN

Cassia stood in the library, staring at the shelves. She had no idea where to start. Libraries usually comforted her, but this one was so vast, so full of knowledge she couldn't begin to understand, that it scared her.

"What are you looking for?" Lucas asked, stepping into the library, his arms crossed over his chest as he entered the room silently. She clearly remembered how loud he was as a kid, a teen too, and yet here he moved around stealthily.

"The *Book of Visionaries*," she replied.

Lucas lifted his hand. The book slipped out of the top shelf and levitated into his grip. "So, now that you have the book, what are you looking for?"

She had been avoiding Lucas. In between his grief and her inappropriate vision, she thought it was better to throw herself into trying to be useful.

"I'm trying to figure out how to get better control over these visions...." she said, sitting down at the desk and starting to flip through the book. There were bookmarks scattered in between the pages. She turned to one of them.

Contacting a Visionary Through a Dream

"Well, this didn't work," she teased, and his deep laugh sounded through the library.

"I was desperate," he replied, the ghost of a smile playing on his lips. "I didn't want to bring you here against your will."

"It says quite clearly that it's impossible without the help of another Visionary."

"I was ready to try anything," he replied, leaning on the desk she was working at. "Is there anything I can help you with?"

She shook her head. She wanted to ask him about Calla, about the suppressant tonic, about his blue eyes, but it wasn't the right time. Instead, she said, "No, I'm good, thank you." His eyes were still sad. "Are you okay?"

He kissed the top of her head and said, "I will be." He turned around and left the library.

She spent hours reading the *Book of Visionaries*, but it was too much. There was too much information and absolutely no time to absorb it all. The book recommended that she touch something to direct or trigger a vision, as if she did not already know that.

She slammed the book closed and sighed.

"Is everything all right?"

Brie's voice took her by surprise and she smiled politely. "Just reading...but I'm done, so go ahead." She stood up and shoved the book into one of the open slots in the shelf.

Cassia exited the library and walked toward the dungeon. She made her way down the narrow staircase and, unsurprisingly, the dungeon door was locked. She cursed and tried her luck again, watching as her blood coated the handle. It remained sealed. She pulled herself back upstairs and walked through the house. She needed someone to open it for her, but did not want it to be Lucas. He had enough on his plate and she wanted to go to him with solutions, not more problems. In a few days she would have to leave this place and leave him. She looked down at the six feathers around her neck. She'd been counting them at least every hour.

Her stomach grumbled as she walked by the kitchen. Nisa stood at the stove, heating a pot of water, her back facing the doorway. Cassia considered, for a moment, asking Nisa for help, but instead she slipped outside and into the garden to pick another apple.

All the apples were higher than she could reach. Complaining silently, she rolled up her sleeves, grabbed the tree, and prepared to climb it.

She heard Min-Jun's recognizable and joyful laugh. "You could ask for help once in a while," he said.

She pointed at the apple. "Do you mind?"

Min-Jun stretched up and picked it for her. Their hands touched briefly as she took it from him. She didn't feel the buzz of his magic. He could have read her, if he wanted to.

"Thank you," she said, polishing the apple as she'd done before. Min-Jun picked one for himself and as he bit into it, she nervously asked, "Will you open the dungeon for me?"

He swallowed the piece of apple he'd been chewing and nodded once before closing his eyes and sending a wave of calmness over her. Xanax had nothing on him.

He led her back down to the dungeon and opened the door. "Good luck," he said, and turned around, leaving her there, alone. It was no longer a dangerous place.

Sitting in the basement, in Jean's cell, she tried to summon another vision linked to the Rahlogs. She touched every part of the floor, including the parts covered in smudges of Jean's blood. There was nothing. She followed the book's instructions and inhaled deeply, focusing her mind on Jean.

A dull ache settled inside her head, likely from using, or attempting to use, so much power, but there was still no vision. She inhaled deeply again and closed her eyes, gripping the metal bars exactly as Jean had done.

It was not working. She cursed out loud, banging her hands on the bars. Tears threatened at the corners of her eyes.

"I think you need to take a break." Lucas stepped into the light where she could see him, his face crumpled in a look of concern.

"How can I take a break when I haven't even achieved anything?" she snapped.

"Stop."

"No."

"Cass, please, you're going to hurt yourself," he said, grabbing her wrist. She pulled out of his grip. He leaned against the bars. "What's going on with you?"

"Nothing."

"Seriously?" He sighed. "Come on, Cass, I know something's wrong. You've been acting weird. Are you PMSing?"

She shot him a dirty look.

He took a step toward her and she moved away. That flutter returned as she remembered the vision, the feeling of her tongue grazing against lips.

"Talk to me," he said, gently touching her elbow.

"Get off me!" she said, and shook off his touch. "Stop it, okay? Stop it. I am doing what you brought me here to do. Stop pretending like you care. You haven't once mentioned Calla or even when we would start on that suppressant tonic, the one you promised. So I figured if I can get this right, after I've helped you, maybe then, maybe then we could start thinking about *my* family, that I need to get back to."

"Cass."

"No, don't 'Cass' me. Don't tell me that I'm overreacting. All we speak about are the Rahlogs," she said, wiping tears off her cheeks with the back of her hands. "And I get that, so just leave me alone so I can focus."

He bit down on his teeth and narrowed his eyes at her. He was about to explode. She had fought with him enough times to know that.

"For fuck's sake, Cass," he said, exhaling loudly, "Brie has been busy with it since you got here. She's collecting the remaining ingredients for the suppressant. I started collecting some of those ingredients before you even got here. I was going to help Calla whether or not you helped us." He shook his head and turned his back to her; it rose and fell with each heavy breath he took. "You know, I thought that no matter how skeptical you became, how paranoid, that you would always trust *me*."

A fresh wave of tears prickled at her eyes. "Luke."

"Oh, no, don't 'Luke' me," Lucas said with a hint of playfulness as he turned around to look at her.

Another feather dropped from her necklace and gently floated downward. They watched it fall as if in slow motion as it landed, soundlessly, on the dusty concrete.

"Five left...." she cracked out.

Lucas walked over and opened his arms. She willingly walked into them and rested her head on his chest, inhaling the ocean. She cried, finally releasing all the tension she'd kept inside her body and mind. She wanted to go home. She wanted to see her sister. But she didn't ever want to leave Lucas either.

Softly, he rubbed her back and kissed the top of her head. "It's okay, it's going to be okay," he whispered. "How cool is it that my best friend came to visit me in another realm?"

She sniffled as her heart rate slowed down. "I'm not PMSing, you idiot."

"Remember when you couldn't solve one of the problems in your physics assignment?" he asked, his hands still rubbing up and down her back, leaving warmth.

"There was never a physics problem that I couldn't solve," she said.

"The one where...I don't know, I didn't care about physics, but it was that day where I came over and you were lying on the floor crying because you were sure you'd never figure it out and your future would be doomed?"

"Ah, yes, I remember that now," she said with a laugh, wrapping her arms around him and realizing how rarely she'd hugged anyone aside from her sister and mother in the last four years.

"Remember what we did?"

She nodded.

"And it helped, right? When you got back you solved it."

She nodded again.

"Come on, let's go for a swim. I know just the place." He released her from his hold and walked out of the dungeon and of course, she followed him.

★ ★ ★

Lucas and Cassia mounted Ruq and Lucas spoke to the wolf. Ruq waited patiently for Lucas to give him permission to move and then they were off. The speed took Cassia by surprise once again.

She leaned back against Lucas, enjoying the heat of his body against the chilled air that whipped past them. He whispered in her ear. "I used to come here for a swim all the time after I just got here, but lately I haven't had a chance. Plus it's not that fun doing it alone."

The Baskian wolf skidded to a halt, nearly flinging Cassia over its head, but Lucas held her in place with an arm wrapped around her waist. He slid off the wolf and guided her down.

She looked upon a large, shimmering stream pool. The heat of the sun sank into her bones as she walked toward the water. Lucas ran past her and pulled off his shirt with one swift motion. He jumped in, pulling his legs up to his chest for extra splash. The water burst out around him, soaking her in the process.

Quickly, she removed the tunic and long pants she was wearing to expose a strappy top with a pair of pants cut short. She climbed into the water and released a small moan.

"That good, huh?" he asked.

"Oh, shut up." She splashed the water at him and he grabbed her, pulling her underwater the same way he had all those years ago. She kicked her legs as she surfaced and placed her hands on both of his shoulders and pushed down. Unlike four years ago, however he barely budged.

"You're gonna have to do better than that," he said, pushing his wet hair away from his face. The shimmer of the water bounced off his dark eyes.

She slipped underwater and pulled on his legs, but that didn't work either. He laughed loudly and it made her giggle. For a moment, she thought they were back at home.

She'd thought she would never be able to do this with him again.

"You never explained about your mom being on this side, but not being with you. And what about your dad?" she asked as they climbed out of the pool on the opposite end. Lucas had beat her there; she used to be the faster swimmer.

He whistled loudly and the wolf howled in response.

"Xo found me when I got here and he took me to the manor. It was just him at the time. He was warned of my arrival by a woman who claimed to be my mother.... She found him when he was lost, scared and starving, and she made him promise that in return, he'd take care of me."

Cassia nodded, following him to a grassy patch. "So, you really trust Xo?"

Lucas nodded. "With my life." He stood as Ruq arrived. "She left him with a letter to give to me and then she disappeared," he said, and threw out the picnic blanket. She started unpacking the basket of food they had brought along. Where she came from, it would be enough to feed five people, but here, she knew it would be just about enough for the two of them.

He rubbed his wet hands on his towel and then dug into his bag. He pulled out a folded piece of paper. It was worn at the edges and browning.

"This is the letter?" she asked, and he nodded. "How do you know it's legit?"

"I know my mother's handwriting. Practiced it for years so I could write those notes for school, remember?" He handed it to her.

She laughed at the memory and unfolded the letter gently. It was blank. She looked up at him quizzically.

"I could only read it once before the writing disappeared," he said. "I keep wondering if it will come back. I was kind of hoping it would come back for you."

"What did it say?"

Lucas bit his lip and looked into the distance for a long time, so long that for a moment she became distracted by the sun shining on the droplets that were sliding down his chest. She searched within herself for that flutter, that feeling.

"She said I was needed on this side," he said, pulling her out of her thoughts, and for that, she was grateful. He looked at her again. "She said that I belonged here and that I could make a difference. She said my powers were special.... But she also said to keep my eyes a secret, my blue eyes. The king wouldn't be happy knowing a Reborn had the power of the Firsts."

Cassia exhaled loudly thinking about those blue eyes. "So, you're a First?"

"Not fully. Turns out my mom was and my dad was a Reborn, but their relationship was frowned upon and the king killed my dad and she fled to protect her unborn child.... Me."

"How are you supposed to make a difference?"

"I don't know, but since being here and seeing everything that is so wrong in this realm, I couldn't just leave. I need to find a way to fight, to activate these powers and use them to do something good...."

"How are you meant to activate your powers?" she asked as she rubbed the towel over her body.

Lucas hesitated and frowned. "I don't know. But what I do know is that I'm hungry and I'm sitting outside, in the sun, after a swim, with my favorite person in all the realms, so can we please eat?"

She stood to eagerly grab some grapes and slipped, landing on her bum on a wet patch of grass. "Ah," she exclaimed. "Now I'm wet!"

Lucas laughed. "That's what *she* said." Then he stuck his arm out to help her up.

"Cass?"

"Yeah?"

Lucas hesitated for a second and then pulled her in for a tight hug. "You have no idea how much I need you here."

She kept her head dug into his chest. She was afraid to look up. The warmth of his body brought comfort, that she was sure of. The longer she thought about their skin touching, the more uncomfortable she became. She exhaled quickly and Lucas moved away, turning around to give Ruq a piece of shredded chicken.

She wondered if she could reach his lips, would she have kissed them?

But then what?

CHAPTER EIGHTEEN

Lucas

Lucas approached Brie in the library with caution. He had accidentally given her a fright once before and it had nearly cost him an eye.

"What do you want, Lucas?" Brie asked softly without turning around as she leaned over a desk in the corner. He hadn't spent much time with her since they had lost Jean. He knew she was still hurting, but he had no idea how to help.

"I'm coming to see how Calla's suppressant is getting along. Cass lost another feather.... She's a bit worried for time," he said, throwing himself down onto one of the old couches. A cloud of dust escaped from underneath him and Brie sneezed dramatically.

She turned to look at him, her eyes red. Whether it was from crying or her extreme dust allergy, he couldn't tell. "About that.... We're down to the worst of the ingredients, the shell of a ring-tailed snail and the feather of a phoenix."

"It's a snail, how bad can it be?" he asked, knowing exactly how bad things could be when magic was involved, but he never wanted to believe it.

"It's not the snail that's the problem. It's where you find them.... They're in Black Hole territory," she explained, walking toward him with a map nearly longer than she was. She sat next to him and opened the map across their laps. "We're here, Thistle. Dandelion is over there," she said, gesturing across the map. "The Black Hole is over there to the far east of where we are. At least it's still on the southern side of the Selli."

"Bit of an ominous name.... Surely it's not that bad?" he asked. It didn't seem very far away. Ruq could get there in a few hours.

"It didn't get the name accidentally, Lucas. Lots of Reborns who go in don't come out," she said.

"And it's the only place where I can get this snail for Calla?" he asked as he scanned the map.

Brie nodded. "According to my books, they like loud, rushing water and are often found near waterfalls, and the Vega Falls is rumored to be the biggest one in Selene."

"Well, then I'm going. Can I take this?" he asked, gesturing to the map.

She sighed, walked over to the desk and brought back a smaller map. "I prepared this for you. I figured you would want to go anyway. I made a few notes about the things that I've heard and marked out the best route in green and the worst route in red. So even if you don't stay on green, don't go on red. Go there and come straight back. Don't stop anywhere, especially not once you enter unfamiliar territory."

"Okay, mother hen, I've survived this long."

"It's truly shocking," she snapped playfully.

"I'll be okay," he said. He stood and touched her wrist gently. "Thank you for this." He walked toward the exit, stretching his arms to loosen the muscles. "Well, I'll be off, then."

"Who'll be going with you?" she called out.

"I'll go by myself."

She ran up to him, her blond curls flung around her face. "Absolutely not."

"It's better that way. I won't be putting anyone else at risk."

"No." She walked out of the library and Lucas followed. As they walked downstairs, he looked toward the ceiling, knowing exactly what she was about to do, but also knowing there was no way he could stop her.

"Hey," she said as she entered the kitchen, "Lucas wants to go to the Black Hole by himself."

"Dammit Brie, I'm not a child," Lucas complained.

"Oh, hell no," Xo said, standing and walking to the closet to collect his weapons. Without question or explanation, he strapped a bow and quiver to his back and slipped a dagger into his holster. He offered Lucas two daggers.

"I've got my mom's dagger," he said, lifting his tunic to expose the copper dagger against his hip.

Cass jumped to her feet, but he held up his hands and stopped her enthusiasm. "No," he said. He'd stand his ground this time. Her hazel eyes lit up with determination and he looked away. It was hard denying her.

"It sounds dangerous," she said, turning toward Xo and using her powers of persuasion on him. "Wouldn't it be helpful to have a Healer with you?"

Lucas walked over to her and pinched her nose. "Nice try, hot shot."

"Heading out on a hunt?" Jun asked as he came out of the kitchen wearing a freshly pressed suit, defusing the Cass bomb that was about to go off.

"Something like that," Lucas said, strapping a bag onto his back.

"Place for a third?" Jun asked.

"Maybe it would be better if you stayed behind and kept the women out of trouble," Lucas said, a wide smile on his face as he waited for the backlash.

All three women jumped up to protest and one of them threw a knife at him, which he managed to dodge.

His guess was Brie.

Lucas walked outside and whistled. Ruq came running out of the stables without his saddle and Xo tutted as he walked into the stables to collect it. The wolf's gray tail wagged happily as he circled Lucas. Lucas reached into Ruq's fur and scratched his back.

Xo walked back up to him with a saddle and Lucas stretched out his hand and summoned it.

"Bow," he said to Ruq, who quickly stopped bouncing around and lowered himself to the ground. Lucas fixed the saddle and climbed on, waiting for Xo to climb up behind him.

Jun walked over, offering Lucas a small plastic container. "Brie says to put the snail in here." Lucas nodded and slipped it into his pocket. He stared at the sketch of the snail Brie had given him earlier. "I'm thinking of training Cassia. She has a lot of pent-up anger.... Are you okay with that?"

Lucas raised his eyebrows and stifled a laugh. Jun had no idea how shielded she really was, but more training could only be beneficial. While he knew Cass could defend herself, he wasn't sure she knew how to do it here, in Selene. "Worth a try. Good luck on that," he said, and smiled to himself as he thought about the stories he would undoubtedly be returning to.

Ruq practically flew along the route. Lucas remembered the first time he experienced a Baskian wolf's speed. Ruq wasn't even fully grown and Lucas had taken him out for a walk and ended up being airborne as Ruq ran straight toward the Rigel River, with Lucas hanging on the leash for dear life.

Once again, he held on tightly, trapped in his thoughts until suddenly, Ruq stopped, waiting for Lucas's instruction. They had reached a crossroads. Lucas studied the route Brie had given him and leaned in and whispered the rest of the route to Ruq. He whined and Lucas took out one of Brie's cookies and fed it to him.

"What's going on between you and Cassia? You think I haven't noticed you're avoiding her?" Xo asked.

Lucas sighed. "I told her about my mom and I didn't tell her about the part that includes her."

"What? That you're bound by magic and she's an integral part in activating your full power? That without her you'd occasionally lose control, threatening to destroy everything around you? I'm shocked that it didn't just come up naturally." Lucas huffed and Xo hit him on the back reassuringly. "She's your best friend, man."

"Yeah, that means I know exactly how she'd react and she won't take it well," Lucas replied.

"I get the sense she doesn't really trust me," Xo said. "Which is unusual, since I am, like, the most trustworthy person who has ever existed. I think it might be one of my powers, except not on her."

Lucas chuckled, Ruq jumped over something and they held on tightly as they both lifted up and landed a second later, grateful for the saddle. "Don't take it personally. Uncle Deo, her dad, was really awesome, but kinda weird too…. He was a homicide detective and I think somehow that warped his view on the world. He managed to convince Cass that she shouldn't trust anyone. It's why she never really had any friends, except me. I forced my way into her life; she and her dad didn't have a choice."

"Sounds familiar," Xo replied and laughed loudly, whacking Lucas on the back again.

★　★　★

As soon as they left familiar territory, Lucas and Xo unsheathed their weapons and Ruq slowed to a speed where they could see their surroundings. Everything seemed…ordinary.

The sky was blue, the sun was out, the birds sang and not a single leaf seemed threatening. It could easily have been a part of the woods near his home.

Lucas knew they were getting closer as the crashing sounds of the waterfall drew him near. They crept through the thick, lush trees and came across the Vega Falls splashing into the Selli River. It was his first time seeing the Vega Falls. Its beauty was often described by the Firsts and the older Reborns. It was one of the many reasons Reborns kept trying to find it.

The stories didn't do it justice. Not nearly. The top of the falls were probably three hundred or four hundred feet up, and much wider than he'd imagined too. The water gushed down, pulling anything in its path along with it and yet it was graceful and calming. A wall of blue, threaded with silver, pouring into the pools below, splashing off the rounded rocks.

The sun shimmered off the water, inviting them in. Lucas felt his clothes clinging to him and noticed Xo eyeing the water lustfully too.

Lucas and Xo jumped off Ruq in search of the snails. Brie had mentioned that the snails often sat on the rocks near the river. Lucas carefully stepped through the long grass. It was clear that no animals had been here grazing.

"Keep watch," he whispered to Xo. Lucas continued to creep toward the water. It was much darker than he was used to.

He didn't see any snails. Not a single one. There were butterflies, crickets, ladybugs and at least six other insects he didn't recognize, but not a single snail.

He climbed on top of the rocks to get a better view. He gripped the hot edges of stone as he pulled himself up another one. Cold wetness splashed across his back and he glanced over his shoulder to see Ruq playing in the water. Lucas shook the water off his hair, and twisted it out of the hem of his tunic, even though the coolness was pleasant.

Sitting on a wet wolf on the way home was not going to be comfortable.

Scanning the area carefully, he noticed that on the other side, near the waterfall, there were a number of snails on the rock face. They looked to be about the right size, approximately that of a regular garden snail. The shell was a dark red. It was too far away for him to see whether it had the black spiral. Lucas stretched out his arm and flicked his wrist, summoning one of the snails, but the snail remained fixed to the surface of the rock. He gestured at one of them once more, but it wouldn't move.

Stupid magic snails.

Finally, a reason to swim. Closing his eyes, he jumped off from the rock and landed in the water. The temperature was perfect, heated up by hours of sunshine to the perfect cool, but not icy cold, temperature. He swam toward the other end of the wide, wide river, but Ruq kept swimming underneath him, pushing him toward the bank. He scratched the wolf's ears and booped his nose. It wasn't time to play, but he couldn't resist it.

He reached the waterfall and stretched out his hands. Perhaps now that he was closer to the snail, his magic would work. He hoped so, since the snails were higher up than he'd anticipated. He gestured at the snail, willing it into his hand, but it still didn't work. He grabbed on to the edge of a rock and pulled himself up.

Fine. If the snail wouldn't come to him, he would go to the snail.

The breeze sent a pleasant chill through his wet clothes as he found his footing and rose completely out of the water. His left hand searched for a grip along the smooth, wet rocks and as he reached up, his foot slipped slightly, sending his heart rate upward, but he managed to regain his stability.

He climbed higher. The sound of the waterfall was deafening up close, but at least now he could see the black spiral on the red shell. It was the right snail. He reached out and plucked a snail slightly larger than a grape off the wall. Now that his free hand was holding a snail, he wondered how he would get it into the plastic container. It came out of its shell and wriggled in his grip. Shuddering and looking away, he placed the snail into his tunic pocket and then reached into his other pocket to grab the container. He used his mouth to bite it open and held it between his chin and neck, while he fished out the slimy snail and placed it in the little box. He sealed it before tucking it back into his pocket and holding his hands under the waterfall to wash off the slime.

Glancing over his shoulder, he attempted to give Xo a thumbs up. But Xo wasn't there. He looked down and saw that Ruq was still at the bottom of the waterfall, his mouth open, and it looked as though he was howling. Lucas couldn't hear him over the thunderous sounds of the waterfall.

"Xo!" Lucas shouted. The entire forest was still, aside from the moving water.

Terror traveled through him.

Lucas climbed down quickly. He looked over his shoulder again. *Where is Xo?* As he lowered his foot, it slipped. This time, he couldn't stop himself from falling and the water splashed around him as he hit the surface and dipped under. He immediately felt Ruq's snout poking him as he tried to come up for air. Ruq opened his mouth and grabbed hold of Lucas's tunic.

"Ruq, stop! I can't breathe!" Lucas shouted, but the wolf wouldn't let go. He was being dragged through the water by an animal that didn't realize he needed oxygen to survive. Swallowing a large amount of water, he coughed, flailing around, but Ruq kept going.

Something pulled on his right leg and he wiggled it, using his left leg to kick at it. Ruq would not slow down.

The pull on his leg turned into a sting. He screamed in pain, gagging on the water he was still trying to expel. Ruq swam faster, still holding on to Lucas's clothing.

The pain traveled up his right leg, pulsating, and his head started spinning. Something tightened around the lower half of his leg. He tried using his left leg to kick at it again, but he couldn't feel his legs. Only pain and pressure. His right leg felt as though it might explode. The pressure traveled up his thigh and spread into his other leg. Numbness followed soon, spreading throughout his entire body.

CHAPTER NINETEEN

"Take a break," Min-Jun warned. "I can sense that you're about to crack."

"Why would I take a break if I am about to crack it?" Cassia asked, her voice shaky. They'd been in the dungeon for a couple of hours.

"Crack. You're about to crack. Not crack *it*. Crack. Sit down, let me get you some tea." He walked out of the dungeon and left her there, wallowing in her self-pity as she tried for the seven hundredth time to summon a vision relating to the Rahlogs.

She lay down with her back on the cold floor and closed her eyes.

"Here," he said and she sat up to receive a cup of tea. Min-Jun was the only one who ever used the pretty teacups. They were white, covered in blue roses and gold-trimmed. The smell alone sprinkled some calmness over her anxiety.

"You can go," Cassia said, sipping the fruity tea. "I don't need a babysitter...I know that's why you stayed behind."

"I was thinking maybe we should take a break from attempting to summon visions and do a bit of weapons training." That lopsided smile found its way onto his face with ease. "I noticed you paid close attention to anyone using a bow and arrow."

A failed attempt at hiding her smile had her whispering, "Fine." She stood carefully to avoid spilling any of the tea and followed him out of the dungeon. While she knew she should focus on her visions, her father had always taught her to never miss an opportunity to learn a useful skill.

They walked out of the manor and through the garden in a comfortable silence. "Where are we going?" she asked, and he quietly pointed to the top of a wooden shed standing out above the line of banana trees at the back of the garden.

Min-Jun turned around to look at her and raised his eyebrows. "I don't think you've been back here yet, have you?"

She shook her head and followed him through a gap in the trees, into the shed. Usually, she'd be afraid to be so isolated with a man she didn't know. Perhaps it was his magic, perhaps it was all the chaos she'd endured over the last few days, but she felt safe. It was a strange, unfamiliar feeling.

Two out of the four wooden walls were lined with weapons of every kind. Cassia spotted daggers and swords ranging from the size of her fingers to the size of her leg. One of the other walls had human- and animal-shaped paper targets.

Min-Jun shrugged out of his cream-colored cardigan, revealing a plain white t-shirt. "I call this one Lucas," he said, pointing at the human target with the most arrows stuck in it. Cassia giggled and he continued, "Are the two of you okay? I don't mean to pry, I just sense the tension."

It was useless lying to an Empath; they sensed the shift in your emotions too easily. She nodded, thinking about how she hadn't told Lucas about the vision, about the kiss. "Yeah, we are. We always will be. We're just a bit stressed, is all...." It wasn't technically a lie.

"Good, because this is his bow, so if you break it, I don't want him to be too mad at me." He smiled in the way that only an Empath could. She suddenly missed Calla deeply. This was all for Calla, after all. She would do anything for her little sister to have just a moment of peace.

Min-Jun handed her the bow and the second she wrapped her fingers around it, her mind buzzed loudly, blocking out every other thought as a vision filtered in.

She saw Lucas lying down, long grass sticking up all around his body. His eyes were closed and his chest barely rose and fell. She saw Ruq howling and pacing around him as the loud sound of water gushing blocked him out. Ruq bowed down alongside Lucas's leg, which was covered in blood, and something else. Something black.

The vision cleared and she dropped the bow and grabbed Min-Jun's arm, opening up her mind to him. "Luke's in danger!" she shouted. Min-Jun's eyes closed for a moment before he broke into a run.

They sprinted to the front of the house and Min-Jun whistled. Willis came running toward them, already saddled. They clambered onto the wolf before it even stopped to bow, then Min-Jun whispered to him, having seen the route Brie had marked out.

The wolf launched forward and the sheer force of air against her eyeballs dried them out. Shutting her eyes, she thought of Lucas. She tried sending her healing abilities through the air to find him, to heal him, to keep him alive. She begged the universe to protect him.

She'd only just got him back.

It was hard to tell how much time had passed; all she knew was that it was too much. Focusing on her breathing and inhaling deeply while imagining his face, his smell, she tried summoning another vision of him. Something. Anything. Her mind gave her nothing except a splitting headache.

They stopped suddenly, surrounded by leafy, aged trees and long green grass. Min-Jun slipped off Willis and she followed after. The sound of water crashing resembled the sound from her vision, pulling her toward it.

Ruq was next to them in a second, howling loudly. He circled them wildly, herding them to where Lucas lay on the ground beside the river.

His clothes were completely soaked, and the pants on his right leg were shredded. The skin was torn open and was bleeding profusely. A spiderweb of black lines radiated from every wound.

Min-Jun and Cassia fell down at his side and grabbed hold of him. Their magic hummed as they closed their eyes and focused on their breathing. Min-Jun let go and said, "Xo is missing. He turned around and Xo was gone. He's got no idea where he went." He dug into Lucas's pocket and pulled out the contained snail. "He said to take this back to Brie."

"What happened to him?" she choked out as the wounds on his legs closed. The black lines remained and each rise of his chest seemed like a struggle.

"I don't know. There was something in the water, a creature of some kind. He thinks it bit him." He stood and cupped Ruq's head, closing his eyes for a moment.

"Ruq is terrified."

"Can you read a wolf's mind?" she asked, pushing more of her healing magic across the black lines, but nothing happened.

He dropped to his knees at Lucas's head once more. "No, just their basic emotions and through touch only."

She cupped Lucas's face and said, "Luke, listen to me. You'll be fine, okay?" His lungs were struggling and she directed her magic there, watching as his breathing eased.

Min-Jun grabbed Lucas's head again. "He says his face and his entire body is numb and he keeps drifting in and out of consciousness." Closing his eyes again, Min-Jun said, underneath his breath, "No, no, no. I won't leave you."

"What's going on?"

"He wants me to go after Xo. He says Ruq should be able to track his scent while it's fresh."

Xo.

He meant everything to Lucas.

Min-Jun and Cassia stared at each other for a moment. While she was terrified of Min-Jun leaving, she couldn't risk losing Xo. "Yeah. Go. Find him, before it's too late. I'll get us home. I can do this. Go. Now. Go!" she shouted, and Min-Jun bowed his head slightly at both of them before mounting Ruq.

"I've sent word to Nisa and I'll leave instructions with Willis to get you home," he said as he looked into her eyes in a way that let her know he could feel her fear. "It'll be okay." Cassia swallowed hard as she tried to convince herself to believe him. Min-Jun whispered to Ruq and went off to find Willis.

Cassia inhaled deeply and gently stroked Lucas's jaw. She couldn't let him die. She would not let him die. "Come on, Lucas," she begged, feeling her tears roll down her cheeks and onto his face. She wiped them off his cheeks and replaced them with a kiss. "Please don't die. Don't leave me again."

She investigated his leg. His wounds appeared to have closed but the black trails bothered her. Something was wrong. Mud spread across the rest of his clothes and skin and she smeared at it, trying to see more of his skin, to see the extent of the black trails. She grabbed her copper dagger, cut off the end of her shirt and ran to the water.

The air cracked and the ground behind her trembled. She spun around and was faced with Lochlan, who landed with a bow, his fists punching the ground and one knee bent as if he had fallen from the sky. He stood up slowly and raised his eyebrows at the cloth in her hand. "I wouldn't do that if I were you," he said, his voice low and calm.

She froze with her hand outstretched above the river. His blue eyes were the first she'd seen since her vision.

"One drop of that water touches you and it immobilizes your magic." Lochlan stepped closer to Lucas and the smirk faded, replaced by a frown. "And you'll need your magic to save him."

"Leave him alone," she said, running to place herself between her friend and the First prince.

"That looks like a beizl bite," Lochlan said, looking over her shoulder. His electric gaze drifted down to hers, stirring something. "It's similar to a jellyfish, except the poison kills you quite quickly. I see he's gone numb already. Pity."

"What do you want?" she said, swallowing the lump forming in her throat.

"I'm here to help."

"Why would you help him when just a few days ago you beat the hell out of him and killed one of his wolves?" she spat. Her heart thumped so loudly she wondered if he could hear it.

He took a step closer to her and said, "Kain takes full credit for the mutt. I, on the other hand, know how to use a whip." The smirk returned, sending an uncalled-for flutter into her belly, which was quickly replaced by bubbling rage.

"Help him," she said.

"Ah, now you want my help," he said. The smirk turned into a full smile, his dimples coming out. "Say 'please'."

"You're infuriating!" she screamed, stomping her foot on the ground.

He took another step closer to her and glanced over to where Lucas lay, then lowered his amused look back to her. "I've been called worse by worse."

Clenching her jaw, she bit out, "Help him, *please*."

"How about, I save your boyfriend's life and you owe me a favor?" he asked. His blue eyes seemed to look into her mind, her soul. She felt his eyes observing every part of her body.

"He's not my boyfriend," she said, crossing her arms tightly over her chest, feeling exposed.

Lochlan smiled in response. "Seems I've struck a nerve."

"What's the favor?" she asked, turning around to look at Lucas. She collapsed next to him and gently touched his cold hand. She could feel his lungs collapsing as they spoke. "Please, anything, I'll do anything. We're running out of time."

"Anything?" he asked, raising his eyebrows suggestively.

Cassia swallowed as a hard knot twisted in her stomach. "Anything."

"Your word is binding in Selene. Not like you people in Talm, who make and break promises like it means nothing."

"Lochlan, please," she begged, standing up and making eye contact with him. "I accept. Please save him."

"If I must." He extended his hand, palm up. "Give me your hand."

"For what?"

"Do you want him to die?"

She extended her hand, placing it in his palm. He turned her hand around, and a shiver traveled up her spine at the heat his hands were radiating.

"This will sting," he said softly. "My apologies." He pricked the tip of her thumb with his dagger and she flinched and pulled it back. "Don't heal it, not yet," he said, while piercing the skin on his own finger. He opened his hand with his palm facing upward. "My lady, your hand."

Gingerly, she put her hand in his.

"A favor for a favor," he said, and waited expectedly. "Now, you say it."

"A favor for a favor," she said, and felt something shift inside of her. Pushing the feeling down, she clenched her jaw and said, "Now save him, your Highness."

"Oh, I like that," he teased as his eyes flickered.

He turned around. His maroon cape whipped behind him as if it had a life of its own. "Very well," he said, looking back over his shoulder at Lucas's leg. "Every time he gets himself into these situations, I'm amazed he's made it this far."

"He did it for me. For my sister," she cried, tears rolling down her cheeks. "For that power suppressant. He was just trying to save her," she said more to herself than anyone else. It wasn't like Lochlan would care.

He exhaled quickly. "He needs the yurip leaf."

Steadying her breath, she looked around at the trees surrounding them. "Where? How do I find it?"

"In what world would you find the antidote alongside the poison?" he said, rolling his eyes as if all this was a joke to him.

She screamed. A scream so loud the birds went silent for fear that she would punish them for singing.

Lochlan vanished and Cassia threw herself on Lucas. She forced her magic into him; she pictured the poison leaving his body; she pictured taking her own life force and giving it to him. She rested her head on his shoulder and cried as she felt his heart rate getting weaker. Lifting her head, she laid her hands on his chest again. If magic wouldn't save him, she'd try everything else.

Before she could start chest compressions, something tickled her hair and she reached her hand to grab it. It was a leaf, the yurip leaf, she assumed.

Lochlan stood alongside her. His face was expressionless. "Get him to chew it, slice open the bites you foolishly healed, take the chewed leaf with his own saliva and shove it into the bites. After that, feel free to close the wounds with the leaf inside. It will heal the damage it's already caused. Simple, really." He pushed his unruly brown hair out of his eyes.

"I don't trust you," she said.

"Personally, I wouldn't either, but you're out of time." He smiled that lazy smile of his and bowed deep at the waist.

"Wait, how did you find us?" she asked, lifting Lucas's head onto her lap. She opened his mouth, folded the leaf inside and manually moved his jaw. As she forced her magic into his lungs once more, his chest rose and fell steadily.

"Between his stench and your scent, I could find the two of you anywhere," he said and she looked up. Their eyes met. Her stomach jumped with an unfamiliar sensation, accelerating her already speeding heart. Lochlan pulled out his sword and swiped it through the air, landing a number of slices across Lucas's legs, cutting open the skin along the fresh scars Cassia had created. "Until next time, little lady." He tilted his head upward and vanished.

While she focused on the task at hand, her breathing slowed and she removed the chewed leaves and shoved them into the fresh cuts across his legs. The black lines had spread across half his chest already. Reaching out, she swiped her hand across the wounds and her magic buzzed softly, barely there. She called on it, inhaling deeply and begging it to work, for the skin to heal. Slowly, the black lines receded and a fresh wave of relief flooded over her senses, a moment before she blacked out.

CHAPTER TWENTY

"Luke!" Cassia cried out as she woke up, throwing her arms out to where Lucas had been lying on the ground next to her. She scrambled into a sitting position, looking around. She wasn't in the Black Hole anymore; she was in his bed, alone. The smell of his ocean scent lingered, but it could be because she was in his room.

She kicked the duvet off her legs and jumped off the bed, swung the door open and ran. Her legs couldn't keep up with her thoughts as she stumbled down the corridor. Her thoughts raced across her mind as she replayed the last thing she remembered. Lucas, poisoned.

Is Luke alive?

Did it work?

How did I get here?

Was it Lochlan?

Is Luke alive?

Is Luke alive?

Please let him be alive. Please let him be alive. Please let him be alive.

She repeated the last thought as a mantra as she took the stairs two at a time, hanging on to the ornate rail to prevent herself from slipping. She landed on the ground floor and stood still for a second to catch her breath, hearing her own heart beat in panic.

There were hushed conversations echoing from the kitchen. The smell of freshly baked bread made her stomach growl. She brushed off her hunger and ran toward the voices, colliding with something hard. She stumbled back and lost her footing, but two hands grabbed her shoulders before she could fall over.

"Hey Cass."

She looked up at Lucas.

He was okay.

She looked down at his legs. He was standing. He was moving.

He was okay.

He's alive.

Her heart squeezed as she released a flood of tears that she had been holding back.

He cupped her face, wiping the tears. "Saved my life. Told you I needed you."

"Luke," she choked out, overwhelmed by her emotions. Her thundering heart and racing mind competed for her attention, along with her growling stomach. It was all too much.

"I'm okay," he said, wiping her continuous stream of tears. "I was just about to eat. You must be starving."

"I'm not," she said.

She absolutely was.

"I'm just so glad you're okay," she said, walking into his arms and holding him tightly.

He stroked her back gently and quietly asked, "How did you save me?"

"Ignorance is bliss."

"Cass."

"Lochlan saved you," she said and he cursed. Feeling his heart rate quicken, she looked up. His eyes flashed blue and her vision replayed through her mind.

She felt safe in that moment, in his arms. Unsure of what persuaded her to do it, she stood on her toes. With shaking hands, she reached up and pulled him down toward her lips, kissing him gently.

Lucas leaned into it, his tongue meeting hers. And then her body froze up.

As quickly as it started, it ended.

She dropped down, flat on her feet, and he straightened. Creating as much distance between their mouths as possible.

His hand shot up to his mouth as his eyebrows nearly reached his hairline.

"Shit! I'm sorry," she gasped out, hiding her face. *What did I do? It was Lucas. It was Luke. What was I thinking?*

She wondered for a moment whether it would be reasonable to pull off the last of her feathers. Then a loud laugh echoed through the hall. The laugh she knew and loved. Her own laughter joined his as it usually did and her muscles slowly loosened again.

Lowering her hands, she found him smiling widely, his cheeks as red as she assumed hers were. His dimples out in full bloom.

"Cass, what the hell?" he asked, his big body still shaking with amusement. Her look of embarrassment quickly turned into a glare. "I mean, I know that I've been working out, but I didn't expect it to work on you."

"Does magic make you crazy? Because that is the only explanation," she snapped, stifling a smile. He wore his freely.

"It actually kinda does when you're a Guest...."

"Momentary lapse of judgment," she said, revisiting her vision of the kiss. "That did not feel the way I wanted it to."

"How did you want it to feel?"

She gestured to her stomach and said, "Like a weird, twisty feeling in my stomach, something to signal that I should have kept going."

"But instead it felt like what?"

"Eating cold food that should have been hot."

Lucas laughed and winced dramatically. "I'm hurt. That's just mean. These lips," he said, gesturing to his mouth, "have made many women very happy."

"I know. I've literally heard their *happiness*. Was hoping it would work on me. Guess not." She turned around, folding her arms across her chest and then shoving them into her pockets and then just shaking them free.

Lucas rested his hand on her back. "Is it okay if I touch you? You're not going to try and kiss me again?"

"Cold food!"

He laughed and led her through the front door and onto the bench on the porch.

"What's going on with you? I never took you for a girl who is, uh, let's say looking for that feeling," he said. "You never really cared about that stuff."

Glancing up, she sighed. "Of course I care about it. I want it too. It's not my fault I don't feel it, is it?"

Lucas shifted uncomfortably and eventually asked, "What happened with Jay? You said I wasn't there when you needed me. I'm here now."

Ruq came running toward them, and her body froze in fear he wouldn't be able to stop and would ram right into them. Lucas pointed at the floor in front of him and Ruq skidded down at their feet, nuzzling against Lucas's leg, howling. "Can we walk and talk? Ruq seems a bit restless."

Cassia stood up and stretched. Ruq hopped up and trotted ahead. She followed behind him with Lucas at her side as they made their way down the path.

Staring at the gravel underneath her boots, she finally said, "I don't know what happened. It just...it wasn't good."

"How so?"

"It was really awkward and really painful and I, well, I didn't feel the need to try it again. Even the thought of having to be that vulnerable with someone, it freaked me out...." she said as she looked away, feeling her eyes tear up at the memory of how much regret she felt after.

"Really painful?"

"It was my first time, it's supposed to be," she said, glancing up at him. "Right?"

A deep frown crossed over his forehead. "Remember my first time? With Lydia?" Cassia nodded in response. "Well...it was her first time too and she said it pinched a bit, something about pressure, but she didn't say it was *really* painful." He ran a hand over his face. "Did you tell him?"

Thinking back, her mind blanked. "I don't know. Anyway, I think I kissed you because it would be so easy with you. You already know every part of me, except that part," she said, bringing the focus back to the matter at hand.

"You can't force that feeling…" he said quietly. "I love you, Cass. I love you more than I love myself, but…." He sighed. "Fuck, this is awkward."

"Sorry."

"Don't apologize…. Our whole lives people have tried to push us together. I'm kinda glad you kissed me. Now I can stop wondering."

"You didn't!"

"Cass, I was seventeen, and you've got great boobs. Obviously I've thought about it, however briefly," he said with a laugh. She punched his arm, noticing a third dark mark circling his bicep. A mark for Jean. She assumed Brie would have the same one.

"Have you had sex since you've been here?"

Lucas scrunched up his nose and nodded. Before she could ask who, he said, "But no one you know." He wrapped an arm around her and pulled her close. Ruq ran ahead and Lucas whistled. The wolf ran back toward them and then spun around and ran away again. He continued, "Listen, you're beautiful. Someone is going to come along and embed themselves so deeply in your mind that every moment that passes will be consumed by them, by what they're doing, by what they look like, by how they make you feel." He tickled her stomach and she slapped his hand away. "Give you that fluttery feeling there."

"What if I'm meant to be alone?" she asked. Ruq threw his head back and howled loudly. Lucas clapped his hands together. The wolf looked over and Lucas shook his head firmly.

"Something tells me you aren't," he said, looking out into the distance where Ruq padded back toward them. "When you get that feeling, that flush just thinking about them, don't let it go. I know you, okay? I know that you think giving in to feelings of lust or love is wasting your time and you're too busy trying to save the world, but… you're wrong."

She stared up at him. He knew very well she was always right.

"No, this time," he said, seeming older than he was, "you're wrong. In a world so full of pain and horror, it isn't a sin to feel happy. It's those moments that keep us going, that keep us sane, that remind us that there's something to fight for."

"We're fighting so you can have sex?" she teased, and he pursed his lips, side-eyeing her.

"Give in to it when it comes, and then come and talk to me. Because I'm telling you, that moment, that overwhelming sense of satisfaction – and Cass, you're going to have to trust me on this, but it is very satisfying –" he laughed, "it takes you out of your mind and I know that of all the people in all the realms, the one person who needs to get out of their mind is *you*."

"When did you become so wise?" she asked. Ruq howled in the distance once more. He was so far away, they couldn't see him. "Again, I'm sorry for kissing you."

"Sorry for making your second attempt at romance a disappointment."

"Third time lucky, right?"

Ruq came sprinting back too fast to keep an eye on him. He ran past them in the direction of the manor and howled again. They exchanged glances and Lucas broke into a run after the wolf. Cassia followed behind them without question.

They nearly bumped into Brie, who was running toward them. Her hair stood wildly, her cheeks red and blood spattered across her beige tunic. "Jun's back...with Xo."

CHAPTER TWENTY-ONE

It wasn't the blood on Brie's clothing that worried them; it was the fear in her eyes.

"Where are they?" Lucas asked, his breathing heavy. His question was answered by Brie spinning around and running back toward the manor. Cassia's stomach turned. She prepared herself for a number of things and none of them were good.

They ran in silence into the manor, down the stairs and into the dungeon through the already open door. They kept going until Brie stopped before they reached the dark corner that Cassia knew as Jean's corner.

Min-Jun was slumped against the wall. His usually clean face and clothes were covered in dirt and blood. His black hair was almost brown because of the amount of mud smeared into it.

He looked up and his eyes, the same eyes that often calmed her anxiety, now triggered it.

Brie grabbed Lucas's elbow, inhaled deeply and stated firmly, "Xo was bitten."

The words echoed through her mind.

Xo was bitten.

It couldn't be.

Brie's voice shook her from her thoughts. "He hasn't transitioned.... Jun found him after they dragged him off and—" Her voice cracked as she spoke and she wiped the tears from her face. "And fought to get him back...."

Lucas stared into the darkness in complete silence. Cassia searched for words but had no idea what to say or what to do. "Why bring him back?" Lucas choked out, finally turning to look at Brie and then

Min-Jun. "So we can watch him die the way we watched Jean die? In a cage?" He blinked furiously as his eyes glistened with tears.

"Hey! I heard that, asswipe!"

The voice traveled through from the darkness and Lucas's mouth twitched into a smile for a split second before being replaced by complete anguish. He walked straight into the darkness and Cassia and Brie followed after him.

When they entered the room, they found Xo lounging on a newly added couch. "Do you like what I've done with the place?" he asked, flashing a smile.

He looked exactly the same. It was hard to believe he had been bitten by one of those monsters. He wasn't screaming like Jean. There was no sign of that animalistic hunger.

Lucas clenched his jaw and offered Xo half a smile. "You absolute idiot. You got yourself bitten?"

Xo laughed. "I've got the scars to prove it." He held up his hands and showed the still-bleeding bites stretching across both arms. "If Jun hadn't shown up, I think I'd have been dinner, not a recruit."

Lucas shook his head violently as if trying to physically shake the thought from his head.

Cassia turned around at the sound of light footsteps and watched as Nisa and Min-Jun came into view, both their expressions twisted and tired. Nisa held on to Min-Jun's wrist and he looked at her, offering her a small smile before leaning against the wall. He slid down the wall and cradled his head in his hands.

"Why aren't you screaming?" Cassia asked, searching Xo's face for any resemblance to the Rahlogs she had seen.

"It'll start in a day or two, when his hunger becomes unbearable," Brie answered quietly with her arms wrapped tightly across her chest.

Xo jumped up and stuck his fingers through the metal bars. Everyone flinched and he laughed heartily. "Oh come on, I've only just been bitten." He looked over at Cassia and said, "What are you waiting for? Grab hold of me and let's find these monsters."

Cassia stepped forward and touched Xo's fingers. His skin was a few shades darker than hers. Lucas's entire body tensed behind her and the room fell quiet as she focused on her breathing. Closing her eyes caused her welled-up tears to spill over and she rubbed her face with her shoulder. They couldn't lose Xo. Lucas wouldn't survive it.

Imagining the buzz of her magic, she willed it into her mind, begging it to make an appearance to give her something.

The buzz started suddenly, tickling her fingertips. The open bites and scratches along Xo's hands and arms closed as she unintentionally healed him, but nothing came to her mind, unlike the last time she'd had a vision.

She shook her head and felt her eyes sting with tears.

"Did you see me die?" Xo asked.

"What? No, I saw nothing."

"Oh," Xo said. "No need to cry then. That's much better than seeing me die." He walked back to the couch and fell into it. "Worth a try, I guess. I'll be here all day, so you can come back later."

"I *will* get it," she replied angrily. "I will. Otherwise what's the point of me even being here?" She stormed out of the dungeon and sprinted up the narrow stairs without thinking. She continued until she ran out of the manor, circled the entire property and ended up in the weapons shed.

She took a sword off the shelf and moved it between her hands, feeling its weight, wondering how anyone could swing it around.

What's the point of having this magic if I can't use it to help people?

"It's okay."

The sound of Lucas's deep voice made her jump. She hadn't heard him enter. For someone so obnoxiously tall, he sure learned to move silently. Keeping her back to him, she put the sword back on the shelf and grabbed a dagger that looked to be made of bone.

"You just got here.... Learning how to control magic takes time. It's been four years and I still don't have access to all of mine," he said, ignoring the fact that she was ignoring him.

Cassia said while investigating the browning bone dagger, "It's hard enough knowing that I have to leave you, but I refuse to leave you here without your new best friend."

"Do I sense jealousy?" he asked, and even though she wasn't looking up, she knew he was smiling.

"Maybe a little…" she said, trailing her fingers along the patterned bone and then gripping the end. It had no actual handle. "I have to save him, Luke."

When he didn't reply, she turned around, swinging the dagger around to get a feel of it. "Did you hear me?" she asked.

"I don't know if he can be saved," he said. Sighing, he picked up the other engraved bone dagger. "I don't think I can do this anymore."

There it was again – Lucas looking defeated.

"I may not know much about real magic, but from all the fantasy novels that I've read and even some of the books in the library, every curse can be lifted," she said. "There has to be a way."

He lifted his eyes from the dagger and met her gaze. "You're right, but Lochlan said that he tried lifting the curse. It wouldn't work."

"Yeah, but that's Lochlan, and you don't trust him, right?" she asked. Lucas spun around and threw the dagger at one of the targets. It landed in the center of the outlined head.

"I don't trust him and I never will," he said and she nodded. She hadn't told Lucas about her vision. Now probably wasn't a good time. Cassia took aim and threw the dagger. It was clear it would hit the wooden wall beside the target and Lucas swirled his wrist and directed it to one of the other targets.

"Although, Jun said it didn't seem like he was lying.…" Lucas groaned and dropped his head into his hands. "I don't know what to believe and they look to me to protect them, Cass. I don't think I can."

Fear laced Lucas's eyes and her tone softened as she spoke. "Come on, we can do anything." Cassia grabbed two swords and gave one of them to him. "We'll figure it out. I promise.… Now teach me how to use this."

*   *   *

Sleeping wasn't an option. Both Cassia and Lucas sat awake in the library, reading everything about the laws of magic, curses and binding spells. Nothing like the Rahlogs were mentioned anywhere. Neither were flesh-eating monsters.

"What are you two up to?" Brie slumped down across from them. Her usually bright blue eyes were dull and the skin below them darker than usual.

"Maybe there's a way to end this, lift it, break it, anything to stop the killing and the dying," Lucas said as he pulled down another spell book.

Brie exhaled. "I read almost every single book in this library when Jean was down there. If there's a way to break this curse, I bet it's in the same book they used to create it."

"But Lochlan tried that," Lucas said.

"Fuck Lochlan, I'll bet he's lying. We need that book."

"Then there's no hope," Lucas snapped.

"Why?" Cassia asked.

"We'd have to break into the palace, find the library, which, I would imagine, is even bigger than this one, and then find the exact book, which I assume isn't labeled *Magic Book to Create and Kill Flesh-Eating Monsters*, and then figure out how to use a spell that is, no doubt, older than all of us put together."

Nisa walked in and sat down next to Brie. Her dark hair was pulled into a messy bun. "I finally got Jun to fall asleep. I think he'll be out for a while and I used a lot of magic to get him there, so I, too, will be out for a while." She yawned loudly, covering her mouth with her hand. "I just wanted to check if anyone needed anything from me before I hibernate."

Lucas's entire expression softened as he shook his head. "We need you to rest. Thanks for taking care of Jun."

"Anytime," she said, before slumping her head forward and falling asleep.

Lucas stood up. "I'll be right back." He lifted Nisa into his arms and walked out of the library. Brie smiled after him.

"How's the suppressant tonic coming along?" Cassia asked. She had been wanting to ask Brie about it, but there was always something else happening.

"We need one more ingredient. I'm consulting all my sources to see where we could get one."

"What is it?" she asked, lazily paging through the *Book of Visionaries* again.

"A feather from a phoenix, but they're almost extinct. There's only a handful left of them. I know King Idis keeps one as a pet, but there are others. I'll find them. I will," Brie said, and rested her head in her hands.

"But you have everything else?" Cassia asked. Brie nodded. "And you're sure it'll work?"

Brie nodded again. "So far, I haven't made anything that didn't work, so yeah, it should." It was strange having someone who didn't know Calla at all seem so invested in her wellbeing. While the doctors at the hospital cared for Calla, after years of trying and failing, they all seemed to have given up. This fresh determination fueled Cassia.

She sat down next to Brie and awkwardly touched her shoulder to scan her for injuries. Physically, she was fine, but her life force was low. Exhaustion. "You need to sleep."

"I can't, we need to save Xo and we need to finish this tonic before your time runs out and—"

"And if you die of exhaustion, you're no good to anyone. Please, Brie, rest. We'll figure something out in the morning."

Brie blinked back tears and wrapped her arms around Cassia, who froze at the affection. "I get why Lucas loves you so much," she said, and then stood up and left.

Cassia stretched her legs across the couch and rested her head on the armrest. The couch cushions molded to her body the way a well-worn couch was meant to.

Heavy footsteps walked back into the library. "Can you people stop falling asleep everywhere except in your beds?" Lucas said, and she opened her eyes lazily. He smiled at her. "Do you want me to carry you too?"

"No, thank you. I can walk," she said, standing up and feeling her head spin. "But maybe you could walk next to me."

"Always have, always will."

CHAPTER TWENTY-TWO

The next morning, Cassia ran up to the library to continue her research, looking for anything that was even adjacent to whatever type of creature a Rahlog was. She wondered for a moment whether eating animal flesh would satisfy Xo, at least temporarily, or whether it would lead to him fully transitioning. It probably wasn't worth the risk.

Lucas walked up and down the aisles with her, summoning books that she couldn't reach and steering her away from books he'd already checked.

"Lucas, Cassia," Min-Jun said as he entered the library, "you have that meeting today."

Lucas cursed under his breath. "I completely forgot."

"Understandably so, but I think you should be the one to go. I'd be happy to join you. I know Xo usually does." Min-Jun slipped his hands into his pocket and met Lucas's hard gaze. It was good to see that the calmness had returned to Min-Jun's eyes.

Lucas sighed heavily and glanced at Cassia. She waited for one of them to fill her in on the details. They were quickly learning it was easier than having her ask a hundred questions.

"Every now and then the Reborns have a meeting to discuss the state of things. We also trade goods. I'm usually the one to go," Lucas explained, sending the book in his hand back to the top shelf. "I don't want to take you with me, Cass. Please don't fight me on this."

"Then go. I'm fine. I'm not as stubborn as you think I am."

"You're way worse," he said without missing a beat and she narrowed her eyes at him. "We'll be gone for about a day, nothing more. Please, please don't spend all your time with Xo. He's only going to get stronger and hungrier."

Cassia pursed her lips and tutted. "Fine."

Shock covered Lucas's expression. "Just like that? You're agreeing with me."

"I'm not that stubborn!"

Lucas offered her a wide grin and a wink, then he joined Min-Jun and exited the library. After they left, Cassia continued walking through the aisles for hours, reading up on Visionaries, on Empaths, on Healers. There was so much she wanted to learn before she had to leave.

"Hey," Brie said, walking up to her. She was shorter than Cassia, not that much taller than Calla.

Her heart ached at the thought of her little sister. "Hey," she said.

"Where's Lucas?" Brie asked.

"Some Reborn meeting. He said he'd be gone for about a day."

"Shit, that's right," Brie said and bit her lip.

"Why?"

Brie hesitated before saying, "Phoenix sighting."

Cassia's heart skipped. "Where? Let's go."

"Excuse me?" Brie said. "Us?" She gestured between the two of them and shook her head. "He'll kill me if I take you with me." She crossed her arms over her chest.

"Can it wait until he gets back or will the phoenix leave?"

Brie bit her lip again. "I don't know. They don't stay in one place for very long." Her eyebrows drew close.

"Please," Cassia said, shifting her weight from one foot to the other and tugging on her tunic nervously. A phoenix. They could get the last ingredient to save Calla. "Please," she said again.

Brie grumbled and threw her slender but toned arms in the air. "Fine, we can go. Together. But you follow my lead, okay?" Her voice carried both weight and fear, but Cassia didn't care.

One last ingredient.

"Deal."

★ ★ ★

Cassia slipped on a pair of black leggings they gave her and a dark brown knee-length tunic. Brie had mentioned that they'd need to blend in as much as possible. While she'd done her research, they had no idea what behavior to expect from the phoenix – other than knowing they were easily frightened. Cassia pulled on the worn-down shoes and stepped out of her room to find Brie waiting for her, wearing leather pants, a matching dark brown tunic and leather boots.

Brie looked down at Cassia's shoes. "Oh, I forgot. I got you a pair of boots that should fit. Size five, right?" Cassia nodded and followed Brie to her bedroom. She found herself wondering where Brie found the time to source almost everything in this place and still have time to do research for everyone on everything. Perhaps *that* was her magic power.

They walked into Brie's bedroom and Cassia was enveloped in shades of pastel pink. Brie blushed slightly, her cheeks matching the walls behind her as she lifted a canvas bag. "Here you go."

Cassia opened the bag to reveal a pair of thick-soled black leather boots. She kicked off her shoes and changed into the boots, tugging on the laces as she tightened them. She wriggled her toes and rotated her ankles. Finally, something that fit her properly.

Brie led her downstairs and walked up to the weaponry closet. She grabbed two steel daggers and handed them to Cassia. She took out an additional two daggers, these two bronze, and strapped them to her thigh. Without saying much, Brie walked outside and whistled, calling for the wolf. Willis ran toward them, already saddled. He twirled around Brie a few times and she raised her right hand. "Bow," she said, and while she was tiny compared to the enormous wolf, the wolf listened. "Go ahead," she said to Cassia, who pulled the reins and climbed on rather inelegantly.

"Do you want to sit up front or at the back?" Brie asked.

"I'm fine at the back."

After climbing up in front of Cassia, Brie leaned forward and whispered to the black wolf. She stretched her hand and offered Willis a cookie. He swallowed it happily and howled quietly. Brie dug into her bag and pulled out another cookie.

"When do I get to learn how to instruct the wolves?" Cassia asked.

"Once your last feather has fallen, Lucas will give them an order to listen to you," Brie replied. "Have you decided to stay?"

"Oh," Cassia replied. She'd always known she'd had to go back home, but it felt as though the reality of it all had only just hit her. "Uhm, no, of course not. I have to get back to Calla."

"Oh yeah, of course," Brie replied, keeping her gaze focused ahead as Willis leapt forward.

The Baskian wolf sprinted through the woods, sending the wind whipping through their hair until Brie held up her hand. Willis slowed to a gentle stop, much gentler than Ruq had ever managed.

"We're here," Brie said and they slid off silently.

"How did you hear about this phoenix?" Cassia asked as she slid her daggers in place and tightened her ponytail. Brie's soft blond curls were pulled into a tight bun, leaving her small face clear and somewhat fearless.

"I keep in touch with the Reborn community. Aewan from the Crabgrass village just north of the Selli mentioned seeing one during one of her hunting trips in Bode Valley," Brie explained as they walked in between the ancient, towering trees.

"And you trust Aewan? You said this place is dangerous. Why would she hunt here?"

"We don't have any other leads," Brie bit back. "And keep your voice low."

They crept closer and Brie whipped out a golden antique monocular. She extended it, peeked through it and then shook her head, gesturing for them to walk deeper into the valley.

The trees became greener the deeper they went, and the grass was longer. Brie's pine scent blended into the surroundings. There were no beaten-down paths and the only sound was that of crickets chirping. It was the first time there were no sounds of birds singing.

They crept through the grass slowly until Brie gasped. She silenced herself with her hands and Cassia followed her gaze.

Cassia had studied pictures of phoenixes beforehand to know what to look out for, but even so, she couldn't believe what she was seeing. Her entire body froze as she was overcome by its beauty.

The phoenix sat perched on the tree above them. Its feathers were deep red and orange, blending into each other, creating the image of a live fire. Its tail curled down the trunk of the tree, nearly reaching their heads.

Cassia lifted her hand slowly but Brie grabbed it and shook her head. Dragging Cassia's ear down to her lips, she whispered so softly, Cassia struggled to hear her, "If you give it a fright, it will spontaneously combust."

Cassia leaned into Brie's ear. "But phoenixes are reborn out of the ashes so…."

"The feather needs to be from a mature phoenix. The ones around your neck are from a chick."

Cassia glanced down at the feathers on her chest before looking up at the majestic creature sitting on a branch. It looked as if it could set the entire tree alight with a flick of its feathery tail.

Brie dug into her bag and lifted out a vial. She opened the lid and the scent of frankincense filled the air. The phoenix above them released a sound similar to a purr. It looked down at them and curled its long tail around itself.

Brie poured some of the frankincense onto the ground. Grabbing Cassia's wrist, she dragged her away from the tree. Cassia opened her mouth to speak but Brie angrily put a finger to her lips.

They sat in silence and watched the bird watch them. Cassia looked at Brie, who mouthed *Wait*, her face firm and frowning.

The phoenix flitted down, landing on the branch below. The branch dipped under its weight, groaning, while the bird stared at them again. Its eyes were golden and glimmering. Cassia looked at Brie and raised her eyebrows. *How long are we supposed to wait?*

Brie replied with a look of annoyance and Cassia pursed her lips and turned her attention back to the fire bird.

After another hour had passed, the phoenix flitted down to the ground and carefully stepped toward the frankincense. Its legs and talons, in contrast to its fiery feathers, were pitch-black. The talons were larger than the pine cones it sidestepped.

It was so close to them now that Cassia could easily leap forward and grab part of the bird. She was sure she could do it. "Don't," Brie whispered as if reading her mind.

Brie stood slowly, her palm up, carrying a few sticks of cinnamon. The phoenix purred again and took a step closer to them. Its golden beak opened and snapped closed as it eyed Brie's palm.

With wobbling legs, Brie took a small step closer and stretched her hand out to the bird.

Up close, the phoenix was even bigger than Cassia initially thought, easily as large as a swan, if a swan looked to be made of fire.

The phoenix paused and observed Brie, tilting its head sideways as it gazed upon the cinnamon sticks in her hand. It purred again and looked between Brie and Cassia. Its golden eyes flashed. Cassia's breath caught; if it weren't for Calla, she might have run in the opposite direction.

Brie stood still. Even her breathing slowed to prevent movement.

The phoenix was within reach.

Something rustled lightly in the bushes behind them and the phoenix took a step back, opening its impressive wings. It hopped up one branch. It was about to flee.

"Don't move," Brie warned.

Cassia was sure she could reach it. She leapt forward as the bird took off and grabbed at its wings.

Just one feather. She only needed to reach one feather.

Brie gasped in horror as Cassia made contact.

The phoenix cawed loudly, a jarring sound knocking the air out of Cassia's chest. Gripping her fingers around the soft feathers, she screamed as her skin seared. Simultaneously, the phoenix burst into a massive orange and red flame. Cassia and Brie stumbled back, away from the growing fire as heat coated their skin. The smoke entered her lungs and she coughed, opening her palm to discover the feather had turned to ash.

"No!" Brie screamed, coughing and doubling over. "What did you do?"

"No, no, no, no, no," Cassia mumbled as she launched toward the died-out flames and the pile of ash. Digging through it, she said, "I had it. I had the feather." She felt her panic build up in a way it hadn't for many years. She couldn't breathe. Her lungs were collapsing.

"I told you not to move," Brie scolded through a stiff jaw. "This was the first sighting in weeks!" Brie pulled at her blond hair and slammed her hands over her face. "You should have listened to me!"

Cassia curled up and sunk her head into her knees. "I—" she started, but Brie had already turned around.

"One order. *One* order. You couldn't follow one order to save your own sister's life and now Calla is—" Brie stopped, but Cassia knew what she was about to say.

Calla was going to die. Because of her. She'd ruined it. She'd ruined their chance of getting the final ingredient for Calla's suppressant tonic.

Brie screamed in frustration and whistled loudly. "Let's go, there's no point in being here now. That thing is useless to us." She pointed at the ash as a small red and orange bird appeared, chirped loudly and hopped around. Brie threw the cinnamon sticks at it and stomped off to the black wolf, who arrived quickly.

Unsure of how she found the will to stand up, Cassia walked behind her quietly. Her hands and knees were covered in ash and burned bits of grass. She didn't know what to say or do. She'd fucked up. That much she knew. The ache in her chest became unbearable. She couldn't go home to Calla without this suppressant. She couldn't face her. Her entire body shuddered as she remembered, clearly, Calla screaming in pain. Cassia's cheeks were hot and wet and she didn't bother wiping them. She didn't care about anything at that moment. The heaviness she felt was unlike anything she'd felt before.

Brie turned around to look at her. How pathetic she must have looked; Brie's expression instantly softened. She sighed heavily and said, "I'll extend my search farther, wider. Reach out to a few new villages. Maybe there's another one out there." She touched Cassia's back for a second before mounting Willis. "Come on, it's getting dark. We should get back before we get ourselves into trouble."

A loud cry escaped Cassia. "I'm sorry," she whimpered.

Brie extended her hand, Cassia took it and climbed on top of the wolf. "We'll figure something out. Maybe there's a replacement. There's no use crying over lost feathers."

Brie pulled off her tunic, revealing a black tank top underneath. Cassia stared at the dark ring around her upper left arm. She looked at her own arm, wondering if her first ring would be for Calla. It would be her own fault.

Her head started spinning. She couldn't hear anything except a thundering sound in her ears, deafening her. There was an incessant pang against the side of her head as she struggled to breathe.

CHAPTER TWENTY-THREE

Lucas

Lucas and Jun arrived at the woods just below the Antares Mountain and offered Ruq some water for his speedy efforts.

The Reborn meeting was being held in the dense woods in the early evening as the sun was starting to set. Every few months they changed the meeting location to avoid being caught by the Firsts. According to one of the older Reborns, the royal guard had discovered one of their earlier meetings and each and every Reborn present had been beaten to a bloody mess for their *attempted coup*. Lucas and Jun navigated to the agreed-upon meeting spot and Lucas waved when he saw Petri in the crowd. Petri raised his hand in greeting, making his way toward them, and before Lucas could say anything, he said, "I never got to thank you for what you did. I'm so sorry, Lucas." A flash of pain crossed over Petri's face. "I'm so sorry about your wolf. We'll have enough next month. We'll have extra."

It was hard to hide the pain it brought Lucas thinking about Zuq. About his white wolf, who didn't deserve to die. The thought of bright red blood soaked into the white fur blocked Lucas's attempt at a reassuring smile, though he knew the guilt was likely eating at Petri. "It's okay. I'm fine," Lucas said. "It was out of our hands." The truth was that he didn't blame Petri at all. He blamed the Firsts. He blamed the king and the princes.

Petri smiled. Then his face twisted in anguish. He bowed slightly before greeting some of the other Reborns who walked by. Lucas and Jun pulled out the bags of fruits and vegetables they usually traded and made their way through the old trees to the makeshift market.

Shoddy tables were set up, each carrying items they would need at some point. Lucas traded bananas for rice, and potatoes for flour. Jun walked back over to him with a bag of sugar. "Brie mentioned running out of rosemary. She's struggling to grow it," Lucas said. "Have you seen any?"

Jun pointed behind him. "I just walked by some. I'll be right back."

Later in the evening, the market tables were collapsed and Vincent, one of the oldest Reborns Lucas had met personally, walked to the center of the circle. He was from the Nutsedge village and often chaired these meetings. Vincent gestured for everyone to quiet down and be seated.

Lucas sat on the grass and crossed his legs.

"We don't have much time, so I'd like to get to the main topics this evening." Vincent turned around, making eye contact with as many of them as he could.

"The first threat is of course our immediate threat, the Rahlogs. We've found that while it is safer to kill someone immediately after they have been bitten, it's almost painless to do it on day three or four when their hunger is more extreme than any physical pain they could feel. It seems more merciful, especially for those of us who have had to put down our own."

A moment of silence swept across the crowd and Lucas's skin crawled. There was no way he could kill Xo. It wasn't fair. Xo was his friend. He didn't deserve this. He wouldn't have even been there, in the Black Hole, if it weren't for Lucas.

"My own village, Nutsedge, survived an attack last week. Only one of us was bitten and uhm," he paused as his voice cracked, "he asked to be killed before he could kill. So, if you knew Asad, I'm sorry for your loss, for our loss."

A woman in the crowd stood up and shouted breathlessly, "Death came for you as it will come for me." She choked on her words and trembled.

The crowd hung their heads and joined in. "Death is not defeat."

Two other women stood and held the first woman tightly while she cried. The crowd finished the greeting. "Rest your soul, my dear friend, until death decides when next we'll meet."

Vincent wiped his fallen tears. "Thank you, Ana, he was a good man. A good husband."

Lucas ground his teeth. There had to be a way to solve this. Something or someone needed to stop them. He stuck up his hand.

Vincent nodded at him.

"We recently found out that killing a Rahlog kills every other Rahlog it created."

Vincent nodded enthusiastically. "Roland suspected that. Thanks for confirming it. Is that you, Lucas?" Lucas nodded and Vincent continued, "Everyone hear that? Spread the word."

"We're working on finding their base and killing their leader," Lucas said.

"How are you going to find their base?"

Jun pinched him. He knew he couldn't tell them about Cass and how she got here. If it came out that he was in any way involved with Lochlan, crown prince of the Firsts, there would be trouble.

"General research, investigating, et cetera."

Vincent nodded. "Keep us updated. Let us know if you ever need backup. Nutsedge will be there." The sincerity in his voice nearly had Lucas admitting everything.

A few other Reborns shouted their support and for a moment, Lucas felt calm. While he never struggled to make friends, he had slipped into this community so easily. They were more than friends; they were family, aunties, uncles, cousins. At least that was what he imagined it would have felt like to have a family.

Diego, another member of Dandelion, stood up next and sighed heavily. His voice shook as he started speaking. "I know that this isn't news. I know that many of you have experienced it. But my little Carlos was taken last night." He slapped his hand across his chest as he winced. "He's just a kid, just like the others. They can't do this," Diego whimpered. "That fucking prince. I'll kill him. I'll kill him myself." A woman stood and held on to him. He dropped his arms and relaxed his shoulders. Jun nodded at the woman. Another Empath, Lucas assumed. The Empaths and Telepaths tended to seek out each other, perhaps finding solace in knowing there were others who lived with the burden of experiencing and managing everyone's emotions.

A number of Reborns stood and told their stories. One was a male Guest who had transitioned, and others spoke about having had their children taken from them in the last few months. Some were telling the same story they had heard before with exactly the same level of pain they felt when first telling it. Everyone listened attentively. The Empaths showed themselves and stretched their powers as far as they could reach. Including Jun, whose breath was becoming ragged.

"Why do they need our children?" a woman with frizzy black hair asked. Lucas recalled meeting her at the last meeting, although he had forgotten her name. "They don't need to use our children as slaves. Children are clumsy and messy. What is the purpose? Why are they doing this?" Her wide eyes opened wider as she fidgeted with her hands.

"It's a power move," Vincent explained, as he usually did. There was always someone who asked. The truth is, they would never understand it. It would always be too much to bear.

"Will we get them back? I didn't even see my girl at the Tribute," the woman said.

An older woman stood up and introduced herself as Liana before saying, "They took my boy almost twenty years ago. I haven't seen him since."

The woman with the frizzy black hair burst into tears once more, shaking her head and mumbling her denial. Her legs wobbled beneath her and her friends gathered around her, calming her, supporting her, consoling her, or attempting to. Nothing would ever take that level of pain away.

"We have to do something!" Zidane shouted, standing up. Everyone clapped and howled in agreement and distress.

Lucas sat up and listened. He would fight alongside these people whenever they wanted him to, but he also knew that they would all die if they tried to start a rebellion now.

Vincent raised his hands to quiet everyone. "We need to bide our time. Reborns are joining our side every day. Our numbers are growing. We need to focus on defeating the Rahlogs and then we will continue to grow," Vincent said. "Soon, soon, we will be powerful enough to take our children back."

Lucas cast his eyes over the crowd and found Zidane staring directly at him. He bowed his head in greeting and received a bow in return.

The next Tribute was discussed to allocate what each community would be bringing. Everyone looked at Lucas, their eyes full of pity. They'd all seen or heard of what had happened with Zuq. With the whipping. But in comparison to what so many others had lost, he didn't feel he deserved their sympathy.

Eventually, when all was said and done, Lucas stood up and watched the crowd dissipate. Some Reborns left immediately; others stayed to mingle. He wanted to leave. He had a Guest and half a Rahlog back home and something about that did not sit well with him.

"Lucas."

He recognized that voice immediately and turned around to see Amani smiling at him. He smiled back instinctively and she bit her bottom lip shyly. She was the first Reborn he'd been romantically involved with on this side. They'd met at a meeting exactly like this, three years ago.

"Do you want to grab a drink?" she asked, her lips full and painted red, reminding him of all the things they did together. He forced himself to look at her eyes instead.

He opened his mouth to respond and heard Jun curse. Jun rarely cursed. "We need to go," he called out to him as he walked over.

"What's wrong?" Lucas asked, smiling politely at Amani. She sighed.

"It's Cassia. She's okay, physically, but uh…. We should go. There's some tension back home and Nisa is struggling with the three of them." Jun waved at Amani. "Sorry," he said to her before dragging Lucas to Ruq and mounting the wolf.

"Jun, explain!" Lucas ordered as soon as they were on the wolf with all their goods packed.

"Cassia and Brie went to find a phoenix. They found one and then Cassia killed it accidentally and she's become almost unresponsive. You know Guests feel everything more intensely, not just hunger and exhaustion. So, I need to get back to help her, to help both of them."

Oh no. Lucas felt his chest twist. "Both of them?"

"Nisa is exhausted from trying to control Xo's pain, Cassia's anxiety, and Brie's pretty angry...."

Cass messed up. He knew she would never recover from this. Every move she made was calculated to avoid having regrets. This was going to kill her.

Fuck.

The only solution he could think of was to find another phoenix feather. As if sensing his own anxiety, Ruq traveled even faster to get him home.

CHAPTER TWENTY-FOUR

Cassia and Brie arrived at the manor after their failed mission. Wordlessly, Brie slid off the wolf, while Cassia stayed where she was, wondering where Willis would run to if she begged him to run away. Anywhere except here and except home; somewhere else where she did not have to face the consequences of her own stupid actions.

Brie walked into the house without looking back to see if Cassia followed. Cassia knew exactly why Brie was angry and couldn't blame her. She simply dug her head into the wolf's black fur.

Brie told me to wait.

She told me not to move.

Why didn't I listen?

The memory played in her mind over and over.

She looked at her inflamed palm, refusing to heal it. The swollen skin and pain were a reminder of her stupidity and carelessness. She flexed her fingers, feeling the crippling pain shoot though her hand, and welcomed it. She deserved it; she deserved worse. Such a minor consequence compared to what Calla was facing because of her actions and would be facing for the rest of her *short* life.

A hand rested on Cassia's elbow and a warm buzz tickled her skin. "Cassia?" Nisa's voice greeted her softly. "Would you like to come inside? Maybe have a bath and something to eat?"

The buzz was just that. A buzz. There was no peace washing over her, no calmness, no happiness. She was void of anything good and light.

There was only regret. Regret that she was here in the first place, that she had missed days, precious days of being with her sister. Her sweet sister, who would be dying soon, she reminded herself, because she could not follow one order.

Nisa grabbed her with both hands and gently tugged her, sliding her off the wolf. Her legs collapsed underneath her, wobbling violently. Nisa pulled her close. The buzz of her magic was louder, but it wasn't landing. Cassia broke free and stomped into the manor. She didn't want Nisa to remove the guilt that ate at her. She hoped it would eat her alive.

After making her way up to her room, she closed the door behind her and debated pulling the necklace off. What was the point of staying, considering there was no hope left to finish the tonic? Brie said something about finding an alternative or another phoenix feather but Cassia had read the *Book of Empaths*; she had researched phoenixes before their trip. Nothing else would work. Her fingers played on the soft feathers around her neck.

There was a knock at her bedroom door and Cassia curled into herself even tighter.

"Cassia?" Nisa called as she entered the room.

Overwhelmed with shame for pushing Nisa away, Cassia turned to look at her, swallowing back tears. It made no sense that her body could even produce this many tears. Nisa walked around the bed and kneeled at her side. "It's going to be okay," she said, and gently unwrapped Cassia's fingers from her necklace. Cassia hadn't realized she was gripping it so tightly. "Don't do it. Lucas deserves a goodbye at least."

More tears streamed down her face and Nisa wiped them gently.

"Why aren't you mad at me?" Cassia asked quietly. "I messed up."

Nisa smiled and stroked her face, each stroke sending a buzz across her skin, but Nisa's magic wasn't doing anything. "It's really tough when you first get here. Everything is crazy and every feeling is heightened…. I was a Guest not too long ago. Xo found me during one of their hunting trips and I was beside myself. I hid in the dungeon, refusing to speak to anyone until that last feather fell." Cassia sniffed, pulling the duvet over her shoulders as she shivered, even though the room was toasty. "Lucas warned us that you have some trust issues…."

Peeking over the edge of the duvet, Cassia found her voice to say, "He said that? Why?"

Nisa sighed. Her expression was soft, her eyes inviting. It was hard not to feel comfortable around her. "I suppose he expected this, and who can blame you for being sceptical when a random woman claims she can save your sister with a feather of a rare and mythical creature? It's a lot to take in...."

"She's going to die because of me."

"We're going to figure something out," Nisa said. "Brie's smart. Like, really smart. And Lucas, come on, he'll make sure you get home with that suppressant." Her hand was firmly planted on Cassia's shoulder now and she started feeling the effects of Nisa's magic, slightly.

Closing her eyes, she willed herself to stop crying, but she couldn't. Calla's little face, which she so desperately missed, kept infiltrating her thoughts. The only alternative to crying uncontrollably was screaming and, well, that seemed worse.

"How about that bath?" Nisa suggested. "It's my solution to at least seventy percent of my problems."

"I don't want to," Cassia said into her pillow.

Nisa stood and soon after, the sound of water running traveled into the room. Nisa walked back in and pulled her up, dragging her into the bathroom. "If you don't wash yourself, I will be forced to do it for you."

Nisa left her alone in the bathroom and Cassia peeled off her clothing, which smelled of ash. She climbed into the already drawn warm bath, allowing the heat to distract her.

She stayed in the bath until the water turned icy and exhaustion teased at the edges of her mind, finally numbing her thoughts. She climbed out of the bath before she could pass out, dried herself off and slipped on a pair of soft, silky pajamas Nisa had set out for her. It was strange being taken care of.

That was usually Cassia's job.

When she finally settled in bed, she pulled the duvet over her head and wished, for a moment, that it would suffocate her.

As tired as she was, sleep would not find her. She lay awake in the dark, on her side, staring at the window at one end of the room. At some point during the evening, she'd opened the curtains and window and the night sky was visible from where she lay.

Ocean air breezed into the room and Lucas climbed into the bed behind her. He wrapped his big arm around her and placed a soft, quick kiss into her hair.

The mattress dipped and another two sets of hands grabbed her. Min-Jun and Nisa sent their magic into her simultaneously and Brie arrived, carrying a bowl of pasta.

Lucas brushed the hair from her face and helped her sit up.

"Why are you all being so nice to me?" she asked, afraid to make eye contact with Brie, who placed the bowl in her lap. "I know why *he's* nice to me." Cassia pointed at Lucas sitting alongside her and he smiled. She didn't need to look at him to know both dimples were out. "He's my friend."

"'You're *our* friend too," Brie answered softly. Judging from her clean face and white dress, she'd had a bath as well.

"But I—" Cassia squeaked.

"A stubborn friend. A frustrating friend. But a friend nonetheless." Brie sighed. "When I messed up, Jean was bitten, so…." Her voice cracked and she stared out of the window. "It could have been worse."

"We all mess up," Min-Jun said. "Some of us ended up on this side because we messed up. Some of us ended up in a cage in a dungeon transitioning into a flesh-eating monster because we messed up."

"Some, and I won't mention any names, created flesh-eating monsters, and wow, did they mess up," Nisa said. Both she and Min-Jun were still casually buzzing their magic into her, taking the edge off.

Brie chuckled and laid a hand on Cassia's knee. "I'm not even sure how I was going to get that feather. My way may not have worked either. Don't beat yourself up about it to a point of uselessness, because then I *will* be mad."

Cassia looked at Brie and felt her mouth twitching upward, but her eyes kept leaking. Their affection and kindness were so foreign to her.

Lucas rubbed her back gently. "We're going to figure something out. Like you said, we always do."

As soon as she ate one forkful of pasta, and the tomato and garlic swirled around in her mouth, her hunger returned and she finished the bowl immediately, blocking out anyone who was talking to her.

With a full stomach and the lingering effects of having two Empaths working on her, she lay down, turning her face to look at Lucas, who lay beside her. There was a warmth radiating from where their shoulders touched. The combination of everything eventually lulled her to sleep, with one thing on her mind.

To repay them, she was going to save Xo.

★   ★   ★

Cassia opened her eyes and immediately realized that she was not awake. It felt the same way as all those *visits* with Lucas. A white light blinded her and she waited for something, or someone, to appear, as Lucas always did.

But instead of Lucas, his mother appeared, her blue eyes wide with relief and a smile spread across her face. "Cass," she whispered, and Cassia gasped at the fact that she could hear her. "Oh, thank goodness. I can finally reach you."

"Aunt Ro, what's going on? Where are you?"

"Listen to me. I don't have much time. I imagine you'll pass out quite soon from overexertion."

"What?" Cassia asked, staring at Aunt Rosheen. Her long blond hair had been cropped short.

"Go to the palace. The book you need to break the curse is there, black leather-bound, no title on the cover."

"What? Wait, how will I find it?"

"It will find its way to you. I've seen it." Aunt Rosheen inhaled quickly. "I have to go. You're our only hope, Cassia."

"Aunty Ro," Cassia started, but her vision blurred and darkened the way it did every time she collapsed.

★   ★   ★

Cassia woke with a fright, shooting upright and waking Lucas, lying beside her. He sat up, eyes wide. His hands patted her arms and shoulders as if checking that she was in one piece.

"I'm fine," she said quickly and he exhaled a breath of relief and fell back down. The mattress bounced underneath him.

"Did you have a vision? A nightmare?"

"I had a visit...from your mom."

CHAPTER TWENTY-FIVE

Lucas sat up again and flicked his wrist; the bedside lamp lit. "What do you mean?"

"She told me to go to the palace. She said the book we need would come to me."

Lucas stared at her. His dark eyes were even darker than usual. "Why? That doesn't make any sense."

"I know what I saw."

"Are you sure it was her?"

She nodded. "It was your mom. Aside from her hair being shorter than the last time I saw her, she looked exactly the same. I know her voice, Luke. It's the same voice that put me to sleep while my mom was working late at the hospital. I'd know it anywhere."

He covered his face with both of his hands and whispered to himself, "Mom, why are you doing this?" He dropped his hands. "Did she say anything else?"

She shook her head.

"Great, so it's just like the letter, a half-baked cake that no one can eat."

Throwing her legs off the bed, she grabbed her new boots.

"Where are you going?" Lucas asked.

"To the palace."

"No. Fuck that," he scoffed.

"I'm going. I have to," she said. "Please, Luke, we need this win."

His head kept shaking. "I don't care what you saw. I'm not sending you into that level of danger. A lamb to slaughter doesn't begin to describe the horrors they'd inflict on you. A female Guest...." Squaring his shoulders, he stood up to his full height.

"You don't get to tell me what to do," she challenged, meeting his gaze.

"I need you alive," he replied, looking away.

She lifted another fallen feather. "Four more feathers with me or a lifetime with Xo?"

Sidestepping him, she ran downstairs and he followed. The dungeon door was open and Brie lay asleep next to the cage that held Xo.

"Hey guys, starting to get a little bit hungry. You might want to ask Brie to move farther away," Xo said, snapping his teeth shut, his eyes wider and wilder than they were the day before.

Lucas bent down and woke Brie gently.

"We're going to the palace," Cassia announced and Lucas sighed.

"It's really dangerous for you, as a female—" Xo started.

"I know, and it was really dangerous for you and Lucas to go to the Black Hole, for me, for Calla, but you did it anyway and look what happened."

"I'd do it again," Xo said easily.

"Let me do this for you." Cassia raised her hands to the metal bars and Xo touched them lightly. She closed her eyes.

"Nothing," she hissed at herself.

"No news is better than bad news, right?" Xo said, laughing lightly.

"This isn't a joke. We could die and that's if we're lucky," Lucas snapped.

Cassia exchanged glances with Brie, who lifted her hands as if to say, *Leave me out of this.*

Wordlessly, Lucas stomped out and Brie went off in the other direction. Cassia followed after Lucas as he angrily filled bags with various items. Daggers, bananas, unlabeled vials were all tossed into the bags. Walking out of the manor, he whistled and she stood silently next to him. Even without being an Empath, she could feel his rage, his fear.

Ruq ran up and skidded to a halt. Quickly, Lucas tied the bags onto Ruq's saddle and mumbled to himself, shaking his head, "This is a bad idea. It's a bad idea." He petted Ruq's head, muttering his thanks to the wolf for all the work he'd done.

Cassia wanted to reassure him, but there was nothing she could say. Lucas turned to face her and wordlessly lifted her onto Ruq and jumped on behind her. Without warning, Ruq launched forward and Cassia leaned against Lucas. His arms were outstretched on either side of her, holding on to the reins, and he rested his head on the back of her head and kissed it gently. "I have to keep you safe," he said, and judging from the low volume, she wasn't sure she was meant to hear it.

After a few hours Lucas raised his hand and Ruq stopped. Lucas hopped off the gray wolf and unpacked a sleeping bag. He surveyed the area, lit a fire and sat in front of it without saying a single word.

"Luke," Cassia started as she climbed off the wolf and woke each of her legs by shaking them. She walked up to Lucas and sat next to him.

He stared at the fire. "Yeah?"

"Will you look at me?" she asked.

"I'd rather not."

"Why's that?" she asked softly.

"Because every time I look at you, I remember I'm leading you to the most dangerous place in the universe and every time I realize that, I want to rip that necklace off your neck and send you back to Talm. At least there you'll be safe."

"But Xo."

"But Xo. I know," he replied, his black eyes still focused on the fire. The orange flames reflected in them.

When the flames eventually died out, Lucas stood and rolled out two blankets. He dragged his blanket up against hers and lay down. "You never got to tell me why Lochlan helped you save me," he said, turning to face her.

"Yeah, I was too busy trying to kiss you."

"Don't remind me," he said and she laughed. "What did he want?"

"A deal."

"And you made a deal with him?" he asked, frowning. His eyes flashed blue for a second.

Turning to look up at the stars instead of his judgmental eyes, she said, "You were about to die. I'd trade anything for your life."

"What did you trade?"

"I don't know yet. He said he'd let me know."

Lucas grumbled, his eyes flashing blue again. "That's not good."

"What's the deal with Lochlan?" she asked as she started drifting off. "Why does he bother helping?"

"He doesn't do anything unless he gets something in return. He wants the Rahlogs gone as much as we do. His father probably instructed him to help," Lucas whispered. "And this way the king never has to publicly admit his mistakes. He makes a mess and we have to deal with it."

"How come they want the Rahlogs gone when they're doing such a great job of killing the Reborns?"

"I asked him that," Lucas said, his teeth clenched tightly. "He said the numbers are growing faster than anticipated and were becoming a nuisance."

"How come I haven't seen any Rahlogs with glowy blue eyes?"

"The Firsts are all safely locked in their villages. The only ones who get bitten are the reckless ones. The Rahlogs are more of an irritation to them than an actual threat." Lucas sighed again. "Once the Rahlogs are out of the way, we'll become their next target. As usual. And then, I'm sure, Lochlan will go back to being the Prince of the Firsts."

"Hmm.... I don't know.... I think he has another reason for helping," Cassia said. The stars were shining brightly around a full moon, reminding her of the emblem on Lochlan's cloak.

"I agree, but I just can't figure out what," Lucas said.

CHAPTER TWENTY-SIX

They could see the palace walls in the distance as the sun was setting the following evening. The orange light glinted off the golden engravings, shimmering in a way that turned it into liquid, making her want to touch it, bathe in it and spread the warm light it cast over all the dark parts of her mind.

It was hard to believe that behind those beautiful walls lived a place of horror far beyond her imagination.

Mesmerized by the walls, she glanced up and up until the gold blended into the orange and red of the sky. Ruq halted suddenly, pulling her back into focus. Lucas tapped the wolf's head and circled his wrist slowly. In response, the gray wolf padded toward the river and trotted along it.

"My mom left me an old map of the palace," Lucas said to Cassia. "She marked a secret entrance through a crack in the Altair riverbed. It's some kind of portal." He sighed, his knuckles whitening as he gripped the reins. "I never thought I would need to use it."

"It seems your mom doesn't do anything without reason," she said, and looked back at him. His jaw was fixed, a deep frown burrowed between his brows. "Well, if anything, we're good at swimming, right?" she joked, and Lucas smiled, although his frown line remained in place.

Following the river, they crept closer and closer to the glimmering boundary until all that stood between them and the palace was the wide, dark river. Lucas released the reins and grabbed her shoulders. "We're here," he said in a voice so soft she barely heard it. He slid off Ruq and grabbed a backpack while offering her a hand to climb down. Cupping Ruq's face, he spoke to the wolf, sending him off into the surrounding woods.

Cassia stood at the edge of the Altair River looking into the water. It was pitch-black. Nothing like the water they'd walked Jean into, or the shimmering water she and Lucas had swum in. Something about this water hinted at the sinister secrets the palace guarded. Everything about this water told her not to enter it.

"Your mom is really a master of mystery," she said, second-guessing her previous determination. "She hasn't told you anything else? Another secret letter maybe?"

"The queen of mystery. We should have known when she wouldn't tell me anything about my father when I was growing up." Lucas stepped into the water and looked back at her. "I don't suppose you're going to let me go in first just to check it out?" She shook her head and he gave her a resigned smile. "Fine," he said, digging into his backpack and pulling out something about the size of a strawberry. "Eat this. It'll help you hold your breath."

Taking the blob from his hand, she popped it into her mouth and immediately gagged as the taste of rotten eggs spread over her senses.

"Swallow," Lucas instructed firmly.

She swallowed and inhaled deeply before saying, "That's what he said."

Lucas smiled and then frowned at her. He stuck out his hand. "Come on, you fool."

He pulled her into the river. The water was ice-cold, even after a day in the hot sun. Lucas pointed down, closed his eyes, inhaled deeply and dropped underwater. She swallowed a mouthful of air then did the same, with the chill entering her bones and threatening to leave her numb. Opening her eyes, she saw a flash of light skin and followed him down to the bottom of the river. He kneeled on the riverbed, placing his hands flat on the ground, but nothing happened. Crawling along with his hands outstretched, he continued touching the riverbed and slamming his palms against it. She swam down beside him, aware that under normal circumstances she would have suffocated by now. Scraping her hands across the river floor, she followed his movements, covering ground, unsure of what she was doing, since she had no idea what a portal would look like.

Lucas stomped his feet on the riverbed, sliding his toes along the sand at the bottom. He turned to face her, shaking his head.

The already dark water soon became inky swirls as the sun set entirely. The riverbed looked to be made of obsidian and seeing Lucas in the water was becoming a challenge.

Spinning around, she searched for him, for his arms, or neck, his face, the parts of his body that weren't covered in dark clothing. She wanted to call out to him, but she couldn't open her mouth, obviously.

She was suddenly extremely aware of how long she'd been underwater as her muscles started tiring and her bones became heavier. *Maybe I'm running out of oxygen,* she thought.

There was still no sign of movement, no sign of Lucas. She could barely see her own hand in front of her face. The water started closing in on her, applying pressure on her chest.

She was definitely running out of oxygen.

Lucas was missing and she couldn't breathe.

Something slimy slid against her leg and she gasped, inhaling a mouthful of water. It rushed into her mouth, filling her lungs. Using the last of her strength, she propelled herself up toward the surface. A cold breeze whipped across the top of her head as her mouth rose above the surface. But before she could inhale the crisp night air, something pulled her under. A hand gripped her wrist and dragged her through the pitch-black depths as she opened her mouth to scream, inhaling more water.

Her magic buzzed as a vision entered her mind and she saw Calla screaming. Alone. Cassia's chest ached at the sight, pulling her out of her vision as she choked. Her body sagged heavily and she was sure she was about to die.

Her toes rubbed against the riverbed as a ring of blue-and-white light blurred through the dark water. She was being dragged closer and closer to it, until she was pulled into the circle, feeling as though her body was left behind.

A hand squeezed her mouth ajar and her eyes opened to see Lucas twirling his wrist, pulling a stream of water from her mouth until she could breathe again. Doubling over, she coughed up the last of it and looked up. He patted her back gently and pulled her into his grip. "Are you okay?" he asked.

"That's pretty cool," she said, steadying her breath.

"Told you telekinesis is the best," he said, his voice shaking slightly with adrenaline. "What the fuck happened down there, Cass? Why'd you swim up to the surface?"

She shook her head, surveying the dark tunnel they crouched in. "I panicked, I couldn't see you and I couldn't hold my breath anymore and something touched my leg."

"I thought I lost you there for a minute," he said, reading her expression. "What's wrong?"

"Calla's in so much pain," she said as she squeezed the water out of her long plait. "I saw her screaming."

He ran his hand through his hair roughly. "We'll figure it out," he said. "I promise."

"Are we in the palace?" she asked, and he shrugged, turning around in the small space provided. It was just about wide enough to accommodate his shoulders.

The tunnel led to a brick wall with a large crack running across a number of bricks. Lucas tapped it again and the same blue-and-white light of a portal appeared and sucked them in. Her limbs felt as though they were separate from the rest of her body as they were thrown into a dimly lit room. Lucas was first to scramble to his feet and check to see if anyone was watching. He raised his hands, ready to attack. But there was no one there. "Coast is clear," he said, offering her a hand.

Cassia took his hand and he pulled her to her feet as the life returned to her legs. "So, did your mom say where the secret tunnels led to?" she asked, squeezing the water out of her dark tunic. She already knew the answer.

"Does it look like I know what I'm doing?" he asked, looking around what seemed to be a bedroom. An unused bedroom, gathering from the thick layer of dust on the floor. The large bed was dressed in maroon-and-gold bedding with cushions of all sizes prettily arranged against a dark wooden headboard.

Cassia closed her eyes, willing another vision, but her mind struck a blank. The image of Calla screaming reappeared but she shook it off. Now was not the time to panic and give in to the heightened emotions that always seemed to be teetering on the edge, waiting to envelop her. "Maybe you should hit me or something?"

"What?" Lucas asked, walking around the room and investigating the furniture without touching anything.

"I don't know, my magic seems to work better when I'm stressed and panicked and an injury is easier to recover from than a panic attack. I'll heal myself after."

"Well, I'm not going to hit you. So let's just go through that door and see what happens," he said, tiptoeing toward the only door in the bedroom.

Lucas cracked open the door and stuck his head out, looking in either direction. He motioned for her to follow behind him as he crept out, unsheathing his copper dagger with his right hand. They leaned into the darkness. Most of the sconces were lit and with a twirl of his wrist, Lucas put the lights out, which made staying in the shadows relatively easy.

A light shuffle echoed from below them and Lucas pulled her into the only thing the passage led to – a narrow service staircase. Cassia climbed the stairs as the footsteps got closer.

The stairway led into another room, different from the one before. The opposite wall was lined with star-shaped windows, the starry night sky flickering inside and lighting up the floor. They were at a crossroads with doorways on their left and right sides. Alternatively, they could go back downstairs and face whoever it was that was walking around.

Cassia and Lucas exchanged glances, but she couldn't stop staring at the star-shaped windows.

"Cass, left or right, we have a fifty percent chance. The odds aren't bad," Lucas said, keeping his voice low.

Her mind tickled, not with magic but with the strangest feeling that she'd been here before. She kept staring at the star-shaped windows. "Do you remember The Adventures of Cass and Luke?" she asked.

"Yeah…. The stories my mom used to tell us when we complained about all the regular stuff?" He took a few steps closer to the doorways and said again, "Come on, Cass, left or right?"

"Do you remember the room with the star-shaped windows?" she asked absentmindedly.

Lucas stopped staring between the doorways and looked at the windows. "What are you saying?" he asked.

"Your mom didn't do anything without reason…" she said quietly, and turned to face him. "Cass and Luke went left, because—"

"Right isn't always right," he finished, meeting her gaze. She went left and he followed, running up to catch up to her. He grabbed her wrist gently. "Cass…. My mom…. Why—" His eyes widened as panic spread across his features.

"I think your mom is a Visionary. It would make sense. How she knew you were needed here. She saw this, us doing this. She said something like that during her dream visit. I mean, it's probably why I could hear her when she visited."

He stopped moving. "Wait a minute, just wait. Why wouldn't she tell me?"

His eyes were dark with fear, with hurt, with disbelief, and Cassia softened her tone. "We'll ask her when we find her, but first, let's get that book and get out of here."

She slipped her wrist out of his grip and let her hand fall in his, leading him down the passage.

"The golden library that Cass always hid in was on the top floor of the castle," Lucas muttered when they reached another flight of stairs.

She grasped onto the railing and ran up as quietly as possible. "I know, I remember all of them. They were my favorite bedtime stories."

As they reached the top of another flight of stairs, they exited into the passage of the castle, illuminated by the lights on the wall. They moved swiftly until they heard voices and pressed themselves against the wall. Lucas pulled her close and turned off the lights.

The passersby stopped. Their glowing blue eyes narrowed as they looked around in the darkness, directly at them. Lucas flicked his wrist, unscrewing a light bulb farther down the passage. The guards fled toward it, giving them a chance to escape into another stairwell.

They climbed every staircase until they reached what had to be the top of the palace. There was only one doorway. The entrance to the library.

"Stay outside, keep watch and buy me some time if you need to," Cassia said to Lucas.

"Do you expect me to let you go in there alone?"

"We don't have time for this, Luke. Your mom said I would get the book. Just keep watch, please. I'll scream if I need you," she said, and he frowned.

"I hope it doesn't come to that." He turned around and said to himself, "I don't like this, I don't like this." He rested his hand on her shoulder. "Be quick—"

"Be quiet, I know."

She stepped through the grand, white entrance. The library was bigger than the one at the manor, as was to be expected. There were shelves that lined the walls from floor to ceiling, and on each shelf, the wood was decorated with gold engravings. The patterns were enchanting, matching the ones on the palace walls.

A moon surrounded by six stars was etched onto every surface that was big enough to show it. The same symbol that was on Lochlan's cloak, she realized.

It was hard to focus on the titles of the books in the soft lighting. The ceiling was covered in paintings, mostly of flowers. Red and blue roses and more felines. A similar white fluffy cat that graced the walls at the manor looked down upon her here.

She ran her fingers upon the shelves until something looked familiar, felt familiar. She hoped she would get that buzz of magic when she touched the right book. But she surely couldn't be expected to touch them all. Revisiting her visit from Aunt Rosheen, she realized there was nothing else. No clues.

"I'm usually the one who comes looking for you."

The voice wrapped around her, tickling her senses and raising the hairs at the back of her neck. Spinning around, she looked into those bright blue eyes as Lochlan crossed his arms over his chest. He wore the same clothing he always wore, except this time, he had on his crown. It was shiny and golden, like everything else in this palace, and perched on top of his wild brown curls. A small smile graced his face.

Something clicked.

Lochlan.

He was the key.

She was sure of it. She also didn't have any other choice but to play his game.

"It took you long enough," she said, crossing her own arms and mimicking his posture as her stomach twisted in nervousness. "I expected you to arrive sooner."

His mouth pulled into a wide smile, but he said nothing. His fiery gaze traveled down her body, an amused look settling on his fine features. "Wet. I like it. I like that," he said, pointing at her plaited hair.

Rolling her eyes, she asked, "Where is the book your father used to create the Rahlogs?" Her nails dug into her arms as she clenched them, attempting to hide the way they were shaking.

"No 'Thank you, Prince Lochlan, for saving my lover'?" he asked, his eyes bright enough to light up the library.

"Please. This isn't for us; it's for everyone. Don't you want the Rahlogs to disappear too?" she asked. "Lucas said you did. Isn't that why you brought me here?"

"And you think you can do it? Something my father failed at? Something I have failed at?" Lochlan scoffed. "You really are full of fire, little lady." He slouched back against the shelves and gestured upward. A small leather-bound book traveled toward him and landed in his hand.

Quickly, she stepped up to him but he pulled it back. "I'm not done with you yet," he said, the light dancing in his dangerous eyes. Footsteps echoed through the library and his smile disappeared. He appeared in front of her within a second, pushing her into the shadows and up against a bookshelf. "Play along or die," he whispered before pressing his hard body against hers.

Every coherent thought in her mind disappeared as his lips landed on hers. The taste of vanilla entered her mouth, igniting something within her. Her stomach fluttered and she opened her eyes, pulling away to breathe as her magic buzzed inside her, threatening to do something. His blue eyes glimmered and her vision came to mind. She leaned back in and he pushed against her, setting her insides on fire in a way she didn't know was possible. His hands landed on her waist, spreading heat throughout her body. Without thinking, she slid her hands into his hair, deepening the kiss. Her body came alive, buzzing, humming, wanting. And then the panic struck. Stiffening her joints. Engulfing her entire body. And just before she could scream, the buzz traveled to her mind as a vision appeared.

She saw the back of a woman, blond hair falling loosely on her shoulders. The woman stalked a roaming rabbit. Crouching down low and pouncing, she transformed into a white cat midair and landed on top of the rabbit. The cat turned around to look directly at Cassia, its eyes the color of a blue flame.

She was pulled out of her vision by an unfamiliar voice.

"Loch, is that a Guest? A *female* Guest?" the voice asked. Lochlan's lips were still pressed against hers, his hands settled on her hips. She twisted as her heart raced.

He broke the kiss and said in a low and threatening voice, "She's mine."

Mine? Cassia wanted to protest and set him straight, but she realized that this was all part of a ruse.

"Have you reported her to Father? He gets them first, you know that," the man replied. Cassia tried peeking over Lochlan's shoulder but he shifted, blocking her view, and then turned around, keeping her in his shadow.

"I'm well aware of the rules, brother. I was here long before you were and, besides, as you well know, I'm bound by those rules. He's already had her and I'm next in line."

Brother.

He was the one who came to look for her when she had arrived. He was the one who killed Zuq. Kain. Lucas had mentioned him.

"She must be a feisty little thing to have caught your attention," Kain drawled. The tone of his voice brought on her nausea.

"Get out," Lochlan ordered calmly.

"Do be quick. I'd like a chance before she leaves."

Lochlan squared his shoulders. "I'll take as long as I like," he said, glancing back at her briefly before adding, "And I have a feeling this one is going to keep me busy for a while."

"Don't get so possessive over a Guest. They're only good for one thing."

Lochlan opened his palms, summoning balls of fire.

"All right, sorry for interrupting. Guest," he called, "don't pull off your feathers until I have a go. I'm a rather generous lover." And with that, she heard his footsteps fade into the distance.

Cassia pushed Lochlan and he spun around to face her. She curled her fingers into a fist and he raised his hands before dropping one of them into his cloak to pull out the book. He offered it to her. "Peace offering," he said.

Swiping it out of his hands, she opened it, and immediately noticed she couldn't read the script. "Give me permission," she said, setting her jaw and inhaling deeply, trying to steady her shaky voice. The flutter in her stomach hadn't stopped, but she chose to ignore it.

"You have my permission to read the book. Read it and go, as far away from this palace as you can, but you can't take it with you," he said, his voice void of the playfulness she had become accustomed to. "My father will track it and in a few moments he'll know that you're here."

As she leafed through the book in a hurry, the words blurred. Lochlan licked his fingers and flipped through the pages while she held the book open. "It's this one," he said.

Cassia read through the spell, memorizing the foreign words and hoping that she could trust Lochlan. She had no other choice at this moment. She looked up into Lochlan's eyes and the eyes of the cat flashed into her mind.

"Who is the woman with the blue eyes?" she asked.

Lochlan raised his eyebrows. "What woman? I assume you've realized we all have blue eyes, or are you not as observant as I thought?"

"The one who transforms into a cat. That cat, I'm assuming," she said, pointing at the ceiling. Lochlan's eyes widened as his lips parted.

"Let her go," Lucas said, stepping into the aisle, his shoulders wide as he prepared to pounce.

"One more step, your Highness, and your lady dies," Lochlan said. He unsheathed his knife and held it to her throat as he pushed her back up against the shelf. The cold metal on her skin made her gasp and her hand flew up to wrap around his wrist, but it wouldn't budge.

"What are you doing?" she bit out, confused by the situation. Was this all part of his plan? To trick her? Her heart raced wildly and her magic buzzed in her mind as she saw a vision of Calla again. Except this time, Calla wasn't screaming. Their mother was. Her mother was leaning over her sister's still body, performing CPR. Screaming and screaming.

Calla.

Calla.

Calla.

"Touch her and I'll kill you," Lucas growled, grounding her in the present. "Let her go."

"No."

"This isn't a game, Lochlan. I'm sick of your games. Just let her go." Lucas unsheathed his own dagger.

"I'm not playing a game. The lady and I have some unfinished business," Lochlan replied, his eyes glancing over Cassia.

"I'd rather die than let you take her."

"It would be my pleasure to see you try," Lochlan purred, summoning a ball of fire.

"Cass can solve the Rahlog problem. Isn't that what you wanted?" Lucas asked, dropping his dagger and raising his hands instead.

"I don't care about the Rahlogs." Lochlan grabbed her wrist with his free hand and whispered, "I just wanted her here."

"Why?" Lucas asked.

"Why wouldn't I take your prized possession?" Lochlan said. "Now, if you'll excuse me."

"I'll kill you," Lucas said, his eyes shifting from fear to aggression. "You lying, worthless excuse of a man."

The smirk fell off Lochlan's face and he straightened his back, turning away from Cassia. "Oh, and you're so perfect. I may have lied to you, but you lied to her," he said, his eyes snapping to hers before focusing on Lucas. "While you manipulate her into staying here so that you can access your full power."

The silence that fell was louder than anything she'd ever heard.

Cassia waited a beat, hoping Lucas would say something. Hoping he'd deny it. "Your full power?" she asked, her heart racing. "What is he talking about?"

"Cass, it's not that simple."

"What's not simple? Is he telling the truth? Did you need me here for your magic?"

Lucas opened his mouth. She knew that look. She knew when he was caught in a lie.

"You've been lying to me this entire time? While I've been thinking you brought me here for Calla?" Cassia shouted, feeling her rage build. "While my sister is dying back in my world?"

The vision of Calla's lifeless body came to mind and Cassia screamed. The scream was born in her lungs and fought its way out of her body. If the king hadn't heard of her arrival, he would know she was there now.

Lucas launched himself at them and Lochlan tightened his grip around her wrist, pulling her apart as the library disappeared.

CHAPTER TWENTY-SEVEN

Lucas

Panic curled in his stomach as his best friend disappeared with one of the most powerful Firsts he knew. Growling loudly as he ran, Lucas bolted through the library, glancing down the aisles in case they were hiding somewhere. But the only noise was what he was making.

"Lochlan!" he yelled with no fear as to whether or not the king would hear him. As long as Lochlan did.

As he skidded across the marble flooring, another doorway caught his eye. The map he'd had of the castle only had one entrance to the library.

"Lochlan!" he called, flinging the door open and racing downstairs. He knew he couldn't trust Lochlan. Everyone knew. Why had he? Why had he let that monster into his home?

He cursed at himself. His power raged within him and he felt that shift in his eyes as they must have turned bright blue. His magic ran through him, buzzing louder than ever before.

He would tear this entire place down if he had to, but he had to find her. He couldn't let the Firsts have her. He'd heard the stories about what they did to Guests. A wave of magic flew out of him as he landed on the floor below. The doors lining the corridor flung open and the chandeliers rattled violently.

Two men clad in maroon and gold with black leather in between ran up to him with their swords drawn. Lucas lifted his head and they froze when their gaze met his and they noticed his blue eyes.

"Ah, a First," one of them said. "Name and village?"

A quick scoff escaped Lucas as he shook his head, forcing his hand forward and throwing them against the wall on the opposite side of the hall. Their bones cracked when they made contact with the wall and tumbled to the floor. He wasn't a First. He would never be.

He felt no mercy as he stepped over their bodies. It wasn't enough to kill a First, but it would take them a long time to recover.

Inhaling deeply, he searched for the scent of firewood and Cassia's original scent, cinnamon. But there was nothing like it. Just the smell of blood. The king's scent of choice.

Lucas ran through the hallway and made his way down another flight of stairs before being faced with four more guards, led by Kain. Before Lucas could react, he was lifted off the ground when Kain raised his hand. "Who are you?" Kain asked.

Lucas struggled in his telekinetic grip, kicking his legs, but it made no difference. He was held firmly, pushed back against the wall behind him. "Where is she?" he bit out.

"Who?" Kain asked, frowning before arching his eyebrows, "Oh, the Guest Lochlan was pressed up against?"

Lucas grunted and felt his knuckles aching as the magic became overwhelming. He was going to kill Lochlan. He was going to kill them all. The buzz in his body roared, flinging out of him once more. Kain was slammed back, taken by surprise. He released his grip on Lucas, who fell to the ground, landing on his hands and knees. Lucas threw his head back and whistled loudly.

Kain scrambled to his feet, unsheathing his sword in one swift motion and swiping it across Lucas's chest. The blade sliced through his skin, sending a splitting pain throughout his body as the blood soaked his clothing. He stumbled backward. Four daggers flew toward him and he swiped his arms in front of him, sending them away. The wound across his chest stung at the movement, but he had to push through. Biting down on his teeth and ignoring the splintering pain, he threw his hands forward, hurling Kain and the guards against the wall. It was his turn to hold them there as his power became deafening.

"Where is she?" he asked again, his voice low as he tried to control his temper. His knuckles ached; his knees screamed. He couldn't let it happen. He couldn't give in. Closing his eyes, he hoped when he opened them, they'd be back to normal.

"I don't know," Kain choked, writhing under Lucas's hold.

"Really, Kain, you are a disappointment."

Lucas spun around to find King Idis staring at him with an eyebrow raised. Their eyes met and the king's mouth parted. "*What* are you?" the king asked, watching Lucas's eyes flashing between blue and black.

A blue-and-orange flame wrapped itself around Lucas's arms. The burning of his flesh broke his focus and he screamed out in pain, dropping his grip on Kain and the guards.

Agony ripped through Lucas's right arm as his skin sizzled under the blazing flame. He fell to the floor. The smell of burning flesh turned his stomach and the pain caused white lights to flicker in his vision.

"Where is Lochlan?" he whimpered as he writhed on the floor. The king approached him on one side and Kain on the other. The space between them was closing fast.

The flame traveled up his arm and across his shoulder. Lucas ground his teeth as the pain, coupled with nausea, threatened his consciousness. He swiped his free hand at King Idis. The king scoffed, his thin lips breaking into a cruel smile. He stood up straight, unmoved by Lucas's attempt.

He tried again, but it was useless. There was nothing else he could do except give in to the magic that built up inside of him.

The air shifted as Ruq raced by them. The gray wolf ran to Lucas at full speed, biting down on his shirt and dragging him through the hall. Lucas grabbed hold of the reins and allowed the wolf to pull him through the royal army that blocked their way. Ruq kept his head low as he barreled through them without slowing down.

Balls of fire flew after them, but Ruq was faster.

"Lochlan! Where are you?" King Idis shouted. "I command you to kill this intruder."

Lucas held on tightly as the pain of his burning flesh numbed his senses. He'd never before used that much magic. If he didn't tie himself to Ruq in the next few seconds, he would lose consciousness and could only hope that Ruq was able to get them home in one piece.

★ ★ ★

The sounds of a wolf howling in distress shook Lucas from his sleep. Brie was at his side as his eyes cracked open, her fingers swiftly untying him. She pulled him off the wolf and threw his heavy arm over her shoulders. He cried out as his sensitive seared flesh landed on her slender shoulders.

"Sorry," she said, struggling under his weight. Ruq bit the back of his shirt once again and lifted him. "Nisa!" she called. "Jun!" She laid him on the floor.

Lucas moaned in pain when his skin touched the cold tiled floor of their foyer. "He took her," he choked out.

"King Idis has Cassia?" Brie asked, leaning over him, her blue eyes wide.

"Lochlan," Lucas said, pushing himself upward using his hands. The pain shot through his arm and shoulder and he collapsed back onto the floor, his head falling into Brie's soft hands before it could hit the tiles. "He took her."

He screamed in pain or anger. He couldn't tell the difference. He needed to get up. He needed to find her. He needed to explain everything to her.

Lochlan would die for this.

"Lucas, please stop moving. Calm down," Brie begged while using her dagger to cut off his shirt. She cursed at the sight of his bleeding chest.

"How can I calm down? He's taken her!" Lucas said. "Kain said he was pressed up against her."

Nisa ran over to them and placed her hands on Lucas. He struggled under her as she forcefully tried soothing him. A low growl escaped him. "Let me go!"

He had to tell Cass the truth.

"It's not working," Nisa said, fear lacing her voice.

Jun stumbled toward them, laying one hand on Lucas and the other on Nisa. They both closed their eyes and Lucas's heart forcefully slowed down. He whimpered as the anger was replaced with heartache. With fear. He stopped writhing as he finally thought about Cass clearly. About Lochlan with her. About how scared she would be. A shudder shook through him. "He's going to hurt her," he said quietly. "He's already hurt her."

The sadness and fear numbed as the Empaths worked on him. "Thank you," he whispered. He felt calmer, but his magic flowed through him wildly, spreading through his chest, his arms, his fingertips, much like the fire had spread, hot and dangerous. It felt as though it would tear through his skin.

"Whoa," Brie said, and Lucas turned to face her. "Your arm, your chest, it's healing...."

Lucas looked down at his arm. The redness of his burned skin was slowly fading.

"How are you doing that?" Nisa asked, lifting her hands from his body.

Lucas shook his head slightly and said as he watched the skin slowly close across his chest, "I don't know."

"Did Cassia share her powers with you?" Nisa asked.

"Sharing magic is extremely complicated and...intimate. I doubt she'd be able to do it," Brie answered. "Besides, Healers heal quicker than this."

"I'm guessing it's got something to do with those," Jun replied, gesturing toward Lucas's eyes. "Firsts heal faster than we do."

"Are they still blue?" Lucas asked.

They all nodded.

Lucas sighed, exhaling slowly, willing his eyes back to their normal color. He pushed himself up and investigated his burned arm. It was still stinging and the skin was inflamed, but he could move. He'd have to deal with the pain until he saw Cass and she could speed up the healing.

He would see her again. This was not how their story ended.

Standing up, he winced in pain and shook off Nisa's and Jun's offers of pain management. "Save your energy," he said. "I need you awake."

Without saying anything else, he made his way downstairs to the dungeon. Jun and Nisa followed him while Brie disappeared somewhere along the way.

"Xo's struggling," Jun said speeding up to match Lucas's pace.

Lucas ignored him and went into the dungeon. He walked straight to where Xo was held and found him curled up on the couch in the fetal position. The warrior who'd so often fought alongside him now looked like an injured child.

"Xo," Lucas whispered, "what else do you remember about my mom? There are some weird coincidences happening and I was hoping…."

Xo uncurled and sat up, his eyes empty. His arms remained wrapped around his abdomen. "Sorry, Lucas, I can't think straight right now. I'm really hungry."

"Xo…."

"Is she going to break the curse?" Xo asked desperately. His grip around himself tightened.

"I'm sure she will…" Lucas said. He wasn't sure, but he had to believe his mother was right. He turned around to face the rest of them. "She had a book in her hand when Lochlan vanished with her."

"What did Lochlan say?" Jun asked, and Brie stepped into the dungeon. She walked up to Lucas with two vials, offering one to him.

"Drink," she said softly. He uncorked the vial and threw the sticky brown liquid into his mouth. It had the familiar berry taste he now associated with pain relief. She uncorked the other vial and emptied its contents onto his burned skin and cool relief spread through him.

"Unfinished business," Lucas said, exhaling as the pain subsided. "He said he had unfinished business with her."

"There's something else," Brie said, rubbing her hands on her clothing and digging into her pocket. She pulled out a large orange-and-red feather, unlike anything he'd ever seen before. "A phoenix feather." She paused. "I found it on my pillow when I woke up."

"What do you mean?" Lucas asked, looking at Jun and Nisa, who both shrugged. "Who put it there?"

"I don't know, but it means I can finish the suppressant tonic," she said. "As much as it unsettles me that someone was in my bedroom while I was asleep."

"None of you heard anything?" Lucas asked.

"Not a sound," Jun said. "Did Lochlan say anything else?"

Lucas clamped down on his teeth at the memory. "He told her about our bond, and her connection to my powers," he said. "He told her I'd been lying to her."

"You weren't technically lying...." Brie said.

"Between Cass and me, it was a lie and I knew it." Lucas stood up. "I'm going to go and find them." He walked toward the doorway. Brie grabbed his wrist, pulling him back inside.

"Right now?" she asked. "You can barely control your eye color. I bet you could do more damage to yourself than to anyone else in this state."

"I don't care," Lucas snapped. "What am I supposed to do? Just let him have her? You know what they're going to do to her. What they may have already done."

Brie paled and her body trembled.

"Exactly. Let me go," Lucas said as he walked out of the dungeon. Brie followed.

"We were kind of hoping that she'd stay and help you control your powers, Lucas. Since she's been here you haven't had any bad episodes," Brie said.

"I should have told her the truth," Lucas replied. "And I'd rather lose myself than be the reason she doesn't get back to her family."

"Let me come with you," Nisa offered. "I could keep your emotions in check and it should make it easier for you to control your powers. It also means Jun and I can keep the lines of communication open in case she escapes the royal guards or Lochlan and comes back here."

Lucas froze and closed his eyes as he remembered his fight against the guards. So much had happened in the last few hours, turning his life upside down.

"The royal guards, Kain and, uh, the king have all seen my eyes," he said.

"What exactly happened?" Jun asked.

"They may have seen it while I tried to kill them."

"Dammit, Lucas," Brie said. "That means they're coming here. Kain knows who you are. We need to go. We all need to go. We can't hold our own if the king and his army come knocking at our door. Especially if you're not here."

"What if Cass comes back and we're not here?" Lucas asked. He knew Brie was right. He knew he had to protect his friends, *but what about Cass?*

"I am sorry, Lucas, but we don't have time to hesitate. Some of them can teleport. They could be here any second. Grab what you need and let's meet outside. I'll gather the wolves," Brie announced.

"Wait," Nisa said. "There's five of us and only two wolves."

"Leave me behind."

They all turned to face Xo.

Xo uncrossed his arms and scratched his chest viciously. The black pants he wore were torn in areas where he'd been scratching himself. "If you open this cage, I'll bite one of you, or all of you. I don't even think I'd turn you. I'd just eat you until there was nothing left."

CHAPTER TWENTY-EIGHT

Cassia's world spun and her limbs felt as though they were being pulled from the sockets before she landed, tumbling on the ground. She opened her eyes and stared up at Lochlan in front of her. He stretched out a hand to help her up but she frowned at him, swatted his hand away and stood up by herself. "Take me back," she demanded, dusting herself off.

"No can do, little lady. I need you to tell me what you saw," he replied in his signature stance, arms crossed, eyebrow raised. All that was missing was the smirk.

"I want to go home," she said and wrapped her fingers around the feather necklace. She didn't care about any of this anymore. She needed to get home to Calla. To help her mother. To be there. She'd already lost the chance of getting the phoenix feather and even if she did, there wasn't much time left.

But there was one thought that shouted louder than all her other thoughts.

Has Lucas been lying to me the entire time?

Much as she tried denying it, she knew he had been lying. Her chest tightened.

The thin silver chain was cool in her palm. She tugged at it, but she was stopped when a hot hand gently gripped her wrist as Lochlan appeared in front of her. She hated that he could teleport.

"Please," he whispered. His tone, soft and unfamiliar, sent a flutter through her body. She pushed it down. It made no sense.

"Where are we?" she asked, looking around at the unfamiliar surroundings. The grass was patchy and overgrown in some places. Birds and bugs chirped and the usually blue sky was covered in gray clouds. A cold breeze whipped by her, sending a shiver through her body.

"What did you see?" he asked, his hand still wrapped around her wrist.

"I won't help you."

"Tell me what you saw."

Cassia grunted in frustration, dropping her hands to her sides and shaking him off. "What is it to you? Who is this woman?"

"That is none of your concern," Lochlan replied, looking up at the sky. He inhaled deeply and crossed his arms again.

"Then I won't tell you anything. For all I know, I'd be leading you to your next victim," she snapped. She turned around and started walking. She'd find her way back to Thistle even if it took her a few days. Or she would simply pull off the necklace and leave all of this behind. It was something she was considering more and more.

"Come back here," he growled. "Or I'll simply come and get you."

"No," she spat, turning around to face him. His jaw was set as he frowned at her. Her blood boiled. "I hate it here. I hate all of you. You are power-hungry, selfish men and all I wanted was to save my sister!" She shouted the last word and the frown fell off his face.

"You will. The suppressant tonic will work. We've used it before, many years ago and well, thanks to me, they have the final ingredient." He inhaled deeply, took his crown off his head and tossed it aside. It bounced lightly as it landed on the grass. "Help me and I'll get you back to that tonic and after that, back home."

"I have no reason to trust you."

He raked his hands through his wild curls, trying to tame them. "You have my word," he said softly. "And you don't have many other options. Now, tell me. What did you see?"

"What do you want with this woman?" she asked, spotting the black leather-bound book on the grass. She walked over to pick it up and hugged it to her chest.

"I'm trying to save her," Lochlan called out, exasperated. "And you're making it very difficult."

"From who?" she asked, turning and walking farther away from him. She spun around. She couldn't see any landmarks; no buildings, no rivers in the distance, no mountains. She couldn't even see the tall golden walls of the castle.

"From my father."

"Why does your father want to kill her?" she shouted back.

"She's my mother."

Cassia stilled. Her breath caught as she searched for a response. "What do you mean?" She turned to face him. "Lucas said the previous queen disappeared."

"She did," he said. A deep frown spread across his face and he ran his hands over his eyes. "But she's here...I can sense her. I just can't find her. That's why I needed you, a Visionary."

"Is that why you brought me here? For your own uses? You didn't want to help Lucas." Cassia huffed. "Selfish. The whole lot of you."

Lochlan shrugged. "Perhaps, but it doesn't change the fact that you're able to help him anyway...and Calla."

"Keep her name out of your filthy mouth," she snapped, turning away from him and continuing her journey. Destination: as far away from him as possible.

Lochlan appeared in front of her and she nearly walked into his chest. "It wasn't that filthy when you kissed me."

"*You* kissed *me*," she bit out and the corner of his mouth kicked up. "Maybe she doesn't want to be found," she said and his blue eyes flashed with anger, or pain; she couldn't tell and she didn't care.

"Regardless, I need to warn her that I'm not the only one who knows she's alive and in Selene. My father has his suspicions and if he's proven right, her life will be in danger." Lochlan grabbed the book she was still clutching and pulled it out of her grip effortlessly. "Have you memorized the spell you need?"

"What?" she asked.

"Have you memorized it? Properly? The way Visionaries are able to memorize things?"

"Uhh, I guess."

"That'll have to do then," he replied and flung the book into the air before shooting a ball of blue fire at it. The book was engulfed by flames and its ashes blew away gently with the breeze as if it never existed.

"What the hell?" she gasped. "What if we needed that?" He was insane. Absolutely insane. There was no other explanation.

"You said you memorized it."

"Yes, but what about the other spells?" she asked.

Lochlan narrowed his eyes. "Personally, I think we're better off without the book that cursed our realm with monsters."

Cassia pursed her lips.

"Books of magic are too easily traced," he continued. "Especially one that is important to my father."

"Does this count as the favor I owe you?" she asked, craning her neck to look up at him and crossing her arms.

"Your audacity amazes me every time." The smirk returned. "This is already paid for. You get your life. Your friends get their lives. Your little sister gets her life. Is that enough motivation?"

Infuriating.

"Fine," she said, revisiting the vision. "I saw…uhm, I don't know. I don't know this place. I have been to, like, three parts of it and well, it wasn't one of those three."

"Hold that thought."

Lochlan grabbed her shoulders and closed his eyes. Once again, she felt her limbs stretch as the air was sucked out of her.

Her body was thrown onto the grass and she landed on her hands and knees. Her stomach turned as it realized it belonged to her.

"Takes a bit of getting used to," Lochlan said and stretched out his hand again.

"You could warn me, asshole," she said, digging her hands into the soft grass.

"I suspected that the book was already being traced. We needed to move."

"Oh and saying, 'Hey Cassia, I'm gonna pull your body apart and put it back together in a different location' was going to take too much time?"

"Precisely."

Cassia huffed and stood up, ignoring his offered hand. She rubbed her hands together to soothe the sting from the fall.

They were surrounded by thin trees that stretched so far into the sky it seemed as though a strong wind would topple them. The branches and leaves at the top of the trees merged into each other, creating a cool, sheltered environment.

"Could you see the ground in your vision? Grassy? Sandy? Soily? Was it indoors?" he asked urgently.

She replayed the memory in her mind, noting as much detail as possible. "Outside. It was grassy, but not grass like this. It had fallen leaves and pine needles. It was crunching underneath her weight. That's why she transformed into a cat, I guess."

Lochlan nodded thoughtfully. "And the rabbit?"

"A gray rabbit. It was about the same size as she was in her cat form," she explained. "Big, floppy ears, little fluffy tail. Looked like a rabbit, or have you never seen one?"

Ignoring the sarcasm in her voice, he chewed on his bottom lip. One of his dimples came out. "Did you hear any birds?"

"Same as here, just chirping." Cassia gestured to the trees around her as a melody of chirping echoed through the forest.

He sucked his teeth and cursed. "Did you see anything useful?"

"There was a mountain in the background, very far in the background."

"Here's your warning," he said before grabbing her shoulders and teleporting.

Cassia tumbled to the sandy ground and pushed herself upright, but doubled over as her stomach projected its insides out.

Lochlan pulled up his nose. "Sorry about that."

"Get away," she cried in between retching.

"That's a lot of vomit for such a small person."

"You're the worst," she bit out. She inhaled deeply and tried to control the violent and involuntary lurches happening inside her.

Lochlan vanished and reappeared, holding a large thick green leaf. "Drink this, it will settle your stomach." He tore it open and a green jellylike substance oozed out.

Cassia shook her head and the movement made her bend over and gag.

"Drink it," he ordered. "It'll also freshen your breath. No one likes vomit breath."

"I hate you."

"You and everyone else," he said, shoving the plant in her direction. She grabbed the leaf. It scraped against her fingertips as she licked the sticky green juice. Surprisingly, it was deliciously refreshing, a combination of mint, lemon and something else.

Lochlan pointed into the distance. "That mountain?"

The mountain he was pointing at looked a lot like the one in her vision, but something was different. "I think it could be, but maybe from that side," she said, pointing to her right and then wiping her mouth with her sleeve as she handed the empty leaf back to him. "Can I have another?"

He received it with a raised eyebrow. "So thirsty."

She made a vulgar gesture and he laughed, then vanished and reappeared with another. He waited while she finished it and then held out his hand, palm up. "My lady?"

Moaning dramatically, she took it and noticed his mouth twist into a smile before he teleported.

At her sudden landing, her legs wobbled and she stumbled, preparing herself for the ground, but Lochlan pulled on their joined hands and stabilized her.

She looked up to see the mountain. "It wasn't this angle either. I think it was more over there." She pointed eastward and Lochlan sighed.

He stuck out his hand. "Come on then."

They traveled through more than eight places before she recognized the outline of the mountain. Another two trips after that eventually perfected the angle.

Cassia exhaled loudly as they landed again. "I want to go home, Lochlan. I don't want to do this anymore.... My sister is dying. She might already be dead. I need to get home." Her voice cracked and Lochlan stared at the ground quietly.

"She's alive. I checked on her before stealing the feather from my father's bedchambers, which is where he keeps that massive fire bird, in case you were wondering how unreasonable he is."

Cassia looked up and locked eyes with him. His blue eyes were clear and bright, reminding her of the way the ocean sparkled on a summer's day. Still, he could be lying.

"Did you really get the phoenix feather?"

"Only one way to find out, isn't there?" he said with raised eyebrows, and then gestured around him. "So, is this it?"

"This is it...kind of," she said and watched as Lochlan's tense shoulders relaxed slightly. His breathing was becoming heavy. "But it's not here. I think we need to go closer."

"Closer? You said the mountain was in the far distance."

"Not this far," she said.

"Can't you summon another vision of her?" he asked, leaning against a tree and closing his eyes.

"It doesn't work that way. It comes spontaneously or from stress, or actually I have no idea, I'm still trying to figure all of this ou—" She stopped mid-word as Lochlan appeared in front of her, cupping her face in his hands.

"A kiss worked last time," he said, leaning downward.

"Nice try," she snapped, pushing him back.

"Thought it might stress you out enough. It was either that or hitting you."

"I'd have taken the punch," she said.

Lochlan's lips curled in response.

"Maybe halfway between here and the mountain. Plus the ground here is all wrong. It had pine needles, remember...? The trees were taller and thicker too and they were obviously pine trees, unless you have another weird magic tree that drops similar needles."

Lochlan hung his head. "All right. Let's go."

"We could walk, I guess," she said. When they'd touched earlier, her magic reached out to him and she sensed his life force was low, but she could not heal exhaustion.

"Just for a little while," he replied, resting his eyes.

"What was her name?"

"Maeve."

"It's a cool name," she said as they walked.

"It means warrior," he answered quietly, "And she was one…. Or *is*, I suppose." He smiled to himself.

It was weird imagining Lochlan as a child. Cassia hazarded a glance at him. His chin was held high, his shoulders squared. He was ready for a fight even though it was only the two of them out here.

Judging from the quality of his cloak and the smoothness of his fingers, she would bet he'd never worked a hard day in his life. The golden palace came to mind and she wondered what he did there all day, while the Reborns worked day and night, producing and creating for the Firsts. Everything was for the Firsts. Including their children.

They walked slowly, the sun beating down on them. Each of them was trapped in their own thoughts. She wanted to save Xo, she wanted to save Calla and as much as she didn't want to think about it, she wanted to confront Lucas.

It made sense. Why else would he be so desperate to get her here that he'd send Lochlan to fetch her and unwillingly pull her into another realm?

But it was Lucas. He wouldn't do that. Would he?

"How long has she been gone?" Cassia asked Lochlan, needing the distraction.

"Longer than you've been alive."

Lochlan kept his head down as he walked.

"What? How old are you?" she asked, her eyes wide in shock. She'd estimated him to be in his late twenties, only a few years older than she was.

"You know we're immortal, right?" he said and glanced up for a moment, stumbling over a small rock. He cursed. "I hate walking. Tedious thing it is."

"Do you teleport everywhere?" she asked as she sidestepped a stone. The terrain changed. Less grass, more stones, no pine needles.

"Do you always ask this many questions?" he replied.

Lucas obviously hadn't warned him.

"I'm just trying to pass the time," she said, looking at him and catching him looking directly at her. Her stomach somersaulted as the kiss replayed in her mind. She could even taste the vanilla from memory.

He must have read her expression, because he bit down on his bottom lip and said playfully, "I can think of many other ways to do that."

CHAPTER TWENTY-NINE

Lochlan paused alongside a tall tree and looked up. He grabbed on to it with both hands and lifted himself. The material on his black tunic tightened around his arms as he pulled upward and climbed the tree. His long limbs made it look easy in just a few swift movements.

He climbed up to the top and the lower branches blocked Cassia's view. She dropped her head and looked down, rubbing the back of her neck. Looking up at trees, Lucas, and now Lochlan was doing a number on her neck.

"Incoming!" he called from above and a moment later he landed in front of her, bending his knees as he reached the ground. The sand beside his feet swirled around him. He straightened his back and opened his hands. In each one, he was holding a red fruit about the size of her fist.

"It tastes similar to a date. Smooth and sweet, but tough…much like yourself." He paused to deliver one of his smirks. "It should stop that terrible noise coming from your stomach."

Cassia flushed and grabbed the fruit. Usually she would question anything and everything, but her stomach was about ready to start eating her intestines, so this fruit would have to do. She bit into it. The flesh was stringy and indeed tough, but it was delicious. Each mouthful melted on her tongue and tickled her stomach as it filled what felt like a gaping hole. "Why'd you only get two?" she complained as she nibbled the last bits of it off the hard pit.

Lochlan offered her what was left of his. "Here, eat it. I'm not hungry."

"How can you not be hungry?" she asked, tossing the sticky pit to the foot of the tree.

Lochlan tore off a generous piece of his own fruit and held it out to her. "Eat this. You're a Guest. I know your kind is willing to eat just about anything and everything. I'll climb up and get myself another."

Her stomach growled loudly. "Are you sure?"

He nodded.

She took the piece and ate it quickly, guilt replacing the feeling of hunger.

"The hungrier you got, the less you spoke and I was beginning to miss the insults you threw at me."

"Piss off," she said, licking the last of the flavor from her lips.

"Aha, there she is," he said, walking ahead of her.

"What about your fruit?" she asked.

"Oh, I lied. Those were the last two up there. The tippils must not have seen them. Nasty little things. They're all teeth and claws," he said. He shook his head in distaste and kept walking. "Come on then, since walking seems to take forever."

Something softened inside her knowing he'd given her his share but she reminded herself that he hadn't done it for her. He needed her to help him. She was a tool, a stepping-stone to get to what he wanted. Just like she was for Lucas. The only people who weren't trying to use her were the ones she'd left behind in another realm.

The trees started getting even taller, the bark thicker, and there were leaves scattered across the grass. "We're getting closer, I think," Cassia said and Lochlan gave her a slight nod. She expected him to look relieved or excited, but instead a look of concern stretched across his face. "Anything I need to know before meeting your mom? What's she like? I mean, considering she raised you, I'm expecting the worst."

His pursed lips relaxed as he spoke. "She's smart, funny and tough. You'll like her and I'll bet she'll like you."

Cassia felt her pulse quicken. She would be meeting a queen. A First queen.

"That man who cornered us in the library, when you, you know...." She paused as her cheeks flushed. "You're brothers, right? How come he isn't out here helping you?"

"Half brother, full pain in the arse," he grunted. "His mother took the throne and brought him in with her before the scent of my mother even left the place. He would probably kill her if he could. Not that I'd let that happen."

The sky darkened and Cassia looked up to see if any stars would bless them, and they did. The night was still and the air cold, but the stars were beautiful. Something tugged at her heart, pulling her toward Lucas, toward her best friend, the one she often stargazed alongside. The one person she could always trust. And yet, he didn't deny it. He didn't deny what Lochlan accused him of.

"You'll see him soon enough," Lochlan said, drawing her gaze toward him. He rolled his eyes.

"Are you telepathic too?"

He scoffed and walked ahead of her. "No, but it's fairly obvious when you're thinking about that big donkey."

That was it. She'd had enough of his handsome face and petty remarks. Unsheathing the copper dagger, she drew it back and aimed for his right ear. "You're such an asshole," she bit out, drawing his attention before throwing the dagger.

Lochlan spun around and rapidly moved his head to the left. His eyes widened. "You could have taken off my ear, you unhinged woman."

"Oh, please, it's not like you use them to listen to anybody," she snapped and he burst out laughing. His dimples crept out and for a moment, she felt herself relax too.

"You would never have got me anyway," he said with a wink.

"My pen says otherwise," she replied, raising her eyebrow.

"That was a lucky shot," he said. He opened his palm and summoned her dagger.

Cassia grinned at the memory as she caught up to him and held out her hand. He placed the dagger in her palm and said, "JW. Let me guess, Joseph Williams, Lucas's father. How romantic of him to give it to you."

"This belonged to his dad?"

"Mm-mm, I suppose," Lochlan said, turning on his heel and walking away. "You can add it to the long list of things he hasn't told you," he called back.

After staring down at the dagger, she ran ahead, catching up to him, only to have him throw an arm out in front of her. "Stay back," he warned, stopping suddenly.

She stopped and looked at him, following his eyeline. But there was nothing there. The forest looked the same in every direction.

Lochlan slid his hand behind her and guided her to their left. His eyes darted back to the same area where she saw nothing. "Someone's left an open portal," he said, his eyebrows furrowed.

"To my side?" she asked, matching his hushed tone. He shook his head. "To where? Another side? Like a third side? The *other* other side?"

Lochlan smiled for a second and then clenched his jaw and nodded. "I think so. There are multiple 'sides'," he said, lifting his fingers to make air quotes. "We call them realms, as I'm sure you know by now. This is the Selene Realm. Yours we call the Talm Realm, but this portal, it seems to be from the Vineas Realm." He kept guiding her away from the invisible portal.

"You seem concerned," she said and became aware of the heat radiating from his hand on her lower back.

"We have wards preventing portals from being opened into our realm," he explained. "It would be unusual for a Vineasian to be able to open this. It would be even more unusual if someone from Selene opened it against my father's wishes." He lifted his cloak and pointed at the symbol, counting the stars as he spoke. "One star for each realm; Selene, Talm, Vineas, Ilios, Eridanus and Vela."

"Have you been to all of them?"

"Briefly visited Vineas, Vela and of course, Talm, but as far as I know, the links between Eridanus and Ilios have been lost." He looked back to where the portal was. "This should be far enough. Wait here and don't move."

Lochlan vanished and reappeared where they had initially stood.

He stretched his arms out in front of him and tapped the air while muttering something, but he was too far away for her to hear it.

The air cracked and a blue-and-white ring appeared, reminding her of the portal they used to access the palace. Her body was tugged at the edges and her clothing pulled toward him. Everything around Lochlan and the portal disappeared, leaving behind only barren land. The trees, the birds, even the fallen leaves on the grass were sucked into the portal. Everything except Lochlan, who dropped to his hands and knees, his back rising and falling as he struggled to catch his breath.

Cassia ran toward him but he stood up slowly, raising a hand for her to stop. "I'm fine."

"You don't look fine."

"It's more energy than I've used in a very long time," he said, standing up. "I'll be fine." He dusted off his hands and knees. "However, your concern is rather touching."

"You're my ride back to Lucas, so don't flatter yourself," she said and glanced at him. As they continued their journey, she was afraid he would collapse at any moment. "If you faint, I can't carry you. You seem heavy and I will leave you behind," she said after a while.

"Fair warning, thanks," he replied, seemingly uninterested in making a witty remark, which she'd become accustomed to. His eyes darted to their right, darkening in color, as he lifted his hand to his lips.

A loud shriek startled her as a Rahlog jumped through the trees, launching himself at her. He was only a bit taller than her, but a lot heavier. His eyes immediately reminded her of Jean; they were filled with the same look. *Hunger.* Cassia unsheathed her dagger but before the Rahlog reached her, a bright blue shield of fire appeared between her and the monster. She stumbled back, away from the flame and landed on her backside. The screams of the Rahlog heightened in pitch as he ran through the fire, setting himself alight. But it didn't stop him.

Lochlan reached out and grabbed her arm, pulling her to her feet. "Run," he said clearly, his shoulders squared. The barrier disappeared and Cassia raised her dagger.

"Go, now," he said weakly. He looked like he was about to fall over.

And then he did.

The monster would likely take long enough to devour Lochlan for her to get away, to find her way back to Lucas. Taking advantage of the moment, she ran, putting as much distance between her and the flesh-hungry being as she could.

But she couldn't just leave him. Spinning around, she saw that the burned Rahlog had reached Lochlan. It grabbed his face and lifted him up.

The Rahlog's teeth neared Lochlan's neck. Her fingers tightened around the dagger she still held firmly in her palm. She took the risk and threw her dagger. If she missed, she'd be defenseless when he attacked her. But she had to try. The dagger flipped through the air and landed in the Rahlog's back. He turned around and looked at her before screaming and choosing her as his next target.

He was in transition. Which meant there was a chance she could save him.

Her mind flitted through the spell she had memorized. She recited the words clearly and loudly. She recited it again as the Rahlog ran toward her, his teeth bared and his long nails pointed directly at her. By the third recitation, her entire body locked in pain but the Rahlog kept running toward her, jumping to cover the last of the distance between them.

Her head slammed against the grass when he landed on top of her and she saw white. The sour stench of his breath covered her senses as he chattered his teeth near her face. Shoving her hands against his neck, she attempted to push him away and he screamed, close enough and loud enough to shatter her eardrum. A lightning bolt of pain traveled through the right side of her head. Her hands reached up to her ears, but the Rahlog leaned in and she returned her hands to his neck and face. He clamped his teeth trying to get a bite of something, of anything, trying to bite her hands where she held him. Her hand slid over his face and his head dipped low, his mouth opening to scream or bite; she couldn't tell and it didn't matter.

She saw her dagger sticking out of his back and slipped one of her hands down his neck. Her other hand was still struggling to keep the Rahlog away from her face. Her right hand gripped the knife and yanked it out. With one swift move she shoved it into the Rahlog's head. The man's blood leaked onto her neck as she lay there, regaining her breath and gagging.

The putrid smell from the Rahlog motivated her to move. After kicking off his lifeless body, she crawled over to Lochlan, touching her ear and feeling her magic buzz as the pain subsided.

Lochlan was slumped on the floor where he'd collapsed. Gently, she touched the scratch along his jaw. It had already started healing, but she sped up the process. Fresh, shiny scars appeared. Standing up, she grabbed his arms and pulled. He barely moved; he was far too heavy and she was tired.

The sky darkened further and the cold breeze turned icy. They'd need a fire to survive the night. She'd need to start it. But her body resisted movement as her eyelids grew heavy. "Lochlan," she said. "Please wake up." He remained still. Had it not been for his beating heart, she would have thought he was dead. "Lochlan," she said again, using the last of her energy as her mind swirled. She couldn't fall asleep, not here, not exposed. There were too many threats. "Please," she said as darkness covered her vision. "Please."

"I do enjoy hearing you beg."

Jerking awake, she opened her eyes to find a pair of blue eyes staring back at her. He looked around, his eyes lingering on the dead Rahlog, and then back at her, a smile playing on his lips. "Fiery little lady," he said and pulled her close, wrapping an arm around her. She was too weak to fight it, unsure if she wanted to. Her bones were heavy and cold and his body was hot, as if there were a flame burning inside of him. Curling against him, she gave up on fighting sleep and heard him whisper, "Thanks for not leaving me behind."

CHAPTER THIRTY

Cassia woke up to the steady sound of Lochlan's beating heart. It beat slower than any heart she had ever monitored. It was even slower than her patients' heartbeats when they were asleep. Slowly, she became aware of the gentle bobbing movement of being carried.

Heat radiated from where he held her, one arm under her shoulders and the other curled under her knees. As the sleep lifted, she moved her head away from his warm chest, feeling the fuzziness clear. She kicked her legs free and he slipped his left arm from underneath her. Her feet dropped to the ground and she wobbled slightly, but still shoved him away.

"Good, you're awake. I was getting bored," he said, as if they hadn't been fighting for their lives a moment ago.

She dizzily searched for her voice. Her mouth was dry and cracked. She threw him a vulgar gesture in the meantime.

He dragged his teeth over his bottom lip and said, "You are terrible at being grateful."

"I saved *you*," she croaked, then swallowed hard. Her saliva stung her throat.

"Ah, now you're aware of the actions you take."

"You could have woken me," she said, ignoring his comment and steadying herself. Looking around, she took in her surroundings. It was still completely dark; she must have only been out for a couple of hours.

"Oh, I tried. You sleep like the dead," he said. "We should get a move on."

She huffed in response. "I don't want you to touch me."

"I have never had a woman say that to me before." He grinned and continued walking. "We're running out of time," he said, turning back to point at her. "You lost another feather."

Her hand shot up to her chest and she dragged her fingers across each feather, counting them. The soft feathers tickled her fingertips. One, two, three feathers left. Which technically meant she only had time to see two more feathers fall. By the time there was only one feather left, she needed to get back to Xo and figure out how to use this spell. It hadn't worked on the Rahlog they had encountered and she was sure she had repeated the spell word for word.

More than anything, she needed to get the suppressant tonic for Calla. Glancing over at Lochlan, she wondered whether he was telling the truth, whether he'd really given them the feather. The final ingredient. Something stirred inside her as she watched him walking. Perhaps he wasn't *that* bad. Perhaps he was telling the truth. *Or not*, she thought as he turned around to frown at her, gesturing for her to walk faster. Even though she was in a hurry, she purposely slowed her pace and enjoyed the frustration that crept onto his cheeks.

Gazing up at the dark sky, she thought of Lucas's dark eyes and part of her wanted to go home without seeing him to avoid the fight entirely, but she knew that this time he couldn't come and find her. He wouldn't be able to stand outside her window and beg her to open up. He would not be able to send his mother over to apologize. He would be gone. Again.

How was she supposed to say goodbye to him again? And this time she'd have to do it willingly.

"And?" Lochlan asked, his lips pursed. "Are we getting any closer? Does any of this look familiar?"

"I don't have night vision," she said in a tone snappier than she intended, immediately regretting it.

"As much as I enjoy your quick little remarks, we don't have much time left," he replied in a hushed whisper. "We're about the distance from the mountain that you said we should be, correct?"

"I still can't see, Lochlan. I am not trying to be a bitch. I literally can't see in the dark."

He took a few steps away from her and she heard something snap before seeing his face illuminated in blue light bouncing off a flame he created in his palm. The fresh scars on his face were larger than she'd initially thought, stretching across the left side of his jaw, starting just underneath his ear, down the edge of his chin and ending on his neck. Two long gashes, just a finger's width apart.

Lighting up the broken-off branch, he handed it to her silently. The fire's bright blue flame burned her eyes and they watered as she furiously blinked back tears and held the branch farther away from her toward the ground.

Pine needles.

Lifting the flame, she saw that the trees looked the same too. Half of them seemed evergreen and the other half were scraggly and cold. Much like she was. A chill ran down her spine at the thought as she looked back at Lochlan, knowing heat was radiating from his strong body.

Turning toward where the mountain should be, she couldn't see anything, not the mountain, not a silhouette. Just darkness extending into more darkness. Slowly, she walked around the area, bringing the flame torch up to the objects surrounding them. Lochlan stood back, observing her silently.

She moved the fire across a large rock and recalled her vision. "It was this rock that I saw your cat-mom jump on."

Lochlan nodded and looked around, chewing on his lip. She'd expected him to make a stupid or flirtatious comment, but he remained quiet. She preferred the stupid and flirtatious comments to the unusual silence.

"Lochlan," she started, "what if she's left? How would we even find her?"

"I don't know," he said. "I don't know." Casting her light on him, she watched him slump down against the tree and rest his head in his hands. "I thought perhaps if I got close enough, she would sense me or I would sense her. I don't know, all right." He stood up and straightened his back. "I didn't think this through. I'll take you back to your friends. I'll bet Lucas wants to kill me."

"He is absolutely going to kill you," she said, sitting down on the rock. "And then, I'm going to kill him." She dragged her fingers across the smooth rock and her mind buzzed. Her hearing deafened as another vision entered her mind. She saw the previously pristine white cat, now covered in splotches of dark red blood, dragging the lifeless rabbit away from the rock toward a large tree. A lattice of tree branches stretched above, covered in leaves, creating a green canopy. The white cat ran straight under the leaves, disappearing from her vision as the shade of the tree blocked her view.

The air rushed back into her lungs and she accidentally dropped the torch to the ground. Bending over, she snatched up the branch, which was still alight. The flame spread to the ground and she stomped on the fire in a panic. Deforestation was not on her list of goals to achieve. It would not go out. "Some help, please?" she said to Lochlan and he looked up, having not noticed any of it. His eyes barely widened as he flicked his wrist, extinguishing the flame.

"I think she might be under that tree," she said, pointing in the direction where she expected it to be. "It's somewhere there. A big, droopy tree with like fifty trunks. You can't miss it."

"I see it," he whispered. "Banyan tree."

He had night vision. Neat.

They edged closer to the tree and he stopped suddenly. "Maybe this is a bad idea. If she wanted to be found, she would have been found. You were right. I should not have come looking for her." He shook his head quickly and spun around. "She's not a damsel-in-distress type anyway. She was almost as powerful as my father. It's part of why he fears her."

"You're telling me I'm about to be faced with the most powerful First I have ever met?"

He extended his hand to her. "Let me take you back. I apologize for wasting your time."

She reached out for his hand, but something about the softness of his voice stopped her. She pulled back and locked eyes with him. "As much as I enjoy being told that I'm right, I think you were right too. If someone wants to kill her, she should know. I think that's why I'm getting visions of her.... I can't ignore them if I know where she is." She turned around to face the tree again. "What if we can save her?"

She heard Lochlan exhale slowly, but he wasn't moving. She lifted her torch to look at him. His jaw was tightly clenched in a way that, had she not been able to sense his physical well being, would have made her think he was in immense pain. Casting her magic over him, she found that he was physically fine, just exhausted, more so than she was.

"Do you want me to go by myself?" she asked. "I could warn her about your father. She won't even have to know you were here...if you don't want her to know."

"What if it's a trap? I have to come with you."

"I can take care of myself," Cassia said. This somehow elicited a small smile from him.

"I know that about you," he said.

"Does she hate Reborns? Like the other Firsts?" Cassia asked as he walked up to her and stood beside her.

"No," he said without hesitation. "Quite the opposite. She fought for their rights, much to my father's dismay.... Unlike his new queen." The leaves crunched loudly as he started moving. He cursed under his breath. "Stupid walking."

He wrapped his fingers around her arm as they reached the tree and she held the torch in front of her. The bark dropped from branches, creating a maze of trunks leading up to one wide trunk, and in the center of the base, there was a hole too small for either of them to fit into. Cat-sized. Leaning downward, Cassia peered into the hole and found a pair of blue eyes looking directly at her.

"Cassia," the cat hissed.

Throwing herself backward at the sound, she dropped the torch. As she landed on her backside, the cat crept out of the hole and transformed into a woman, who stood in the shadows. The leaves crunched again as Lochlan shifted on his feet.

"Cassia? Lucas?" the woman asked in a voice far too familiar to Cassia.

Lochlan scoffed, stepping forward. "I am afraid, Mother, much to your disappointment, it's your other son. The one you abandoned."

CHAPTER THIRTY-ONE

Other son?

Other *son?*

No. It couldn't be.

Staring in the darkness, Cassia looked at where she assumed Lochlan and Aunty Rosheen were standing. She grabbed the torch and held it up in front of her as Aunty Rosheen stepped into the light. It was really her.

"Loch," she breathed, stepping forward. The blue fire lit up her face and the resemblance was undeniable. Aside from Aunty Rosheen's blond hair, Lochlan looked exactly like her. "What are you doing here? Did you give Cassia the book? Where is my Lucas?"

Lochlan's face twisted for a moment before relaxing into a cool, polished expression. "You're not going to take one minute to at least pretend to be happy to see me?" The leaves crunched as he turned around. "After all these years," he said to himself. The fury lacing his voice made her shudder.

"Lochlan," Rosheen sighed, her tone softer. The sound of the leaves crunching stopped underneath Lochlan's weight. Cassia stood frozen, holding the torch and watching as Rosheen, his *mother,* Lucas's mother, walked up to Lochlan and cupped his face. He leaned his head down and rested his forehead on hers. "I simply wasn't expecting you. I only saw Cassia in my vision and where there's a Cass, there's usually a Luke." She glanced over at Cassia, smiling softly.

"Mother," Lochlan breathed. "I knew you were alive. I knew you were back. Even before Cassia saw you in her vision." His voice caught. "Because he couldn't command me anymore."

"Does he know that I'm here?" she asked. The softness that filled her voice had vanished.

"I don't know. He suspected it and I came here to warn you. Although, I imagine by now he must have called for me and when I didn't show up, he either knows you're here or assumes I'm dead.... I do hope it's the latter."

She cursed loudly and looked at Cassia. "Oh Cass, I'm sorry that we're reuniting under these circumstances. But I have to ask, did you manage to get the book?"

"Uhm, sort of." Cassia hesitated, glancing toward Lochlan. He shifted on his feet. "I memorized the spell."

"Great, that's good enough. I couldn't get it myself. He would have sensed me immediately, even with my new scent." She pulled Cassia in for a tight hug and the smell of the ocean filled Cassia's senses. "Look at you, you're beautiful."

Cassia melted into her arms as if being hugged by her own mother. "Thank you, Aunty Ro."

"Aunty Ro?" Lochlan scoffed.

"I go by Rosheen now," she said, releasing Cassia and turning to Lochlan. "Take us to Lucas."

Lochlan's blue eyes flashed. "That's it, then? No explanation? No apology?"

"We don't have time."

"You just left me," Lochlan said, his voice raspy, scraping on Cassia's skin, instead of the cool, smooth voice she'd become accustomed to.

"I did what I needed to do, Lochlan," Rosheen answered calmly. "You know what your father used to do to me."

Lochlan swallowed, squaring his shoulders before saying in a worryingly calm voice, "Who do you think he did it to after you left?"

Cassia stood quietly, observing this warrior unravel while Aunty Rosheen, the same woman who fetched her from school and iced cupcakes with her, stood her ground against him. Rosheen looked down for a moment, her eyes clear and cool, and said, "We don't have time for this. Lochlan, I—"

"Don't you dare, Mother," he interrupted her. "I need to rest, just for a moment."

Rosheen bit her lip. "I'm sorry, Loch, I am." Lochlan dropped his head. "But I command that you take us to my manor."

Lochlan's entire body stiffened. He reached out both of his arms, touching Cassia on the shoulder and his mother on her elbow, without saying anything.

Cassia felt the familiar sensation of being disconnected from her body as they teleported away.

★ ★ ★

A sharp bolt of pain traveled up her right arm as she collided with a rock upon landing. Grabbing her right shoulder with her left hand, she howled in pain and Aunty Rosheen, who landed on her feet, reached out to touch her shoulder. With a slight tickle and buzz, the pain disappeared. Cassia stood up and rotated her shoulder freely.

"Thank you," she whispered as Min-Jun's words echoed through her memory. *First one since the previous queen.*

"Come on," Rosheen said as she walked up to the front door. Before she reached it, the door swung open gracefully. She turned around, held out a hand and whispered, "Wait here," before transforming into a cat and creeping inside soundlessly.

Lochlan was exactly where he landed, crouched on the ground with his eyes closed and his breathing heavy enough for Cassia to hear it.

"Are you okay?" she asked, walking back toward him.

"I'm fine," he snapped, his eyes still shut.

"Your life force feels low."

Lochlan looked up and the fire in his eyes sent a chill down her spine. "I said I'm fine."

Rosheen came back out, transforming back into a human as she exited the house. "They're not here, but Xo is," she said, "barely. Come Cassia, we have work to do." She walked back into the house and Cassia ran after her, reaching the bottom of the stairs as Rosheen grabbed the dungeon door handle.

"It's charmed," Cassia said.

"Who do you think charmed it?" Rosheen said with a smirk that reminded her so much of Lochlan. She looked behind them to find a smirkless Lochlan standing at the top of the stairs. A hard and frightening look settled on his face.

They walked into the dungeon, straight to where Xo lay curled up on the floor. The image of Jean dying appeared in Cassia's mind and she ran forward, gripping her hands around the metal bars. "Xo!"

Xo leapt to the bars, wrapping his hands around hers and digging his nails into her wrists. She screamed as he drew blood. The scent of it drove Xo into a screaming, raging fit and he pulled her hand through the bars. Her chest pushed up against the cage, sending a dull pain where the metal pushed against her ribs. She pulled back, but he was too strong. Too desperate. Xo opened his mouth, prepared to bite, and was flung back into the wall behind him.

Lochlan's breath rasped as he exhaled and lowered his hand before Cassia could thank him. Xo jumped to his feet, threw his head back and screamed. "I'm hungry, Cassia! I can't take it anymore. Kill me. Kill me! Kill me or I'll kill you." The smile she was so used to seeing on his face was gone. His brown skin was covered in scratches with red blood caked on it. His lips were cracked and bleeding and his eyes seemed wider, filled with fear and something else that terrified her.

Dropping to the floor, he howled. Tears created visible paths down his dusty, dirty face.

"Xo," Rosheen said calmly, "you did so well keeping my boy safe, now it's my turn to save you." She leaned out and touched Cassia's hands, healing the wounds instantly. "Tell me the spell," she said to Cassia, who recited it without hesitation. Rosheen corrected her pronunciation several times and then nodded at her, before turning to Xo and gesturing to the bars. "Come over here."

"I can't, I can't, I can't," he said, and screamed. It was the same deafening scream Cassia associated with the Rahlogs.

"Lochlan, I command you to go in there and hold him up against these bars. We need to channel our magic into him while breaking the curse."

Wordlessly, Lochlan stepped up to the cage, gripped the handle and said, "It's blood-locked, obviously." He lifted his now bleeding palm.

Rosheen grabbed the lock, and with her blood, the gate clicked open and Lochlan slipped inside. Xo was on top of Lochlan before Cassia even lifted her eyes from the handle. Lochlan summoned a ball of fire and held it on Xo's chest until he stumbled back, screaming.

"Stop! You're hurting him!" Cassia shouted.

Rosheen locked the cage and Lochlan looked at her, an unfamiliar expression crossing his face. Before Xo could attack again, Lochlan teleported and reappeared behind him, grabbing his arms and twisting them behind his back. Xo screamed loudly, throwing his head back and turning his neck as he tried to bite Lochlan. Effortlessly, Lochlan pushed Xo up against the metal bars. "How long is this going to take, Mother?"

Rosheen ignored him and held Cassia's hands. "The night you were born, I gave you some of my magic and it saved you, and now I need you to help me save him."

She gave Cassia no chance to process what she said, to process what it meant. She stood on Cassia's left and entwined her right hand in Cassia's left. They stretched their free hands onto Xo's burned chest. "Don't let go of me and don't let go of him, do you understand?" she asked. Cassia nodded, already feeling her magic buzz, louder than usual. "Focus your magic into your hands, into healing."

Rosheen nodded and they started reciting at the same time. Xo struggled in Lochlan's grip. His screams became louder and louder. Throwing his head back violently, he slammed the back of it into Lochlan's nose, causing him to almost lose his footing. He pushed Xo even harder against the cage, his leather boots sliding against the dusty concrete floor. Lochlan spat as the blood from his bleeding nose reached his mouth. Xo's nostrils flared and he jerked his head forward, banging it on the metal bars in front of him. Dark red blood oozed out of a fresh wound on his forehead. Wincing, Cassia looked away, but she kept reciting the foreign words and she kept holding on to Rosheen and touching Xo.

They finished the spell and Rosheen squeezed Cassia's hand and said, "Again."

Cassia recited it word for word, using the pronunciation she'd just been taught. She felt her magic buzzing at her fingertips. She imagined a string being pulled from her brain, down to her heart, across her shoulders and through her fingers to where she held Rosheen's hand and touched Xo's chest.

He screeched, lifting his feet off the ground and stomping down on Lochlan's boots. Growling, Lochlan shoved him harder. A deep frown etched into his bloodied features.

"Again," Rosheen commanded.

Cassia felt a sense of power overwhelm her as she recited the spell for the third time. She forced herself to focus, to keep her contact with Rosheen, to keep her contact with Xo. She looked into Xo's brown eyes but he shut them as he screamed again. His voice was hoarse and almost gone, but he opened his mouth and attempted to scream once more. Her determination wavered. She couldn't do this. It wasn't working. Lifting her gaze, she found Lochlan's blue-flame eyes. He clenched his jaw and nodded at her. *You can do this*, he mouthed.

As they finished the spell for the third time, Xo collapsed in Lochlan's arms, but Lochlan continued to hold him tightly. Rosheen smiled, releasing Cassia's hand, and then leaned her head against the bars, onto Xo's chest. The scratches on his skin and the open wound on his head healed instantly. He opened his eyes. They were clear, just as she remembered them when they had first met. "Ro," he mouthed, and winced. His throat was raw from screaming and his voice had almost abandoned him.

Rosheen nodded and gently touched his throat, before unlocking the cell. "It worked," she said, a wide smile crossing her beautiful face. "You can let him go," she said to Lochlan.

"How can you be sure?"

"Lochlan," his mother sighed, and he let go, raising his hands in surrender.

Xo limped out and wrapped his arms around Rosheen. "It worked, it worked," he said into her light hair.

Rosheen rubbed his back for a moment and stepped back to smile at Cassia. "Our work isn't done just yet." Lochlan closed his eyes and shook his head. "We need to find Lucas. Do you have any idea where he'd have gone?" she asked Xo.

"They left in a hurry, said something about the royal guard wanting to find him. He had a proper fit without you, Cassia." Xo collapsed onto the ground. Cassia bit her lip and looked away. "I'm so hungry," he said.

"For food, right?" Cassia asked as Lochlan reached for his dagger. Xo nodded.

"What the fuck are you doing here?" Xo asked, looking up at Lochlan.

"Helping to save your life apparently," Lochlan snapped, lifting the bottom of his tunic to wipe the blood on his face. It simply spread it, rather than removed it.

Xo side-eyed him and turned to Rosheen. "You know," he said, "I have a bit of an idea where he could be. But without the wolves it'll take a while to get there."

"Lochlan will take us."

"Mother," Lochlan started and Xo's eyes widened at the term.

Cassia widened her eyes and nodded, mouthing: *Oh yeah.*

Xo's eyebrows bounced up in return. Good. So she wasn't the only one who hadn't known about this.

"I physically can't. I don't think I would be able to take myself, let alone three extra people."

"You'll be fine," Rosheen said, lifting her chin and offering him her hand. "I checked your life force. It's not that low yet."

"You know that you're not supposed to overuse your magic. Plus I would certainly lose consciousness. I won't be able to defend myself."

"Maybe we could take a small break?" Cassia asked and Rosheen sighed, shaking her head.

"Where is it?" Rosheen asked Xo, pulling him back up to his feet.

"Clover village had been attacked by Rahlogs a while back. It's a ghost town now. Lucas and I had previously discussed that it would make for a good hiding place." Xo limped out of the dungeon and upstairs. He led them to the library, stopping only to grab a banana from the kitchen. They each took one too and followed.

Rosheen stopped midway as she climbed the stairs to the library and traced her fingers along the portrait of the big, black-furred animal. She looked down at Cassia on the step below her. "Joseph, Lucas's father, was magnificent. He was the most powerful Reborn I ever met and the kindest. Lucas gets that from him." Without waiting for a response, Rosheen turned around and continued into the library. Lochlan lowered his gaze to the ground and followed quietly.

Xo pulled out a map and opened it up across the desk. "It's around here," he said, pointing east from where they were. He looked up at Rosheen, who nodded.

Lochlan sighed. "All I'm asking for is a couple of hours, Mother."

"Lochlan, I command you to take us there," Rosheen said firmly. Lochlan looked up at his mother and his eyebrows drew close. It reminded Cassia of Lucas as a young child.

Cassia reached out for him instinctively, but he held out his arms and said, "Hold on."

Cassia grabbed his arm tightly; she refused to be thrown to the ground again. Her world spun as they teleported and she landed on her feet, although her knees complained at the impact. Xo rolled into the dust and Cassia smiled smugly.

Clover village was eerily quiet and dark. The only light in the area was cast by the moon. The houses had doors flung open and windows broken; shattered glass littered the front of each and every house.

Surrounding the town were large boulders, piled on top of each other. From the pathway, she would never have known the village existed.

Xo led the way and Rosheen and Cassia followed. After a few seconds, she realized Lochlan wasn't beside them. Turning around, she saw that Lochlan had collapsed, his chest barely rising and falling. She walked back to him and kneeled down. "Lochlan," she said, but his eyes remained closed. "Help me lift him. We can't just leave him here in the dirt, exposed."

Xo tutted. "We can."

"Xo," Cassia warned, and Xo walked over and threw one of Lochlan's arms over his broad shoulders while he complained.

"Can't believe you're guilt-tripping me into helping a First."

"Rosheen is a First," Cassia said.

"Yeah, but he's the worst First," Xo said, as they carried him deeper into the village.

"I wouldn't say he's the *worst*. He saved your life," she said, and Xo threw him down against the wall between two small houses.

Cassia shot him a dirty look. "Oh, he'll live," Xo said. "Which is more than we can say for the thousands he's killed." She tried to think of something to say to defend him, but there was nothing she could say to that. "Ssh," Xo said, bringing his finger to his lips. "Someone's here."

CHAPTER THIRTY-TWO

Lucas

Lucas held out his hand and stopped Ruq. He had a feeling they would be safe here, at least until they came up with another plan. Jun dismounted quickly and scanned the area. He came back and gave Lucas a thumbs up to let them know the coast was clear. Lucas slid off the wolf. They needed to move fast and get inside before anyone saw them. He started untying one of their bags and threw it across his shoulder. They had brought enough food for a few days, but he knew he'd need to hunt if they were going to eat enough to regain their powers before facing Lochlan.

Before *killing* Lochlan.

His eyes flashed blue at the mere thought of the First prince, and he distracted himself by petting Ruq. Cassia wasn't here. He couldn't give in to that power.

Brie immediately hurried off into one of the empty homes and came out shaking her head. "Not that one. Covered in blood." She ran into another. "That one's got a hand."

"Forgot to warn you about that," Lucas said as she scurried out. "The stables seemed okay the last time we were here. Soft place to rest, I suppose, and enough space to keep the wolves close."

Brie, Jun and Nisa nodded and they led the wolves to the stables and continued unpacking. Brie pulled out a tiny cauldron, about the size of a soup bowl, and started adding all the ingredients he was now familiar with. She was making the suppressant tonic for Calla.

His mind raced to Cass. He was going to get her back, even though he had no idea how he was going to explain everything to her. He needed to make her understand. Truthfully, he wasn't even sure if he understood it all.

But he couldn't shake the way she'd looked at him before Lochlan took her away. The hurt and distrust in her hazel eyes had never been directed at him before.

"I hope they won't hurt Xo," Nisa said quietly.

"Even the Firsts are afraid of the Rahlogs. I bet they don't even know he's down there. The dungeon is well-concealed," Lucas said, attempting to sound calm and confident.

Everything was falling apart. He could feel himself unraveling. He was losing control of the power that lurked within him and neither Cass nor Xo was here to help him.

Jun silently collected firewood and the scent of the wood triggered him once again. Stupid chosen scent.

"Lucas," Jun warned, taking a step closer to him, but Nisa was quicker and laid her hand on his. He felt himself calm down.

"Maybe we shouldn't stop him. Maybe he needs to give in to that feeling," Brie said distractedly while crushing a lily into her cauldron.

"What are you talking about?" Nisa snapped.

"He won't hurt us," Brie replied, looking up at him. "You won't hurt us, you never have. So why do we keep resisting it? Maybe you can control it. We haven't tried."

"I need Cass."

"Are you sure?" Brie asked, looking up briefly. Her cauldron was almost overflowing. She placed it gently on the fire and muttered a few words over it.

"She's my other half. We were born on the same night. My mother shared her magic with Cass. She gave Cass life and now Cass is tied to my life, my power.... I needed an anchor in Talm, and my mom chose Cass. At least that's all she told me."

Brie stood up and started slicing bread. "I hear you. I just think your body is trying to tell you something every time your eyes go blue. I'm worried that suppressing it might do more harm than good."

Lucas sat down and she passed him a sandwich. He ate it in three bites and immediately wished he had savored it instead.

"Do you love her?" Brie asked as the contents in the cauldron reached boiling point.

"It's not like that. We're bonded by magic. I can feel it.... Using my powers feels different when she's around," Lucas said and Brie handed him another sandwich.

She sighed and nodded. "Then we'll find her...." Brie took out the large phoenix feather and folded it into the cauldron which had started bubbling over. "She'll understand, Lucas, she loves you too."

"She has trust issues."

"Oh, don't I know it," Brie said and smiled. "Gave her a simple instruction and yet...."

Lucas chuckled, despite his stress. It was typical of Cass to act on impulse, on her instincts and to be fair, he'd generally trust her instincts over his own.

He spread himself out on the hay and hoped Brie was right. He wished he could talk to Cass. The longest fight they had ever had lasted about two days and it was awful. They promised each other they would never fight like that again, never leave anything unresolved and never keep secrets from one another. Full transparency. Always.

He lay awake for hours, looking at the trusses in the stable roof. Ruq snuggled up against him, providing the perfect amount of heat. Willis lay in between Jun and Nisa, keeping both of them warm.

The sound of voices traveling in from the courtyard made his heart skyrocket. Lucas jumped up. Everyone else was asleep. Crouching low, he crept to the open stable door and peeked through. It was dark and quiet. Maybe he'd imagined it. But just in case, he unsheathed his dagger and stepped outside, listening closely.

He turned around slowly, listening for movement, any movement. The sound of a stone shifting across the sand came from behind him and he spun, swinging his blade.

His knife was blocked by the same arm that taught him how to use it.

Xo smiled widely, his eyes clear of pain and hunger. "I told you that attack is too easily blocked."

A gasp of relief escaped Lucas. He threw his arms around Xo, squeezing him tightly. His heart raced as comfort flooded through him. "What happened?" Lucas asked. "Is it really you?"

"Your mom saved me, man," Xo replied, the familiar grin still fixed in place.

"My mom?"

"Yeah, and Cassia."

Lucas looked over Xo's shoulder. His mom stepped out of the shadows and before his brain registered what was happening, he leapt toward her. The intense need to be close to her at that moment, of ensuring that she was real, was indescribable. Wrapping her in his arms so tightly, he stopped a moment when he thought he might crack one of her ribs.

She slipped her arms around his chest. "Lucas. My boy."

It was her. It was her voice. Her touch. It was his mom.

"Mom." Lucas held her tightly and wiped away his tears with his sleeve. "What are you doing here? Did you heal Xo? What's going on?" His voice caught as he looked across the courtyard and saw Cass walking toward him, observing him, a sad smile on her face, her arms wrapped around herself.

Rosheen let go of him and he lowered his head, placing a quick kiss on his mother's cheek. His gaze fell on Cass as he straightened. "Go to her. You know I would never try to keep the two of you apart," Rosheen said.

Lucas raised his brows. "That much is clear." His mother only smiled in response, lifting her chin in Cass's direction.

"Go."

Cass stood firmly in place as he walked toward her. Her arms tightened around her chest the way they always did when she was uncomfortable. "Are you okay?" he asked.

She frowned deeply. "I'm fine."

"Cass?"

She huffed.

"Cass."

"Explain yourself, Lucas!" she yelled. He was in trouble whenever she used his name like that.

"What did you want me to say? That we were bonded by magic at birth and that I need you to stop me from completely losing control?"

"Yes!" she shouted, stomping her foot on the ground. Lucas inhaled quickly and released a low growl. "It's better than lying to me, Lucas. You promised, promised me you would never lie to me."

"And I didn't," he replied. "I just didn't know how to explain it, where to start, and I knew you had to go back to save Calla and I would never risk her life for this. I was going to tell you, I swear."

Cass bit her lip and looked away. A silence stretched between them. Something that was rarely there when they were around each other.

"Bonded by magic?" she eventually asked.

"Yep, best friends deluxe."

"We're not supposed to, like, be soul mates or something, are we?" she asked, looking up at him.

"Hope not. That kiss was awful," he said, risking a joke and holding his breath as he watched her respond.

"Cold food," she said and let out a chuckle. If she was joking, then she wasn't that mad anymore. His eyes traveled over her and landed on her scarred hands. He touched them.

"Did he do this? Did he hurt you?" he asked. She had so much dirt and blood smeared on her cheeks that he couldn't see any of her freckles.

"No. He didn't hurt me, he just wanted...." She paused, looking almost frightened.

His rage grew. "He wanted what?"

Cass glanced between Lucas and his mother. "I think you should talk to your mom and with Lochlan too, when he wakes."

"He's here?" Lucas asked, feeling his shoulders tense. Cass's eyes widened and she glanced at his mother and Xo, before looking toward the shadows behind them.

Lucas let go of her and ran to the shadows, fueled by something bigger than his anger, bigger than his hatred. They chased him, but he was fast.

Lochlan was slumped against a wall. Lucas grabbed his collar, shaking him violently. "Wake up, you asshole."

"Let him go!" Cass shouted.

Lochlan's eyes cracked open and Lucas dropped him to the ground. He flicked his wrist and sent Lochlan flying against the brick wall. Lochlan groaned as he landed, his head lolling forward. Lucas thought about everything the Firsts had done to them. He thought about Zuq, about the children, what they did with Guests, what he might have done to Cass. Lucas pounced on him and punched him in the center of his face.

The satisfaction that came with his knuckles breaking that nose was unbeatable. He wanted to do that for a long time.

"Enough," his mother ordered.

Lucas hit him again. "Fight back," he said to Lochlan, who barely stirred.

"Luke!" Cassia shouted, running in between them and pushing Lucas back. "He's your brother!"

CHAPTER THIRTY-THREE

Lucas froze and turned to face her with eyes so bright blue, it looked nothing like him. Cassia immediately regretted her outburst, but she was sure that if she had not said anything, Lucas would have killed Lochlan.

"You're lying."

"I don't lie to you," she said, raising her hands. She stepped out from in between them, giving Lochlan a chance to speak.

He looked up at Lucas and smiled before saying, "You heard correctly, your Highness."

Idiot.

Cassia narrowed her eyes, which only made him smile wider. Lucas straightened and turned toward his mother, his blue eyes shining as brightly as Lochlan's. "What is she talking about?"

"It's true," Rosheen said, swallowing hard. "I'm sorry, Lucas, but Lochlan is your…brother."

Lucas shook his head. "There is no way I'm related to *that*."

"Oh, I'm hurt," Lochlan said sarcastically, rolling his eyes. Lucas threw a dangerous glance in his direction. "Hit me again, baby brother. I'm not afraid of you. Do avoid my handsome face, though. I quite like it."

Lucas growled and Rosheen raised her hands. "It's a lot to take in, I understand, but what's important is that—"

Lucas interrupted her. "But Lochlan's a First prince. His mother was the queen, many many years ago…."

Rosheen nodded. "You're a prince too."

Lucas froze, his voice dropping so low, it was merely a vibration that echoed through the ground. "Is the king my…."

Rosheen shook her head. "No, absolutely not. Your father, Joseph, was a Reborn. He was the best person I knew, the complete opposite of Idis…. He was kind and soft. Lucas, it's why you're so gentle."

Lochlan scoffed again and gestured to his broken nose. "Gentle, yes."

"My eyes, Mom, they're because of you?" Lucas asked. "Why can't I control them?"

"I told you. Your power is tied to her." Rosheen pointed at Cassia. "The night you were born I threw my power over her to protect her, but you, Lucas, as a newborn baby, you were already compassionate, you felt her fear, and in that moment of life and near death, your magic bonded with hers. A magic that was not meant to be in Talm. It needed something to anchor on to. The minute you saw her, you stopped screaming and I knew, she was your anchor."

Cassia looked up at Lucas and found him looking at her.

Rosheen turned to face them both. "Haven't you realized that you have always found comfort in each other, that you felt whole when you were together? That was your magic, calling to each other, calling to itself." Cassia stood wordlessly, unable to figure out what to say. "We'll have a lifetime to catch up. For now we have Rahlogs that can be saved, just like Xo…and the clock is ticking," she said, pointing at Cassia's chest. "We need to save as many as we can before Cass leaves, and you" – she turned to Lucas – "you need to kill their leader while she's still here."

Lucas looked between his mother and Cassia, and walked away. Rosheen went after him. Cassia decided it would be better to let them talk alone. She knew she would need some time alone with her mother if she came back from the dead, said she was a queen and that she had a new sibling who she'd spent years hating. It was a lot to take in. Besides, Cassia needed a moment to digest what she'd heard.

She was his anchor.

Best friends deluxe.

Lochlan dropped his head and groaned. Cassia sat down next to him, lifting his chin to observe the damage. He brushed her hands away. "I don't need your help. It will heal."

"Oh, stop being a baby," she replied and rubbed her fingers along his broken nose and reddened eye. "I can heal it quicker."

She grabbed a flask of water and cut off a part of her shirt using her dagger. She soaked the torn cloth and handed it to him,

"Least you could do," Lochlan said, "is wipe off the blood your magically bonded boyfriend brought forth."

"Such a baby," she said as she wiped his forehead. "Go easy on him, okay? It's an unusual situation." Lochlan closed his eyes and she wiped the cloth gently across his eyelids and down his straight nose. After cutting off another piece of her clothing, she drenched it again and wiped his mouth and chin. Her breath caught as her fingers grazed his lips, sending a twisting tension deep in her abdomen. Her entire body started beating quickly, as fast as her heart.

"Thank you," he said, his eyes still closed, as he rested his head back.

The cloth was soaked in blood by the time she was finished with him, but his face was clean and aside from the seemingly permanent grimace and his red-stained clothing, it was as though Lucas had never laid a hand on him. Lochlan opened his eyes and shook her off, raising his eyebrows and gesturing behind her. She turned around and found Lucas standing there, glaring at them. Cassia sighed and stood up.

"You okay?" she asked Lucas.

"What are you doing?" he asked. His glare remained fixed on Lochlan, and Lochlan, who had no sense of self-preservation, returned the look.

"I just fixed him up," she said.

"Why?" he growled.

"Why not? He's on our side."

"Is he?" Lucas asked, looking at Cassia. "It's the same guy who took you away from me without warning, who has tormented me for the last few years until now, when he needed your help. Before this, the Firsts treated us like animals. We starved, we begged them for mercy. He's the one who shows up and pulls Reborn children out of their parents' arms. Has he told you that?"

Cassia flinched, gasping, and Lochlan appeared in front of Lucas, facing him. His blue eyes reflected Lucas's, laced with threats of violence.

"Do it, I dare you," Lucas said. "It's nothing you haven't done before."

"It would be my absolute pleasure," Lochlan replied.

"Lochlan, I command you to protect Lucas...."

Lochlan's body froze. They all turned to look at Rosheen, who stood behind Lucas. "We need Lucas alive. He is the only one powerful enough to defeat an army of Rahlogs and eventually, the king."

"Mom, I'm not that powerful."

"Baby, next time you feel that power building, give in, as long as she's around." Rosheen pointed at Cassia and then said to Lochlan, "Protect him, whatever it takes."

"Whatever it takes?" Lochlan spat and walked away.

"Lochlan," she said and he paused, turning around to face her. "Don't go too far. I command you to stick around and keep watch tonight."

"I wouldn't have trusted any of these fools to keep watch anyway," he said before disappearing into the darkness.

Cassia looked forward to resting, finally. She lay down on the hay and exhaled the day, feeling her body buzzing from all the magic she used. Her mind raced even as she closed her eyes. Lucas sat down next to her and offered her a sandwich. She sat up and took it. Her stomach grumbled as she gobbled it up, and though Lucas offered her some fruit too, two bananas and an apple, she was too tired to eat any more.

"I'm still mad at you," she said and Lucas wrapped his arm around her and pulled her close.

"I thought I was going to lose you when he disappeared with you."

She leaned into his embrace and felt tears prick at the corners of her eyes. "Now you know how it feels," she replied, hearing her own voice crack.

"Are you okay?" he asked quietly. She nodded, but sniffed. Lucas lifted her head and looked at her shining eyes. She bit her lip and the tears escaped. "Are you okay, Cass? Did he hurt you?"

"This isn't about him," Cassia said, blinking back a fresh wave of tears. "I'm going to have to leave you."

Lucas sighed and his lip trembled. He leaned down and kissed the top of her head gently. "Let's not think about it."

"It's hard not to." She looked up at him and wiggled out of his embrace. She lay back down and he lay down next to her. She studied every feature, locking them in her memories, knowing she would revisit them regularly, knowing that these memories were all she would have of him for months, or years probably, if she was lucky.

"Your connection to Selene will live through your magic and it'll bring you back here. We'll see each other again. I know it."

"I don't want to live wanting to die," she said. "All that stuff you said about love, I want it. I want to get married. And have kids, or one kid, at least. Maybe not the kids thing, but I definitely want a life. How am I going to live it when all I'll look forward to is getting back here…especially knowing that you need me here."

"I'll be okay, Cass," he whispered. "Don't worry about me."

"What if I reach the last feather tomorrow, amid the chaos?" she said. Lucas frowned, his eyes shining as hers were. "I won't even get to say goodbye, Lucas."

"Why the hell are you calling me *Lucas*?"

"You're not the same Luke I remember from four years ago."

He smiled. "That may be, but you'll always be my best friend. You'll always be Cass."

★   ★   ★

She tossed and turned that night and eventually gave up. Sleep was a hopeless cause. She grabbed the fruit, stepped over Lucas gently and went for a walk.

The sun was slowly beginning to rise, casting a light pink glow across the wrecked houses. Lochlan stood at the town entrance with his back facing her. The sunlight lit him, glimmering across his golden-brown curls. She walked up to him and said, "What are you doing up?"

He glanced at her. "You reek of him."

"Oh, shut up," she snapped.

He crossed his arms. "What are you doing up anyway?" His eyes fell on the banana in her hand.

"Couldn't sleep." She offered him the banana and he raised an eyebrow. "You weren't at dinner. Have you eaten? Have you slept? Your life force still feels pretty low."

He took the banana without answering any of her questions. "Thanks."

"You need to sleep," she said. "I can keep watch if you want, but you need your energy for tomorrow."

"I'm delighted that you care," he said. His sarcasm seemed to have returned.

"You're a First. We don't stand a chance without you."

He pursed his lips and looked away. "I have been commanded to keep watch, so that's not an option." He bit into the banana.

"I don't understand. Is it a power of compulsion?" A cold breeze flew across her skin and she wrapped her arms around herself.

"Firsts are sired by their parents, by default, by their mothers. For carrying them, birthing them and generally being the primary caretaker.... If the mother dies, or in my case, abandons you to start a new family and leaves this realm, you become sired by your father." Lochlan exhaled slowly, looking into the distance, his expression hard, softened only by the pink-and-orange light cast against it. "When she reappeared, the sire defaulted back to her."

She passed him the apple and he took it without question, rubbing it on his shirt. He bit into it, quickly wiping the juice that trailed down his chin with the back of his hand.

"I'm sorry," she said softly.

"I don't need your sympathy, Cassia. Please go to your lover and leave me be. I do fine on my own. I always have." He polished off the apple, including the core, and spat out the stem.

"I don't like it when you call me 'Cassia'."

He glared at her. "You don't like it when I call you '*Cass*' either. What am I meant to call you?"

She chewed on her lip and looked away. "I think…." She paused, realizing it as she said it. "I think I like it when you call me '*fiery*'." She smiled weakly as embarrassment crept into her cheeks. Lochlan turned to face her, his eyes filled with amusement. She frowned at him. "Oh, don't get any ideas. It just makes me feel tough and right now, I'm pretty scared. I need to be really tough tomorrow. I don't know how many people I'll have to heal and whether I can, and ugh," she shuddered, "the Rahlogs are terrifying. I don't know if I can do it. What if I collapse? With an entire pack of Rahlogs around? My powers aren't even offensive. I mean, I know I'm not completely useless…."

"I have the scar to prove that."

She turned to him, and he smiled devilishly.

Resisting a smile, she said, "I'm scared and I need to know that I'm fiery and tough and everything other than being Cassia, because Cassia is just a med student."

"Give me your hand," he said.

"Why?"

"Don't you trust me?" he asked.

"Should I?"

"Probably not," he said with a laugh.

"Fuck it," she said and offered him her hand. He very obviously suppressed a grin as he took it. The heat in his fingers woke her up, spreading throughout her body.

He lifted her hand to his lips and whispered, "You are fiery. Remember that. Especially when you're scared. Give in to the fire you feel." Gently, he kissed her fingers. His lips were hot, like the rest of his body. "You can do this."

Cassia felt her hands tingle where his lips met her skin. She pulled her hand away, but the tingle continued to travel up her arms and she felt her heart flutter. Her entire body lit up. She crossed her arms, suddenly feeling exposed. Vulnerable. As if he could sense her reaction to him. "I should get some rest. See you later, Prince Lochlan," she said quickly, already walking away.

"Sleep well, fiery little lady."

CHAPTER THIRTY-FOUR

"I know where their camp is. I had a vision of it a while back, but I couldn't face them alone," Rosheen announced when everyone started waking up.

"Mom, why all the mystery? Why couldn't you be honest with us?" Lucas asked.

Cassia huffed. "You're one to talk," she said to Lucas.

"Cass," Rosheen said, "you'll learn that not every vision will materialize as you saw it. One action could change everything and I needed things to go in a certain way to get you here and keep you here long enough to get that spell. I still can't tell you everything I've seen."

It was a strange feeling, realizing that Rosheen knew things about Cassia's future that she herself might never know. She could also tell, judging from the tone Rosheen used, that there was no point in arguing.

Brie and Xo distributed breakfast. Hard-boiled eggs, a few cubes of cheese and some of her homemade bread that she'd brought along.

The bread was still soft, melting in her mouth as she ate it, with a few blocks of cheese in between. Glancing around, she saw Lochlan leaning against the stable door, a small plate in hand. He raised it as their eyes met and she frowned at him, eliciting a smile in response.

Brie approached her carrying a small vial. "This is for Calla."

"You finished it?" Cassia asked. "The suppressant tonic? But the feather...."

"It somehow found its way to me. I don't know how," Brie said, and Cassia looked over at Lochlan, a warmth of gratitude spreading through her chest. She had hoped that he was telling the truth. His blue eyes flickered in her direction and Cassia's body tingled the way it did whenever he looked at her like that. Brie followed her gaze and said, "But I have my suspicions." Brie turned back to Cassia. "She needs to drink all of it. It won't taste good, but it'll work and keep her magic suppressed until she turns eighteen or enters Selene. After that you can heal the damage that's already been done to her body."

"Thank you so much," Cassia replied, shoving it into her pocket with the worn and folded pamphlet Min-Jun had given her when they had first met. An unfamiliar feeling of affection overwhelmed her and she reached out to hug Brie. After about one second, she'd had enough of the physical touch and released her. "You don't even know me and you did so much for my family. I know I haven't been the easiest person to get along with."

"A friend of Lucas's is a friend of mine," Brie said, smiling.

"Lochlan," Rosheen called, "I need you to take me here." She pointed at the map. "I command it."

"For goodness' sake, Mother, you could just ask me," he complained, walking over to where everyone else was seated. He threw the plate and it floated down to the floor where the other plates were stacked.

"We don't have time to waste, Loch."

"Wait, Mom, where are you going? Let me come with you," Lucas said.

"I need to make sure I have the right place. Cassia will come along with me and the rest of them will stay with you. You can meet us there. The wolves should get you there quickly and quietly."

"There's too many of us for the wolves," Xo announced.

"I could come with you," Nisa offered. "It would be easy to keep in touch with Jun, and I could let him know where we are once we get there." She cleared up the empty dishes and handed out another round of hot black tea.

"Good idea," Rosheen replied.

"Great, another person to carry." Lochlan sighed and stretched out his arms. Rosheen and Nisa grabbed one arm each and Cassia touched his back gently. Her fingers tingled as her magic buzzed. But nothing happened.

"Hold your breath," he announced, before transporting them to the base of the mountain Cassia and Lochlan had seen previously.

Even though it was early in the morning, it felt like it was in the middle of the night; the sky was dark and the air was cool. The mountain, up close, seemed like any other mountain, dark brown and rocky. Nothing about it told her that the entire camp of Rahlogs was lurking inside.

"They should be in there," Rosheen said. "It's a maze of tunnels and caves, so try not to get separated. If you get lost, we may not find each other again, not before a Rahlog sniffs you out."

Everyone nodded and Cassia felt her heart quicken. Nisa stroked her arm and slowed it down. She smiled at Nisa, who returned the smile, their hands finding each other in the dark.

They stepped inside. It was pitch-dark and quiet. No chirping of a lost bird or scurry of an insect, or more concerningly, no screams of a Rahlog. Perhaps Rosheen was wrong. Or perhaps they had moved. Rosheen continued on and they all followed closely behind. As they went deeper in, the faint sounds of screams started and each step took them closer toward it. The screaming became louder, echoing off the mountain walls and hitting them from every direction. It was hard to tell whether they were already surrounded or whether the echo of the tunnels made it seem that way.

Rosheen grabbed her shoulder. "Stay calm, Cassia, we need you to be in control of your powers and emotions. Multiple lives depend on it." Nisa stretched out her hand to calm Cassia but Rosheen intercepted it. "Save your energy, Nisa. Cass, get it together." Cassia swallowed and walked close to Rosheen. Rosheen nodded at Nisa. "You can tell them where we are. Keep Min-Jun updated. Tell them we're going in and getting started because Cassia's lost another feather…. We're down to two."

Lochlan's head snapped down to her chest, where two feathers were hanging.

It felt as through her world was collapsing around her. What could she possibly do in the time it would take for two feathers to fall? Technically, *one*.

Lochlan's gaze drifted upward and met her eyes. He offered the same reassuring look he'd given her when they broke the spell and healed Xo. It worked then and for some reason, it worked now.

They kept moving through the dark tunnel until they reached a small cave where an eerie white light reflected off the walls, providing a cold but lit atmosphere. The peaceful sound of water dripping echoed in between the terrifying screams. They continued forward, toward the screams and the dripping water.

Drop.

Drop.

Drop.

It was easier to focus on that and block out the terror.

They reached a fork in the tunnel and went left; another fork took them farther left until they entered a cave with a male Rahlog, leaning over a woman.

The woman stood and screamed, throwing herself at Cassia. She stumbled backward, landing hard on the rock while the male Rahlog stood up slowly. "Breakfast time," he growled, pushing the female Rahlog away. Lochlan grabbed her and pulled her back.

"Don't kill her, she hasn't transitioned!" Rosheen shouted as she buried her dagger in the other Rahlog's head. "Hold her down! *He's* transitioned." She wiped her dagger on the fallen Rahlog. "Kill the ones who seem in control. Save the others, understood?"

Everyone nodded.

"Can we get the ball rolling here?" Lochlan asked as he pushed the screaming woman down on the cold ground. Cassia and Rosheen leaned down in front of her, joined their hands and touched the back of the Rahlog's head. They recited the spell over and over, just as they had done with Xo. Cassia felt the same sensation of magic washing over her while the Rahlog screamed and struggled, until she stopped. Lochlan tumbled off her, stood and exhaled loudly. He brushed the dust off his knees, a look of distaste on his face.

The woman stood. Her green eyes were wide with fear, but they were clear. "What's happening?" she asked.

"How do you feel?" Nisa asked.

"Fine…thank you," she said, turning to Rosheen and Cassia. "Thank you." She gasped when her eyes met Rosheen's and Rosheen smiled at her. She gasped again when she saw Lochlan and bowed quickly.

"Finally, some respect," Lochlan tutted.

Rosheen handed her a knife and a banana. "Show us your gratitude by helping us out. Kill the transitioned. Save the ones like you."

The woman nodded, gobbling up the banana. "Anya." They all nodded in acknowledgment; there was no time for pleasantries.

They crept through the tunnels, finding two Rahlogs in the next cave as well; one who had transitioned and one who hadn't. Lochlan was quicker the next time, pinning the Rahlog who hadn't transitioned to the floor before it could attack. Rosheen was fast enough in killing the other. Anya stood with her knife outstretched and her mouth agape. Her life force was still low and she very obviously did not know how to use a knife.

They snaked through the tunnels, checking each cave and collecting the people they'd saved along the way. The next one had another pair of Rahlogs. Instinctively, Cassia started reciting the spell as soon as she had hold of Rosheen's hand. But before they could finish it, another three Rahlogs entered the cave and attacked Anya. Nisa leapt forward, digging her knife into one of them and then spun around and stabbed her knife into the other as he sunk his teeth into the man they had just saved in the previous chamber, tearing through his neck.

Lochlan summoned a ball of fire and shot it at the third Rahlog, who screamed and ran toward them. The spell wasn't finished and Lochlan kept the Rahlog pinned underneath him. He flicked his wrist, sending the other one flying against the rock wall. The sounds of bone cracking bounced off the walls and traveled up Cassia's spine.

The spell worked and the young man stood. Anya ran over to him and filled him in on what had happened. His name was Deneshen.

He was a Reborn, much like Anya and the rest of the people they had saved.

Lochlan slumped down, breathing heavily.

"We need to move," Rosheen said, and Lochlan pushed himself up.

They exited the chamber and found a group of Rahlogs waiting for them. Half of them were screaming and the other half licked their lips as they took in each and every one of them.

"The Master would like to see who dares to come into his caves and kill his people," one of them announced, stepping forward. Had it not been for his blood-smeared face, he would have been handsome. He had light brown skin and green eyes; his dark hair was shoulder-length and messy.

Anya whimpered. "Frederick."

"Anya, they reversed the transition?"

"They can save you too. Come with us," she said, taking a step closer. He took a step back, his face twisted in pain.

"I can't. I'm sorry."

Cassia knew that Frederick was beyond saving. The second they had the chance, they would have to kill him, but there were three Rahlogs for every one of them. There was no way they would be able to defeat them. Cassia squared her shoulders and prepared to fight, but to her surprise Rosheen raised her hands in surrender.

Terror crept over her skin as the Rahlogs grabbed her, their fingers tight around her wrists as they pinned her arms behind her back. They were dragged to the center of the mountain to a vast chamber. The large space was lined with Rahlogs on each side and at the end of it, a Rahlog sat perched on a throne, a body strewn across his lap as he chewed into a human leg. Cassia heard the *drip, drip, drip* echo through the room. It was not water, as she'd initially thought; it was the blood of the body dripping into a bucket. Rahlogs scooped out handfuls for themselves and drank it thirstily.

Nisa stretched out to touch Rosheen and Cassia. *Jun says that they are almost here*, she said in their minds. Rosheen nodded subtly.

Lochlan's eyes started drooping and Cassia kicked him. He winced but his eyelids fluttered open.

"Wake up. This isn't the time for a nap," Cassia whispered, and Lochlan groaned, his eyes flickering closed and open again as he fought it.

"What have we here?" the Master asked, biting into the calf of the body and tearing at the muscle. Blood dripped down his chin and he wiped it up with his hand, licking every drop as it trailed down his fingers and wrist. The Rahlogs holding on to Cassia sucked on their tongues and she shuddered at the sound.

"We've come to make a deal," Rosheen announced.

"Oh," the Master cooed, "I'm not interested. I just want to taste you."

"Who tastes the best?" Rosheen asked.

"The Firsts are certainly richer than the Reborns and much, much harder to come by. I do enjoy a Guest," he said, eyeing Cassia, "but they are far and few between." The Master shifted on his throne. The white-and-brown throne contrasted with the dark cave. It was then that Cassia realized it was made of bones.

"I have both a First and a Guest for you," Rosheen said. "Not just any First, but a prince."

CHAPTER THIRTY-FIVE

Lochlan exhaled, closed his eyes and collapsed after his mother offered them up to the Master. Cassia struggled to get out of the Rahlog's grip and looked over at Rosheen as she tried to figure out her plan. She ripped her arm free, but the Rahlog quickly grabbed her, pulling her close. She felt his tongue trace along the back of her neck.

The Rahlog that held Lochlan sniffed him, his mouth open wide, exposing his dull teeth.

"Ah, ah, ah, ah, he's mine," the Master snapped and the Rahlog bowed. "Why should I make a deal with you when I could just eat you?" The Master's dark eyes lit up with excitement. He tossed the lifeless body from his lap. When it landed on the floor with a heavy thud, five Rahlogs attacked it, ripping off limbs before retreating back to line the walls.

Cassia shut her eyes and squeezed them; she couldn't bear to watch. The memory of this would haunt her forever.

"Because I could keep them coming," Rosheen said and lifted her chin. "I'm Maeve, Queen of the Firsts. I will bring you all my subjects who misbehave and I can easily fetch you some Guests, if that is what you desire?"

The Master licked his thin, cracked lips. He raised an eyebrow as he considered it. "What do you want in return?"

"You spare my life and do my dirty work. Cull the Reborns as King Idis intended for you to do and once we're done with them, you can kill the king."

"Bring me the prince," he drawled, crossing his legs and leaning back into the bone throne. The Rahlog carried Lochlan to the Master and he sniffed him, closing his eyes momentarily. "This one will be decadent."

Cassia struggled and glared at Rosheen. There was no way she would sacrifice her own son for the rest of them. Cassia wouldn't let it happen; it was cruel, too cruel. Asshole or not, he didn't deserve this. It had to be part of Rosheen's plan, but she remained unmoved as the Master leaned in to bite Lochlan. Before Cassia could free herself, the sound of wolves howling echoed through the tunnels. The Rahlogs flinched and all their heads shot upward. It gave them just enough time to spin out of their hold. Cassia unsheathed her knife and dug it into her attacker's heart. Rosheen flicked her wrists, flinging about ten of them at the walls.

Ruq launched into the center of the room and Lucas and Brie jumped off, their weapons already drawn. Ruq threw his head back and howled loudly as Willis skidded into the cave.

At the same time, Lochlan pulled out of the Rahlog's grip and unsheathed his dagger. He launched forward with the dagger pointed at the Master's heart, but a group of nearby Rahlogs created a barrier in front of their master. Lochlan lit up his palms and the Master stood and shouted, "Attack! Bite! Kill! I don't care, but get them out of here!" The Rahlogs that lined the walls of the chamber attacked and the Master slipped out of the chamber.

Cassia felt their hands on her from every direction and almost instantly felt them being pulled off. She spun around as they were flung across the room, whether it was by Lucas or Rosheen, she couldn't tell. She searched the room for Lochlan and found him facing her, a smile on his face, as he spread out his palms and sent a wall of fire toward a group of Rahlogs. They screamed as the blue flames reached them, burning them into ash.

"Lucas!" Rosheen shouted. "Find their master and take him out! It'll kill his entire line."

"What about the ones in transition? The ones we can save?" Cassia cried.

"They'll die," Rosheen said. "So we need to work fast."

Lucas growled as he fought off a number of Rahlogs, his eyes shifting between Rosheen and Cassia and flashing between dark and bright blue. Cassia watched as Lochlan unwillingly threw himself in front of every blow directed at Lucas. His hands moved effortlessly as he switched between knifework, telekinesis and summoning fire. That was the warrior they spoke of. The one they feared.

Min-Jun pinned two Rahlogs to the ground and used his powers to calm them. "These two are in transition!" he shouted. Lochlan twirled his wrist, throwing a ring of fire around them as Rosheen and Cassia kneeled next to the transitioning Rahlogs and recited the spell. Rosheen tore the sleeves off her shirt and sat with her shoulder against Cassia's bare shoulder. They each laid their hands on both Rahlogs.

Lucas struggled to keep up with the Rahlogs attacking him. Lochlan was at his side, fending them off, landing his knife in hearts and heads. "If I can't find your master, I will kill you all one by one," he said calmly.

Min-Jun pinned down another Rahlog who hadn't transitioned and Lochlan protected them with more fire.

"Order the wolves to get these people out of here. They're too weak to fight," Rosheen said to Min-Jun, and he nodded, whistling to call the wolves.

A group of Rahlogs attacked Lucas and Lochlan flung them away. Lucas and Lochlan turned to face each other before raising their hands in unison and pushing forward, sending an entire row of Rahlogs crashing into the wall.

Streams of Rahlogs entered the cave as they broke another curse.

"Find the Master!" Rosheen shouted. "We can't keep this up for much longer."

Lucas shook his head a minute. Then he collapsed.

Cassia felt panic rise as Rahlogs made their way to her unconscious friend. Letting go of Rosheen, she fought through a group of Rahlogs, her skin being clawed at in the process.

When Cassia landed next to him, Lochlan was already in front of him, fighting off the Rahlogs with the last energy he had to spare.

THE LAST FEATHER • 267

He doubled over. "There's too many of them and I'm out of magic."
Lochlan took a shaky breath and unsheathed his sword. Even without
his magic, he had to continue fighting them off.

"Lucas, wake up, wake up," Cassia whispered.

"He's used too much power!" Lochlan shouted as he pushed his
sword through the chest of an approaching monster.

Cassia sent her magic through Lucas and felt her head spin.

"Luke, come on," she begged, and the scratches along his face
disappeared.

A Rahlog attacked and Lochlan swung his sword, slicing off the
Rahlog's outstretched arm. More approached and he ran forward,
lifting his sword as if it weighed nothing.

A female Rahlog appeared from the opposite direction and Cassia
stood, putting herself between the Rahlog and Lucas. She picked up
Lucas's dagger and squared her shoulders. The redheaded woman
attacked and Cassia tumbled away. She scrambled to her feet and
shoved her dagger into the woman's chest, but as she pulled it out,
more Rahlogs appeared.

Cassia spun around, surveying the area. They were severely
outnumbered. In the distance, she saw a blur of grey as Ruq re-entered
the cave and snarled. Cassia whistled, hoping to get Ruq's attention,
but the wolf was immediately surrounded by a crowd of Rahlogs.

The cold fingers of a Rahlog wrapped around Cassia's right hand
and shook the knife out of her grip. Lochlan rushed toward her, but
the Rahlog was just a few inches from her shoulder and there was
another one approaching.

Lucas lay unconscious at her side. She needed to protect him, but
she wasn't the only one. Lochlan had been ordered to protect him too.

Lochlan pushed his way through multiple Rahlogs to get to them,
but he was too far away. Cassia screamed, writhing out of the Rahlog's
grip, but he was too powerful. Her hand slipped across her pocket and
she felt the vial. Her heart raced, roaring in her chest for something
to happen, to save her. She needed to survive this. Screaming again as
terror engulfed her heart, she felt her magic buzzing loudly.

Lochlan threw his knife and it landed in the back of one of the Rahlogs attacking her as he grabbed his sword and continued fighting his way through to her. The buzz of her magic thundered, heating up her entire body, and a wall of blue fire surrounded her and Lucas.

Leaning over Lucas, she shouted, "Wake up, please!"

His eyes flung open, blue as the flame around them. "Cass."

"We need to find the Master."

"Cass."

"What?"

"You have to go," he said, reaching up to touch her chest. She looked down and noticed a single red feather dangling at the end of her chain. She couldn't leave now. "I've got this," he said, whipping his arms out and sending Rahlogs flying against the walls. Lochlan gestured and killed the wall of fire, a tired smile perched on his face.

Lucas stood and gestured with his hands, spinning around. His eyes were still bright blue. The Master was pulled into the room and thrown across it. Lucas lifted Cassia to her feet and kissed the top of her head. "Goodbye Cass," he said softly. Cassia reached out to him. She wasn't ready to say goodbye to him.

Lucas threw his head back and growled, louder than she had ever heard him growl before. "Rip it off, rip it off, now!" he shouted as his nails grew into claws. He hunched over. "Rip it off, Cass!"

Cassia watched as Lucas transformed into a black beast that reminded her of the beast she had seen in his father's manor. He looked more like a black lion than the one in the manor, but larger, and much more deadly it seemed as he pounced onto the Master just a moment before she ripped off the chain and opened her eyes in the hospital break room.

CHAPTER THIRTY-SIX

Lochlan

Lochlan inhaled deeply, slowly. He could feel his entire body collapsing but at the same time he could not rest. Protecting Lucas was a command. He had no choice but to stand and fight. Besides, it was the one thing he knew he could do.

He was raised to fight, raised with violence.

Cassia vanished. She vanished before he could register that it would be the last time he saw her. She vanished a minute after creating a wall of fire to protect herself, to protect Lucas. It didn't come as a surprise that she summoned that much fire on her first attempt. *Fiery*, that's what she was. His skin tingled unfamiliarly when she used what he'd given to her.

A growl vibrated through the chamber as Lucas transformed. His nails grew into claws as his clothing shifted into black fur. Lochlan had seen something like that beast before. He was there when his father walked into the palace carrying its head.

The beast's muscular legs beat off the ground as it pounced forward, pinning the Master down. Opening its mouth, it revealed long, sharp teeth, which tore into Rahlog's neck. Blood sprayed across the cave floor. The nauseating sound of muscles tearing and thick blood being splattered silenced the room as everyone froze.

The beast threw its head back and roared. Lochlan had faced many animals and monsters, but nothing that threatening.

A group of Rahlogs leapt on top of the big beast and Lochlan launched himself at them, burying his dagger into any part of them he could reach. And then they all collapsed.

The Rahlogs lay lifeless, scattered across the cave like fallen flies. Every single one of them. Lochlan exhaled, his knife still raised in defense. He peeked underneath the black beast's body to see what was left of the Master and saw his head had been ripped off his neck.

Lucas's beast turned to face him with the head hanging in his large mouth.

The large brute did it, Lochlan thought, and smiled at Lucas before bowing mockingly. "Your Highness, you have earned your title."

The beast lifted its blue eyes to Lochlan's, its fangs long and sharp. It opened its mouth, releasing the head. The light thud echoed through the chamber.

Lochlan took a step backward. "Lucas?"

"Lochlan!" their mother screamed. "Get away from him!"

Lochlan turned around as Lucas pounced and landed on top of him. Lochlan inhaled and used the last bit of magic he could to teleport out from underneath Lucas's clawed grip. The beast spun around viciously, its growl shattering off the walls.

"Lucas," their mother said gently, approaching him with her hands raised. "I command you to calm down. I command you to transform back into yourself."

It seemed the beast was not sired by their mother, because Lucas attacked and their mother threw herself out of the way.

"Where's Cassia?" their mother asked, looking around.

"Gone," Lochlan answered as they backed away from the beast. She cursed. She was scared. Lochlan had never seen fear in her eyes. The beast roared again, its blue eyes contrasting its black fur.

Lochlan stepped in front of their mother and unsheathed his sword. Lucas pounced. Lochlan was unable to stab him; the command of protecting Lucas prohibited it.

Lucas's sharp teeth clamped near Lochlan's neck and Lochlan gripped the beast's head and pushed it back. His biceps ached as they struggled to keep the beast's teeth away.

The beast turned its head quickly, clamping down. Lochlan screamed as the blood gushed out of his arm and pain shot through his entire body.

Xo approached, a small dagger in his hand as if he had a death wish.

"Lucas," Xo called, "listen to me. Come on, calm down." He swiped at the beast but another dagger flew by and landed in the beast's shoulder. Lucas looked up and focused on his next target, the owner of the dagger.

The small blond, whose name Lochlan had never bothered to learn. Immediately she broke into a run and the beast chased her. She was fast, and perhaps she would have escaped had it not been for the pool of blood she slipped in. The beast landed on her and her bones cracked loudly, louder than her screams.

One of the Empaths threw himself on top of the beast's back. "Calm down!" he shouted, his voice cracking with pain.

Lochlan was on his feet again, his knife drawn, as he ran to join them. The female Empath got there first and placed her hands on him. "Calm down!" she said as well. The two Empaths hung on, whispering to the beast until it collapsed. Whether their magic made a difference, or Lucas ran out of energy, Lochlan wasn't sure. It didn't matter, though, because the blond lay very still.

CHAPTER THIRTY-SEVEN

Cassia woke up in the same break room that Lochlan had taken her from. She fell onto the floor, her mind spinning as sleep nearly overwhelmed her. But she *couldn't* sleep. That wasn't an option. The break room light flickered and washed a familiarity over her. Using the last of her energy, she stood, gripping the small table for support. It shook underneath her. Her hand traveled to her pocket and felt the vial. She launched herself out of the break room and into the hospital corridors.

"Where's my mom?" she asked one of the nurses passing by, but they looked at her confusedly. She looked down at her bloodied, torn clothes. "Where is my mother?" Cassia asked again, urgently.

"Maya's with Calla, in room 108. She's not doing well. Cassia, where have you been?"

Cassia pushed past the nurse and ran through the hospital toward room 108. She flung the door open and found her sister laying still on the hospital bed, barely taking up any space. Her chest rose and fell slowly. Her eyes were closed and her brown skin was unnaturally pale. The hospital lighting made it worse.

Her mother jumped to her feet and wrapped her arms around Cassia, shaking with sobs of sadness and relief. Cassia shrugged off the hug and moved to Calla's side. "Cassia," her mother started but Cassia wasn't ready to confront her mother about Rosheen just yet. Her mother choked on tears as she said, "She's in a coma. I don't think she'll wake up." Cassia took out the vial. It would work. They said it would. It had to. She lifted Calla's head and opened her mouth. "What are you doing?" her mother asked. "Where have you been?"

"I think you know," Cassia snapped, immediately regretting her tone. Gently, she emptied the vial into Calla's mouth. Calla coughed but managed to swallow it all. Laying her head back down on the pillow, Cassia collapsed onto the hard plastic seat in the room. She hung her head and cried for what felt like the first time in years.

"Cassia," her mother said again.

"Why didn't you tell me about Aunty Rosheen? About Lucas and me?"

Her mother stood next to her and rubbed her back gently. "I'm sorry for not telling you. I didn't know how." Cassia was tired of hearing that excuse.

She stood, shrugging out of her mother's touch again, and placed her hands on Calla. "Come on, this better work," she said to herself. She felt the last of her magic escape through her fingers and into her sister. She could feel all the damage, all the inflammation. She imagined the physical pain her sister had been experiencing. She stood there for a long time, healing each and every organ, each and every cell, until Calla opened her eyes.

"Cassia?"

Cassia smiled at her sister with fresh tears streaming down her face, burning as they ran across the open scratches. "How do you feel?" she managed to ask.

"Am I dead?" Calla asked, her eyes wide in fear, but clear. The color had already returned to her cheeks.

Cassia shook her head. "No, you're very much alive. How do you feel?"

"There's no pain."

Words Cassia had thought she'd never hear. Relief washed over her, warming every part of her body, and her knees wobbled. The first taste of relief since Calla's first scream.

★　　★　　★

Every muscle in Cassia's body ached. She could barely move. She felt her sister playing with her hair and heard her humming. Opening her eyes and squinting at the bright fluorescent lights, she said, "Hey."

"You awake?" Calla asked.

"I'm not sleep talking..." she said, smiling weakly.

Calla chuckled. Her usually dull hazel eyes were lit up with life and Cassia couldn't contain the way her heart fluttered with joy. Her mother stood and checked Cassia's pulse.

"Mom, I'm fine."

"What happened?" her mother asked.

"Let's go home. I have a lot of stories to tell you," Cassia said as she pushed herself off the side of the bed. Her muscles screamed in reluctance. "Maybe give me a few more minutes." Cassia fell back onto the bed and gave in to the drowsiness once more.

When she was eventually strong enough to leave the hospital, her mother drove them home. Sleep took her again the second she sat down on her couch. The comfort of something she was so used to overwhelmed her, sinking her deeper into its cushions.

As a pleasant surprise, he was there again. In her dreams. *Visiting* her. Except this time, she knew it wasn't a dream. He smiled and she smiled back. Lucas's eyes were black, not the blue she had seen when she had left him behind.

They'd survived it. Even without her, they'd survived it.

"Hey Cass," he said, and she could hear him.

"Can you hear me?" she asked. He nodded. "How?"

"My mom's helping. She says to say 'Hi' to your mom."

Cassia chuckled. "What happened?"

"We won, the Rahlogs are gone. Every last one of them."

"You did it," she whispered as she felt her tense muscles relax.

"We did it, Cass, you and me. Another story to add to The Adventures of Cass and Luke." He laughed lightly, offering her two dimples, despite looking exhausted. Fresh scars covered his arms and jaw and his ear looked as though it had been sliced apart and put back together.

THE LAST FEATHER • 275

"I hope the story doesn't end there," she said.

He shook his head. "I'm here, whenever you want to talk. I'm here."

"Is everyone okay?" She reached out and he reached out for her, but she couldn't feel him. It was worth a try.

Lucas sighed.

"Luke, what happened?"

Lucas pursed his lips and looked down. Something was wrong. Her heart froze as she assumed the worst. "It's a mess, Cass." He looked down at his hands. "Everyone's okay...alive, my mom's busy patching them up as best as she can. She's still busy with them. It was bad, Cass, I nearly—" He cleared his throat. "Anyway, we're okay. Are you? Is Calla? Everyone wants to know."

"She's perfect," Cassia said, feeling her eyes well up again. "Please, thank Brie for me. She's amazing. I think I might be in love with her."

Pain flashed across his eyes. "I will." He ran his hands over his face and his eyes flashed blue. "I need you. I really need you." His voice caught.

"Luke, are you okay? What's wrong? Tell me."

He shook his head. "I just need you. I already miss you."

"I miss you," she replied without hesitation.

His expression changed as he looked away. He looked back at her with fear covering his features. "I have to go, Cass. Until we meet again?"

"Lucas, what's wrong?"

"This story doesn't end here," he said, offering her a reassuring smile.

Then he disappeared.

ACKNOWLEDGMENTS

If we take it back to the beginning, I have to start off by thanking my parents, Yacoob and Gadija, and sisters, Tasneem and Layla, for always encouraging me to read, to tell my stories and to be as me as I needed to be. Hey Mom, thank you for letting me take out library books on both our library cards.

For someone who doesn't enjoy reading fiction, my husband sure enjoys cheering me on. To Michael, thank you for letting me bounce ideas off you even though your suggestions are so ridiculous that there isn't a story I could come up with to accommodate them. If it weren't for you, my novel may never have landed in Flame Tree Press's hands and I may have given up somewhere along the way.

To my darling daughter, you're three years old at the moment and haven't read this book. You don't pay rent and you take up ninety percent of my time, but I just know you'll be the best cheerleader in a couple of years and without you, I wouldn't know what to be.

I feel the urge to acknowledge my cats, but they won't be reading this and so all I'll tell you is that Charger is sleeping peacefully beside me while Turbo eyes my cables. If you ever find me complaining that my headset isn't working, know that Turbo chewed through the wire with her tiny, sharp teeth and then probably innocently curled up in my arms after.

Life works in mysterious ways and up until a few years ago, I had never met Nuhaa and Zayaan and yet, when they waltzed, or more accurately, scrambled into my life, they fit perfectly. I can't picture my life going forward without them. They are, as Susan Dennard would put it, my threadsisters. I could not have finished this book without them. Thank you for listening to my rambling voice notes, for reading the very first version of this thing, chapter by chapter, line by line – actually, you stood behind me reading as I wrote word for word. Thank you for that. For the squeals. The laughter. The tears. Thank you for falling in love with my characters before I did. Cassia, Lucas and the rest of the gang would not have existed as they do if it weren't for your support. And yes, I appreciate that everything you buy me has been vanilla or sea salt scented since.

Yumna, thank you for reading this book even though you don't read fantasy. Thank you for always believing in me, even when I didn't believe in myself.

It's impossible for me to mention all the people who cheered me on, who contributed to the way this book ended up, but to name a few: Kauthar, Raffaella, Cassey, Bhavna, Jacqui, Michelle, Fiona, Zaid, Isa, Jaylynn, Najwah and Natheefah – your support, your comments, your gifts and gifs are everything to me.

When Flame Tree Press made me an offer, I had absolutely no hesitation. I didn't need the two-week period to think about it. There was something about Don D'Auria that pulled me in immediately and I'm so pleased that *The Last Feather* and the entire *Selene* trilogy has found a home there. Working with Don, Josie and Imogen has been a treat (for me, probably not for them). A big shout out to the rest of the Flame Tree team, who I know are busy behind the scenes, making sure this book will reach as many readers as possible. Sarah and Maria, thank you for dealing with all my questions, of which, I know, there are plenty.

There is no way I could do this without the readers. I would like to thank everyone who purchases this book, reads it, loves it, reviews it or talks about it. Your opinion is the most important to me. I hope you enjoyed reading this as much as I enjoyed writing it. And finally, by the blessings of God, I've done it! I've managed to convince people that my stories are worth reading and I will forever be grateful for that.

FLAME TREE PRESS
FICTION WITHOUT FRONTIERS
Award-Winning Authors & Original Voices

Flame Tree Press is the trade fiction imprint of Flame Tree Publishing, focusing on excellent writing in horror and the supernatural, crime and mystery, science fiction and fantasy. Our aim is to explore beyond the boundaries of the everyday, with tales from both award-winning authors and original voices.

•

You may also enjoy:
The Sentient by Nadia Afifi
The Emergent by Nadia Afifi
Junction by Daniel M. Bensen
Interchange by Daniel M. Bensen
American Dreams by Kenneth Bromberg
Second Lives by P.D. Cacek
Second Chances by P.D. Cacek
The City Among the Stars by Francis Carsac
Vulcan's Forge by Robert Mitchell Evans
The Widening Gyre by Michael R. Johnston
The Blood-Dimmed Tide by Michael R. Johnston
What Rough Beasts by Michael R. Johnston
The Heron Kings by Eric Lewis
The Heron Kings' Flight by Eric Lewis
The Sky Woman by J.D. Moyer
The Guardian by J.D. Moyer
The Last Crucible by J.D. Moyer
The Goblets Immortal by Beth Overmyer
Holes in the Veil by Beth Overmyer
The Apocalypse Strain by Jason Parent
A Killing Fire by Faye Snowden
A Killing Rain by Faye Snowden
Fearless by Allen Stroud
Resilient by Allen Stroud
Screams from the Void by Anne Tibbets
Of Kings, Queens and Colonies by Johnny Worthen

•

Join our mailing list for free short stories, new release details, news about our authors and special promotions:

flametreepress.com